D0104909

Here's What Readers Are Saying about the Christy Miller series...

"I started reading the Christy Miller series when I was fourteen. I read all of them in a matter of weeks, and they changed my life. I truly feel that your books have helped me through some of the hardest times of my life."

"To me Christy is a friend. She is so real to me. I can really relate to her...I feel that my relationship with God became so much stronger as I read the Christy Miller series."

"After I read *Summer Promise,* I realized what a real Christian was, so I prayed along with Christy and now I know I'm a real Christian."

"My friend told me I should read your books. I had never really asked Jesus into my heart... You showed me, through Christy, how to really be a Christian."

"Last year I read the Christy Miller Series...Christ is in me and is here to stay because of your books."

"Your books helped me take the first step in giving my heart to the Lord. They inspired me to stay pure."

"I am a hurricane Katrina survivor... During the time when I was in the hurricane, the Bible and the Christy Miller series were my comfort... Thank you for all the hope you have given me through those books."

Christy Miller

COLLECTION

VOLUME 3

TRUE FRIENDS

STARRY NIGHT

SEVENTEEN WISHES

ROBIN JONES GUNN

Multnomah Books

This is a work of fiction. The characters, incidents, and dialogues are products of the author's imagination and are not to be construed as real. Any resemblance to actual events or persons, living or dead, is entirely coincidental.

THE CHRISTY MILLER COLLECTION, VOLUME 3
published by Multnomah Books

International Standard Book Number: 978-1-59052-586-9

Cover image by PixelWorks Studios, www.shootpw.com

Compilation of:
True Friends

Starry Night

Seventeen Wishes

Published in the United States by WaterBrook Multnomah, an imprint of the Crown Publishing Group, a division of Random House Inc., New York.

Printed in the United States of America

For information:
MULTNOMAH BOOKS
12265 ORACLE BOULEVARD, SUITE 200 • COLORADO SPRINGS, CO 80921

Library of Congress Cataloging-in-Publication Data
Gunn, Robin Jones, 1955-
The Christy Miller collection.
v. cm.
ISBN 1-59052-586-8
[1. Friendship—Fiction. 2. Christian life—Fiction.] I. Title.
PZ7.G972Chr 2006
[Fic]—dc22

2005025580

13—10

TEEN NOVELS BY ROBIN JONES GUNN

The Christy Miller Series

Volume 1

Book 1: *Summer Promise*

Book 2: *A Whisper and a Wish*

Book 3: *Yours Forever*

Volume 2

Book 4: *Surprise Endings*

Book 5: *Island Dreamer*

Book 6: *A Heart Full of Hope*

Volume 3

Book 7: *True Friends*

Book 8: *Starry Night*

Book 9: *Seventeen Wishes*

Volume 4

Book 10: *A Time to Cherish*

Book 11: *Sweet Dreams*

Book 12: *A Promise Is Forever*

The Sierra Jensen Series

Volume 1

Book 1: *Only You, Sierra*

Book 2: *In Your Dreams*

Book 3: *Don't You Wish*

Volume 2

Book 4: *Close Your Eyes*

Book 5: *Without a Doubt*

Book 6: *With This Ring*

Volume 3

Book 7: *Open Your Heart*

Book 8: *Time Will Tell*

Book 9: *Now Picture This*

Volume 4

Book 10: *Hold On Tight*

Book 11: *Closer Than Ever*

Book 12: *Take My Hand*

BOOK SEVEN

True Friends

In memory of my mother-in-law,

Katherine Beckman Gunn.

You were and always will be my True Friend.

1

A Lightning Bolt from Heaven

"Over the years many people have given their opinions on friendship. I would like this class to work off the handout I've given you and write a three-page essay. Begin with the phrase, 'A true friend is.' You may use the rest of the class time to work on it. Any questions?"

Sixteen-year-old Christy Miller glanced across her English class and noticed that her friend Katie had her hand up.

"Is it okay if we use some of the quotes from the list?" Katie's red hair swished as she tilted her head.

"Of course you may. Now, no talking. This is project time."

Christy adjusted her long legs under the desk and studied the handout. The page was full of quotes from people like Constantine and Aristotle. She smiled when she read what Charles Dickens had to say about friends: "Friendship? Yes, please."

Taking out a fresh sheet of paper, she wrote at the top of the page, *A true friend is...*

Only one word came to mind: *Todd.*

That was not the word she was looking for. Christy pushed the thought aside and scolded herself. *Come on, you have lots of friends. What are you doing thinking of Todd? He's not even part of your life anymore. Think, think, think. What is a true friend?*

She began to write. *A true friend is someone who sticks up for you and...*

Todd, her mind said again.

...and they always look for the best in you. A true friend likes you even when you don't like yourself very much. Then, without meaning to, she wrote, *My true friend is Todd Spencer.*

There. She finally admitted it to herself. By writing it down, it was as if she admitted to the world that Todd was her true friend. How did Todd say it almost a year ago when he placed the engraved "Forever" ID bracelet on her wrist? *Here's my friendship; I promise it to you. It's yours forever.*

Christy thought of how Todd had backed up that statement about two months ago. It was morning on a deserted beach. The night before, without really wanting to, Christy had agreed to start going out with Rick Doyle. There she was, in the early morning California fog, trying to explain it to Todd.

Christy tried to give back the bracelet, but Todd wouldn't take it.

"No matter what happens," he said, "we're going to be friends forever."

Then he announced that he was going to Hawaii to try out for the world-tour surfing team. She hadn't heard from him since.

Christy drew a tiny heart in the corner of her paper and let memories of Todd fill her mind. Each memory prompted a little doodle. Soon the margins danced with sketches of a tandem bike, a picnic basket with seagulls circling over it, a bouquet of carnations, an old Volkswagen bus, and down the entire right side of her page, a waterfall crowned with a bridge across the top.

The shrill bell jolted her back to her Friday morning English class. Snapping her notebook shut, Christy grabbed her books and waited at the door for Katie.

"Did you get yours done?" Katie asked, her green eyes sparkling as though she had a secret.

"Not really." Christy pushed back her nutmeg-brown hair. The new shampoo she had used on it last night made it too silky, and it kept falling in her face today, driving her crazy. "Did you?"

"Almost," Katie said as they walked down the noisy hallway. "Who did you write about?"

"Well, I didn't come up with anything final yet. I guess I'm going to have to work on it this weekend."

"I wrote about the person I consider to be my truest friend in the whole world." Katie's eyes kept twinkling. "I want you to read it, but not until I'm finished."

A horrible feeling hit Christy. *Katie's acting like she wrote about me! Like I'm her best friend. Katie has been a true friend to me, and I've taken her for granted.*

By lunchtime, Christy had formed a plan. She wanted to do something that would let Katie know how much she appreciated her. They met at their usual spot outdoors. Kelley High was an older school, and their cafeteria was small and tended to be dominated by the freshmen. Most of the upperclassmen went off campus for lunch. Christy and Katie had gotten into the routine of bringing sack lunches and meeting on the grass under one of the large shade trees.

Being able to eat outside most of the year was one of the things Christy liked best about living in Southern California.

"Katie, I'm going to ask you something, and I want you to give me a straight answer," Christy said once they'd sat down, away from the noisy crowds at the picnic tables.

"Okay, shoot."

"I want to know what you'd like to do together sometime. Just you and me."

"What do you mean?" Katie asked.

"What is something you'd like to do? Would you like to go shopping or what? Name it."

"You're sounding like something's wrong, Christy. We do stuff together all the time. Why do we need to make special plans to do something together?"

Christy took a deep breath and stuffed the remainder of her sandwich back in her lunch bag. She hadn't figured it would be this complicated. "Can I be honest with you?"

"No, I want you to lie to me." Katie pushed Christy on the shoulder. "I'm only kidding! What are you being so serious about? You're scaring me."

"Katie, you have been such a good friend to me. I feel like I haven't been as good a friend back to you. You're the most gracious friend I've ever had."

"Gracious?"

"Yeah, you know. Like last year when my aunt and uncle took me to Palm Springs. You didn't get to come because of the football game. You were so gracious about it—"

"But—" Katie started to interrupt.

Christy kept going, not letting Katie have a chance to disagree with her. "Then this summer when I went to Maui.

You know I wanted to take you, but I had to take Paula with me because she was visiting that week. It was all set up by my aunt, and I didn't have any say about who went with me."

"I know, Christy. You don't have to explain."

"That's what I mean! You're always so supportive. You were gracious about Palm Springs and Maui. You were even gracious when Paula was a snip to you—"

"Christy," Katie finally cut in, "you're making it sound as though I was being heroic. I wasn't. It killed me that I didn't get to go with you those times."

"But you didn't act like it. That's what I'm trying to say. You've always been supportive of me. Always."

"Well, almost always," Katie said. "If you will recall, I wasn't exactly supportive when you were dating Rick."

"Yes, you were. You just had a strong opinion about him."

"I still have that opinion. I didn't need to say all those things to you about him though," Katie said thoughtfully. "You handled the situation fine without my nasty comments."

"No," Christy disagreed, "I needed you to say whatever you wanted to say. I needed to hear your opinion. And, as I've said before and will probably say a thousand times, you were right. Going out with Rick was a huge mistake."

"And as I've told you a thousand times, going out with Rick was not the problem. Going steady with him was...well, if you want my opinion, it was about the stupidest thing you've done in your entire life."

Christy laughed as Katie's honesty brushed over her. "Okay, well, I guess some things I have to learn the hard way. You know, it still hurts when I think about him."

"Why? Because he was such a jerk, and he treated you like slime?"

"No, Rick didn't treat me badly; you know that."

"Oh, right. He only stole the bracelet Todd gave you, hocked it to a jeweler, and is now making you buy it back with every paycheck until Thanksgiving. Silly me!" Katie slapped her forehead for emphasis. "I guess that's the way every girl hopes her boyfriend will treat her. I just haven't reached a level of maturity to be able to understand such deep, caring, emotionally enriching relationships."

"Okay, okay!" Christy threw her hands up in surrender. "You're right! Okay? Rick was sort of a..."

"...grade-A, first-class, total jerk," Katie filled in for her.

"I guess you could put it that way," Christy gave in. "But he wasn't like that all the time. There's a tender side to him too. I'm not saying I want to go out with him again. It's just that I don't feel like my relationship with Rick is resolved."

"You told him to get lost. What more needs to be resolved?"

"I can't explain it. I'm not sure I really know. I want him to understand why I broke up with him. One of these days I'd like to sit down with him and talk everything out."

Katie ventured slowly, "You mean the way you talked things over with Todd that morning on the beach? I mean, can you honestly say you now feel your relationship with Todd is over and resolved?"

Christy shook her head, feeling her hair tumble over her shoulders as she lowered her eyes. Uninvited tears brimmed behind her lower lids. "No," she said softly. "It's not over with Todd. I think about him all the time."

"So?" Katie perked up. "Why don't you write him?

Send him a card. One of those cartoon ones. You told me your uncle gave you Todd's address last week. What are you waiting for?"

"I don't know." Christy blinked back a tear. "A lightning bolt from heaven, I guess."

"Then here," Katie said, playfully bopping Christy on the head with a foil-wrapped Ding Dong. "Consider this your lightning bolt from heaven, and this is your message: 'Goeth thereforeth and writeth to Toddeth.'"

Christy laughed, her clear blue-green eyes making contact with Katie's. "Since you put it that way, okay, I will. I shalt goeth and buyeth a card todayeth."

Katie smiled her approval, "You know, an occasional bonk on the head with a Ding Dong seems to do you some good. Remind me to do that about every fifty thousand miles."

Not until Christy was sitting in her Spanish class after lunch did she realize that Katie had never answered her original question. Christy still didn't know what Katie would like the two of them to do together.

About the only time they had spent together during the summer was at church. Then school started, and Christy's job kept her busy every weekend.

When Christy started going out with Rick, Katie had talked about having the annual back-to-school slumber party at her house. Only Christy hadn't been able to find a free weekend for the party since she worked every Friday night and then had gone out with Rick on Saturdays after work. With Rick out of the picture, Christy thought maybe she could help Katie plan a slumber party with a bunch of girls like they'd had last year.

Christy drove right from school to the mall, where her job at the pet store started at four. Her boss, Jon, greeted her with a big smile.

"Guess what?" Jon said.

His long hair was pulled back in its usual ponytail, and he had on his typical jeans and T-shirt. Christy didn't notice anything different about Jon. It must be something about the shop.

She glanced around but didn't see anything that had changed. "I don't know. I give up. What?"

"I sold Walter this morning." Jon beamed.

Even the mention of Walter gave Christy the willies. She would never forget the night when the fifteen-foot python escaped from his cage and slithered out into the mall.

"You seem pretty happy about selling him. Beverly told me you'd had him forever. I didn't think you'd ever sell him."

"I did have him forever. Not because I was fond of Walter, but because nobody wanted to buy him. This morning some guy from Fallbrook came in and paid full price. Walter has a new home, and I couldn't be happier for him."

Jon picked up a clipboard from under the counter and said, "I've been meaning to ask you. Are you still happy with your hours, or do you want to change them so you can spend more time with your boyfriend?"

Christy felt her cheeks turn red. "Oh no," she said quickly. "My hours are fine. I don't need to change them. Really."

Jon looked Christy in the eyes with the same scrutiny a doctor uses when checking a patient's throat. Then, as if he had found what he was looking for, he looked back at his clipboard. "I'm sorry."

Christy felt a little confused by his examination. "You're sorry that I don't want to change my hours? I can change them or trade with somebody else if you need me to."

"No, your hours are fine with me. As a matter of fact, they're great. I'm sorry you broke up with...what was his name?"

"Rick." The moment Christy said his name, she felt as though she had bitten into a wild, tangy raspberry.

"His name is Rick," she added, hoping to purge herself of the raspberry sensation. "We broke up about a week ago. But it's fine, really. We're just friends."

Jon looked her in the eyes again. Then he flashed her a big grin, snapped the clip on top of the clipboard, stuck his pen behind his ear, and turned toward the back of the shop. "Well, I guess there comes a time when you have to say good-bye," he commented. "It's not always easy, but you've got to let the ol' snake go. Let somebody else have him for a while."

Christy was about to jump in and defend Rick when Jon turned back to face her and said, "You know I'm talking about Walter, of course. That ol' snake, I mean."

"Right." Christy smiled back. "Walter. Of course. I knew that."

She slipped her backpack under the counter and took her position behind the register.

Guys. Who needs them? Not me.

Christy began to straighten the countertop, ready to concentrate on work.

I'll show Jon and Katie and everyone else that I don't need a guy in my life.

Taking a deep breath, she mumbled, "Now, if I can only convince myself, I'll be fine."

2

The King of Returns

"Excuse me," the customer in front of the register said to Christy.

She had been working for more than an hour, but this was the first customer who had talked to her. All the rest had responded to her smile and "Have a nice day" with grunts and mumbles.

"Could you tell me when you're going to get more birdseed mix? You seem to be out; the bin is empty."

"I'm not sure, but let me ask the manager." Christy pushed the red button under the counter, and Jon came trotting up to the front.

As Christy explained to Jon about the birdseed, out of the corner of her eye she spotted Katie entering the shop.

"Our shipment comes in Monday," Jon told the customer. "Would you like us to call you when it arrives?"

"No, I would not like you to call me when it arrives," the man answered. "I would like it if you stocked your store well enough so you don't have to offer lame excuses and make me wait. What kind of a manager are you? You can't even keep your birdseed stocked."

With that, the man turned and marched out of the store.

"What's with that guy?" Christy asked.

"Oh, didn't I tell you? He's one of our best customers," Jon answered.

"Then I wouldn't want to meet one of our worst customers!"

"You know what they say, 'The customer is always right.' Best thing to do is let it roll off you and keep going," Jon advised.

"But Jon, he was rude to you, and he said a bunch of mean things."

"Weeds," Jon answered simply. "Maybe he was trying to toss a bunch of weed seeds in my garden. I don't need them."

"So what do you do? Ignore them?"

Jon looked at her as if she were young and had so much to learn. "If I ignore a bunch of weed seeds, they might take root and grow, right?"

"Right."

"And I'm certainly not going to fertilize and water those kinds of seeds for the fun of seeing what they look like when they sprout."

Christy nodded.

"So I pluck 'em and throw 'em away," Jon said, using the appropriate hand motions. "Weeds belong at the dump, not in my garden."

Christy thought about how unassuming Jon appeared. She never would have guessed that her boss, the manager of a pet store, would come up with such insights into life.

Glancing at the clock behind the register, Jon said, "It's about time for your break. Why don't you take it now while your friend is here."

"Okay. And by the way, her name is Katie."

Pulling her backpack out from under the counter and looping it over her shoulder, Christy called out, "It's okay, Katie. He's on to you. You don't have to act like a customer anymore."

Katie was standing behind a tall wire rack loaded with paperback books. She stuck her head around the rack. Only her green eyes showed above the book in her hand, titled *How to House-Train Your Rabbit in 20 Days.*

"Nice to meet you, Katie," Jon called out as the girls scooted out of the shop.

"You too," Katie called over her shoulder.

Giggling, Christy asked, "Did you hear that man who came in right before you and wanted the birdseed? Could you believe that guy?"

"I think he was having a bad day." Katie pulled Christy by the arm. "This way. We're going to the gift shop to find a card for Todd."

"Boy, between you and Jon, nothing in my life is a secret!" Christy teased.

They entered the gift shop and walked down the greeting-card aisle.

"Let me pick out the card, okay?" Christy said.

"Of course," Katie agreed, stopping in front of a display of humorous cards. "I'm only here to offer my support."

"And your opinion," Christy added.

"And my opinion. But only if you want it." Katie lifted a card from the display and scanned it.

"Look!" Katie practically shouted, holding up the card. "This is it! This is perfect. The search has ended. I've found the perfect card. Read it."

"Katie," Christy scolded.

"I know, I know. You only wanted my opinion. Well, in my opinion, this is perfect. Didn't you tell me that Todd has an orange surfboard?"

Christy snatched the card from Katie's eager waving fist and looked it over. On the front was a drawing of a lone surfer on a bright orange board riding the crest of a huge wave and shouting, "Surf's up!" All the cartoon surfers on the beach were grabbing their boards and scrambling over each other in a muddled attempt to join the surfer.

Christy opened the card. Inside it said, *So, what's up in your end of the world?*

"Well," Katie said eagerly, "for a guy who left civilization to surf all winter on Oahu's North Shore, is this the perfect card, or what? And can you believe it? It even has an orange surfboard! Now is that odd, or is that God?"

Christy was laughing by now. "All right, you've convinced me. This is the perfect card for Todd. Let's pay for it, and then I'll treat you to a frozen yogurt next door. Remind me to ask you something."

A few minutes later, they were both scooping chocolate yogurt from their small cups and heading back to the pet store.

"So, what did you want to ask me?" Katie said.

"You never answered me at lunch today about what you want to do together. I thought maybe we could organize that yearly slumber party you were talking about a few weeks ago. I know it's October already, but we could still pretend it's a back-to-school party."

Katie shook her head. "I've tried at least three times to organize it, but it just isn't going to happen. I guess we've all grown up. Maybe high school juniors are too old for sleep-overs. You know, our first party at Janelle's was the year we started sixth grade. Most of those girls aren't interested any-more."

"Why not?"

"Some of them have moved. Most of them have boyfriends or they work. Nobody wanted to have one this year except me."

"And me," Christy added. "I admit I was too busy with Rick and my job and being on restriction and everything when school started. But I really want to have a slumber party now. Even if it's just the two of us."

Katie brightened. "Do you really? When? Any night is fine with me."

"How about tomorrow night? Could we pull it together that fast?" Christy asked.

"Sure! I can make a few calls to some girls and pick up a few bags of chips, some TP, and M&M's. What time can you be there?"

"I get off work at six, so if my parents say it's okay, I'll come right from work," Christy suggested.

"Perfect! I'll go home and clear a space in the freezer—you know, all the usual pre-party preparations."

"Why do you need to clear a space in the freezer?" Christy asked.

"It's tradition to freeze someone's underwear. Whose did we do last year? We try not to get the same person two years in a row."

"I don't remember, but can we just say it was mine so they won't do it to me this year?"

Katie laughed, and Christy knew that Katie was happy and excited about the party. It made Christy feel glad that they were going to do it. But it also made her feel bad that she had put Katie on hold so many times in the past.

"I'll order the pizza at six," Katie said, "so it'll be there when you arrive. This is going to be great!"

The next afternoon, while Christy was at work, Katie called with an update on the party plans. Christy was in the back of the store marking prices on cans of fish food, which made it convenient for her to keep working while she talked.

"I have my sleeping bag and everything in the car," Christy said. "My parents were super nice and said I could keep the car all night. I don't have to be home until after church tomorrow. The only thing is, they don't want me to drive tonight if we go out papering houses. I can only drive to your house and then to church in the morning."

"Sounds good," Katie said. "I've called about fifteen girls. So far only three can come, but you never know. Some of them might show up later."

"Sure." Christy tried to sound optimistic. "You never know who else might come. Who is definitely coming?"

"You, me, and Teri."

Christy's heart sank when she realized that she and Katie were two of the three. Katie deserved better. She deserved a house full of adoring friends who appreciated her for the true friend she was.

"Teri's coming? Really? That's great!" Christy said,

covering up her disappointment. She had tried out for cheerleading with Teri last spring and had wanted a chance to get to know her better ever since.

"Teri's coming for part of it, but she probably can't spend the night. You know, her dad is a pastor. He doesn't like his kids staying out late on Saturday nights because one time Teri's brother was up late and fell asleep in the front pew on Sunday morning. I guess he tumbled onto the floor or something and disrupted the whole service. Anyway, Teri said it's a family rule now that everyone has to be in bed by eleven on Saturday night."

"Ouch!" Christy said.

"What happened?"

"I was trying to open this shipping box, and I smashed my thumb. Oh no!" Christy started to laugh. "Katie, you're not going to believe this."

"What?"

"Guess what's in the box?"

"What?"

"Birdseed! It's a huge box of birdseed, but someone wrote 'Fish Food' on the side of it. Just think, we could've satisfied that birdseed man last night after all. I have to tell Jon. I'll see you around six-thirty. We'll have a great time tonight. You'll see."

Christy hung up the phone and went to find Jon. Her coworker Beverly was standing behind the register helping a young boy. He was counting out his pennies to see if he had enough to buy a plastic treasure chest for his aquarium.

"Is Jon around?" Christy asked her.

"He should be right back. He went to return a shirt," Beverly explained, her silver bracelets clinking on the counter as she helped to count out the pennies.

"Didn't he return a shirt last week?"

"I think that was a pair of pants. Haven't you noticed how Jon shops? He buys stuff first and then decides if he likes it. He's the king of returns. All the department stores here at the mall have his credit card numbers memorized from seeing them so often, first when he buys the stuff, and then when he returns it." Beverly turned to the boy and said, "Looks like you need 27 cents more."

The little boy's face fell. "That's all I have."

"Here," Christy said, reaching for her backpack under the counter. "I'm sure I have a quarter and a couple of pennies. Go ahead and ring it up, Beverly."

"Thanks," the boy said, shooting Christy a big smile. "And if I change my mind, can I return it?"

Beverly and Christy both laughed, and Beverly said, "If you do, make sure you ask for Jon. He's the king of returns around here."

Just then Jon walked in with a bag in each hand.

"I thought you were going to return something," Beverly teased.

"I did. Now I'm trying to decide what to get my sister for her birthday."

He held up the bag in his right hand and said, "It's either a vase or—" holding up the bag in his left hand—"perfume."

Looking to Beverly and Christy for advice, he asked, "Which do you think would be best?"

At the same moment, Christy answered, "Perfume," and Beverly said, "The vase."

"You two are a lot of help." Then, heading toward the

back of the shop, Jon added, "Oh well, I don't have to mail it until next Friday. I should be able to decide by then. I'll just take the other one back."

"What did I tell you?" Beverly swished her long braid back to where it belonged, trailing down her back. "The king of returns."

Right then Christy caught a glimpse of a guy in the mall. He looked a lot like Rick.

Making her way over to the front window, she pretended to work on the dog cage's latch while she scanned the mall for Rick. But she didn't see him anywhere.

Maybe I have my own king of returns returning to my life. Rick said he wouldn't be back from college until Thanksgiving, but I wouldn't put it past him to secretly check up on me.

Letting go of the latch on the dog cage, she realized her hands were shaking. *What's wrong with me? I shouldn't feel this way about seeing Rick. We live in the same town, so we're bound to run into each other. I have no regrets and nothing to hide.*

Christy clenched her fists, realizing she suddenly felt mad. Rick had had this strange power over her ever since she first met him, more than a year ago. As a matter of fact, it had been the night of Katie's slumber party. The girls had papered his house, and he chased Christy down the street. For a whole year he had pursued her. She finally dated him and then broke up with him. But obviously thinking about him still caused her stomach to flip-flop.

Why am I like this? Is this normal? I hate this feeling. I never know when it's going to strike, and it's so hard to make it go away.

"Christy," Jon said, coming up behind her. "What's this I hear about a box of birdseed?"

Her feelings about Rick disappeared quickly. As Christy

followed Jon into the back of the store to show him the box, everything switched from heart-pounding to normal in a matter of minutes.

But that evening, after work, the sweaty-palm feeling hit again.

3

Pass the M&M's

"I'd like to make a payment on a bracelet you're holding for me," Christy said to the salesclerk at the jewelry store.

She stopped in every Saturday after work to pay off Todd's bracelet, which Rick had used as a down payment for a bracelet he had bought her. "It's under Miller. Christy Miller."

"Just a moment," the tall blond woman replied. She made her way to the back of the store, where she spoke to the manager in hushed tones.

The manager looked up and, recognizing Christy, picked up a box and came out to the counter.

"Christy Miller," the older man said with a toothy smile. "How are you?"

"Fine, thanks. I just came in to make my weekly payment." She couldn't figure out why he was being so friendly and grinning at her that way.

"No need," he said, holding out the box. "It's all yours. Paid in full."

"I-I-I don't understand," Christy stammered. "I still have five more payments."

"Nope." The man placed the long, slim box in her hand. "A certain party, who wishes to remain anonymous, has paid it off. You can take it with you today."

"Who? What certain party?"

"Sorry. Can't tell you. He wishes to remain anonymous."

"He?" Christy whispered to herself. *Not Rick. Rick would never have done this. Or would he? He knew how upset I was that he stole it. Is it possible Rick returned the silver bracelet he gave me to get my gold one back?*

"Go ahead," the man said. "Put it on. I cleaned it for you this afternoon. No charge. It's a beautiful bracelet."

Christy couldn't believe she was getting Todd's bracelet back! She felt as though this was almost a sacred moment. It certainly wasn't one she wanted to share with the jewelry store manager.

"Thank you very much," she said, tucking the unopened box into her backpack. "I really appreciate it. Thank you." She backed up and quickly made her exit so she wouldn't feel forced to open the box in front of him and have him offer to help clasp the bracelet to her wrist.

She hurried back to the pet store, where she planned to slip out the back door and into the parking lot. Jon was sitting at the card table in the back room, going through the day's mail.

"Good night," she called out as she breezed past him. "See you next week."

"Glad to have your bracelet finally?" Jon asked, without appearing to look up from his letters.

Christy stopped and spun around, astounded. "How did you know?"

Then it struck her that Jon knew she was making payments because the jewelry store manager had called him to check on her credit.

"You didn't pay for this, did you? Because if you did, well, I was paying for it, and I'll pay you back."

Jon looked at her as if he didn't understand a word she was saying.

"You can take it out of my paycheck—really—every week until it's paid off." Christy caught her breath. "I appreciate it, but you didn't have to do it."

"Do what?" Jon looked amused at her ramblings.

"You mean you weren't the one who paid off my bracelet?" Christy asked slowly. "Then how did you know?"

Jon shook his head and smiled. "I saw the jewelry box sticking out of your backpack when you walked by. I knew you'd been making payments on a bracelet at the jewelry store. I figured that must be the one."

"Oh," was all Christy could manage to say.

"Have a good time at Katie's tonight." Jon went back to his stack of bills.

"I will. Thanks." Christy reached for her keys in her purse and headed for her car.

Wait a minute! How did Jon know I was going to Katie's?

Deciding that her boss worked as an undercover detective in his spare time, Christy unlocked the door to the small blue car she shared with her mom and slid onto the seat.

Inside the warm car, she held the bracelet box solemnly in her hand before opening it. At this moment it didn't matter who had paid off the balance. The gold ID bracelet was hers once more.

"Father," she whispered, "thank You. Thank You for letting me get my bracelet back, and thank You for Todd. Please keep him safe in Hawaii. And please fix our relationship so I can feel like we're close friends again. Thank You that You always listen to me and You care about every little thing in my life. I love You, Lord!"

Opening her eyes, Christy raised the lid on the jewelry box. The instant she saw the bracelet—perfect, shining, with its engraved "Forever"—she felt jubilant.

Katie could hardly believe Christy's story a short time later when Christy proudly held out her right arm for Katie to inspect.

"Do you think Rick paid for it?" Katie asked.

"No, not really. I kind of think it might be my boss. He seems like the sort of person who would do something nice in secret."

"Well, whoever paid for it, I think it's a total God-thing. I hope you never, ever take it off again."

"I don't plan to," Christy said with a confident smile. "So, where's Teri? Is she coming?"

"No, she called about an hour ago. I guess her mom is sick, so she thinks she'd better stay home and help out. Looks like it's just you and me."

Katie pointed toward the kitchen table covered with snack food and said, "Do you think we'll have enough to eat?"

"That's not all for us, is it?"

"My mom said my brothers could eat whatever we left, but they're both out with my dad and probably won't be back till late. Go ahead and grab some pizza and something to drink. We can eat in the living room. I rented a couple of movies."

Katie sounded like she was looking forward to their evening together, but Christy could tell she was disappointed that it was just the two of them.

For the first two hours, they kicked back on the couch, eating and watching an old movie about a VW bug with a mind of its own. It was kind of funny, but not really.

As soon as the film ended, Christy felt the sadness in Katie's voice again as she said, "Do you want to watch another video or play a game or what?"

"Doesn't matter to me. What do you want to do?"

"Are you hungry?" Katie asked. "There's lots more food."

Christy puffed out her cheeks and patted her stomach. "I'm so full I couldn't eat another chip if you forced me."

"We could try new hairstyles," Katie suggested.

"Oh, please! Don't even look at my hair. I've given up on it. I keep trying different shampoos and conditioners, but haven't found anything I like. I don't know what to do with it anymore."

"I like it the way it is right now. It looks more like the real you. More natural. No offense, but when you had it short, it didn't really fit you, if you know what I mean."

"I used to have really long hair, almost down to my waist," Christy said.

"Why did you cut it?"

"My aunt Marti talked me into it two summers ago when I first came out from Wisconsin. She told me I needed a 'California look.'"

Katie tilted her head, examining Christy's hair. "Yes, I definitely like you better with long hair. Didn't you tell me once that Todd said he liked your hair long?"

Christy nodded, smiling at the memory of Todd's comment.

"Speaking of Todd, did you send his card yet?" Katie asked.

"I sent it this morning from work."

"What did you write in it? I mean, only if you want to tell me. If it's too personal, that's okay. I understand."

"Don't worry. It was definitely not too personal," Christy said. "I didn't write much. I told him I was praying for him and thinking about him. I told him about my job at the pet store. Stuff like that. I said I hoped he had done well in the surfing competitions. He's always quoting verses, so I thought I'd send him a verse I liked. Only I just wrote the reference, so he'll have to look it up himself."

"That's so cool," Katie said. "It's like sending a message in secret code. What verse was it? Or is that too personal to ask? You don't have to tell me if you don't want to."

"No, it's not too personal. I found it in Philippians, because that's one of my favorite books in the Bible. I don't remember the exact verse. Is your Bible around? I could show you."

Katie uncoiled herself from the couch and returned from her bedroom a moment later with her Bible.

"Here it is." Christy found Philippians and pointed to chapter 1, verse 3. "Beginning here to the first part of verse 7."

Katie read aloud: "'I thank my God in all my remembrance of you, always in every prayer of mine for you all making my prayer with joy, because of your partnership in the gospel from the first day until now. And I am sure of this, that he who began a good work in you will bring it to completion at the day of Jesus Christ. It is right for me to feel this way about you all, because I hold you in my heart....'"

"Oh, Christy!" Katie exclaimed. "That is so romantic!"

"Romantic?" Christy said with a laugh. "It's a Bible verse!"

"I know, but that last part, 'I hold you in my heart,' is so tender. When Todd reads that, he's going to drop his surfboard, hop the next plane, and come running to your doorstep."

Christy laughed. "I doubt it. Hopefully when Todd reads it, he will feel encouraged and know that I really care about him."

"And that you hold him in your heart," Katie added.

"Oh stop it, Katie! It's not just about Todd. It says 'you all' a bunch of times. Those verses apply to you too. You're my friend, and I thank God for you all the time."

"I thank God for you too, Christy. It seems that good friends are harder and harder to find." Katie closed her Bible and set it on the coffee table.

"I know what you mean," Christy agreed. "I guess that the more things change, the more we have to hold on to true friends."

Katie nodded.

"You know," Christy said, "I'm sorry this didn't turn out to be much of a slumber party, like the ones you used to have. Let's think of something else you and I can do together. What's something you'd really like to do or somewhere you'd really like to go?"

Katie thought for a moment. "Well, there is one thing I've always wanted to do, but I didn't want to do it by myself. I wanted somebody to go with me."

"I'll do it with you." Christy quickly added, "As long as it isn't bungee jumping or skydiving."

"No, nothing that wild. It's skiing. I've always wanted to go skiing."

Christy swallowed hard. To her, skiing was right up there with bungee jumping and all those other sports where you travel at a high speed with no control over your body.

Katie looked at Christy, her freckled nose all scrunched up in anticipation. "So what do you think? We could join the ski club at school and go on the trip with them to Lake Tahoe at Thanksgiving. Wouldn't that be great? You asked what I really wanted to do, and that's what I've always wanted to do."

Christy knew the credibility of her offer to strengthen her friendship with Katie now rested on her answer. She knew it was within her power to bless her friend or pull the dream out from underneath her.

"Is there still time to join the ski club? Haven't they met already?" Christy said, stalling her answer.

"This Monday is the last day to join. They meet after school in Mr. Riley's class. I went last week because I wanted to join, but I didn't particularly want to spend a ski weekend with any of the kids who are in the club."

"You didn't tell me you went."

"I didn't think you'd be interested. I guess it was just a wild thought."

"No, it's a great thought. We could do that. We could join the ski club together. I've never been skiing before though. Do they let people like me join?"

"I've never skied before, either," Katie said. "So I asked last week. They said at Squaw Valley, where they're going for the club trip, they offer ski lessons to beginners like us. We could take lessons together."

Katie looked so excited that Christy reluctantly said, "Well, okay. Let's go Monday and sign up."

"This is great!" Katie plopped the bowl of M&M's in her lap and tossed a handful into her mouth. "You wait and see. We're going to have the absolute best time! Finally we get to go on a trip together."

Christy tried to ignore all her uncertain, nervous feelings about this. She was doing it for Katie, so it was the right thing to do. She shouldn't be such a chicken when it came to adventure. Hadn't she survived driving the Hana road this summer in Maui? Certainly she could survive ski lessons.

"What do you want to do now?" Katie asked. "It's only nine-thirty. Do you want to go toilet-paper somebody's house? We could give each other egg white and oatmeal facials maybe. Or we could watch *Gone with the Wind.*"

"That's the other movie you rented? You didn't tell me that! I thought it was another car movie. I'd love to watch *Gone with the Wind*!" Christy exclaimed. "I've only seen it once, and I missed the end because I fell asleep. Let's watch it, okay?"

Katie jumped up to pop the movie into the machine. "So your choice for the evening is a marathon movie and more junk food. I knew there was a reason we got along so well! We have the same taste in slumber parties."

Returning to her nest on the couch, Katie threw her sleeping bag over her legs. She turned to Christy, who now held the candy bowl in her lap, and said, "Come on, future ski bunny. Pass the M&M's."

With a laugh, Christy thought, *Ski chicken is more like it.*

4

Friendship? Yes, Please!

"How much is this trip going to cost?" Christy's dad asked on Monday evening.

"It's around $150, but we're having a fund-raiser, so it won't cost that much really." Christy tried to sound confident. She felt a little more positive about the trip after the meeting that afternoon. It sounded like it would be a lot of fun, and Katie was excited about it.

Christy's dad was on his knees with a screwdriver in his hand, trying to repair the upside-down, disassembled recliner chair in the living room. He scratched his reddish-brown hair with the end of the screwdriver. "That's a lot of money, Christy. How much do you expect to raise, and how are you going to do it?"

"We're selling candy bars for two dollars apiece. A dollar goes toward the cost of the candy, and a dollar toward the trip. Would you like to buy one?" she asked with a childish grin. She knew that her dad could pull the plug on the trip if he didn't think she should go.

"I want a candy bar." David spoke up from his corner of the couch, where he was attempting to do his math homework. "Can I have one?"

"You'll have to ask your mother when she gets back from the grocery store," Dad answered. "She's the one with the secret cash around here. I don't know where she hides it."

"It's in the freezer. I'll show you," David scooted off the couch. "She keeps it in that old tin that says 'grease.'"

"Stay where you are, son. Get that homework done."

Dad went back to work on the chair, muttering to himself, "Imagine that. All these years, and I never knew where she kept it. Even my ten-year-old knows that what I thought was frozen bacon grease is really her stash."

Just then the phone rang, and David jumped up. "I'll get it!"

"Don't bother, David. I've already got it," Christy said, reaching for the phone in the kitchen.

"Christina dear," came the voice on the other end. "How are you? Bob and I were just saying we hadn't heard from you or your folks for a while and wondered how everything was going there."

"We're all fine, Aunt Marti. How are you guys?"

"We're both fine. How's school going for you? Are you finding new groups to get involved with since you dropped out of cheerleading?"

Christy cringed at the jab about cheerleading, but she was glad to report to her aunt that she had joined the ski club. She knew it was the kind of club Aunt Marti would approve of.

That news was all Aunt Marti needed to set into motion a string of plans. First she told Christy she would take three boxes of the fund-raiser candy bars and sell them at her next women's meeting. Whatever portion of the necessary $150 Christy couldn't raise, Aunt Marti would gladly supply.

Of course, Christy couldn't go skiing without the right attire. Aunt Marti said she would go shopping tomorrow for ski clothes and have the outfits sent directly to Christy's house.

"The clothes should arrive this weekend at the latest," Aunt Marti stated. "That should give you plenty of time to try them on and decide if you need any more."

"Aunt Marti, you really don't have to do all this for me, you know."

"Why are you always trying to spoil my fun, Christina? You know I love helping you out like this. Goodness knows, your mother would love to provide these things for you if she could. But we all know that's just not possible on your father's salary. Let me do this for you, and please stop acting as if it's such a huge favor. It's nothing, really."

Christy sighed. She had learned long ago not to cross her aunt. "Thanks, Aunt Marti. Do you want me to mail the boxes of candy to you?"

"Actually, Bob is playing golf in Rancho Santa Fe this Wednesday. I'll have him stop by and pick up the candy. I might even be able to send some of thc ski clothes with him. That is, if I can find everything we need by tomorrow. Say, is your mother home? I need to talk to her."

"She just walked in the door," Christy said, holding out the phone to her mom.

Mom's round face looked flushed as she placed two big bags of groceries on the counter and brushed back her short graying hair.

"It's your sister," Christy said.

Mom smiled, took the phone, and answered brightly, "Hello, Martha. How are you?"

With her free hand, Mom motioned for Christy to unload the rest of the groceries from the car.

"Come on, David," Christy called as she marched through the living room. "Help me carry in the groceries."

"I can't," David said, pushing up his glasses. "I have to finish my homework."

Oh brother, Christy thought, *you'll jump up to answer the phone and to reveal Mom's freezer secrets, but when I ask you to help, you suddenly have to do your homework.*

"Go on, David," Dad said. "You can take a quick break and help your sister. I think I'll take a break too." He laid down the screwdriver and joined Christy and David in unloading the car.

A few minutes later, the kitchen counters were covered with nine bags of groceries. Mom had hung up the phone and begun the challenge of putting everything away.

"How come you never buy any good stuff?" David asked. "All my friends at school get cupcakes and candy bars in their lunches. All I ever get is an oatmeal cookie."

"I'm trying to keep our family healthy," Mom said. "We all eat too much junk food as it is. I'm not going to pay good money for that stuff when a homemade oatmeal cookie is much better for you."

Dad turned to Christy and said under his breath, "Sounds like your mother read another one of those health food articles. Just watch. Bet you anything we're having tofu and bean sprouts for dinner."

"I heard that," Mom said. "And no, we're not having tofu. We're having stir-fry."

"With beef?" Dad asked, looking hopeful.

"No."

"Chicken?"

"No, just vegetables. Lots and lots of vegetables."

Dad looked disappointed.

Mom tried to convince him. "We don't need to eat meat at every meal. Besides, it saves money on our food bill, and it's good for us to pork out on vegetables every once in a while."

"Pork," Dad repeated. "Now, that's a good idea. You could throw some pork chops in with those vegetables, and we'd have a real meal."

Mom gave Dad a look Christy knew well. It was a mock-stern look in which she stuck out her chin and lowered her eyebrows. But all it did was make Dad laugh.

"Okay, okay." In two steps he was across the kitchen floor and scooping Mom up in a bear hug. "We'll be your vegetarian guinea pigs tonight. And tomorrow night, if you want to test out a huge slab of prime rib on us, hey, we won't complain a bit, will we, kids?"

"Yeesh," David said. "They look like they're going to start kissing. I'm going to do my homework."

Christy kept putting away the groceries. Out of the corner of her eye, she watched her parents snuggling. She thought it was kind of cute the way they still teased each other and acted a little goofy, especially after being married for so many years.

"Oh, leave those out," Mom said when she saw Christy loading the celery and carrots into the refrigerator. "That's part of our stir-fry for tonight."

"I'll leave you two to your chop-sueying." Dad headed back to his project in the living room. He still had a grin on his face.

Christy thought about how her dad came across so gruff and stern most of the time. Then at moments like this, she wondered what he was like as a teenager and what her mom was like when the two of them first met.

While they spent the next twenty minutes chopping up vegetables, Christy asked her mom questions about how she met Dad and what things had been like for them. Most of Mom's answers Christy had already heard. She knew the stories of their engagement and wedding by heart.

"What about when you were dating?" Christy asked. "What made you so sure you liked Dad more than that other guy you were seeing? What was his name?"

"Well, you know, in a small town everyone knows everyone else," Mom explained. "I had known your father since we were in grade school. The other kids said he was a bully because he was kind of big for his age. I thought he was shy though. And I liked him as a good friend for many years."

Mom opened a new bottle of all-natural canola oil and poured some into the hot electric skillet. "So when he finally asked me out, it just seemed right because we'd been friends—good friends—for so many years."

"How did you know he was the one you wanted to marry?" Christy asked, scraping the carrots off the cutting board and watching them dance in the hot skillet.

Mom's worry lines disappeared. "Because I couldn't picture myself spending the rest of my life with anyone else."

Christy thought about her mom's statement for the rest of the evening. After dinner she attacked her homework. The first paper she pulled out was her English essay on true friends. The class had slid by without them having to turn in their essays that morning because they'd had a substitute who didn't know anything about the assignment.

The night before Christy had thrown away her first draft and put together a couple paragraphs on how a true friend was someone you can trust. Reading her essay now, it sounded flat.

"A true friend is..." she repeated, lifting her stuffed Pooh Bear and balancing him on her knees. "What is a true friend, Pooh?"

Deciding to work from what she had already written rather than start over, Christy continued to write about how you can always trust a true friend. She thought it would be nice to include Katie in her essay, since Katie seemed to be writing about her.

A true friend will tell you what you need to hear, Christy wrote, *even when what she or he has to say might not be what you want to hear.*

After several minutes of work, Christy reread her essay and started to critique her grammar. She wondered if it was okay to end one of her sentences with *is*. She knew the teacher would squawk because she had used the word *totally,* so she changed it to *sincerely*.

Then she noticed she had used *sincerely* a few words later. Using the same word twice, so close together, was another no-no with her English teacher.

This is a lot harder than I thought it would be. But I sure could use a good grade in this class.

It took her at least fifteen minutes to rewrite her sentences. By the time she had finished, she had lost any previous creativity.

I don't think it's possible for my right brain and left brain to work together. How can I be creative and critical at the same time? This writing business is hard!

Forcing herself to go on, Christy tried extra hard to capture a good description of a friend. It seemed to take forever. She decided that writing three full pages was entirely too long an assignment for such a simple topic.

At least Christy had nice handwriting in her favor. When she finally finished, she recopied the paper so it would look neat. She liked the final line of her essay: *I would have to agree with Constantine, who said, "My treasures are my friends."* It was her favorite quote from the list her English teacher had passed out.

"What do you think, Pooh?" Christy held up her finished paper for him to see. "Think I'll get an A?"

Christy tucked her paper into her notebook and got ready for bed. Before turning out the light, she reached under her bed and pulled out a shoe box covered in floral wrapping paper. She opened it and peered at the three letters inside.

This was her secret box, containing letters written to her future husband. She had written the first letter on her sixteenth birthday. The other two she had written during the past few months when she had something on her heart she wanted to write down for the guy she would someday marry.

Every time Christy wrote to him, she prayed for him. Her goal was to present this box to her husband on their wedding day. He would see that for years she had been praying for him and thinking about how to be the best partner in the world for him.

Christy lifted the pad of plain, white writing paper and in her best handwriting wrote,

Dear Future Husband,

I was thinking today about friends and about how I want us to always be good friends—before and after we're married. I think I still have a lot to learn about how to be a good friend, but I'm trying to be more encouraging and supportive of my friend Katie. I actually let her talk me into going skiing! Do you like to ski?

I just wanted you to know that I'm praying for you and thinking about you.

Your friend,

Christy

She carefully folded the letter and added it to the collection in the box. Then, slipping the box back under her bed, she held her Pooh Bear tightly and prayed for her future husband—whoever and wherever he might be.

5

You Go, Girlfriend!

On Wednesday, Christy hurried home from school and finished her homework before dinner. Her youth group met on Wednesday nights for Bible study, and the agreement with her parents was that she had to have her homework done before she could go. She had been to the Bible study only once before because she had never managed to complete her homework in time. Tonight she had a good reason for going—Katie.

Christy grabbed her Bible and car keys, eager to rush out the door at ten minutes before seven.

Her mom called after her, "Be sure you're home by nine. Don't give anyone a ride. Lock the doors, and call us if you have any problems."

"Okay, Mom," Christy answered. "I'll be fine. See you at nine."

Smiling to herself, she thought, *I'm only going a few miles to church. My parents make it sound like I'm going on a safari!*

She made it just in time and found Katie in the back row, saving a seat for her.

"Did you see that new guy over there?" Katie whispered, pointing toward the front of the room. "He just moved here from Ecuador. I heard his parents are missionaries."

Christy saw the guy Katie was pointing at. He was nice-looking with light brown hair, broad shoulders, and fair skin with a sprinkling of freckles.

"He sure doesn't look like a missionary kid," Christy whispered back.

"Why? Because he looks normal?" Katie asked.

"I guess. You know what I mean. He looks like any other guy here."

"Let's talk to him afterward, okay? I bet it's not easy to make friends and fit into a new culture and everything after living in the jungle."

"Did he really live in the jungle?" Christy asked.

"Sure! Where else would a missionary live in Ecuador?"

The Bible study leader, Luke, asked everyone to find a seat so they could get started.

Christy watched the new guy sit down in the front row and thought, *That missionary kid doesn't look like the Tarzan type. I wonder if he really lived in a rain forest.*

After opening in prayer, Luke introduced Glen to the rest of the group and had him stand and say a few words.

Glen looked nervous as he quickly explained that he and his family were missionaries in the city of Quito and that his dad worked at a Christian radio station there.

Christy and Katie exchanged glances, and Katie whispered, "And I thought he lived in a hut and ate tree bark?"

The study that night centered on what it meant to be a missionary. At least four times, Luke said, "Each of us is a missionary right where we are. We don't have to go to a foreign country to tell others about the Lord. Start seeing your high school as your mission field." Toward the end, he asked if anyone had any comments to add.

To Christy's surprise, Katie's hand shot up.

"I want to ask you guys to pray for us—for Christy and me—because we're sort of going on a missions trip."

Christy gave Katie a puzzled look, feeling a little embarrassed that Katie had included her name in this announcement, especially since she wasn't sure what Katie was going to say.

With a grin, Katie explained to the group, "We've joined the ski club at Kelley High, and we're going on a trip with them over Thanksgiving weekend. I think it's going to be a real opportunity to witness to a lot of the people, because none of them go to church as far as I know."

"That's great!" Luke said. "It's a chance for you both to see what it's like to be in the world but not of it. We'll be praying for you both."

He turned around and wrote on the board, *Katie Weldon and Christy Miller—school ski trip.*

"Does anyone else have something they'd like to add?"

I wonder what he meant by "in the world but not of it"? This ski trip is such a big deal for Katie! Now she's turned it into a missions trip. I hope she doesn't get too disappointed if it ends up we can't go.

"I have something," said a girl in the middle of the room.

Christy had seen her before, but she went to a different school, and Christy didn't know her name. She seemed really nice. Christy had thought once before when she saw her in Sunday school that she was the kind of girl Christy would like to get to know.

"Sure, Lisa, go ahead," Luke said.

"I have a list I started a couple of weeks ago, and I've

been carrying it around in the back of my Bible. I guess you could call it a hit list."

Some people sitting near Lisa laughed. She didn't look like the kind of person who would have a hit list. Tall and gentle-looking, Lisa had long brown hair that hung in soft curls. She appeared to be the sort of person who had a kind word for everyone.

Lisa's cheeks began to turn pink as she explained, "It's not a list of people I'm trying to get..." She paused and said, "Well, I guess maybe it is."

Lisa looked flustered. Luke jumped in and encouraged her to keep going. "That's okay," he said. "I think I know what you're getting at. A hit list is probably the best way of describing it too. Go ahead and explain what the list is for."

Looking a little more courageous, Lisa went on. "See, what I did was ask God to show me who He wanted me to witness to this year at school. Then, when certain friends came to mind, I wrote down their names. I have six names on my list, and every night when I have my quiet time, I pray for them."

"Is your plan to simply pray for these six friends?" Luke asked.

"Well, I really wanted to start witnessing to my friends, but I wasn't sure exactly how to do it. A couple of weeks ago you taught about how prayer is the key that unlocks any door. So I'm starting by praying for them. Then, when opportunities come up, I want to tell them about the Lord."

"That's a great idea, Lisa. Let me ask you something. Do you feel it's your personal responsibility to make sure each one of those six friends gives his or her heart to the Lord?"

Christy thought of how she might answer if Luke had directed the question toward her. She probably would have said yes. It seemed to her that if she were willing to make that kind of commitment to pray for six friends, then she should be willing to keep at it until they all became Christians.

"No," Lisa answered.

You're a lot braver than I am, Lisa, to admit that in front of everybody!

"I mean, I feel it's my personal responsibility to pray for them every day and to tell them about the Lord. But I know the way they respond to it all is their own responsibility. Theirs and God's, really."

"Good," Luke said. "I'm glad you see the difference. That's what witnessing is all about. We need to be faithful to pray and faithful to share, but we must leave all the results up to God. If we've done all that, and they're still not interested, we have to try not to take it personally. If they reject the message, remember it's our heavenly Father they're rejecting."

Luke turned and added Lisa Huisman's name to the list on the board.

"We'll be praying for you, too, on your missionary journey. I'd encourage all of you to start your own hit list. Remember, the foundation has to be prayer." Luke took a deep breath and crossed his arms across his broad chest.

Then he looked at his watch and said, "We need to wrap it up. Let's pray for Katie, Christy, and Lisa."

Luke prayed for them and then closed the Bible study by saying, "Everyone, be sure to introduce yourself to Glen. One more thing. There's a sign-up sheet at the back door for the pizza feed Friday night after the football game. It's three dollars for church kids and free for any friends you bring."

Everyone started to talk. Luke spoke over the rumblings. "This is exactly what we've been talking about, you guys. A chance to bring your friends to a place where they'll hear about the Lord and have fun at the same time. Don't just come by yourself or with your church friends. Consider this your missionary opportunity of the week." Then, sounding like a football coach, he shouted, "Now everybody go out there and give 'em heaven this week!"

Christy felt bad because she had to work Friday night and couldn't come to the pizza feed. The whole lesson that night had made her think though about how few friends she had outside her church friends. If she were going to the pizza feed, who would she invite? Maybe this ski club was a good idea because she could meet some new people and invite them to church with her.

"Come on," Katie urged, standing up and tugging on Christy's arm. "Let's meet Glen."

"Do I detect a girl with a crush on a guy here?" Christy teased.

"I'm only trying to be friendly," Katie said with a gleam in her eye. "Luke told us to make Glen feel welcome, didn't he?"

Just then Luke came up and said, "I'm glad you told us about the ski club, Katie. It's a great opportunity for both of you."

His warm smile made Christy feel welcomed into the group as he turned to her and said, "I'm glad to see you here, Christy. I hope it works out for you to come all the time."

"I hope so too." Christy felt a little guilty for not getting involved earlier. "I wanted to come to the pizza feed on Friday, but I have to work."

"Maybe you can stop by after work," Luke suggested. "We'll be cranked up here until around midnight."

Christy felt silly explaining to Luke that her parents had a strict curfew of ten. She smiled. "Maybe."

Katie looked over Christy's shoulder, obviously trying to track Glen. "We probably should get going, Christy."

"Can I ask you both a question first?" Luke asked.

Katie glanced over at Glen and then back at Luke. "Yes?"

"Do either of you see Rick Doyle anymore? I thought someone said he was dating one of you."

"Not me!" Katie said in quick defense.

Christy shyly admitted, "I was. I went out with him last month. He isn't around anymore though because he's going to San Diego State."

"I knew that," Luke said, "but I was trying to see if he was spending time with any Christians. He sort of dropped out of everything toward the end of last year, and I haven't seen him around. I thought I'd see who keeps in contact with him and find out how he's doing."

"I don't really know much about how he's doing," Christy said. "But he moved into an apartment with some Christian guys, and one of them, Doug, is a friend of mine. Doug's a really strong Christian."

"Well, good. That's encouraging. If you see Rick, tell him I asked about him and that I'm praying for him."

"She probably won't see him," Katie blurted out, giving Christy a "let's get going" look. Then quickly she added, "I need to sign up for the pizza feed. Excuse me." With a swish of her copper hair, she turned and made a beeline for the clipboard by the back door.

Christy noticed that Glen was by the door with pen in hand, ready to sign up, when Katie practically pounced on him. She must have said something funny to him, because he smiled at her, and they began a conversation.

You go, girlfriend!

Christy glanced at the clock on the wall and realized she had only ten minutes to make it home by nine. She caught Katie's eye, waved good-bye, and headed for the less-crowded front door.

All the way home she thought about how cute it was seeing Katie with a crush on Glen. She hoped he was a nice guy and wouldn't break her heart. She couldn't wait till the next day at school so she could ask Katie how everything went with him.

"Okay, so tell me your opening line," Christy said the next morning when she entered her English class and found Katie already at her desk.

"What opening line?"

"With Glen! You had him laughing in ten seconds. How did you do it?"

"Oh, that," Katie said with a laugh. "You noticed, huh?"

"Yes, of course I noticed. Tell me what happened."

"I just asked him if he ever ate bug larvae in Ecuador."

"Katie, how gross!" But Christy had to giggle. "Why did you ask him that?"

"I wanted to be original," Katie said with a smile. "It worked! He said he'd look for me tomorrow night at the pizza feed."

The teacher interrupted their conversation by saying, "This is not a social club. Will you please find your seat, Miss Miller, so we can begin our class?"

Why do I get the feeling this teacher isn't exactly crazy about me?

Christy hurried to her seat and made a special effort to perform as a model student for the remainder of the class.

At lunch Christy caught up on the rest of Katie's story. It sounded like she and Glen had really hit it off, and Katie was excited about seeing him Friday night. Christy felt a little left out since she had to work. She was determined to be enthusiastic and supportive of Katie, the same way Katie had always been supportive of her.

"What do you think I should wear?" Katie asked. "Jeans would probably be good, right? And what? A sweatshirt or sweater or T-shirt? I could wear that University of Hawaii one you got me, or is that too cheesy?"

"No, I think that would be great."

"You're just saying that. I can tell. Your words are saying, 'That's great,' but your face is saying, 'Katie, girl, go buy yourself a new shirt.' And can I just say that I think that's a very good idea and that you have been elected to come shopping with me to help pick it out?"

Katie caught her breath and looked at Christy expectantly. "How about it? Can you go to the mall after school?"

"I don't know. I'll have to ask. If you think about it, you already have some really nice outfits you could wear if you didn't have the money to buy something new." Christy chose her words carefully, since a few weeks ago Katie had said that all she had to spend on back-to-school clothes was the seventy-five dollars her grandmother had sent her and that had barely paid for her new shoes.

"I've got twenty dollars from babysitting that I was going to use for the ski trip. This seems much more important though."

"How are you doing on selling your candy bars?" Christy asked. "Do you think you'll be able to sell all fifteen of your boxes in the next three weeks?"

Katie quickly turned the question back on Christy. "How about you? How many have you sold so far?"

"Well, my uncle came by last night while we were at youth group. He was going to take three of the boxes for my aunt to sell at her women's group."

"So you sold three boxes without doing a thing?"

"Actually, he ended up taking all fifteen boxes. He said he'd pass them out to all the trick-or-treaters on Halloween."

"Let me get this straight," Katie said. "Your uncle bought all fifteen of your boxes last night, and now you have your total amount for the ski trip raised?"

"Well...yeah, I guess I do." It hadn't hit Christy that way until this minute. She now had even fewer reasons to back out of the trip.

"All you need is for your aunt to buy you a couple of new ski outfits, and you're all set."

"I told you she was doing that, right?"

Katie threw her hands up in the air. "Don't tell me. She already bought you a new outfit."

"Come on. I told you she was going to buy some ski stuff. At least I thought I told you."

Christy couldn't believe how upset Katie was acting over Uncle Bob and Aunt Marti's generous involvement. "My uncle left the outfits last night, but I haven't tried them on yet."

"Christy, I was being sarcastic about the outfits! You mean your aunt actually bought you some?"

"You have to understand what my aunt is like. This is nothing to her. It's her way of being a part of my life or something. It's not like I go around asking her to buy me things."

Katie shook her head. "You are spoiled rotten by your rich relatives, Christy Miller, and you don't even know it."

Now it was Christy's turn to get huffy. "I am not! I have to work just so I can have money to put gas in the car. Did you forget that? And you've seen where I live. My family can't even afford to buy a house; we're renting that little house. Your house is three times as big as ours, you have your own car, and your dad pays for your insurance and your gas."

"Okay, okay." Katie bowed her head in surrender. "You're right. It is ridiculous for us to get all hyper over nothing. I guess I didn't expect you to have your money this soon, especially when I'm dealing with negative funds..." Her voice trailed off.

"What do you mean?"

"I kind of, well, I sort of haven't sold any, really."

"Wait a minute," Christy said, reaching for Katie's fund-raiser candy box next to her and opening the cardboard handle. "There are only two left in here. That means you sold eight. That's eight dollars toward the trip. What's wrong with that?"

Katie's voice became softer as she looked down and said, "I didn't exactly sell eight candy bars."

Christy counted again. "There are only two left in here. With ten in a box, that means you sold eight, right? You've earned eight dollars."

Looking up and biting her lower lip, Katie confessed, "Actually, I owe $16."

Christy's blue-green eyes widened, and she said, "Katie Weldon, you didn't!"

"Well, see, I have this thing about chocolate. I can't be in the same room with it. It starts calling my name and says, 'Eat me! Eat me!' In the middle of the night, it wakes me up. When I'm trying to do my homework, it keeps bothering me. Really, Christy, I've tried ignoring it, I've tried telling myself that it's calling to some other Katie, not me. I've tried everything! The only way to shut it up is to eat it."

By this time Christy was giggling at Katie's confession. "Eight jumbo chocolate bars in two days?"

"Three days," Katie corrected. "We got them on Monday, remember?"

"Aren't you sick?"

"Actually, I feel pretty good," Katie said, her mischievous smile returning. "I kind of feel like I'm in love. Isn't that what they said in science class last year? Chocolate releases some chemical in your brain and makes you think you're in love?"

"I don't know about that, but you'd better lay off the candy bars tonight and tomorrow. Otherwise, when you see Glen tomorrow night, you won't know if it's true love or the chocolate double-crossing you!"

"I think you're right," Katie said somberly. "What should I do about the fund-raiser, though? I mean, this is like the worst-case scenario. We're supposed to go on this trip together, and so far you have all your money, as well as new outfits, and I owe the ski club sixteen bucks. You wouldn't go skiing without me, would you?"

Christy laughed some more before offering her solution. "How about if you give me all your chocolate bars, and I'll see if we can sell them at the pet shop? Jon is cool about stuff like this. Then, instead of buying a new shirt for tomorrow night, why don't you borrow one of mine so you'll feel like you're wearing something new? Then give me sixteen of your twenty dollars so your fund-raiser account will be brought back up to zero."

"I guess you're right. That only leaves me with four dollars, though."

"So? That will get you through the weekend. The pizza feed costs three dollars, and you have a dollar left over for...for the offering on Sunday!"

"Good idea," Katie said. "I was thinking of giving to a special church fund, anyway."

"Let me guess. Could it be the missionary fund?"

Both girls started to laugh.

"You know, those missionaries need all the support they can get," Katie said.

"And I'm sure you'll see to that by socially supporting your very own favorite missionary tomorrow night!" Christy teased.

"We all must try to do whatever we can," Katie said with a mock straight face. "And this is my little way of helping out."

6

Peculiar Treasures

That afternoon Katie and Christy set out to find a shirt of Christy's for Katie to borrow. Forty-five minutes into the project, Christy's bed was covered with clothes, and Katie still hadn't decided on one. She had tried on nearly everything Christy owned, but nothing seemed to suit her.

"I still like the green one on you." Christy lowered herself to the floor and rested her back against her bed.

Katie held it up and gave her honest opinion. "It looks like old-fashioned long underwear."

"I know. It's supposed to. It looks good on you."

Katie slipped it back on and studied herself in the mirror. "But it's long-sleeved. What if it's really hot inside?"

"Push up the sleeves. Yeah, like that. It looks sporty on you."

"I always look sporty. I don't want to look sporty; I want to look cute. No, take that back. I want to look attractive. No, change that to stunning. No, actually..." Katie spun around and spurted out, "I don't want to look like me. I want to look like you!"

"Like me?" Christy stammered. "Why? You're adorable, Katie. Look at you. You've got the total aerobic body, unique red, swishy hair, and wildly green eyes. I mean it, Katie. You're adorable."

"I don't want green eyes. I want guys to call them 'killer eyes,' like they do yours. And unique red hair is great only when you're a groupie at a rock concert. I'd rather have shiny brown hair like yours."

Christy was silent. She had never compared herself with Katie before, and she didn't know how to deny the things Katie was saying about her.

"Face it." Katie let her true feelings out. "With your looks and your personality, you have guys like Rick and Todd clamoring for your attention. Not me. I've never had a guy be even slightly interested in me. Remember the disaster last year when I asked Lance to the prom? I can't believe I even went with him."

Christy nodded in sympathy, remembering Katie's green carnation corsage and the way Lance had ignored her all night and then sent her home alone in his rented limo.

"Who am I kidding?" Katie slumped onto the floor next to Christy. "Why do I think Glen would be interested in me?"

"Because you're you," Christy said. "You're wonderful, and God made you a peculiar treasure."

"A what?"

"My grandma used to say that. She showed it to me in her Bible once. It's in the Old Testament somewhere. Exodus, I think. God called His people His 'peculiar treasure.' That's what you are, Katie. That's what we both are—God's peculiar treasures. So what if there isn't a guy in your life yet who appreciates you for who you are? Just keep being yourself, and hold out for a hero, okay?"

Tears brimmed in Katie's eyes as she leaned over and gave Christy a hug. "If I didn't have you as my closest friend, Christy, I would be totally miserable!"

"No, no, no," Christy said. "It's the other way around. If *I* didn't have *you* as my closest friend, I'd be totally miserable."

"I guess we're just a pair of unmiserable peculiar treasures," Katie said with a laugh.

"And this unmiserable peculiar treasure," Christy said, pointing at Katie, "is going to look adorable tomorrow night in an old-fashioned, green long underwear shirt with the sleeves pushed up. And she is going to be herself, and she is going to have a wonderful time!"

"If you say so," Katie said, her grin returning. Glancing at all the clothes on the bed, she teased, "Are you sure there's nothing else I can try on?"

"Oh, wait here. As a matter of fact, there is! I'll be right back."

Christy scurried out of the room and returned a moment later with three big shopping bags. "The ski outfits from Aunt Marti," she announced.

The two friends laughingly tore into the bags and were soon modeling the skiwear.

"Is this outfit wild or what?" Katie asked, checking out the black ski bibs with a matching black and dark pink jacket. A black turtleneck with bright pink squiggles on the neck and cuffs completed the outfit. "People actually wear this in public?"

"Here." Christy lifted a pair of black snow pants from the last bag. "These are pretty basic. Why don't you try these instead?"

"Good idea. I'm sure these would look much better on you. I'm not exactly the hot-pink-super-heroine type." Katie handed over the wild swirl pants and matching turtleneck.

Christy tried them on. She felt flashy and daring. She decided that looking the part of an experienced skier might be half the battle in persuading herself to actually hit the slopes. Yes, she would definitely keep the hot pink outfit.

"That looks much better on you," Katie said, pulling on the black ski pants. "These fit me pretty well. What do you think? Could I borrow them for the trip?"

"Of course. Here, try on this sweater." Christy tossed Katie a white turtleneck sweater. "That looks great together. Very classy. Just like you."

"Look at us," Katie said, examining their reflections in the full-length mirror. "We look like we know how to ski already. Hand me those black gloves."

Christy scooped up the new gloves off the floor and grabbed a pair of ski goggles from the bottom of the bag.

Katie put on the gloves and goggles, and striking a ski pose, she shouted, "Look out, Lake Tahoe! A couple of peculiar treasures are coming your way!"

Aunt Marti called later that night to see if Christy liked any of the new ski clothes.

"They're all great, and they fit. I'm going to let Katie borrow the black pants and white sweater if that's okay."

"Well, then, will you still have enough outfits? You're going to be there an entire weekend," Marti said.

"I'm sure I won't need anything else."

"I'll pick up another pair of the black ski pants and a red sweater to go with them. I almost bought the red sweater the other day, but I remembered how you once told me that Rick liked you in red. I didn't want to make you feel bad since you broke up with the poor guy. But since you do need another outfit, I'll go ahead and get the red sweater. Just know, Christy dear, that I'm not buying it to remind you of Rick."

Oh brother! Did my aunt ditch school the days they taught tact or what? "I appreciate the outfits, Aunt Marti. You don't have to get me anything else, though. Really."

"Nonsense! I'll send the pants and sweater tomorrow, and I'll send an extra pair of goggles for your friend."

"Thank you, Aunt Marti. And tell Uncle Bob thanks for buying all the candy bars."

"Oh, he's sitting here at the kitchen table right now, sticking orange pumpkin labels on them. You know your uncle. He likes to have a special treat for the kids around here on Halloween. Are you going to dress up this year?"

"I don't think so."

"We really should throw a costume party for you next year. Wouldn't that be fun? When I was your age, your mother and I had a costume party, and I dressed up like a flapper."

"You dressed up like Flipper the dolphin?"

"No, dear, I said a flapper. You know, a dancer from the Roaring Twenties. I probably still have the costume. Well, you think about it, and decide when we should have that party for you. It could be a fun welcome-home party for Todd. You don't know when he's coming back yet, do you?"

Christy swallowed hard. "No, I don't know."

"I see. Well, all in good time. I want you to know I'm

very proud of you for joining this ski club. It'll give you a chance to meet other young people, and as stylish as you're going to look, who knows what might happen!"

Right! Who knows? I might break every bone in my body. But thanks to you, Aunt Marti, I'll look stylish doing it.

The next day at work, Christy asked Jon about selling the candy bars for Katie.

"Fine with me. Put a sign on the box, and don't leave them where a kid could walk off with one," Jon suggested. "How much do they cost?"

"Two dollars each. There are ten in each box," Christy explained.

"Really?" Jon's expression brightened. "I'll take a box."

"A whole box? For yourself?"

"No, for my sister. She's a chocoholic. I'll send her a box for her birthday. Saves me having to decide what to get for her. And it's already boxed. This will be easier than trying to mail the vase or the perfume."

Jon lifted one of the boxes of chocolate from Christy's shopping bag and pulled a twenty-dollar-bill out of his pocket. "Thanks, Christy. You made my life a little easier today!"

Christy looked at the easy twenty and then back at Jon. "It was nothing, really. Glad to help out." She pulled an envelope from her purse and stuck the twenty-dollar-bill in along with the sixteen dollars Katie had given her for the eight bars she had eaten. *Katie, we just might end up going on this ski trip, after all. Only 132 more bars to go!*

Finding some marking pens on a shelf in the back, Christy made a sign for the box of candy bars and took them out front to the register. Beverly was standing there, handing change back to a customer.

"Hi," Christy said. "I'm going to put this up here. Jon said it was okay."

"Smells like chocolate," Beverly said. "A very welcome change of fragrance from the usual pet store smells. They should sell well here. Jon left for a few minutes. He said he was going to mail his sister's birthday present. I forgot to ask if he ended up deciding on the perfume or the vase."

"Neither," Christy said. "He's sending her a box of chocolate bars."

Beverly laughed and shook her head. Her long braid wiggled down her back like a little girl's jump rope. "You never can tell with that guy. What did I tell you? The king of returns. Watch, he'll take back the vase and the perfume, and he'll buy something else. What do you think it'll be?"

"A tie maybe?" Christy guessed.

"No, I've never seen him wear a tie. Maybe he'll get a leather belt or something wild, like one of those new Billings Cycle Machines. It's an exercise bike and stair-step machine in one. He's been talking about keeping one in the back so he could exercise in his spare time."

"What spare time?" Christy asked. "The guy never stops!"

"Oh, there's the phone. I'll get it. Are you ready to take over the register?"

"Sure." Christy watched Beverly hotfoot it to the back room and thought of how little she knew about Beverly and Jon. They both seemed like nice, low-stress people. But where did they stand with the Lord? After Luke's talk at the Wednesday night Bible study and Lisa's "hit list," Christy felt concerned about finding ways to be a missionary to those around her.

During her break, she made a quick trip to the Bible bookstore at the other end of the mall. She bought two little booklets that told how to become a Christian and a card for Katie that said, *Our God is an awesome God.*

Back at the pet store, she tried to decide the best way to deliver the booklets to Beverly and Jon. She thought about casually leaving them at the back table. That seemed chicken. Maybe she should personally hand the booklets to them and say something like, "This is regarding life and death. Please read it." No, that sounded too dramatic.

By the time she left work that night, she had worked herself into a frazzle trying to figure out how to deliver her urgent witnessing message. She had thought of at least twenty different ways to give them to Jon and Beverly, but she had said none of them, and the booklets were still in her backpack.

I hope Katie had more success on her mission tonight than I did, Christy thought as she fell into bed. She smiled at the thought of Katie asking Glen if he ate bug larvae. She'd have to ask Katie what lines she'd come up with at the pizza feed to impress Glen.

Katie called the next morning at nine-thirty with a mixed report.

"He kind of talked to me. Sort of. It was weird. It was like neither of us knew what to talk about, so we just sat there. It was pretty noisy, so it was hard to have a conversation. But he sat by me for most of the time. Actually, he sat across from me. He didn't say anything about seeing me on Sunday or next Wednesday. I guess he was just being polite."

"Or," Christy suggested, "he was nervous and didn't know what to say. Did you ever think of that? Guys can get nervous too, you know."

"I don't know," Katie said. "I saw him talking to a bunch of guys in the parking lot before we went in, and he was real yakety-yak with them. Then he came in and sat across from me and hardly said anything."

"Don't you see? He was talking to *guys* out front. Guys, Katie. That's different than trying to talk to a girl—especially a girl he's interested in. I'm sure Glen was nervous, and that's why he didn't talk much."

"You think so?"

"Yes. Look at all the positive things that happened. He left a bunch of guys and came over and sat by you."

"I hadn't thought of that."

"Right there is proof, I think, that he's interested in you. And the second thing is that he stayed for a while. He could've left at any time. I think he stayed because he wanted to. He was being shy or nervous or unsure of himself. I think in another setting, maybe where it's quieter, Glen will open up more."

"I hope you're right, Christy. He seems like a nice guy with a really tender heart. I hope we have another chance to talk sometime."

"You will. I'm sure you will. I think it went well for your first time together. You'll probably see him on Sunday. What are you going to wear?"

"Don't make any jokes, but I think I'll wear a dress," Katie said. "I know it'll be the first time most of my friends have ever seen me in anything other than shorts or jeans. It could be a little mind-boggling for some. They'll probably think Katie's long-lost twin is visiting the youth department. But hey, sometimes you have to step out and be brave."

"Speaking of being brave," Christy said, "I was planning on witnessing to Jon and Beverly last night at work, only nothing happened. I guess Glen wasn't the only one who was too nervous and shy to speak up."

"Wait until there's a natural opportunity to say something. It'll work out," Katie said.

"And it'll work out for you too. With Glen, I mean. You wait for a natural opportunity to say something to him too."

"There's nothing in the rule book that says I can't wait in a dress, is there?"

Christy laughed. "Nope. I think the dress will be a nice touch."

Later Christy wondered what might add a nice touch to her witnessing attempt. Maybe a card from the Bible bookstore with a verse on it. That way she could slip the booklet inside the card and seal the envelope.

The morning at work went fast because they were busy doing a lot of restocking in the store. For the first hour, Christy ended up in the back, opening and pricing boxes of pet food.

During her lunch break, she made a quick trip to the Bible bookstore. For twenty minutes she scanned every card on the rack. None of them seemed to be just right for Jon and Beverly.

In the end, Christy bought two cards that had garden scenes on the front and were blank inside. She thought she would have better success thinking up her own message.

All afternoon she ran ideas through her mind, trying to come up with the right phrase for the witnessing cards. Only snappy lines came to mind. It was like she was trying to enter some Christian bumper sticker contest or something.

Have you considered your eternal destiny lately?

Did you know heaven is just a prayer away?

Get right or get left!

Here's a word from our Heavenly Sponsor.

Please don't die without God.

Did you know you needed a heart transplant?

When the roll is called up yonder, will you be there?

You need Jesus.

Can I just share that...

Instead of feeling inspired, Christy felt frustrated.

Witnessing shouldn't be this hard. What's my problem? The most important thing in the world is whether a person understands how to be saved and have eternal life through Christ. Why can't I figure out a way to say that so it sounds natural?

When she arrived home from work that night, the two cards and the booklets were still in her backpack, untouched.

But before she went to bed, a page of flowery stationery was folded in half and slipped into the back of her Bible. At the top of the page appeared *Christy's Hit List*. Two names were written below.

7

The Little Mouse

The next two weeks were filled with homework, ski club meetings, Wednesday night Bible study, and Christy's usual Friday night and Saturday hours at the pet store. The blank cards and unused booklets remained in her backpack.

"Do you think I'll raise all the money in time?" Katie asked Christy as they walked down the school halls after their ski club meeting. "We're leaving in ten days, and how much more did they say I needed? Fifty dollars?"

"Must be, because we've sold about six boxes of the candy bars at the pet store. Jon bought a box, and then your first box you basically paid for. And you sold some last week. I think Mr. Riley said you needed fifty-two dollars more."

"I can get that by next Monday, right?" Katie looked hopeful. "I'm babysitting on Thursday night, and if more candy bars sell this week at the pet store, I should be able to come up with the fifty-two dollars, right?"

"I'm sure it'll work out," Christy said as they paused in the school parking lot in front of Katie's car. "How much homework do you have?"

"Not much. A chapter to read for government and a dialogue to memorize for Spanish."

"Do you want to come over to my house, and we could do our homework together?"

"I probably should get home so I can, well, you know, work on my Spanish." Katie's expression lit up. "Did I tell you I got an A on my last Spanish test?"

"Could it be the result of a certain Spanish tutor from Ecuador?" Christy teased.

She felt happy for Katie's budding friendship with Glen. He definitely had found a place in her life.

It all started when Katie bravely called Glen one night a few days after the pizza feed to ask a question about the pronunciation of a word in her Spanish dialogue. Glen not only gave her the answer, but he also talked with her for more than two hours.

The next Sunday he remained timid around Katie. Christy thought he seemed shy and unsure of himself. But the day after that, Glen called Katie and they talked for another two hours.

Their relationship seemed a little peculiar to Christy. Katie, however, appeared content with how things were progressing, and Christy thought it best to stay out of it.

"I probably should get going," Katie said. "I told Glen I'd call him if I got stuck with my Spanish, and it looks like I'll need to call him early. Our last conversation went until after ten-thirty, and my mom said I shouldn't be on the phone that long." Katie smiled brightly and said, "See you tomorrow. Happy homework!"

Yeah, happy homework all by myself.

A barrage of weird thoughts bombarded Christy. Now she sort of knew how Katie felt when Christy was dating Rick. It was a strange, almost competitive feeling, as if she should be mad at Glen for taking Katie away from her. She hadn't expected to feel this way, and she hadn't ever expected Katie to be so preoccupied with anything or anyone else that she would put Christy off this way.

Christy drove home, went inside, and pulled a jacket from her closet. "I'm going for a walk around the block before I start my homework," she explained to her mom.

"Are you okay?" Mom asked.

"I'm fine. I've been sitting all day, and I need to get some oxygen to my brain before I tackle the books."

"Well, be careful."

"I'm only going around the block."

"The wind has kicked up, and it's chilly out. Did you get a jacket?"

"Yes," Christy called out as she pulled the front door shut and let the screen door slam in the wind.

A few crinkled brown leaves skipped across the yard, and the air had a bit of a nip to it. It was good thinking weather.

She walked briskly and contemplated the ski trip, only a week and a half away. It looked like she would really be going. There was no turning back now. Christy told herself it would be fun and a good experience. A little part of her felt the disappointment she had seen on her mom's face when Mom realized this would be the first time their family wouldn't be together for Thanksgiving.

Instead of turkey, stuffing, and cranberries next Thursday, Christy figured she would be eating corn dogs and cocoa. It certainly wasn't enough of a reason for her to back out of her promise to Katie. Nevertheless, the realization made her sad.

The only good part about being gone over Thanksgiving was that since Rick would probably be home, she wouldn't have to see him or talk things through with him. Deep down she knew she had done the right thing by breaking up with him. It was disappointing though that their relationship had turned into an "all or nothing" one. She would have liked to be friends with him, even better friends than they were during the last school year.

The change in her relationship with Katie disappointed her too. Christy knew it was crazy to be jealous of Glen, yet she recognized the feeling, and at least to herself, she admitted that was exactly what she felt.

It'd be different if I had a boyfriend now too. Or at least someone I was going out with occasionally. I wonder if Katie and I will ever have boyfriends at the same time. I wonder if we'll ever double-date.

The thoughts she had pushed down for the last few weeks began to stir up to the top as she turned the corner and headed up the block, back to her house. The wind was now in her face, and she pushed into it, pushing her heart's feelings to the surface at the same time.

I wonder when I'll see Todd again. Will things be like they were, or have both of us changed so much that we can never go back to how it was? I wonder if he received my card. I wonder if he liked it. I wonder if I should write him again or wait until he writes me back.

She lowered her head and pushed forward. The oncoming wind made her eyes water, and aloud she told herself, "Why do you think he'd write you? He's never written you before. Todd is Todd, and his life doesn't include you right now. It might someday. And then again, it might not. You have to go on, Christy."

She walked up the steps to her front porch and righted a plastic planter that the wind had knocked over. It reminded her of the first time she and her family had seen this house. The screen on the door had been torn, and a smashed clay pot had lain scattered across the porch. That was only a little more than a year ago. One year, and so much had changed in her life.

Why do things have to change? Why can't anything stay the same—just for a little while? Why does God blow His reckless, raging wind through my life and scatter everything and everyone around?

She tugged open the front door. As soon as she entered the warm house, Christy was aware of her wind-buffeted cheeks turning rosy and of the wonderful, strong smell of Mom's meat loaf and baked potatoes in the oven. Christy knew her dad would be thankful that Mom was adding meat back into the family diet. The last few weeks they'd eaten a lot of pasta and vegetables.

Even though it was still a week and a half before Thanksgiving, the day when people were supposed to think of all they were grateful for, Christy decided to do a preliminary rundown. She headed straight for her room, took off her jacket, plopped onto her bed, and began a list in her diary.

I'm thankful for my parents, this house, my health, and all the blessings God has given us, like food and clothes. I'm thankful for my friends and...

Christy paused. The thought had come so quickly that she wasn't sure if she should write it. She decided to go with the flow and wrote:

...I'm thankful for Todd. And Rick. And Katie. And for my job, my church, my relationship with Jesus, and the way I can talk with Him anytime and anywhere.

Then, because it somehow ended up sounding like a prayer, Christy wrote *Amen* at the bottom of the page.

Wednesday night, Luke had the high school Bible study do almost the same thing. He passed out paper and pens and had everyone think of something they were thankful for that they had never consciously thanked God for. Then they were to write Him a letter, thanking Him for whatever it was.

Christy thought hard and finally wrote, *God, I'm thankful for my eyesight. I've always taken it for granted. I'm thankful I can see.*

Luke gave everyone another piece of paper and told them to think of someone they were thankful for and to write a note to that person, explaining why they were thankful.

Christy thought at first she should write her note to Katie. Sneaking a peek at Katie's letter, she noticed Katie had gone right to work, writing Glen a thank-you note for his help in Spanish. Somehow she lost her zeal to write to Katie. In the end, Christy wrote hers to her parents, thanking them for all they had done for her.

Even though she and Katie were sitting together for the whole Bible study, it seemed like Katie barely noticed Christy. As soon as the study ended, Katie sprang from her chair like a panther.

Christy watched as Katie slipped between the haphazard rows of folding chairs before striking up a conversation with Glen. He seemed to enjoy the attention.

The minute Katie handed him the thank-you note, Glen's face turned red. He stuck the note in his pocket without reading it. Then he stood there, his face still a bit rosy, while Katie talked on, using her nonstop hand motions to demonstrate everything she was saying to him.

Even though Christy felt some twinges of jealousy over Katie's attention to Glen, she couldn't help but feel happy for Katie. Glen seemed to benefit from their friendship, and Katie definitely was too.

Christy drove home thinking about how much fun they were going to have on the ski trip. At the same time, she felt guilty for thinking it. She knew that one of the reasons they were going to have so much fun was because neither of them was interested in any of the guys who were going.

Now if Glen were going on the trip, Christy probably would have decided to stay home. She wasn't sure if that was immature or not, but she was sure she and Katie would have a lot more fun without any boyfriend problems for the weekend.

When Christy arrived home, Mom had already gone to bed, but Dad was watching TV in the recliner. Christy handed him the note and waited for his reaction.

Her dad read the thank-you. He smiled at her and pulled the side lever on the recliner in order to make the footrest pop up. Instead, the backrest reclined almost all the way to the floor. For a minute, it looked like Dad might be hurled over the back of the chair.

Christy jumped over to his side, prepared to try to block the launch. But her dad had managed to balance the recliner with no damage done to the space capsule or the astronaut.

"Well!" He chuckled. "Thanks for the note of encouragement. With all the things I do wrong around here, it's nice to know somebody thinks I do a few things right!"

He patted the side of the recliner for emphasis, and Christy remembered him dismantling and "fixing" it a few weeks ago.

She hugged him around the neck. "You do a lot of things right. I don't always remember to thank you, but I should."

"You know," Dad said solemnly, "your mother and I are letting you go on this ski trip, but neither of us feels too comfortable with the whole thing."

"Why?"

"You've never skied before, you're going with a bunch of people we don't know, and as far as we know, you and Katie are the only Christians. We just don't feel certain that it's the best thing you could be doing."

Christy panicked. "Are you saying I can't go?"

"No. We've discussed it, and since you're so sure about it, we agreed you should go. Your mother and I don't feel comfortable with it, that's all."

Christy wasn't sure how to respond. Were her parents hinting that she should withdraw from the trip on her own? Were they sending her but withholding their blessing? Were they really leaving the choice up to her? What should she say?

"I don't think the school would let us take a trip like this if anything bad had ever happened," she ventured. "Mr. Riley is the sponsor, and he said he and his wife have taken the club every year for the past four years. I'm sure I'll be okay."

"I suppose you will. You've been on greater adventures than this, no doubt. I just wanted you to know I have some reservations."

Dad pushed himself out of the recliner and, turning off the TV, said, "Well, that's all I wanted to say. Thanks for the note."

Christy followed him down the hall, remembering when she was a little girl on their Wisconsin farm. One of her favorite pastimes had been to follow her dad around in the barn. He was so big that she could easily hide behind him. When she walked softly in the hay, he never knew she was there.

Sometimes his long strides would suddenly come to a halt, and she would bump into him. Then he would scoop her into his arms, lift her over his head, and bellow for the cows to hear, "Look, I've found a little mouse! Listen to her squeak."

He would say that because by then Christy would be giggling, squealing, and pleading to be put down.

Following her dad down the hall tonight, she realized that she was now only six inches shorter than he was. At sixteen years old, she would never be scooped up in his arms again to be held over his head and called his little mouse. She was almost a woman, and he was almost treating her like one.

On impulse, right before Dad opened the bedroom door, Christy spoke. "Dad?"

He turned to face her, but she wasn't sure what she wanted to say. Instead of trying to find the words, Christy wrapped her arms around him and pressed her cheek into his chest.

Dad returned the hug. They looked at each other and smiled. Christy was certain he knew exactly what she had been thinking.

He brushed back her long bangs with his rough hand, kissed her on the forehead, and said, "Good night, my little mouse."

8

96817

"Make sure you've turned in your medical releases, otherwise we'll leave you in the school parking lot on Wednesday. Nobody goes without a signed medical release form!" Mr. Riley made his announcement loud and clear as the ski club was breaking up after its final meeting before the trip.

"And don't forget that you're each responsible for your meals on the way up and back. Did I leave anything out? Oh, right, your luggage." Mr. Riley raised his voice. "Everyone, listen! Bring your luggage to school on Wednesday morning, and take it to the teachers' lounge. One bag each, one sleeping bag, and one carry-on, like a small backpack, that you'll keep with you in the van. Okay, any questions?"

"Yeah," one of the guys asked from his perch on top of Mr. Riley's desk. "Is there any snow?"

"I heard a storm's coming in tonight. Let's hope it dumps a ton on the mountains for the next two days and that it clears up by the time we hit the slopes on Thursday."

"I hope we don't have to drive through the snow," Christy confided to Katie. "Our family got stuck in a blizzard once when I was seven, and we had to spend the night in our car."

"Really? How scary! I've never even seen snow."

"What?" Christy asked, stopping Katie in her tracks. "How could you live to be sixteen years old and never see snow?"

"I've lived in Southern California all my life, and my family doesn't travel much. That's why I've always wanted to go skiing."

"I can't believe this, Katie. Do you have any idea how cold and wet and miserable snow can be? Do you have any idea how hard it is to walk in or keep your balance on an icy sidewalk?"

"Nope," Katie said honestly.

"This is going to be quite a trip. I can tell already. Are you sure you have enough warm clothes? And did you get your money all straightened out?"

"My parents gave me the last twenty dollars I needed, and whatever we get from the candy bars you still have at the pet store will be my meal money for the trip."

"I'm stopping by there on the way home. Jon's so nice, he's even giving me my paycheck early so I'll have extra spending money."

"Just think," Katie said, "you were planning on using all those paychecks to buy back your bracelet."

"I know. I still have no idea who paid it off." Christy rubbed her thumb over the thin gold band. "Anyway, I'll get the rest of your candy money and give it to you tomorrow."

Christy hoped the remainder of the candy bars had sold. On Saturday she had noticed at least a box and a half left.

When she entered the pet store that afternoon, Jon was standing by the register, swatting the air with a small goldfish net.

"What are you doing?" Christy asked. "Trying to catch a flying fish?"

"Very funny. No, I'm trying to catch a fly. I like feeding my lizards the old-fashioned, organic way. Whoa!" Jon swooped the net through the air inches from Christy's face, then squeezed the opening closed with his fingers.

Christy peered at the goldfish net he held before her. Sure enough, he had caught a fly.

"Can you watch the register while I take this to the lizards?" Jon asked as he walked away. Then turning around, he said, "Wait a minute! You're not working today, are you?"

"No. I came in to pick up the candy bars and..." She let her sentence trail off, deciding it might be rude to assume Jon was still planning to give her paycheck to her early.

"That's right. I almost forgot. Could you watch the register anyway? I'll be right back."

For some reason, Christy felt funny walking behind the counter and standing by the register when it wasn't her day to work. It almost seemed like she was sneaking into a place she didn't belong.

Just then a man who had been in the back of the store came up to the register with a large bag in his arms. He looked slightly familiar, but Christy wasn't sure where she had seen him before.

He dropped the bag onto the counter with a thump and said, "Glad to see you finally got someone around here who knows how to order your stuff for you."

The label on the bag said "Birdseed." Then Christy remembered when she had seen this man before.

Without letting on that she recognized him, she quickly rang up the sale and hoped he would leave quietly, without causing a scene like last time.

"Two dollars for a candy bar?" the man bellowed when he read the sign on the box. "What kind of highway robbery is that? And what kind of a pet store sells food for humans? There's probably some city ordinance against that. What kind of city would let some jerk sell food for humans and food for animals over the same counter?"

"Here's your change, sir," Christy said, her hand shaking.

He snatched the three one-dollar bills from her and, grappling with his bag of birdseed, stormed off.

"Another satisfied customer, I see," Jon said, coming up to the front.

"What's with that guy? And by the way, thanks for letting me be the one to wait on him." Christy slung her backpack over her shoulder and stepped away from the register, indicating she was now off duty.

"Aw, don't let him bother you. He likes being miserable. He's in here at least once a week, and he always finds something to gripe about. What was it this time?"

"The candy bars. But that's okay, because I'm taking them, and he won't be able to call the city officials and have them fine you for selling dog food and chocolate over the same counter." Christy did a quick count of the bars left in the box and asked, "Are there any more in back?"

"That's the last of them," Jon said, reaching in his pocket. "My sister called and said they were good, so here."

He stuck a wad of money in Christy's hand. "I'll buy the rest of them."

"You don't have to do that," Christy protested. Uncrumpling the bill in her hand and realizing it was a twenty, she said, "This is too much. There are only three candy bars left. That's six dollars, not twenty."

"Keep the change," Jon said. "Buy yourself a snow cone or something this weekend. Buy one for your friend too. What's her name? Katie?"

"Yeah, Katie. Thanks, Jon. This is really generous of you."

Jon reached into the box and pulled out the three remaining candy bars. "Here," he said, tossing one to Christy. "Have a candy bar. And here." He tossed her another one. "Give this one to Katie."

Then he unwrapped the third bar and bit into it. "Your paycheck and the envelope with the candy money are in the cash register. Let me get it for you."

Christy decided to join Jon in devouring the final candy bars. She unwrapped the one he had tossed to her and discovered it had almonds. She hated nuts. Then she remembered how she had tried macadamia nuts on her frozen yogurt when she was in Maui. She had liked them. Maybe she would like these almonds.

She let the first bite melt slowly in her mouth until all that was left was the almond. Then, with a crunch, she chewed it up and swallowed.

"Here you go." Jon handed Christy the two envelopes. "Have a great time, don't break any bones, and see you back here at work next Friday."

"Thanks again," Christy said, taking another bite of the

chocolate-and-almond experiment. She decided her dislike of nuts must have been a childhood thing. To her sixteen-year-old palate, there was nothing about nuts to dislike.

"Oh, before you go, I wanted to ask you something," Jon said. "What church do you go to?"

Christy couldn't believe he was asking her. This might be the opportunity to witness she had been praying for. She quickly swallowed the chunk of chocolate and almonds.

After she told Jon the name of her church, she watched as he pulled out a piece of paper and a pen.

"How do you get there?" he asked, carefully writing down the directions. "And what time does church start?"

Christy gave him all the information. Then because her curiosity was killing her, she asked, "Why? I mean, how did you know I was a Christian?"

"When you applied for this job," Jon stated, "you wrote on the application you wouldn't work on Sundays, so I figured you went to church somewhere. Then I've been watching you to see if you lived all those things they teach in church about being honest and not stealing and all that."

Christy's eyebrows went up as she waited for him to finish.

"So far, so good. I like what I see."

This is too good to be true! God is answering my prayer about witnessing to Jon. And I haven't even said anything.

Feeling excited and a bit proud of her strong Christian example, Christy said, "So you're saying that because you see Jesus in me, you're interested in going to church?"

"No," Jon answered.

Christy tried not to let the disappointment and puzzlement show on her face.

"I asked about church because I have an old friend from

college who's coming to stay with me over Thanksgiving. He's one of those 'born agains,' and I know he's going to want to go to a church around here on Sunday, if not on Thanksgiving too. You're the only one I know who goes to church."

She didn't want this witnessing opportunity to die such a humiliating death, so Christy mustered her courage and said, "Why don't you go with him, Jon? I think you'd like my church."

A slight smile crept across Jon's face. "You've got me targeted now, don't you? I guess I don't mind a little nudge toward heaven every now and then. Just promise me you won't be like one girl who used to work here. She never said a word about being born again or anything. She just left these little...what are they called? Tracts? Well, she left them everywhere around the store, only she did it in secret. Guess she thought nobody would figure out who they were from."

Jon shook his head, still grinning. "We used to call her the Easter Bunny."

Christy breathed a sigh of relief that she hadn't tried the same technique with her cards and booklets.

"I say if you're going to believe something, then believe it enough to take a stand and not be sneaky about it." Jon looked directly at Christy.

Words bubbled up in Christy's heart and tumbled out of her mouth before she had a chance to critique them. "I believe you need to turn your life over to God."

"Oh, you do?" Now Jon was laughing.

Christy knew him well enough to realize that he was genuinely amused.

"Well now, I like that, Christy. You believe something strongly enough to say it. I admire you for that. You might try a little tact with your honesty. But I wouldn't be surprised if you told me you're praying for me."

Christy's boldness began to evaporate, and she could feel her cheeks flushing under Jon's intense gaze. In a much smaller voice, she said, "As a matter of fact, I *have* been praying for you."

Now Jon was surprised. "I guess it can't hurt," he said, slipping behind the counter to help a customer who was approaching the cash register.

"Have a great weekend." Jon smiled his good-bye.

The next day at lunch, Christy delivered to Katie the money from Jon, along with a rundown on her witnessing opportunity.

"Can you imagine what would have happened if you had given him that card and tract?" Katie asked.

"I know. Makes me think how much easier my life would be if I wouldn't try to run ahead of God," Christy said, sticking her hand into her lunch bag.

"Oh, look what I have for you!" She presented Katie with the candy bar. "A gift from Jon."

"Looks like you and I are going on a ski trip tomorrow!" Katie said excitedly. "Let's celebrate. I'll share the final candy bar with you to salute our victory over the near-fiasco fund-raiser."

Katie broke the bar in two, handed the larger piece to Christy, and then held up her half. "Here's to the best friend anyone could ever have—Christy Miller! I couldn't have made it without you, Chris."

"Sure you could have. I wouldn't have made it without

Aunt Marti. I never thought I'd say this, but here's to Aunt Marti."

The two girls chomped into their chocolate at the same time.

"So are you beginning to feel those chemicals affecting your brain yet?" Christy asked as soon as she swallowed the first bite.

Katie blushed and said, "He called me again last night. I'm kind of sorry we're not going to be around for Bible study or church. I think Glen might be getting a little more confident. After all these long talks on the phone, he's bound to sit by me at church pretty soon, don't you think?"

"Well, if you feel that strongly about seeing him, we could back out of the ski trip," Christy ventured.

"Are you kidding? After all we've been through with the fund-raiser and everything? No way! We're committed to this trip, Christy." Katie added with a twinkle, "Glen will just have to wait for me to return, because I'm the kind of girl who is worth waiting for."

"You are, Katie. And don't you ever forget it!"

Christy began to pack for the trip the minute she arrived home from school. She rolled the ski clothes because they fit better in her bag that way. The tough part was deciding what else to bring. She started with two pairs of sweats, but they were too bulky. She managed to narrow it down to one pair of sweatpants and two sweatshirts. The turtlenecks and T-shirts fit easily. The choice of sweaters became tricky, and in the end, she took only one and decided to wear the other one to school tomorrow.

"How's it coming?" Mom asked, popping her head into Christy's room.

"I think I have it all stuffed in." Christy wrestled with the big black zipper on top of her bag.

"Did you include some tights? And how about your mittens?"

Christy let the zipper go and flopped backward on the floor. "No," she moaned. "I forgot all my underwear too."

"Looks like you need a bigger bag," Mom said with a chuckle.

"We're only allowed to bring one."

"Yes, but it doesn't have to be a small one, does it? I think there's one in the garage that's a little bigger. I'll be right back."

Mom returned with an old, beat-up green army duffel bag that was definitely bigger than the newer slick black one Christy had been cramming her stuff into.

"Mom, that old thing is falling apart, and it's totally ugly. I wouldn't want to be caught dead carrying that thing."

Even though Mom looked like she was about to correct Christy, she only dropped the green bag on the floor and said, "Then you work it out. Dinner will be ready in fifteen minutes."

Now Christy sat alone on her bedroom floor, half of her wanting to pout like a little girl and the other half demanding that she act like an independent young woman packing for a ski trip. It was up to her to decide if she wanted to take everything she needed and be seen with the ugly bag or take fewer clothes in the cool-looking bag.

Dumping everything out on the floor, she reevaluated what she actually needed and what she could leave behind. She needed everything, and more. It looked like the ugly bag was the only way to go. How frustrating and how humiliating. It even smelled disgusting.

As they were finishing dinner, Mom casually asked if Christy had managed to work out her packing situation.

"Yes," Christy mumbled into her forkful of peas, "I'm taking the green bag."

"I think you'll be glad you did," Mom said, standing and beginning to clear the table. "Oh, by the way, this came in the mail today for you. Any idea what it is?"

Mom picked up a small slip of paper off the cluttered part of the counter and handed it to Christy. It was a notice from the post office indicating there was a package being held for Christy Miller, and the package had postage due.

"It doesn't say who it's from," Christy said, turning the slip over and examining the back. "All it says is 57 cents is due on a package."

"Let me see it. Who's it from?" David asked.

"I don't know. I haven't ordered anything lately. I have all the ski stuff Aunt Marti was sending."

"It should have the zip code it was sent from on it," Dad said, putting out his hand. "May I have a look?"

Christy handed him the slip, and Dad said, "It was sent from 96817. Has to be somewhere on the West Coast. I thought maybe your grandmother had sent something, but her zip wouldn't start with a nine."

"Can you pick it up for me tomorrow?" Christy asked. "I'm leaving right after school for the ski trip, so I won't be able to get to the post office until Monday."

"Sure. Leave it where I'll see it," Mom said.

I wonder who sent me a package. What could it possibly be?

9

The Inside-Outsider

Paying attention in class proved to be nearly impossible by fifth period Wednesday afternoon. The teachers were already in vacation mode, and the students, whether they had weekend plans or not, were talking about anything and everything but class work.

When the final bell rang, Christy hurried to the teachers' lounge and found Katie already there, digging her luggage out of the heap.

"I have your bag, Christy. It's over there by the couch. Do you have your backpack and your jacket?"

"My jacket is still in my locker. I'm going to run and get it and put these books back. Do you need anything from your locker?"

"I'm all set. I'll wait here for you."

Christy bustled her way through the loud, crowded hallway, surprised that her heart was beating so hard and fast.

I guess I thought this day would never come. I thought something would happen, and we'd never actually go on the trip. But now it's here, and I'm going—green bag and all. So I'd better make the best of it and stop being a chicken.

She spun through the combination on her lock,

grabbed her jacket, crammed in her books, and met Katie back in the teachers' lounge, all in about five minutes.

Katie had on her backpack, her jacket was tied around her waist, her bag was slung over her shoulder, and her sleeping bag was tucked under her arm. "Mr. Riley said to carry our stuff out to the van in the parking lot. Are you ready?"

"I think so." Christy grabbed her bulky green duffel bag and looped her carry-on over her shoulder. With the other hand, she snatched her sleeping bag and jacket.

"No offense," Katie said, eyeing the drab monster bag, "but didn't you have any other suitcases or anything? You look like you're going to boot camp."

Christy did take offense at the comment—not because it was Katie who said it, but because she had almost convinced herself that the duffel bag was not a big deal and that no one would even notice it. To have Katie comment on it meant all her fears of being rejected by the entire ski club were, in fact, well-founded.

"Let's just go." Christy pushed past Katie to the door. Maybe if they hurried, Mr. Riley would load their stuff first, and no one else would notice her bag.

But by the time they arrived at the van, they were the last to deliver their bags. To Christy's chagrin, her bag was placed on top of the heap. The van door was slammed shut, and her bag was the only one showing. In fact, it took up the whole back window.

The worst part was that her dad had decided last night to mark the bag for her, as if someone else would happen to bring a bag that looked exactly like hers. With a black permanent marker he had written "MILLER" in huge letters across the side. Of course, that was the side facing out. Not only would the whole school know that Christy Miller belonged to that ugly green bag, but all who drove past them from here to Lake Tahoe would also know.

Everyone else had already claimed a seat inside the van. Christy and Katie found two tight-squeeze spots left on the front bench seat, right behind the driver. Definitely not the cool place to sit.

Christy slid in first, next to the window, feeling like everyone was watching her. It was one thing to show up at a meeting for the ski club with these people scattered around a classroom. There it didn't matter that no one knew her name or paid attention to her. But it felt completely different to be jammed into a van with these same people and to know that they would be together in tight quarters for the next four days.

Feeling hot from embarrassment and from the warm ski sweater she was wearing, Christy tried to open the window next to her. She pushed and pinched but couldn't figure it out.

Katie leaned over and released the catch in an instant. The window slid open easily. With a laugh and in a loud voice, Katie said, "You have to be smarter than the window, Miller."

Christy bore her eyes into her sudden traitor-friend and kept shooting visual darts until Katie caught on that her comment had hurt. It was bad enough that the slam had been inflicted in front of all these strangers, but Christy wondered why Katie suddenly called her "Miller." Was it so they would all know she was the Miller who went with the green monster bag?

"Hey, it was only a joke," Katie said. "Take a chill pill, Christy. You're not freaking out on me, are you?"

What are you doing, Katie? What's with this slang all of a sudden? Are you trying to show these people you're cool, and I'm not?

Just then Mr. Riley climbed into the driver's seat, and his blond, athletic-looking wife joined him in the front passenger seat.

"Hey, Don, I need your medical release form," Mr. Riley yelled to the back of the van.

"Oh, man!" Don rose from his prime spot and said, "It's in my locker. I'll be right back."

"Hustle, Donald!" Mr. Riley called after him. "It's not fair for you to keep the rest of the group waiting."

Mrs. Riley turned around and introduced herself to Katie and Christy. "You girls can call me Janet this weekend. I know Lou still wants everyone to call him Mr. Riley, but I prefer that you call me Janet."

She seemed sweet, and Christy felt a little relieved that their woman leader was so approachable.

"Have you girls ever been to Tahoe before? It's so beautiful up there."

For some reason Christy responded, "Katie's never even seen snow before." It sounded like a jab, and Christy realized she must have said it to get back at Katie for the earlier slams she had made on Christy.

But the remark didn't faze Katie a bit. She unashamedly admitted that she had never seen snow and began to draw all kinds of ski advice out of Janet.

Don returned with the medical form, Mr. Riley started up the van, and soon they were on their way. For the first forty-five minutes or so, Christy looked out the window and listened to Katie ramble on with Janet and Mr. Riley as if they were old friends. The guy sitting on the other side of Katie had turned around in his seat and was involved in a conversation with the girl right behind him. The rest of the group settled into their conversations and natural groupings.

The three cool guys had taken over the back of the van. They were all popular, and Don seemed to be the leader of the three. They already had on their skier sunglasses and were stretched out on the backseat, talking loudly about moguls and how much air they had caught on certain ski runs at Squaw Valley. Don said that one year there had been so much snow that he had skied at Squaw Valley on the Fourth of July. No one questioned him or his skiing expertise. Don and the other guys brought their own skis and poles. Their collection of expensive equipment was tied down on top of the van.

In front of the guys were the rich girls. There were three of them too, and they all wore their hair the same way—shoulder-length with blond highlights. They all had straight white teeth and perfectly clear skin. Christy didn't know any of their names, but her guess was that they probably all had the same name too.

In the middle was a couple and a girl named Julie, who looked like she was about to become part of another couple with the guy sitting next to Katie.

It didn't take a genius to figure out that Katie and Christy were the leftovers. Funny how a person could be part of the "in" group and still feel like an outsider.

They drove for hours, and Christy slept a good part of the way. Her jacket worked as the perfect pillow against the closed van window. She regretted coming on the trip. With Katie treating her the way she had, Christy was not looking forward to the thought of four more days of the same.

It was dark when they stopped for dinner. Christy stumbled out of the van and saw that they were at Jacques' Café, a little restaurant in an even littler town. Someone asked why they hadn't gone on to Bishop for dinner.

"This is our traditional stopping place," said Mr. Riley. "They have great food, and I always like giving Jacques the business. Go on in, guys."

The group filed in and waited to be seated. The hostess showed them to three large booths. Everyone scrambled to find a place. Katie scooted in right next to Janet in the booth with Mr. Riley and the three popular guys. Before Christy could wedge in, all the places were filled.

The booth next to them held the two couples, and she wasn't about to interfere with that foursome. All that was left was a spot with the three rich girls.

"May I squeeze in here?" Christy asked the girl on the end, expecting rejection or at least a disdainful look.

To her surprise, the girl said, "Sure, Christy."

Scooting over, she introduced Christy to the other girls. "I'm Shannon," the girl said. "And that's Jennifer and Tiffany."

Christy was surprised at their sudden friendliness. At the same time she felt suspicious of their willingness to accept her into their group.

"You know," Shannon said, handing Christy a menu, "I've been wanting to tell you this for a long time, and I guess this is the perfect opportunity."

Now Christy was really surprised. Not only did this girl know her name, but she also had something she wanted to tell Christy.

"I thought what you did last year at the final assembly when you gave up your cheerleading spot to Teri Moreno was a really cool thing. I've always wanted to tell you that, but I didn't know you or anything, and you're always hanging out with that other girl who used to be a mascot."

Jennifer and Tiffany snickered behind their menus. One of them mumbled, "If you're not coordinated enough to be a cheerleader, I guess the next best thing is a mascot."

"That way you can hide in a cougar costume, and when you fall all over the football field, everyone thinks you're doing it on purpose."

Christy didn't join in their giggling. She opened her menu and looked down for a long time, trying to sort this out. It hurt her that these girls were making fun of Katie, yet at the moment she was still miffed at Katie. The amazing thing was that these girls had noticed her and accepted her into their group.

Maybe this is going to be a missions trip, like Katie said. If these girls are willing to let me be friends with them, maybe they'll let me tell them about the Lord. This could be a God-thing. If only Katie would support me a little here.

When the waitress came, all three girls ordered the chicken club sandwich. Christy was the last to order. She had planned on having a hamburger and French fries but at the last minute told the waitress, "I'll have the same thing."

"Mayo on the side, like the others?" the waitress asked.

"Sure, that would be fine."

The girls all smiled at Christy, and she felt like she had

passed some sort of secret initiation. Was it the mayo on the side or the chicken club?

Chicken club, Christy thought. *If that doesn't perfectly describe me, I don't know what does!*

10

Up Close and Personal

The van pulled up in front of a condominium complex somewhere on the north shore of Lake Tahoe well after midnight.

"Okay, everyone," Mr. Riley said, turning off the engine and turning on the lights inside the van. "We have numbers four and five. Let's put all the girls in number four and the guys in number five. Grab your own stuff, and then you guys come back to help me with the ice chests on the roof."

Christy, still squinting from the sudden bright light, climbed out of the van and stumbled on the gravel driveway to the back. The first thing she noticed was the white blanket of snow covering the ground in front of the condo. The parking area and walkways had been cleared, but everything else under the streetlight's beacon looked as though it had been spread with white frosting.

"Snow!" Katie cheered. "Look, there's snow!" She scooped up a handful and playfully tossed the loose powder into the air. "Whee!" she squealed, pressing together a snowball.

The three girls stood beside Christy at the back of the

van, and one of them asked, "What's with her?"

"She's never seen snow before."

"In her life?"

"No, this is the first time."

The girls gave each other knowing looks, and Christy realized what they were thinking. Katie wasn't rich like they were. She didn't travel and wear designer clothes like they did. She clearly wasn't "one of them."

Christy wasn't sure why they accepted her though. Was it just the cheerleader thing or something else?

Christy pulled on her jacket and was aware of the cold creeping through her tennis shoes and socks. It was a familiar Wisconsin-winter feeling, and one she hadn't missed since they had moved to California. She hated having cold feet.

Don started handing out luggage, and since Christy's bag was the first to come out, she thought, *If these girls think I'm on their same social level, this duffel bag ought to set them straight right away.*

"Is that your bag?" Tiffany asked, sounding surprised.

Oh boy, here it comes. Oh well, the popularity was nice while it lasted.

"Yes," Christy admitted, "it's mine."

"Where did you get it?" Tiffany asked, touching it as if to test its authenticity. "I looked at Goodwill, the Salvation Army, and the Army-Navy Surplus, and they didn't have any more."

Christy thought Tiffany was mocking her and was about to get upset when she noticed that the other two girls were looking at her bag with the same admiration. Not one of them was smirking.

"I...I got it out of our garage. It's my dad's. I don't know where he got it."

"You are so lucky," Tiffany said sincerely. "All I could find was a pair of army boots. My mom had them resoled and waterproofed for this trip. They're in my bag; I'll show them to you when we get inside. You're going to bunk with us, aren't you?"

Christy couldn't believe it. These girls were serious. Apparently, old army gear was "in," and she didn't even know it. Why else would a rich girl, who could buy any pair of boots in the mall, hunt down an old pair in the thrift stores and have them fixed up? Christy had a lot to learn about this group of girls.

Janet led the seven girls into the two-story condo and flipped on the lights. It was much more spacious than Christy had expected. There were three bedrooms and three bathrooms, and an upstairs living room and kitchen that looked out on the lake.

"This is huge!" Katie exclaimed. "Where do you want us, Janet?"

"If you girls don't mind, I'd like to take the little bedroom upstairs. It only has a double bed in it. These two downstairs bedrooms have four beds in each, so there's plenty of room for you."

"Let's take this one," Katie said, preparing to dump her bag in the nearest bedroom.

"This room is already taken," Tiffany said. Jennifer and Shannon slid past Tiffany and tossed their bags on the floor to visually back up Tiffany's statement.

"Fine, we'll go in the other room," Katie said, heading down the hallway. "Come on, Christy."

Christy felt torn. She had made inroads with the three rich girls, and there was an extra bed in with them. They had invited her to stay with them. It was the perfect witnessing opportunity. And yet, after all, the reason she had agreed to come on this trip was to support Katie.

"I'd better go in the other room," Christy said quietly to the three girls. "Katie and I kind of planned this trip together, you know."

"Well, if you change your mind, you're welcome in our room anytime," Shannon said.

Christy started to lug her stuff down the hall.

"Hey," Tiffany called out after her, "as soon as you unload your stuff, come back, and I'll show you my boots."

"Okay," Christy agreed. Somehow she felt like a traitor, yet it was hard to tell which side she was betraying.

"Look!" Katie exclaimed as Christy entered the room. "Daybeds! Do you want to be on top or on the pullout?"

"Doesn't matter to me. Which do you want?"

The other two girls entered the room, their boyfriends carrying their luggage. They said hi, dumped their stuff, and left with the guys.

"Guess we won't be seeing much of them this week," Katie said. "I'll take the bottom bed. You can have the top."

"I don't mind the bottom," Christy said. "Besides, the bottom pops up if you want to be higher."

"No, this is fine. I don't mind, really."

"Christy," came a call from down the hallway. "Are you coming?"

Katie gave Christy a questioning look.

"Tiffany has a pair of boots she wants to show me," Christy explained.

"Oh, well then let's go." Katie led the way down the hall as if she had been invited as well.

I have a horrible feeling about this! Christy thought. She latched on to Katie's shoulder and pulled her back toward their room. "Katie," she said, "remember how you said a few weeks ago at Bible study that this trip was like our missions trip?" She spoke in a soft voice and hoped Katie would be open to what she was trying to convey.

"Oh," Katie said, nodding her head. "Right! You think these three might be the ones we've been sent to witness to."

"Something like that," Christy said, keeping her voice low. "I think we should try to be open in case we experience some, you know, like hostility or something. Don't take it personally."

"Good point," Katie agreed. "I know these girls, and they can be really snobby. I'm glad you recognize that about them, because I'd hate for you to get your feelings hurt the first night."

My feelings, Katie! I'm trying to protect your feelings here.

Katie had already begun to march down the hall like a crusader. All Christy could do was follow. As she expected, when they approached the room, all three girls gave Katie a what-are-you-doing-here look. Katie seemed oblivious.

"Are those your boots?" Christy asked quickly, hoping to divert the girls' attention from Katie. She bent down and picked up one of the clunky-looking fossils. "Do these really fit you?"

"They're a little big. Plenty of room for my wool socks though. What are you going to wear tomorrow?"

Christy noticed that all three girls had turned their backs on Katie and were gathered around Christy. It made her feel nervous and on the spot, not at all like the center of attention in a popular way.

"Well, I, um...I guess some ski clothes. We're going skiing first thing in the morning, aren't we?"

"We leave at six-thirty," Katie said.

The three girls ignored her.

"Six-thirty," Christy repeated. "Boy, that's early. Guess we'd better get some sleep. I think I'll go get my sleeping bag ready." Christy gently broke out of the cocoon surrounding her and headed for the door.

"Girls?" Janet called, coming down the stairs. "I have everything set up for making tomorrow's lunches. Could you come and help me?"

"Sure," Christy said, eager to change locations. "What can we do?"

Katie joined her, taking the stairs two at a time. The others followed slowly behind.

Janet explained the assembly line she had set up on the kitchen counter. "Everyone gets one sandwich. Try to get two sandwiches out of each packet of lunch meat."

"I don't eat processed meat," Tiffany said, her arms folded in front of her.

"I remembered that from last year, Tiffany. I brought peanut butter and jelly especially for you."

Tiffany made a face.

Janet went on with her instructions. "We need to make a total of fourteen lunches. Here's a pen to put names on them. At the end of the counter by the lunch bags is a box of apples. Here are the cookies, and drinks are in the ice chest. Any questions?"

"Let's make a production line," Katie said. "I'll start down here with the bread and mayonnaise. Christy, why don't you be the meat slapper?"

"The meat slapper," Shannon mimicked, and the three girls laughed.

Christy moved into position and bravely said, "Okay, one meat slapper coming up."

The other three reluctantly began to write names on the lunch sacks and stuff cookies into plastic bags.

Katie tried to pry the lid off the mayonnaise jar. It was stubborn and didn't cooperate with her muscular twists and turns. Shannon came over to see what was holding up the line.

"Here," she said. With a flick of her long fingernail, the plastic seal broke loose.

At the same moment, the lid popped off due to the change in altitude. A spray of mayonnaise squirted out the side, splattering Katie's face and shirt.

It was a hilarious sight, and without thinking, Christy blurted out, "You have to be smarter than the mayonnaise jar, Katie."

All the girls burst into a chorus of laughter, while Katie fumbled for a paper towel to wipe her face.

Why did I say that? Where did it come from? I didn't mean to humiliate her in front of these girls.

The girls laughed much longer than the joke deserved. By the look on Katie's face, Christy knew she had done some major damage to Katie's feelings. Christy quietly worked on dividing up the lunch meat.

The lunches were completed with a lot of chatter and uninvited directions from the guys, who suddenly appeared and gave special orders on how they liked their sandwiches. Christy kept quiet, afraid her untamed tongue might rebel on her once more before the night was over.

Maybe Janet assumed Christy's silence was a result of the guys' taunting, because she came up behind Christy and whispered, "Tomorrow night they'll make the sandwiches, and you can get even by bossing them around."

Christy smiled and let Janet think that's what she was clammed up about. She finished her part of the lunch making and slipped out of the group so she could go down to her room and get ready for bed. Katie came in about ten minutes later and silently laid out her sleeping bag.

"Katie?" Christy said softly, already in her pajamas, with her hair back in a clip and her face freshly washed. "Katie, I'm sorry I said that. I apologize."

"That's okay," Katie said without looking up from her bed preparations. "Don't worry about it. I deserved it."

"I still had no right to say it, and I'm sorry. Will you please forgive me?"

Katie looked up slowly. A smile forced its way across her face. "Sure. I forgive you. Don't worry about it."

Christy probably would have stayed awake for a long time rehashing the whole situation, except she was so tired that the minute her head hit the pillow she was gone.

A shrill alarm clock startled her into an upright position. Her eyes darted around the dark room. It took her a while to remember where she was.

"It's five-thirty, you guys," Julie announced from the other bed. "Who wants to get in the shower first?"

"I'll be second," mumbled Katie. "Give me five more minutes of sleep."

"I'll go," Christy volunteered, realizing this might be her only chance with so many girls getting ready. She felt like her head was full of cotton balls. All the early-morning noises seemed to bounce off her. She was quick in the shower and tried to be quick with the blow dryer since it seemed like the noise would wake up the whole building. With a towel around her, she returned to the darkened room and tried not to trip over Katie while searching for her duffel bag.

"You done?" Katie muttered.

"It's all yours," Christy whispered back. "Do you mind if I turn on a light?"

"Go ahead," Julie said from the bed. "We need to get going." Then she added to Katie, "I hope you're fast in the shower too."

The light snapped on, and Christy felt awkward standing there with only a towel on, and the other three girls sitting up in bed looking at her. She quickly pulled out her new ski outfit. By the time Katie returned from her shower, Christy was dressed and ready to go.

The other two girls took their turns in the bathroom. Katie suggested that she and Christy help with breakfast since they had extra time waiting for everyone else to get ready.

Upstairs they found Mr. Riley and his wife putting out bowls and spoons on the table. On the stove, the tea kettle whistled.

"Good morning, early birds!" Mr. Riley said. "I'll go see if the guys are ready. You two can help yourselves to some instant oatmeal."

"We also have juice and doughnuts," Janet added. "And hot chocolate and hot apple cider if you want something to warm you before we face the icicles outside."

Within twenty minutes, everyone had made an appearance at the breakfast table. Some ate, others only grabbed their lunches and stuck a dooughnut between their teeth as the group loaded into the van.

No doubt about it, it was cold. It took eight attempts before the engine on the poor van could turn over. Everyone huddled on the cold vinyl van seats, rubbing their hands and exhaling great puffs of air.

Christy did a final check in her backpack for her sunglasses, lip balm, and wallet. She found that she had everything except her courage. Somehow she had thought if she made it this far in the process, the adrenaline would kick in, and she would feel wild and daring. She only felt cold and nervous.

"You look so cute," Shannon commented from her seat behind Christy. "I love your outfit."

"Thanks," Christy said.

During the next half hour, Christy played different scenarios over in her mind. She told herself that many people skied all the time, and not all of them broke bones. Some of them must even like skiing, because they apparently kept coming back every year. If she started to go too fast on the skis, she could always sit down in the snow. That seemed like a safe technique. After all, how dangerous could ski lessons be?

By the time she and Katie were outfitted with boots, skis, and poles, it was almost nine and time for ski school. They were the only two from the group who were taking lessons. At first that was embarrassing. Then Christy felt thankful for the time to be alone with Katie, without all the pressure from the other girls.

They took the gondola by themselves to the ski school location and followed the signs to where their class was to meet on the side of a slightly sloping hill.

The sun had broken through the morning clouds, and everything around them looked ultra-bright as the sunlight reflected off the snow. The girls carried their skis and crunched through the white powder. They took their places with the nine other students, who were of all ages, shapes, and sizes.

"Yoo-hoo!" called a voice from the ski lift overhead. "Have fun, you two!"

They looked up and saw Mr. and Mrs. Riley on their way to the mountaintop, their ski-fitted feet swaying as they rose.

Christy waved. Katie fumbled for her goggles to block the bright sun and asked, "Was that Janet?"

Christy nodded and asked, "Do you think we'll ever graduate from ski school and be brave enough to actually ride in one of those things all the way to the top?"

"I'm counting on it," Katie said. "So where's our ski instructor?"

"Right here," said a deep voice behind them.

They turned and saw a tall, tanned, smiling man who looked like a movie star playing the role of every girl's dream of a ski instructor.

"Maybe I don't want to be in such a big hurry to graduate," Katie whispered.

"I'm Dawson," the man said, addressing the group of novices. "I'll be your instructor today. The first thing we'll work on is how to put on your skis."

What Christy would have guessed to be an easy procedure turned out to be awkward. It took everyone in the class four or more tries before each of them managed to get the skis on. With their poles holding them steady, the class waited for further instruction.

Dawson began with showing them how to stop, demonstrating how to point the skis in a pie slice or wedge shape, how to balance, and how to plant the poles in the snow for support. Next the class was shown how to walk sideways up a hill. They all began to practice.

"So far so good," Christy said to Katie.

"I don't know about you," Katie said, "but I think I might need some personal instruction after class. You know, some up-close-and-personal instruction."

"Okay, that's good!" Dawson called out. "Everyone stop where you are. Now try turning halfway around, keeping your skis together in a wedge. Remember, balance. Stay in control."

Christy lifted one long ski and put it down. But it landed across the top of the ski on her left foot. She lifted the right one again and pointed it straight. She tried to lift the left foot. As soon as she did, the right ski began to move forward. She quickly put her left foot down. Now both skis were beginning to move, and both were pointed straight downhill, right at Dawson.

"Yikes!" Christy called out. "Stop me, Katie!"

Katie lunged her hand forward in an effort to grab Christy's leg. Instead, the point of her ski pole made contact, slicing a two-inch hole in the right side of Christy's ski pants.

Christy kept moving downhill, picking up speed.

"Plant your poles! Wedge your feet!" Dawson yelled.

Christy tried everything at once, but in her panic she lost all sense of balance. Shrieking, lurching, and flailing her arms, Christy sped forward, running face-first into Dawson's chest.

It seemed his firm stance was enough to break her fall. The problem was, Christy's skis had slid between Dawson's legs, which were planted in a firm A-frame. Even though her face had stopped with as much finesse as if it had hit a brick wall, her legs kept going, pulling the rest of her body with them.

Just as she was about to slip between his legs and slide down the rest of the hill on her backside, Dawson grabbed her under both arms and pulled her back to an upright position.

"You okay?" he asked, his arms still supporting her, their faces only inches apart.

"I...I think so."

"Hey, Christy!" came a call from the overhead ski lift.

Christy looked up and saw Shannon waving her camera and yelling, "I captured that one on film."

Dawson smiled.

Christy smiled back, letting out a nervous giggle. "Sorry!"

"No problem. Now I'm going to let go of you and step to the side. I want you to try sidestepping back up to the rest of the class. Think you can try that?"

Christy laughed nervously again and said the only thing that came to mind. "Guess I have to be smarter than the skis, huh?"

"You're doing fine," Dawson said without laughing at her dumb joke. "Try to remember to balance this time. There you go. You've got it."

Christy sidestepped uphill while the rest of the class watched. As soon as she managed to make her way back into the line next to Katie, Katie said, "Very sneaky!"

"I did not do that on purpose! You know that."

"You'll never convince me of that, you ski-instructor-stealer, you!"

"Hey, be my guest. He's all yours!" Christy teased back. "Try the same thing I did. If you like running into a brick wall at full speed, with an audience, my technique works great!"

"Maybe I'll wait until lunch and see if he wants to join me for cookies and cocoa," Katie said. "What do you think? Does he look like the cookie type or the apple type?"

Christy adjusted her goggles and rubbed her sore nose. "Bricks. He looks like the bricks-and-cement type. Believe me, I'm speaking from the up-close-and-personal view-point. The guy eats bricks."

11

A Little Mouthwash Goes a Long Way

By lunchtime Dawson had disappeared, and Christy and Katie were on their own with their sack lunches and cups of hot cocoa. After removing their skis and getting their booted feet back on solid ground, they found a picnic table and reviewed for each other the morning's events.

"Can I just say that you were about the funniest looking snow bunny I've ever seen?" Katie asked.

"Oh, well you were a lot of help. Trying to harpoon me with your ski pole!" Christy ran her finger over the tear in her ski pants. "The purpose of ski poles is to balance yourself, not skewer your neighbor."

Katie laughed "You should have seen the look on Dawson's face when you were coming at him! Did you see him?"

"No, I was too busy trying to 'wedge,' and then all I could do was examine the knit pattern on his ski sweater."

"Up close and personal," Katie quipped.

"Very up close and personal," Christy said, still laughing. "I felt like such a total klutz!"

"Well, can I just say that you—"

Christy cut in and finished the sentence for her, "—that I *looked* like a total klutz."

"How did you know that's what I was going to say?"

"A wild guess."

"I can see the report on TV tonight," Katie teased. "Innocent ski instructor maimed for life by a total klutz—news at eleven."

They both laughed until the cold air stung the tears in their eyes.

"You have to admit," Christy said, "that for our first time ever on skis, we didn't do too badly."

"We?"

"Okay, you didn't do too badly. And I conquered a whole bunch of fears. I'm willing to try again after lunch."

"Should be easy to find our ski instructor. He's the one with the indentation on his sweater in the shape of Christy's goggles," Katie said.

They burst into another round of laughter.

"He's probably going to run when he sees us coming back for more," Christy said.

"When he sees *you* coming back for more. I, so far, have not yet had an up-close-and-personal encounter with the guy. However, the day isn't over yet!"

"We make a great tag team," Christy said. "I'll terrorize him in the morning class; you terrorize him in the afternoon class. Maybe they'll give us a brand-new instructor tomorrow morning, and we can start the relay all over again!"

As soon as Katie stopped laughing, she pulled her sandwich out of her bag and said, "We should have at least insisted on turkey sandwiches. It is Thanksgiving, you know."

"That's right! I wonder if my family has eaten yet. Probably not. We always go for a long walk while the turkey bakes. It feels strange not being there. Happy Thanksgiving, Katie."

"Happy Thanksgiving to you too. And thanks for coming on this trip with me. It's exactly what I thought skiing would be like."

"Katie, we haven't exactly skied yet."

"All in good time, Christy. We have two more days of this."

"How many ski instructors is that, if I keep up my present rate of mutilation?" Christy asked.

Katie laughed so hard, she nearly choked on her sandwich.

In spite of all their joking, they both did well in their afternoon ski class. Christy, however, felt ready to turn in her skis by three and let her aching legs have a rest.

They met the group back at the van at four-thirty and humbly listened to everyone else tell exciting stories of swooshing down Siberian Express, Shirley Lake, and some of the other more treacherous runs. Somehow, Christy's announcing that she had completed her first successful snowplow didn't seem like worthy news.

Mr. Riley drove to a Mexican restaurant at the Boatworks in Tahoe City, and the group waited twenty minutes before being seated at a long table.

The baskets of chips were instantly devoured, and everyone ordered combination plates. The conversation flowed in and around Christy. From her seat between Katie and Mr. Riley, she found it easier to listen to all the clamor rather than to try to jump in and add to it. It seemed that everyone was having a great time. Even in her weary state, Christy was enjoying all of it as well.

When they arrived back at the condos, there wasn't a lot of complaining when Mr. Riley asked everyone to go right to bed so they could be ready to leave at six-thirty again the next morning.

Christy headed for her bed, eager to make contact with her pillow. But Shannon called to her from the other bedroom, where the three girls were sitting on the floor, pulling off their boots and rubbing their feet.

"We want you to come skiing with us tomorrow," Shannon said. "We've all talked about it, and we'll only take you on the bunny slopes until you're ready for more."

"I kind of already decided to go back to ski school with Katie tomorrow," Christy said. "I'm not very good yet."

"Yes, you are," Shannon protested. "We saw you, and you're good enough to try a bigger hill."

"You saw me all right! You saw me colliding with the poor ski instructor. By the way, I want that picture and the negative when you have it developed."

"I hope it comes out," Shannon said with a giggle. "It was kind of funny."

"Will you come with us tomorrow?" Jennifer asked.

"Maybe I could ski with you part of the day. I could attend ski school in the morning, and then Katie and I could come with you guys for the afternoon."

"We weren't exactly inviting Katie," Tiffany said. "We thought it would be more convenient with you because you'd make it a foursome, which makes it a whole lot easier on the lifts and everything."

"I guess I'll have to see how things go tomorrow,"

Christy answered cautiously. She didn't want to blow an opportunity to get "in" with these girls, but at the same time she didn't want to put any strain on her relationship with Katie after they'd had such a fun day together.

"Okay," Shannon agreed, "we'll meet you at the snack bar after your morning class, and you can tell us then."

For the last few minutes, Christy had been hiccuping. With each hiccup came the taste of Mexican food. "Can I get a drink in your bathroom?"

"Sure. Go ahead."

Christy filled her hands with water since there weren't any cups around and drank quickly, hoping to shake the hiccups. She noticed a bottle of mouthwash on the counter and called out, "Is it okay if I use some of your mouthwash? I've heard that gargling sometimes helps hiccups."

"I don't think—" Jennifer began, but Shannon interrupted.

"It's okay," Shannon said. "It's not really ours. It was here when we got here, but I'm sure you can use it."

Christy could hear the girls murmuring in the background as she took a quick swig of the green mouthwash and bent her head back to gargle.

Suddenly, her throat was on fire. Her whole mouth felt torched. She quickly coughed and spit out the mouthwash. Then she stuck her mouth back under the faucet to let the cold water soothe the numbness.

Christy thought she heard one of the girls say, "I told you guys!"

She grabbed a towel to dry off her face but kept coughing. Her mouth still felt tingly. "What is that stuff? That's the worst mouthwash I've ever used."

"Why? What happened?" Tiffany asked.

She and the other girls joined Christy in the bathroom.

"I only tried to gargle with a little bit, but my whole mouth lit on fire!" Christy explained, still coughing. "I've never tasted mouthwash like that before."

"I wonder what it could be?" Tiffany said. She opened the large bottle and sniffed its green contents.

"It doesn't really smell like anything. Maybe we should put it back under the counter where we found it," Tiffany suggested.

Her two friends agreed.

"I'm sure it's old or something. We probably should have left it there," Shannon said.

Tiffany was about to stash the bottle under the counter when Katie appeared. "There you are! I wondered where everyone went."

Spying the big bottle in Tiffany's hand, she said, "Are you having a bad breath party, and you didn't invite me?"

"There's something wrong with it," Christy said. "I used some, and I felt as though I was about to choke to death."

"Really?" Katie said. "Let me smell it."

"We already smelled it," Shannon said briskly. "We're going to put it back where we found it. I don't think you should mess with it, Katie."

Undaunted, Katie reached over and took the bottle out of Tiffany's hand. "I'm only going to smell it, you guys. What's the big deal?"

She unscrewed the white lid and took a whiff. "Hmmm." She sniffed again.

Christy noticed that Shannon and the other girls were

exchanging glances, which showed their obvious disapproval of Katie.

Katie stuck her finger into the bottle and tasted the green liquid. "Vodka," she announced. "It's not mouthwash at all! Someone filled this bottle with vodka and added green food coloring to make it look like mouthwash."

Christy was shocked.

Shannon looked at Christy and then said, "Who would do such a thing? It was here when we got here—right, girls?"

The other two agreed, and Katie said, "I think we should give the bottle to Janet right now."

"Good idea," Tiffany said, grabbing the bottle back and tightly screwing on the lid. "I'll take it to her."

"Let's all take it up," Katie suggested. "We can go right now."

"We'll do it later," Tiffany said firmly. "The guys are up there now, making lunches for tomorrow, and I don't want to cause a big scene."

Christy thought the reasoning sounded legitimate, but Katie wasn't buying it. "So what if the guys are there? I say we take it up now."

"Look," Shannon said firmly, "we said we'd turn it in, and we will."

Jennifer stepped between Shannon and Katie and said, "Katie, you don't understand. You and Christy didn't go on this trip last year. The three of us did. You see, last year they had some problems. I don't want it to appear that we're going to cause any trouble this year."

"Why? What happened?" Christy asked.

Tiffany spoke up. "Several couples came last year, and

Mr. Riley found they were sneaking off at night to be together, if you know what I mean."

"What does that have to do with us finding a bottle of green vodka?" Katie challenged.

"You don't understand. Last year Mr. Riley found out at four in the morning what was going on. He woke everyone up, had us pack all our stuff, and drove us back home after only one day of skiing. It ruined the weekend."

"I remember hearing about that," Katie said.

"So don't you see?" Jennifer pleaded. "If he even thought this bottle of liquor was ours, he could cancel the rest of the trip right here and now. Everyone would be super mad at us for making a big deal over nothing."

"I think the best thing for us to do is pour it down the drain ourselves and not say anything about it," Shannon suggested.

"Great idea," Tiffany said, gently nudging the girls out of the bathroom with one hand while still holding the bottle in the other hand. "If you all will excuse me, I need to use the restroom."

Before Christy knew it, Tiffany had pushed them all out of the bathroom, and they stood together in the bedroom, looking at each other.

"I don't know about you guys," Jennifer said, "but I'm ready for a good night's sleep. Good night, Christy and Katie."

"Good night," they both said on their way down the hall to their room.

Katie switched on the light, and their two roommates, who were already in bed, cried out, "Hey, do you mind?"

With a snap the light was off, and Katie led Christy to their adjacent bathroom.

Once inside with the door closed, Katie turned on the light and whispered to Christy, "I know they're lying."

"How can you say that?"

"I know they are. They brought the vodka. I just know it."

"They said they found it under the counter when they got here," Christy protested. "If they brought it, and it was supposed to be a big secret, then why did they leave it out on the counter?"

"Because it's camouflaged in that bottle and with the green food coloring. They never expected you to use it. Didn't they act a little hesitant when you opened the bottle?"

"Not that I remember," Christy said. "They said they would pour it out, and I think we should believe them and trust them. If they don't pour it out, then we can tell Janet. I'd hate to be blamed for ruining this whole trip over a misunderstanding."

"You're too trusting, Christy. You're only worried about your precious reputation with those girls, aren't you?"

"What's that supposed to mean?" Christy raised her voice.

"I mean, you want them to like you so much that you're willing to believe a lie!"

"I am not! I'm trying to give them the benefit of the doubt. You're too judgmental. That's your problem!"

"Judgmental! Ha!" Katie spouted.

Before Katie could continue, Christy put her hand on

Katie's shoulder and said, "Wait a minute. I'm sorry. I take that back. I don't want to get in a fight with you. We've never fought like this before, Katie, and I don't want to start now."

Katie's red face slowly toned down a shade. "You're right. We shouldn't be arguing. Those girls are the problem, not you and me."

"Actually," Christy said, taking a deep breath and trying to calm down, "I think the problem is that we're supposed to be witnessing to those girls, and we've ended up being divided over them."

"You're right again," Katie said, all the fire extinguished from her eyes. "You're probably right too about the judgmental part. I tend to form hard-and-fast opinions of people."

"I shouldn't have said anything. I'm sorry. And you're probably right about my being too trusting. I tend to be too naive about things. I mean, I practically drank the stuff and choked on it, but I never would have known it was vodka. I've never tasted anything like that before."

"You know," Katie said, "I think there's a way for us both to find out if they're telling the truth or not."

"How?"

Katie's green eyes narrowed to catlike slits. "Listen," she said. "I have a plan."

12

Traitor

The next morning, Christy and her roommates followed the same wake-up routine as the day before. After Katie and Christy dressed, they went upstairs and helped Janet prepare breakfast.

The guys made their appearance first, followed at last by the rest of the girls. The kitchen was a muddled flurry of breakfast preparations and lunch bag sorting.

Christy made eye contact with Katie across the room and nodded her head once. Katie then slipped away from the group and disappeared downstairs.

"Did you get your lunch yet, Christy?" Janet asked, startling her out of her concentration.

"Oh, no. Thanks. I'll get it."

"There's one more bag," Janet turned it so she could see the name. "Katie," she read aloud. Looking around, she asked, "Where is Katie?"

"I'll take it for her," Christy offered.

Shannon apparently overhead Janet asking Christy about Katie. She called to Christy from the kitchen table, "Where is Katie? Did she give up on skiing after yesterday's lessons? Is she going to stay in bed all day?"

"No," Christy answered, her heart pounding. "She's going. She just had to go downstairs for a minute."

Shannon turned, whispered something to Tiffany, and then hopped up from her chair and hurried down the stairs.

Oh no! Katie, look out! Shannon's going to catch you snooping.

Christy quickly slipped around the counter to the kitchen and flipped on the garbage disposal switch. Immediately, everyone stopped their conversations and turned to look at her.

"Oops!" Christy said, shrugging her shoulders. "Wrong switch."

Just then Katie appeared at the top of the stairs and looked around the room anxiously until she spotted Janet. Motioning for Christy to follow her, Katie went over to where Janet sat at the table and leaned down to say something to her in private.

Janet rose from her chair and led Katie to her room. Christy waited until they came in her direction before she joined the procession. All the while she was aware of Tiffany and Jennifer, who were still seated at the table, watching Katie's every move.

Just as Christy slipped into Janet's room, she noticed Tiffany and Jennifer heading down the stairs. Janet closed the door, and Katie started in breathlessly. She sounded like a spy who had returned from a successful secret mission.

"I found it," Katie said to Christy. "And I was right. They didn't empty it out. It wasn't under the sink, and that's why it took me so long to find it. I got your signal, though. Thanks!"

"Would you mind backing up here?" Janet asked. "I seem to have missed something."

Katie talked fast, gesturing with her hands, her face expressive. She explained how the "rich girls" had a bottle of vodka in their room, and how even though they said they were going to pour it out, the bottle was still there this morning.

"So you found the full bottle just sitting on their bathroom counter?" Janet asked.

"No, it was in the shower. I almost didn't see it, but then when Christy turned on the garbage disposal I knew that was the signal that someone was coming. I turned around really fast and spotted it through the shower's glass door. I barely made it out of there before Shannon came in."

"Why didn't you girls tell me all of this last night?"

"They said they would pour it out, and I believed them," Christy said.

Katie gave her an I-told-you-so look.

"We can't let this go," Janet said. "Not after what happened last year. You girls stay here. I'll get Lou, and we'll bring the other girls in too."

Christy sat on the edge of the bed with Katie beside her. Her hands were shaking, and she felt her throat closing up. She hated being in situations like this. Why hadn't those girls kept their word and poured the stuff out? Was it actually their bottle of camouflaged vodka after all? Was Katie right about them?

Mr. Riley entered the room with Janet and the three girls and closed the door behind him. All five of the girls crowded onto the bed. Christy focused on her hands folded in her lap, not willing to look anyone in the eye.

"Katie says you girls had a bottle of vodka in your room last night. What do you have to say about that?" Mr. Riley asked, his arms folded across his chest.

Shannon, looking innocent and offended by the accusation, said, "It was a bottle of mouthwash we found under our sink. Christy had some, and it made her cough, and then Katie came bursting into our bathroom and said it was vodka with green food coloring."

"Was it?" Janet asked.

"How would we know? We didn't try it," Shannon said.

"Where's the bottle now?" Mr. Riley asked.

"We poured it out and threw the bottle away last night. We didn't want any misunderstandings, like last year," Jennifer answered.

"That's not true!" Katie burst out. "The full bottle is still in your bathroom. I saw it in the shower this morning!"

"What were you doing in our bathroom?" Tiffany asked.

"Checking to see if you kept your word, which you didn't," Katie stated firmly.

Christy felt more and more uncomfortable as the accusations continued. She didn't know what to say.

"Let's all go downstairs and have a look in your bathroom. We'll settle this once and for all," Mr. Riley said, opening the door.

Don was standing right next to the door, apparently listening to the conversation.

"Oh, hey!" Don said when Mr. Riley opened the door. "We were just going to ask how soon until we load up the van. It's almost seven."

"We'll leave in about ten minutes," Mr. Riley said. "Excuse us." Pressing past the eager skier, Mr. Riley led the parade of girls downstairs.

The seven of them squeezed into the bathroom.

"Okay, Katie," Mr. Riley said, "where did you see the bottle of mouthwash?"

"In the shower," she said. "Behind the glass door there."

Mr. Riley opened the shower door and picked up a bottle filled with green liquid. He held it up for his wife to see and read the label. "Herbal Garden Shampoo. You used to use this brand, didn't you, Janet?"

She nodded and said, "Maybe you should take the lid off and smell it."

"It wasn't shampoo," Katie protested. "It was mouthwash. A big bottle, and it was in there this morning."

Christy watched as the three girls looked at each other, shrugging their shoulders and exchanging expressions of innocence.

Mr. Riley twisted off the lid from the shampoo and poked his finger inside. Rubbing his thumb and fingers together until they formed a lather, he sniffed at the liquid and said, "This is shampoo, Katie. One hundred percent shampoo."

"I know," Katie said, exasperated. "I'm talking about mouthwash, not shampoo. Check under the cupboards and in their luggage. It was here twenty minutes ago."

"Christy," Mr. Riley turned to her, "what was it that you drank last night?"

Feeling all eyes on her, Christy said, "I didn't really drink anything. I was trying to gargle. See, I had the hiccups, and I came in here to get a drink of water. I saw the mouthwash on the counter and asked the girls if I could have some."

"And they didn't try to stop you or say, 'That's not mouthwash'?" Mr. Riley asked.

"No, I mean, I don't think so. I don't remember. I just took a little bit, and my mouth felt on fire, so I spit it out and rinsed my mouth with water."

"It got rid of her hiccups," Shannon said with a smile.

"You don't know if it was vodka or not though, do you?" Janet asked.

"No, I've never tasted vodka before, or anything like that, so I don't know what it tastes like," Christy said.

"Katie was the one who drank some and said it was vodka," Shannon offered.

"I didn't drink any. I only tasted it, since it didn't have much of a smell."

"Okay, okay," Mr. Riley said, looking irritated and putting the shampoo back in the shower. "Where is the mouthwash bottle now?"

"There," Shannon said pointing to the trash can. "Since Katie made such a big deal over it last night, we poured it out and threw the bottle away."

Mr. Riley lifted the empty bottle from the trash can, untwisted the lid and sniffed. "Nothing," he said, handing the white cap to Janet. "It doesn't smell like anything. I don't know what was in here."

Janet smelled the cap and shook her head. "It seems like a big hassle over nothing. It's poured out, and that's all that matters. I'm no psychologist, but I'd say maybe, just maybe, you girls are quarreling over something else here.

Something completely unrelated, like territory or friendship loyalty. Can we drop this whole thing and finish the trip without any more hassles?"

"I agree," Mr. Riley said. "We've held up the whole group over this. I appreciate your concern, Katie. Sounds as though it was a case of someone leaving an old bottle of mouthwash under the sink for too long. You girls came along and happened to use some, and it had a kick to it. You poured it out and threw the bottle away, and that's that."

"But Mr. Riley," Katie said, looking frantic, "I know what I saw. You can't just drop the whole thing like this. Christy will back me up. I'm telling the truth."

Mr. Riley paused for a moment and looked at Christy. She froze under his intent gaze. "Do you honestly think it was vodka?" he asked.

Everyone was staring at her. All Christy could say was, "I don't know."

Turning to Katie, he said, "Maybe it's time to stop forcing the issue here. No rules have been violated. If you want to keep pressing it, then maybe I'll have to ask you why it is that you, a girl under the legal drinking age, even know what vodka tastes like."

Then pointing his finger at the three girls in front of him, he said, "And if I find out that you do have liquor on this trip, you need to know, young ladies, that the consequences for all three of you will be extremely serious. Is that understood?"

"Yes, sir," they all answered, nearly in unison and with somber faces.

"Okay. Let's load up and get out of here. The snow is

melting while we stand here bickering in the bathroom. This is crazy!"

They all filed out. Christy went to her room to get her backpack and jacket. Katie was right behind her.

"Traitor," Katie muttered under her breath as she entered the room and slammed the door.

Christy felt as though her heart had just broken. Why would Katie say that to her? She started to cry and turned to face her angry friend.

"Why didn't you stick up for me?" Katie asked, tears now coming to her eyes too. "You made me look like an idiot in front of everyone, and you know I was right! Why didn't you tell them it was vodka?"

"Katie, all I could say was the truth. I don't know what it was! I don't know what vodka tastes like. I was not trying to betray you! How can you say that to me? I only told the truth!"

Katie wiped her eyes with the back of her hand. With quick, jerking motions, she yanked off the black and white ski sweater and peeled off the black ski pants.

"I don't feel like wearing these today," she said, throwing the ski clothes onto Christy's bed. Grabbing a pair of jeans and a sweatshirt, she stormed into the bathroom and slammed the door.

Christy wanted to throw herself on the bed and cry her eyes out. But from the hallway she heard Don yelling for everyone to hurry up because it was already seven-thirty. Numbly gathering her things, she wiped her eyes and headed for the door.

13

Guilty

Christy spent the rest of the morning in ski class with Katie, yet they couldn't bring themselves to speak to each other. It made the session quiet and uncomfortable.

How can it be that I'm only a few feet from my closest friend, but I've never been so lonely in my life? This has to be the most horrible, miserable, alienating experience ever! What am I going to do? How can I mend things with Katie?

Cold, wet, and unable to concentrate, Christy excused herself from class and plowed her way back through the snow to the lodge. She went to her locker and pulled out her backpack, searching for a tissue for her leaky nose. No such luck. The bathroom was close, and she was glad to find a tissue box in the wall near the paper towels.

Having blown her nose and taken a few extra tissues to stuff in her pocket, Christy was about to leave when she heard her name mentioned.

Someone behind one of the closed stalls said, "It was a good thing Christy was on our side, or else Mr. Riley might have believed Katie."

"Oh, I know!" a voice from another closed stall

answered. "That little snoop almost ruined everything. Are you sure Christy's totally on our side?"

"I'm going to make sure before the day is over. She's supposed to go skiing with us this afternoon. I'm going to be super nice to her just to cement her friendship."

A stall door opened, and Christy froze, expecting it to be one of the girls. It wasn't. With her heart pounding, she slipped into the vacated stall to listen to the rest of the conversation.

She heard another stall door open, and from the way the voices moved and from the sound of running water, Christy guessed that at least one of the girls was out of the stall and over by the sink, washing her hands.

"Do you really think Christy has never tasted any liquor before? I mean, did you see her? She played innocent better than we did!"

"Who knows? She could be telling the truth. I don't know. At least she isn't a truth crusader like Katie."

"I don't think we have to worry about Katie anymore." The voice paused and then said, "Ugh! Why didn't you guys tell me my hair was such a mess! Did you bring a brush?"

"There's one in my locker. Come on. Let's pick up our lunches, and I'll get the brush for you."

"So you really think we're not going to have any more problems with Katie?"

"To quote Christy's classic line with the mayonnaise blowout, 'You have to be smarter than the bottle of mouthwash, Katie!'"

"Then it looks like we're safe."

Muffled giggles followed the girls as they exited the bathroom.

Katie was right; it was vodka! And they sound like they still have it! What should I do?

It seemed the only thing for Christy to do was meet the girls at lunch, as planned. Surely she would be able to think of some way to confront them with this whole thing then.

Throwing her backpack over her shoulder, Christy marched to the appointed meeting place at the snack bar. The girls weren't there yet, so Christy decided to act casual, find a place to sit down, and start eating her lunch. She settled in and unzipped her pack, only to find that she had no lunch. She had left it back at the condo.

I don't believe this! This day keeps getting worse and worse. What next?

What came next was the appearance of Shannon, Tiffany, and Jennifer. She wasn't ready to face them.

"Hi!" Shannon called out, waving as she approached. "Did you forget your lunch? I saw it on the counter and brought it for you. Are you getting hungry?"

Christy smiled and meekly accepted her forgotten lunch. "Did you get Katie's too?"

"No. Are you sure she forgot hers? I only saw yours on the counter. Did I tell you how much I like your jacket? That color looks great on you."

Christy knew her lunch had been right next to Katie's. She was not in the mood to play any more games with these girls.

"Which run do you want to try first, Christy?" Tiffany asked. "Do you want to take it easy or dive right in and go to the top?"

"I'm still not sure," Christy replied, stalling. "I'm still signed up for ski school for the afternoon session."

"You're not going, are you? Why waste your time when

you could be really skiing?" Shannon asked.

"Yeah," Jennifer added, "with us."

Christy bit into her sandwich so she wouldn't have to answer and slightly shrugged her shoulders.

I can't pretend I don't know what they said. I could find Janet and Mr. Riley, but then these girls would never speak to me again, and I'd feel awful. Christy kept chewing slowly. *What am I thinking? Do I care what they think of me? No, I care about what Katie thinks of me. And I guess, ultimately, I care about what the Lord thinks of me. I have to say something. Lord, help!*

"Shannon," she blurted out, not sure of what she was going to say next. "Ym, can I ask your opinion on something?"

"Sure."

"Actually, I'd like it if all of you could give me your advice. I kind of have a problem."

"Does it start with *K* and end with *atie*?" Tiffany asked.

"I'll just say it's about a girl I know," Christy began, still not sure of what she was doing, gingerly making it up as she went. One thing was certain—these girls loved to give advice. They had all stopped eating and were intently waiting to hear Christy's problem.

"This girl was sort of talked into buying some cosmetics from this friend of hers, who was trying to sell them," Christy began.

"We've all done that before, right?" Jennifer asked, and the others nodded in agreement.

"Well, this girl was told how great the products were, and if she didn't like them, she could return them anytime and get all her money back. So she tried them, and they didn't seem that great. But the friend who sold them to the girl kept flattering her and trying to make her feel good about it. About the cosmetics, I mean."

"That's how it usually goes," Jennifer commented. "Then what happened? Did she totally break out or what?"

"Actually..." Christy continued, her heart pounding. She was quickly making up this story as she went along and wasn't sure she could pull it off. "The girl found out the cosmetics company was under investigation for fraud. Her friend promised that none of it was true, and she even tried to sell her some more of the stuff. The girl believed her friend and bought a bunch and even tried to convince some of her other friends that the products were good."

"What happened?" Jennifer asked.

"The girl accidentally overheard a conversation and found out that her friend had lied to her. The friend knew all along that the company was in trouble and the cosmetics weren't that good. She'd been using this girl the whole time."

"That is the lowest," Tiffany said. "I'd make the liar give me all my money back, and I'd never speak to her again."

"I'd sue the company," Shannon said.

"That's why I wanted your advice," Christy said. "Because the girl is thinking of going directly to the authorities and reporting the whole thing. Except she doesn't want to lose her friend who lied to her and used her. How can the girl work things out so that her friend won't use her anymore and yet expose the truth at the same time?"

The girls all looked at each other, and Shannon said, "Trash the friend. Go right to the authorities, and get justice."

"I agree," Jennifer said. "What kind of friend would set

her up like that and keep up the front even when she knows it's a lie?"

"Friends like you," Christy blurted out.

"What are you talking about?" Shannon asked.

"Yeah, what is this? You're not talking about makeup, are you?" said Jennifer.

Christy forced herself to look directly at the girls. Her stomach was in a huge knot when she said, "I accidentally overheard you guys talking a little while ago in the bathroom. I know there really was vodka or some kind of liquor in the mouthwash bottle, that it was yours, and that you still have it." Her voice began to quiver. "And I don't know what to do about it. If I followed the advice you all just gave me, then I should go right to Mr. Riley and totally dump all of you as friends because you set me up, lied to me, and used me."

"We never lied, and we did not set you up," Shannon said. "You went for the mouthwash on your own. We didn't give it to you. Then we let the situation run its natural course. None of us told a lie."

"You're saying you honestly did find that bottle underneath the sink?" Christy questioned.

"Well, no," Tiffany admitted. "We had to make up that part. Except for that, we didn't lie."

Jennifer added, "If Katie hadn't come snooping around, everything would have smoothed over, and no one would have gotten hurt."

"Well, I got hurt," Christy said, feeling her emotions rising. She wasn't sure she could push them down much longer. "And I'll be honest with you guys—I don't know what I'm going to do about it. Your advice to me was to go right to the authorities and throw away the friendship. That might be the best advice, but I don't want to throw away any of my friendships—not with Katie and not with you."

Because she thought she was going to burst into tears or throw up or both, Christy excused herself and fled for the refuge of the restroom. She emerged from the stall fifteen minutes later, having had a good, long, quiet cry in private.

The last thing she felt like doing was going back out on the ski slopes. Collecting all her gear and checking her red, puffy eyes in the mirror, she left the restroom and headed for the huge fireplace in the lodge.

Finding an empty chair, Christy planted herself near the tall window, her feet pointing toward the fire. Outside, the afternoon sun was now hidden by a block of clouds that looked as if they had aprons full of snow and were waiting for the signal before dumping it on the earth below.

Then, as if God had given the signal for the matronly clouds to gleefully shake empty their aprons, tiny snow babies began to float to their new homes. Some were eagerly adopted by the sturdy evergreens stretching out their arms to receive them. Others caught rides on the shoulders of determined skiers snowplowing their way down to the lodge. Most of the silent snowflakes found their places on the slopes, where they huddled together with those that had come before them.

Somehow it all has a purpose and a place, Christy thought as she settled into her chair and watched the world outside turn white. *The only comforting part of this whole mess is that God knows the beginning and the end. I know He cares about what I'm feeling, and I know that somehow, every time, He works it out for His good. Everything has a purpose.*

"Did you give up?" a voice said behind her.

Christy turned around and saw Mr. Riley holding a cup of hot cocoa.

"Just taking a break," Christy said. "Looks a little too cold out there for me."

"It's getting colder, and the visibility up on top is pretty soupy. If the rest of the group ends up huddled by the fire here, we might as well go back to the condo. We could rent a couple of movies and make some popcorn."

"That sounds like fun." Christy smiled up at him.

"I'm glad you're here by yourself for a minute," Mr. Riley said. "I've thought about something, and I wanted to run it past you."

"Good, because I have something I wanted to talk to you about too."

"I realized that when I smelled the lid of the mouthwash bottle this morning, it didn't have any kind of odor. If it had been filled with mouthwash, it would have smelled minty. I use that brand, and it's very minty. Christy, do you think there's any chance the bottle did have some kind of liquor in it?"

Christy readjusted her position in the chair and decided this was the moment to tell all.

Just then Katie's voice called out behind them, "Mr. Riley, your wife is looking for you." Katie apparently hadn't seen Christy in the chair, because when she did notice her, she added, "Oh, I didn't know you were busy."

"Tell Janet I'll be right there. Christy was about to tell me something."

"Then I guess I'd better leave you two alone."

Christy could hear the bite in her tone. Katie was still hurting, and Christy knew she had every right to be.

"No, I'd like you to stay, Katie. I'd like you to hear this too."

Katie hung back, not looking at Christy. Waiting for Christy to speak, she took a stance that said, "I dare you to melt me."

Christy looked up at Mr. Riley and began. "Katie was right. There was vodka in the mouthwash bottle. It was probably there in the shower this morning too just as Katie said."

"Oh, fine!" Katie threw her hands in the air. "Now you're on my side. What brought about the big change? Did your new friends suddenly dump you?"

Christy kept her gaze on Mr. Riley as she explained that she had told the truth during the confrontation. She honestly didn't know what she had tasted the night before. What changed her mind was when she overheard the girls talking.

"I wasn't trying to discredit you at all this morning, Katie. I was only trying to say what was true." Christy kept looking at Katie until Katie finally made eye contact. As soon as Katie's bloodshot eyes met hers, Christy said, "I'm sorry."

"No, it's my fault," Katie said in a small voice. "I never should have doubted you were telling the truth. Can you forgive me for calling you a traitor?"

"Of course. And can you forgive me for not being braver and standing by you when it really counted?"

Katie smiled and nodded. "Of course," she said, bending over and giving Christy a hug. "It takes a lot more than that to break up a couple of peculiar treasures like us."

"Well, if you two have managed to mend your friendship, I think I'll go find Janet, and we'll get this whole thing cleared up. Thanks, both of you, for your honesty. You'd be surprised how hard it is to find a high school student these days who tells the truth. My opinion of you both just shot up 100 percent. I wish more of my students were like you two."

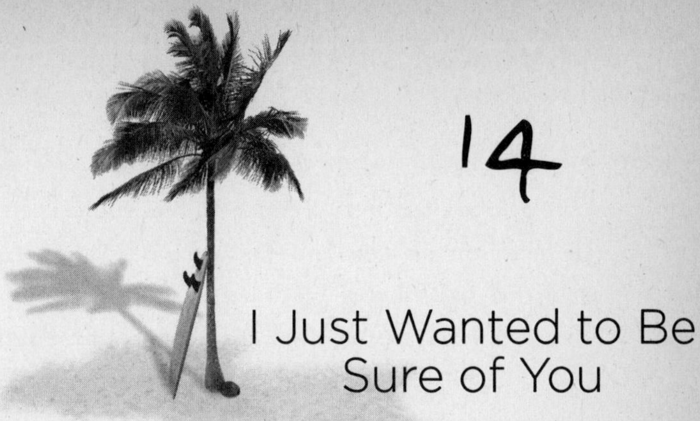

14

I Just Wanted to Be Sure of You

"Christy," Mom called softly. "Wake up, Christy. You have some visitors."

Christy rolled over on the couch and squinted at Mom. "Did I fall asleep? What time is it?"

"It's four," Mom said. "You fell asleep right after we got back from church this morning. You know, it's probably a good thing you came home a day early from that ski trip. Otherwise you wouldn't have made it through school tomorrow."

Christy sat up on the couch and untwisted her red ski sweater. "I really conked out, didn't I? Did you say someone was here?"

"Yes," Mom hesitated. "I think you might be surprised."

"Who is it?" Christy released her hair from its ponytail clip and quickly ran her fingers through it. "Did Katie come by with Glen? She was hoping he'd stop by her house this afternoon."

"Why don't you come see?" Mom said. "They're out in front, talking to Dad."

Christy rose from the couch, slipped on her shoes, and ran a finger under each eye in case her Sunday morning makeup had smeared while she slept. Opening the front door, she stepped out onto the porch. She could hear her dad talking to someone around the corner of the house, but she couldn't see who it was.

Giving her hair one more quick shake and taking another tug at her sweater, she walked down the steps and curiously rounded the corner of the house.

"Rick? Doug? Hi! What are you guys doing here?"

"Whoa," Doug teased. "It's *Sleeping Beauty, Part Two*! And don't you look like the sun-kissed snow bunny. Did you have a good time?"

Doug, her friend from two summers ago at the beach, had no qualms about stepping up and giving her a big hug in front of her dad and Rick. Christy had never figured out whether Doug really was clueless or just so genuine that he had nothing to hide, and that's why he freely acted on his impulses.

Christy accepted his enthusiastic hug and then, because it only seemed right, she turned toward Rick. He hesitated at first, but gave her a noncommittal side-squeeze without saying anything.

The instant Rick put his arm around her, she smelled his aftershave. She didn't know what kind it was, but it was the same heady fragrance he had worn on every date they had gone on.

Instantly, she felt her stomach tighten and her heart swell with mixed feelings. She could tell by Rick's nonverbal greeting that he was either embarrassed to touch her in front of her dad or else being here was all Doug's idea.

"Yeah." Christy tried to remember Doug's question. "The ski trip went well. Not great, but well."

"If you kids will excuse me," Dad said, holding up a screwdriver, "I'm trying to fix the recliner."

Poor Dad! I wonder if the chair will cooperate with him this time.

"Your dad said you came back a day early because a storm was coming, and you didn't want to get snowed in," Doug said, leaning casually against the side of his yellow truck, which he had parked in the driveway.

"That was part of it." Christy gave a quick rundown of the confrontation with the girls over the liquor and how they finally confessed to bringing it with the expectation of having a party on the last night. "I guess the ski club had a similar problem last year with some couples who snuck off."

Rick snickered and said the first words to her since he had arrived. "Did Shannon, Jennifer, and Tiffany happen to mention they were the ones who snuck out last year?"

"No," Christy said. "They didn't happen to mention that."

She cautiously shot a glance at Rick. It felt odd being here with him with no warning that she would face him today. He looked the same—tall, broad-shouldered, with wavy dark hair and chocolate-brown eyes. Yet he looked a little different. Was it that he was somehow more reserved, or was he mad?

She would have liked to say so many things to him, but none of them seemed possible with Doug standing a few feet away. It especially felt awkward since Doug was Todd's best friend, and now Doug and Rick were sharing an apartment and going to school together at San Diego State.

What surprised her the most was that at this moment,

Rick no longer seemed to have that strong, overpowering effect he had had on her in the past. But she felt a strong desire to be friends with Rick. Good friends.

"We were stopping by to pick up some of Rick's junk on our way back to school. I told him I couldn't be this close to you without saying hi," Doug said. "You sure look great! I'm glad to hear you're doing well. I like your hair that way too."

Christy sheepishly smoothed down her wild mane. She could feel Rick's stare as she faced Doug. Rick always told her she looked good in red. Funny how she just happened to be wearing a red sweater the afternoon he decided to pop back into her life. She thought of the gold "Forever" bracelet on her right wrist and wondered if it showed under the cuff of the sweater.

Would Rick notice? Would it even matter to him? And was it possible that he was the one who had bought it back for her?

"Do you guys want to come in? Do you want something to drink or anything?" Christy asked.

"We probably should get going," Rick said. "We have to get back by six for God-Lovers."

"God-Lovers?" Christy repeated, trying to remember where she had heard that expression before.

"God-Lovers," said Doug with a smile. "You like the name? I picked it out. It's a bunch of Christians who meet at our apartment every week. I've been doing the teaching, but tonight Rick is teaching for the first time." Doug gave him a playful punch in the arm. "Getting a little nervous there, buddy?"

Rick tagged him back, and the male sporting ritual

began. Christy watched as the two competitive, over-six-foot-tall "little boys" sparred with each other in her driveway.

She couldn't believe how well Rick and Doug got along. She had only seen Todd in that "best bud" position with Doug. Todd and Rick were so different from each other, yet Doug seemed to get along great with both of them.

Guys sure do this friendship thing differently than girls do.

Competitive Rick appeared to emerge victorious from their round, which was not a surprise to Christy. She decided some things about him might never change.

"I'm sure glad you guys came by. Sorry you couldn't stay longer," she said, not feeling ready to say good-bye to either of them.

She would have loved to jump into the truck with them and go down to San Diego to their God-Lovers fellowship. She would have loved to hear Rick lead a Bible study and see firsthand what was going on in his life. Could it be that he really was getting serious about God?

"We'll all have to get together and do something during Christmas break," Doug said. "Are you going to be around, Christy?"

"Yes, I'll be around. We should do that. It would be fun!"

Doug gave her another bear hug before hopping up into his truck's front seat. "You can come down and see us anytime. Or if you can't come, send cookies!"

Christy laughed.

"I'm serious," Doug said. "Remember those cookies you made for Todd and me last Christmas? Those were the best cookies I've ever had."

"I'll see what I can do," Christy said with a smile. "Oh, but wait! I don't have your address."

Doug scrounged underneath his seat for a piece of paper and pulled out an empty French fry wrapper. "Here," he said, handing the wrapper to Rick along with a pen from his glove box. "Give her our address."

Rick scribbled down the address. When he handed it to Christy, she reached for the paper with her right hand, and her bracelet came into plain view.

She watched Rick's face for any indication that he had noticed. He seemed to be looking at it, but the only change on his face were the corners of his mouth, which moved slightly upward. He didn't look at her. He didn't say anything.

Without even a good-bye hug, Rick hopped into the passenger side of the truck. He reached for his sunglasses on the dashboard, slipped them on, and rested his arm on the rim of the open window.

"Bye," Christy said, sad that they were leaving after such a short visit. "I'm glad you guys came by. Next time stay longer, okay?"

Doug revved up the engine. Right before he backed out of the driveway, he called out, "Don't forget about sending those cookies!"

"I won't." Christy waved the French fry wrapper in the air. "I'll send you some. I promise!"

Rick held up his hand, all five fingers outstretched in a frozen wave, as they backed up and headed down the street. She couldn't read his expression because the dark glasses covered his eyes. Very unsettling.

The encounter left her full of questions. Rick didn't

seem like his old, domineering self. He didn't really seem mad. Was he hurt? Was it hard for him to be around her with Doug there, since they hadn't talked in so long? Did he feel the same way that Christy did, that things weren't completely cleared up between them?

She decided to go inside and call Katie to get her opinion.

"She's not here," Katie's brother said when he answered the phone.

"Could you please tell her I called and I'll see her tomorrow at school?"

The next morning, as Christy grabbed her lunch off the counter on her way to school, Mom said, "Why don't you take that post office notice with you and pick up your package? I didn't get there this weekend."

Christy had forgotten all about the mystery package from 96817. She found the slip, stuck it in her purse, and rushed out the door.

In English class, her teacher finally handed back their essays on "A True Friend Is..." Christy got a B-minus, with a note that said, "Try working a little harder on sentence structure."

This shouldn't have been that hard. Why is it so tough for me to put my feelings into words? I guess it doesn't help much that I'm being graded for sentence structure instead of what I said.

The teacher gave them the last fifteen minutes of class to work on their next reading assignment. Christy pulled out her book and began to read, determined to finish in class so she wouldn't have more homework.

The girl behind Christy tapped her on the shoulder and slipped her a note. It was from Katie, and it said, "Do you want to read my paper? I got an A!"

Christy turned her head in Katie's direction and, with a smile, nodded her head. The paper was passed up to Christy while the teacher wrote on the board.

Sure enough, at the top of the page was a big A. Katie's first line was a quote:

> *Piglet sidled up to Pooh.*
> *"Pooh!" he whispered.*
> *"Yes, Piglet?"*
> *"Nothing," said Piglet, taking Pooh's paw. "I just wanted to be sure of you."*

Her paper went on to describe a true friend as someone who is there for you all the time, no matter what. Someone you don't have to impress because you always know you can be yourself and that person will still accept you. She even quoted Proverbs 17:17: "A friend loves at all times."

The last few lines of Katie's paper said, *I feel I am more blessed than many people because I have this kind of friend in my life. A friend who is always there for me no matter what. A friend who accepts me as I am but loves me too much to let me stay that way. Yes, I would say I am blessed because I have a true friend.*

Christy bit her lower lip, feeling self-conscious and guilty. She didn't exactly measure up to all the qualities that Katie had listed as true friend characteristics. She would be a better friend to Katie.

Christy handed the paper back to Katie at lunch and said, "It's really good. I have to tell you that it made me feel guilty though."

"Why?" Katie asked.

"The way you described your true friend as always being there for you and accepting you in every situation..." Christy hesitated. "I mean, that's really a strong statement."

"You think it was too strong? I thought I watered it down too much." Katie examined the paper. "I even changed the last line before I handed it in. At first I had, 'I have a true friend, and His name is Jesus Christ.' But then I thought she might lower my grade."

Oh! That makes sense. The Lord is always there, and all those other things Katie wrote about Him are true too. Man, am I arrogant or what, to think Katie wrote about me!

"By the way," Katie said. "Can you give me a ride home today? My brother borrowed my car again."

"I'll have to call my mom and ask, but I'm sure it'll be okay. I have to stop by the post office anyway. I received this strange notice that a package was sent to me with postage due."

"It's probably that free sample of sunscreen we sent away for last summer," Katie suggested. "I still haven't gotten mine."

"Could be," Christy said.

"Why? You think it's from Rick or something?"

"No. Oh! I didn't tell you yet! Did your brother mention I called last night?"

"Mr. Message Messer-Upper? No, not likely."

"Where were you? Did Glen come by?"

"No, I was at the grocery store with my mom. Glen didn't even call. Or maybe he did, and my brother forgot to give me the message. I'll see Glen Wednesday night at Bible study, and I'll find out then. Why did you call?"

"No big reason. Only to tell you that Rick and Doug came by yesterday."

Katie stopped eating her sandwich, and her eyes grew huge. "Why didn't you tell me? What happened? Did he notice your bracelet?"

Christy gave a detailed rundown of the situation.

Katie presented her evaluation. "If you ask me, Rick is still hurting over your breaking up with him. And if you want my opinion on that, it was good for the boy. About time someone showed him what it feels like."

"That's not why I broke up with him."

"You broke up with him because he was a jerk, right?"

"No, Katie. He's not a jerk. He's just Rick."

"Same thing," Katie muttered.

"No, it isn't. It's hard to explain why I broke up with him. At the time it was based a lot on my feelings, and I knew I was doing the right thing. The only way I can describe it is that Rick didn't have a spiritual dimension to him, and I really missed that, since Todd is 90 percent spiritual and 10 percent emotions. Rick was like 90 percent emotions, and I don't know how much of anything else. But when I saw him yesterday, he seemed more spiritual. He definitely wasn't the same guy. I think Doug has been a good influence on him."

"That's great. Really, I mean it. I know we're not supposed to judge, but with Rick it always seemed like he was playing Christian. You couldn't tell if it was real to him, or if it was all stuff he was role-playing since he's been going to that church ever since he was a baby."

"I'd like to believe it's becoming real to him," Christy said. "That's what I'm going to start praying for. I put Jennifer, Shannon, and Tiffany on my prayer list. Maybe I should add Rick too."

"The one you should be praying for is Todd," Katie said. "You never heard back from him after you sent that card, did you?"

"No."

"Don't look like that, Christy."

"Like what?"

"You have that look that says, 'Todd has forgotten about me, and I'm never going to see him again in my entire life.' You know that's not true," Katie chided.

"Sometimes it's hard to know what's true." Christy tried not to sound sad. She looked down and spun her bracelet around her wrist. "I guess it's all the stuff on the true friend essays and being reminded of it today. I guess I feel like Piglet. Sometimes I just want to be sure of Pooh, you know what I mean?"

"Yeah, I know what you mean. But the Lord is the only one who is always going to be there for us every single time. You know that."

"I know that about the Lord, but I never know what to think about Todd."

"If you want my opinion..." Katie hesitated.

Christy smiled, "You know I always want your opinion, or at least almost always."

Katie smiled back, "Well, whether you want it or not, my opinion on Todd is that you should always go back to what you know is true and repeat it to yourself. That way you won't get so confused with all these uncertainties."

"What do you mean?"

"Like those verses you wrote him from Philippians about how you thank God for him and how it's only right for you to feel that way because you hold him in your heart.

He said he'd be your friend forever, remember? He promised you that."

"You're right. I need to remember a quote I used in my paper." Christy pulled out her essay and showed Katie. "'My treasures are my friends.'"

"Right," Katie added, "and some friends are 'peculiar treasures.' I'd say Todd falls into the 'peculiar treasure' category."

The bell interrupted their pondering. Christy shoved her paper back in her notebook and said with a sigh, "I hope you're right, Katie."

"Of course I'm right. You know I'm right. Well, at least most of the time."

Christy smiled. "See you after school. I'm off to Spanish."

"My favorite subject lately," Katie said with her comical glint. "Don't forget to call your mom to see if you can take me home."

The remainder of the day went quickly, and Christy met Katie at her car. "My mom said it was fine for me to take you home. Is it okay if we stop at the post office first?"

"You're the driver," Katie said, dropping her backpack on the floor of the car. "How do you manage to keep your car so clean?"

"Mom's orders. She has a thing about dirty cars."

"I guess it doesn't hurt that your brother isn't old enough to borrow it yet," Katie said.

When they were in front of the post office, Christy parked the car and asked Katie if she wanted to come in.

"Are you kidding? You've got my curiosity going on this mysterious package. Do you have the claim slip?"

"Right here." Christy pulled it out of her backpack.

Four people were in line ahead of them, and soon five more people filed in behind them. When Christy reached the window, she handed the clerk the slip of paper and said, "I have a package with postage due. Here's the 57 cents I owe on it."

"Just a moment." The clerk took off for the back with the slip in his hand. He returned right away with his hand behind his back and a funny grin on his face.

"Are you Christy Miller?" he asked.

"Yes."

"Do you know anyone named Phil?"

"Phil?" Christy turned to Katie to see if she recognized the name. "No, I don't think so."

"Just wondering," the clerk said. "Here you go." He plopped a big, egg-shaped, greenish object on the counter. Her address was written on one side in thick black letters. "It's all yours."

"What's that?" Katie asked. "Some kind of overgrown kiwi?"

"No, it's a coconut," Christy said. "That's what they look like when they fall off the trees in Hawaii."

As soon as she said "Hawaii," her eyes grew big. She and Katie locked gazes, their mouths dropping open in unison. The girls quickly moved to the side wall, out of the way of the gawking customers.

"Turn it over, turn it over!" Katie urged. "What's written on the other side?"

Her heart pounding, Christy obediently turned over the coconut and spotted some more black letters. Aloud she read, "'Phil. 1:7.' What does that mean?"

"Philippians!" Katie practically screamed. "Phil is short for Philippians. Don't you get it? He's sending your message back to you. I can't believe this! This is so incredible! What are those other words? They're kind of smeared. Can you read them?"

Christy held the coconut in the light, with Katie's face right beside hers. "I think it says, 'I...hold...you...in...my... heart...too.'"

"Ayhhhhhhhhhh!" Both girls screamed and grabbed each other by the shoulders. Suddenly aware of their curious audience, Katie pushed Christy out of the post office and into the parking lot.

"What did I tell you? What did I tell you?" Katie said, starting in a whisper and getting louder. "This is such a Todd-thing! Who else would ever think of mailing you a coconut? And sending back your message in Bible-verse code! This is so incredible!"

Christy looked at her coconut and then at her enthusiastic friend. Her vision turned blurry. She didn't know if the tears were from laughing or crying, because at this moment she wasn't sure which she was doing.

"Now that," Katie said with a complete air of confidence, "is what I was talking about. You hold in your hand evidence that Todd is always going to be your true friend."

"He *is* my true friend, Katie." Christy blinked back the tears and hugged the coconut close to her heart. With her other arm, she hugged Katie and said, "And you're my true friend too, Katie."

"True friends, no matter what happens," Katie said.

"No matter what happens," Christy agreed. "Because peculiar treasures have to stick together." Then smiling at

Katie and feeling as if she were about to burst with joy, Christy added, "And that's why I hold you both in my heart...forever."

BOOK EIGHT

Starry Night

To my sister, Julie Ann Jones Johnson,
who has stood by my heart many times as
I've counted stars.
With special appreciation to Rich
Mullins, Margaret Becker, and Bryan Duncan, who
have each brilliantly put to music the starry-night
thoughts I've attempted to write in this story.

1

Car Trek: The Next Generation

"Don't laugh," sixteen-year-old Katie said to her best friend, Christy Miller. "Just keep driving, and don't laugh."

"I'm not laughing." Christy pressed her foot on the brake pedal as she turned into the mall parking lot. "Honest. I'm not laughing."

Christy brushed back her nutmeg-brown hair and glanced at Katie out of the corner of her eye. "Is it okay if I park behind the pet store?"

"That's fine. Do you think anyone will see us? I mean, anyone we know?" Katie's bright green eyes scanned the parking lot.

"Probably not," Christy said, aware that her voice carried a hint of laughter. She pulled into a parking space and turned off the engine before cautiously clearing her throat and asking, "Are you going to put on the rest of your costume in the car or when you get inside?"

"You've been waiting for this, haven't you?" Katie said briskly. "You're going to crack up any minute. Admit it. Not all of us can have cushy jobs at the pet store like you."

Katie yanked a pair of felt shoes from her duffel bag

and slipped them on. The toes curled up, and bells hung from their ends.

"It's a job, all right?" Katie defended, pulling a matching felt hat from the bag and adjusting it so the bell hung down on the right side of her head. She reached for a pair of plastic pointed ears and secured them in place. "And if you want to know the truth, I'm proud to be one of Santa's elves," she declared.

Christy could barely hold back her laughter at Katie's elf appearance. She quickly tilted the rearview mirror toward herself. "I think I have something in my eye." She tried to quench the laughter bubble in her throat.

One peek in the mirror at her sparkling blue-green eyes warned Christy that the laughter bubble had sprung a leak and was escaping as tiny tears.

She quickly dabbed them away and tried to maintain control for the sake of Katie's self-image.

"Let me see that," Katie said, turning the mirror in her direction and bobbing her head to get a full view of her green hat and pointed elf ears.

She turned to Christy, "What kind of best friend are you? Why didn't you tell me I look like the bride of Spockenstein?"

Both girls burst into uncontrollable laughter.

"Beam me up, Santy!" Katie joked.

Christy could hardly breathe she was laughing so hard.

Katie reached for a tissue and spouted in her best Scottish accent, "I cain't hold her together much longer! Captain, I think she's goin' to blow!" With that, she put the tissue to her face and faked blowing her nose so hard that one of her elf ears fell off.

"Stop, Katie!" Christy forced the words out over her laughter. "We're going to be late for work."

"Okay, okay," Katie said, calming down. "You're right. This is my first day, and I'd better not be late to Santa's house."

Christy caught her breath and, positioning the mirror back so she could view herself, did a quick fix on her eye makeup. "Come on, Katie. You're going to be the best elf this mall has ever seen. Are you ready?"

"Ready as I'll ever be." Katie grabbed her bag, stepped out of the car, and then immediately ducked back in. With a muffled shriek, she plunged her head beneath the dashboard.

"Duck!" she yelled. "Get down, quick. Maybe he didn't see me."

"Who?" Christy followed Katie's orders and scrunched down in the seat.

Before Katie could answer, Christy heard a gentle tap against her window.

She looked at her friend's terror-stricken face as Katie moaned, "Oh no! Too late!"

Christy turned to see Rick Doyle's smiling face peering in her window.

Quickly sitting up, Christy smiled back and pressed the button to roll down the window. It didn't work because the engine was turned off. Without thinking, she opened her car door and bashed Rick in the knees.

Rick, ever the athlete, absorbed the blow as if she had only tapped him.

"Oh, I'm sorry! Are you okay, Rick?"

"Sure." He looked past Christy to the curled-up elf in her passenger seat. "I thought I saw Katie."

"Rick!" Katie said brightly, pulling herself up. Her hat tilted all the way to one side, and she looked pretty silly. "I was just, ah...I...ah, I lost a contact!"

"Lost contact with your home planet is more like it," Rick teased.

Katie smirked. "Har, har. I forgot what a funny guy you are, Rick Doyle."

Katie had never been a fan of Rick's. Even when he was voted "most popular" last year at their high school, Katie had written "As if!" across his picture in her yearbook.

"Yeah, I'm real funny," Rick said. "Too bad I don't have a pair of green tights and some alien ears so I could be as funny as you."

"I happen to be an elf," Katie stated, gathering her things and pushing open the car door. "And I'm proud of it. I also happen to be late for work, so if you'll please excuse me..." Katie slammed her door and hurried into the mall.

"I need to get to work." Christy looped her small leather backpack over her shoulder.

Rick held the car door for her, and she slid out. She was only inches from him. They hadn't been this close since they dated a few months ago.

Why is Rick being so friendly all of a sudden? What's he up to? Christy wondered.

"Mind if I walk you to work?" he asked. "Or would that make you feel uncomfortable?"

"No, not at all." Christy started toward the mall with Rick beside her.

Why is he asking if I'm uncomfortable? Why is he looking at me so...so tenderly?

"So, what brings you to the mall?" Christy asked, trying to appear casual. "Some Christmas shopping? Only fourteen shopping days left, you know." *Oh, brother, Christy, do you know how stupid that sounds?*

"Actually, I was on my way home from college for the weekend, and I remembered that you work on Fridays. I stopped by to see if you were here."

"Well, here I am!" Christy realized how nervous and ridiculous she sounded. But how was she supposed to interpret Rick's sudden appearance, as if silence and tension hadn't existed between them ever since they'd quit dating?

Rick smiled at her as he held the door open, and she slid past him. She didn't dare look up into his chocolate-brown eyes. She even held her breath so she couldn't smell his familiar aftershave and be whisked back into a swirl of memories. She would be strong. She would resist him.

The pet store was only a few yards away, and Christy walked quickly. It was as if once she hit the doorway she would be in the safe zone, and he couldn't confuse her anymore.

This is crazy! What am I thinking? For weeks I've been telling Katie how much I wish I could sit down and talk with Rick to resolve everything. Yet, now that he's only inches from me, I'm running from him, just like I have since the day we met.

With sudden boldness, Christy turned to Rick. "I have to get to work now, but I have a break around six. Can you meet me back here then?"

Rick grinned, but he was visibly surprised at her boldness. "Thanks for the invitation, but I already have plans for the evening. I'd like to get together sometime. To talk."

"I'd like that too," Christy answered softly.

"Okay." Rick nodded. "That's what we'll do then. We'll get together sometime and talk."

"Is that why you stopped by to see if I was here? Were you thinking we could set up a time to talk?"

"Actually, I told Doug I'd remind you about those cookies you promised to bake for us." Rick stuck his hands in his pockets and looked a little sheepish. "Doug is, well...he's a cookie freak, you know. I've even seen him go into Oreo withdrawals."

Christy smiled at his joke. Doug was a great guy. She had hoped that when Rick and Doug became roommates, Doug would have a good influence on Rick. It looked as though maybe he had.

"Doug also wanted me to see if you could come down to our God-Lovers Bible study Sunday night. It's from six to nine. I'll draw you a map if you want to come."

Christy wasn't sure how to interpret the invitation. Was Doug inviting her? Or Rick? She knew her parents wouldn't be in favor of her making the forty-five-minute drive to San Diego by herself.

"I'm not sure I can come," she said, quickly adding, "but I'd like to! Ever since Doug first mentioned your group, I've wanted to come, but I'm not sure my parents would let me drive down by myself."

Christy hoped Rick would pick up on the hint and offer to take her. It would be the perfect opportunity for them to talk. "Oh, right. Those strict parents of yours. I almost forgot," Rick said. "You could invite Rudolph the red-haired elf to come with you."

Pulling a scrap of paper from his pocket, Rick offered it to Christy. "Here's our number. Doug wanted me to give it to you. He'll be there all weekend. Call him if you decide you can come down. I have to go. I'll see you later."

"And we'll get together and talk sometime, right?" Christy hoped she wasn't appearing too eager.

"Right," Rick said, taking small steps backward, as if being sucked into some great mall vacuum. "We'll do that. We'll get together and talk sometime."

He lifted his right hand like a quarterback winding up for a pass and waved at her over the heads of the Christmas shoppers. Then he was gone.

Christy sighed and headed for her safe haven behind the cash register at the pet store, where Jon, her boss, stood helping a customer. Two more were in line.

"So glad you could join us, Miss Miller," Jon said without looking at her. Then to the customer he said, "That will be $17.53, please."

Christy forced herself to look at the clock and grimaced when she saw she was fifteen minutes late. Her boss, Jon, was usually easygoing. He wore his hair in a ponytail and had more than once done nice things for Christy. He did like all his employees to be prompt though.

"I'm sorry, Jon. Do you want me to do that?"

"Sure," he answered as he stepped back to let Christy accept the twenty-dollar-bill from the customer. Christy counted back the customer's change. By then three more people had stepped in line.

Christy had a feeling she wouldn't get her usual six o'clock break. Maybe Katie would pop in during hers, and Christy could hear how the elf business was going.

But Katie didn't appear at the pet store until closing time. Her face glowed.

"Congratulate me," she said. "I earned a 10 percent bonus tonight!"

"That's great! How did you do it?"

"They said they'd give me a bonus if we sold a certain number of photo packages," Katie explained. "My job is to get the kids to sit on Santa's lap and smile. Of course, the parents are watching, and when they see their kids laughing and looking so cute, they buy more pictures. We did a record-setting amount of business tonight."

"The world's most successful elf," Christy praised her spunky friend. "And to think I knew her when she was merely a high school student."

"Good for you, Katie." Jon pulled down the metal cage door that locked up the shop. "What's your 10 percent bonus based on?"

"Based on?" Katie asked.

"You know, based on," Jon said. "You're going to get 10 percent of what?"

Katie blushed. "I don't know. I didn't ask him. I was too excited, I guess."

"You can find out tomorrow," Christy suggested. "I'm glad your first day went so well."

"It was perfect, except for Slick Rick," Katie said, following Christy to the back of the store. "He came over to Santa's house and stood there for at least half an hour just smiling at me."

"Rick did?" Christy asked. "Why would he do that?"

"To drive me crazy. Why else?"

Jon, with the cash drawer in his hands, had joined them in the back room. Christy noticed a wry grin on his face.

"The old tease-her-best-friend trick," he muttered. "Worked a few times for me."

"What?" Katie asked.

"I don't think we want to know," Christy advised, pulling Katie out the back door. "Good night, Jon. See you tomorrow."

When they reached Christy's car, Katie said, "So, when are we going to make the cookies? We should make them Sunday afternoon; then we can take them with us to the Bible study that night."

"What are you talking about?"

"You know, the God-Lovers group at Rick and Doug's apartment. We're going this Sunday night, aren't we?"

"Katie, where did you come up with all this?"

"Rick told me."

"When?"

"Well, I sort of talked to him on my break. He told me all about the weekend plans. Why? Didn't he tell you?"

Christy looked at Katie in disbelief. "Rick actually waited around for you, and you spent your break with him?"

"Yeah, so?"

"And he invited you to God-Lovers, and you really want to go?"

"Sure. Don't you? I think it'll be fun. I want to meet this Doug I've heard so much about." Katie plunged her felt hat and shoes into her bag and looked at Christy, who sat frozen in the driver's seat, the keys in her hand. "What's wrong?"

"Nothing," Christy snapped, swallowing all her confusion and surprise in one huge gulp. "Nothing at all."

Jamming the keys into the ignition, she started the car with a roar. Then she forced herself to ask calmly, "So, what kind of cookies should we make?"

2

Chocolate Chip Rescue

"*Well, what did your parents say?*" Katie asked the next morning on the phone. "Can you go to God-Lovers?"

"I haven't asked them yet," Christy said with a sigh. "I have a feeling I already know what they'll say."

"Tell them I'm going," Katie urged. "My parents said it was okay. They even said I could have the car, and I don't have to be home until eleven. Maybe if you tell your parents I'm driving, they'll let you go."

Christy felt a tinge of jealousy over Katie's freedom. She knew she shouldn't compare. Still, it didn't seem fair.

"I was thinking," Christy said, "maybe we should try to go next Sunday night because Christmas break starts then, and we won't have any school on Monday. This Sunday is still a school night for me, and I'm supposed to be home by nine."

"Why don't we go both weeks? Or at least try to go both weeks. I'm really looking forward to it, and I'd like it if you could come with me this week."

Christy realized Katie planned to go whether Christy went with her or not. That hurt. After all, Rick and Doug were her friends. Why should Katie feel so welcomed into their group without Christy there?

"I have to get ready for work," Christy stated abruptly. "I don't want to be late again like yesterday." She said it with a jab, as if she wanted Katie to take the hint that it was her fault Christy had been late.

"Oh, you're right! It's already after ten, and I'm not dressed yet. Hey, do you want to meet at the food court on our lunch break?"

"Okay," Christy said. "I usually have my break at one."

"Great! I'll meet you at the doughnut bar at one unless I can't get away then. Bye!" Katie said cheerfully before hanging up.

Yeah, or unless Slick Rick comes to bug you again. Christy had thought through the situation with Rick a dozen times. None of it made sense. She could believe the part about Doug wanting Rick to invite Christy to God-Lovers, but why did Rick wait around to have dinner with Katie—especially since he had told Christy he couldn't meet her during her break?

She jumped into the shower and quickly washed her hair, debating whether to approach her parents this morning about driving to San Diego with Katie or to wait until that evening. She knew they would say no either way. Why bother asking at all?

It ended up taking a half hour to get ready for work, which meant she barely had enough time to fly out the door with a "See you later" tossed over her shoulder to Mom and Dad.

Her morning continued at a frenzied pace. She couldn't believe it was already one when Jon asked if she wanted to take her lunch break.

Christy arrived at the doughnut bar at 1:04. Katie wasn't in sight. After waiting ten minutes, Christy realized if she didn't get in line and order lunch, her break would be over. She was starving and had no trouble deciding on the French bread pizza, even though that line was one of the longest.

While she waited in line and then sat down to eat her pizza, Christy kept scanning the noisy plaza for Katie. For some reason, she half expected to see Rick as well. She saw neither and had to hurry back to the pet store. If she had had more time, she would have visited Santa's house to watch Katie in action. Or maybe even spot Rick there.

Stop it! she reprimanded herself. *Why are you thinking like this about Rick and Katie? Get your head out of the garbage can, girl! It stinks in there.*

From the minute she stepped back into the shop until she left at six, business remained steady. She felt glad the afternoon had zoomed by. Since Katie never appeared, Christy thought she had better check in on her before going home.

The line at Santa's house wrapped halfway around the large snow scene. In the middle of the display stood a three-sided cottage complete with fake snow, icicles, and mechanical elves who were wired to continually wrap presents and paint red stripes on candy canes.

Christy thought the snow looked funny at this Southern California mall, where most of the shoppers wore shorts. The jolly, rotund Santa sat on his throne with a camera positioned in front of him.

And there, next to the camera, danced Katie. The eyes of the toddler on Santa's lap followed her antics with obvious glee. "Look at Rudolph!" Katie said in a squeaky voice, holding up a reindeer hand puppet. "He's about to fly!"

Katie swooped the puppet forward, beeping Rudolph's red nose on the little boy's nose. She ducked as the bright flash went off, capturing the child's big smile.

No wonder Rick stuck around. I could watch her for hours too. She sure has a knack for this. Why was I getting so jealous and worried about Rick being interested in Katie? That's ridiculous!

As the next child approached the place of honor, Christy caught Katie's attention and called out, "I'm going home now. Call me, okay?"

Katie called back, "We've been so busy! I'll be here another hour. Do you want to bake cookies at my house tonight or tomorrow?"

Aware of the photographer's disapproving glare, Christy shrugged and said, "Call me when you get home, okay?"

Katie nodded and waved. She reached into a basket next to the camera, pulled out a squeaky snowman, and went back to her make-the-baby-smile routine.

Katie finally called Christy at nine-thirty, full of excitement. "I just got home, and you'll never believe what happened! You know the photographer? He offered me a job! After Christmas. He wants me to work at his studio when he does children's portraits. He says I'm the best assistant he's ever had! And get this: He offered to pay me double what I'm getting now!"

"That's great, Katie! Good for you." Christy tried to make her voice sound light and sweet, even though she didn't feel that way. No one had ever said she was the best at anything or offered to double her salary.

"And the best part of all is that I don't have to wear a costume." Katie laughed. "I did tell him the ears were real though, but he promised me his company didn't discriminate against big ears. I'm so excited! I can't believe he hired me just like that."

"That's really great, Katie."

"Sorry it took me so long to get home. I know it's too late to make cookies tonight, but why don't we do it tomorrow? Can you come over here right after church?"

"Hang on," Christy said. "Let me ask my mom."

Christy covered the phone and called to her mom in the other room, "Mom, is it okay if I go to Katie's after church tomorrow to bake cookies?"

"Sure, that would be fine," Mom called back. "I have some butter and chocolate chips in the freezer you can take with you."

The next afternoon, as the girls began their cookie baking, Christy realized it was a good thing she had brought the extra chocolate chips. Katie, who admitted being unable to stay in the same room with any form of chocolate without devouring it, had already made a dent in her supply.

"Pretend they aren't there," Christy advised, "and measure the flour for me."

"You're asking me to ignore them?" Katie looked longingly at the chips spilling from the open bag. "Look at them, Christy. Look at those sad little chips with their tiny, little brown elf caps. Can't you hear them?"

Katie bent closer to the counter, her hand cupped behind her ear. "They're saying. 'We're cold out here, wearing nothing but our tiny elf caps. Please let us come inside your warm tummy!'"

With her most sympathetic expression, Katie pleaded

with Christy. "How can you be so cruel as to leave them there, alone in the cold, shivering?"

"Oh, all right!" Christy scooped up the bag and twisted the top to lock the remaining chips inside. "Just these orphans here on the counter. Their brothers and sisters are mine! And I shall keep them as my prisoners while you measure the flour."

"Oh, thank you, thank you! I knew you had a tender heart. Come, little chips." Katie brushed them into her hand. "Time to go for a ride on a big slide! Ready? Go!" She dropped the handful into her mouth.

"Murf eill bumph dhl grayde," Katie said.

"What?" Christy asked.

With a swallow and a lick of her lips, Katie repeated, "I said, they feel better already."

Christy shook her head. "You know, Katie, you really should be in drama. You're going to be the next Lucy, I just know it."

"It's my red hair. When the first word you recognize as a child is *carrottop,* you quickly figure out you're not in line for the future Miss America."

"Oh yeah? Well, that's not what Glen seemed to think this morning. Isn't this the first time he's actually sat by you at church?"

"You noticed, huh?"

"Noticed! How could I not notice? He acted like you were the only one in the whole Sunday school class. I'd say that shy guy has come a long way!"

"Going a long way is more like it," Katie said with a sigh. "He's leaving as soon as school is out this Friday. His parents are going on a two-week trip to Oregon to raise their support so they can go back to Ecuador in the spring."

"Then he won't be around for Christmas," Christy said, feeling sorry for Katie. Glen was a nice guy, and Christy thought he and Katie were good for each other.

Katie poured the flour into the mixing bowl. "I bought him a CD yesterday at the Christian bookstore. I was going to give it to him this morning, but he didn't get me anything, and I felt strange giving him a present, so I didn't."

"Wait a minute." Christy paused from her batter mixing. "If I remember correctly, you were the one last Christmas who convinced me to give a gift to Rick, even though I barely knew him. I think it's your turn to give a guy a present in the church parking lot."

"No, no, no. You see, you provided both of us with a very good learning experience last year. I learned from your embarrassment, and therefore, I do not need to repeat the same mistake you already made on behalf of both of us."

"Oh, right! That is such a wimp out, Katie. First of all, Glen is not Rick, so it won't be the same kind of mistake. Second, Glen probably didn't give you a gift because he has no money, right? And third..." Christy hesitated. "I forget what third is. But I still think you should consider it missionary support and give Glen the CD. He'll have something to listen to on his long trip to Oregon."

Katie thought for a minute. "I guess you're right, as always. Christmas is supposed to be about giving, not receiving, right? I hate it when you like a guy, and you can't tell if he likes you back."

"Believe me," Christy agreed, "I know how that feels. You should do what you've told me to do—be honest about your feelings and see what happens."

"All right, I'll give Glen the CD. But when? He's leaving on Friday."

"He usually goes to church on Sunday nights, doesn't he? Why don't you give it to him tonight?"

"What about the trip to San Diego?"

"Katie," Christy confessed, "I can't go to San Diego tonight. I never even asked my parents. I knew they'd say no."

"I thought you worked it out with them!"

"No," Christy admitted, shaking her head. "But I still wanted to make the cookies. I thought we could mail them to the guys. Or if you go by yourself tonight, you can deliver them."

Katie pulled the cookie sheets out from the cupboard and slammed them on the counter. "What you're really saying is that you don't want me to go down there by myself because Doug and the others are all your friends. If you can't go, then you don't want me to go. Right?"

"It's not like that, Katie." Christy caught herself before she made up a lie. "Well, maybe that's part of it. I do feel left out. But I only know Doug and Rick. I don't know anyone else there. I just wanted us both to be able to go. That's all."

Katie had been staring at the floor while Christy was talking. She looked up and flashed her green eyes at Christy. "Okay, I'll wait and go when you can. And I'll give Glen the CD tonight."

"Are you sure?"

"Yes, I'm sure."

"Thanks, Katie. You're the most understanding friend in the world."

"Wait. There's a condition. If I can do all that, then you can at least ask your parents about going to San Diego next Sunday."

"I will," Christy promised. "They'll say no, but I'll ask anyway."

"Christy, you won't know until you ask!"

Two hours later, as Christy walked in the front door with a plateful of cookies in her hand, the phone rang.

"I'll get it," she called out, reaching for the receiver and placing the cookies on the kitchen counter. "Hello?"

"Hi, Christy? This is Doug."

"Doug, hi! Guess what I have for you?"

"I hope it's cookies!"

"Yep. Katie and I made them this afternoon for you guys. I'll mail them to you tomorrow."

"I was hoping you were bringing them with you tonight. Rick said he gave you the message."

"He did," Christy said. "But I can't come. I'm sorry, Doug. I really wanted to, and hopefully I'll be able to another time." She lowered her voice. "My parents aren't in favor of my driving all that way at night and everything."

"I wish I'd known that," Doug said. "I could've given you a ride."

"That's okay, Doug. It's kind of a long way for you to have to come."

"I wouldn't have minded a bit. Actually, I should have called you earlier. You see, tonight is our last God-Lovers. We won't meet again until next semester starts up. Probably the end of January."

"Oh, I didn't know, Doug. I'm sorry. Now I really feel bad."

"I should have called you earlier," Doug said. "But hey, we have a huge Christmas break starting next week. We can all get together and do something then. Are you going to be at your aunt and uncle's in Newport Beach like you were last year?"

"I'm not sure yet what we're doing. I could probably make arrangements at work and ask my aunt if I could stay with her." Christy thought of how fun it would be to get together with her Newport Beach friends again. Last Christmas she had had breakfast on the beach with Todd.

Todd was so different from any other guy she had ever known. The last two years of her life were filled with memories of him: her first kiss, a trip to Disneyland on her birthday, the vacation last summer on Maui, long talks, and many ups and downs. She thought of New Year's Eve last year, when she and Todd went to a party in Newport Beach at their friend Heather's house. At midnight Todd had given her a gold ID bracelet with the word "Forever" engraved on it and kissed her.

While she was dating Rick, he had "borrowed" the ID bracelet and traded it for a clunky silver one that said "Rick." Her relationship with Rick had its share of rough water, but when she found out he had taken Todd's bracelet and sold it, she broke up with him immediately.

Christy had faithfully made payments at the jewelry store to retrieve her gold bracelet. Then one day she went to make a payment and found out that some guy, who wished to remain anonymous, had paid it off.

She still didn't know who it was. At first she suspected Jon, her boss. He denied it when she asked him. Katie thought it might have been Rick, trying to make up for being such a jerk. For a while Christy wondered if somehow Todd had found out and paid it off.

She glanced at her bracelet, now secure on her right wrist, and asked Doug, "Have you heard anything from Todd? Did he say when he's coming back from Hawaii?"

"No, I haven't," Doug answered slowly. "We need to be praying for him though, because the next two weeks are his big competition weeks at Waimea. He'll either make the pro surfing circuit or drop out."

"If he doesn't make it, does that mean he might come home?" Christy tried not to sound too hopeful.

"Who knows. He might stay at U of H for the next semester. Or he could be on a plane back right now. You never know with Todd."

Well said, Doug. I couldn't have expressed it better myself. You never know with Todd. Looking at her bracelet again she thought, *He could be on a plane right now. You never know!*

3

Opposites Don't Attract, Do They?

Christy woke up Monday morning with a sore throat and thought about how wonderful it would be to stay in her cozy bed all day. But she knew that, with only five more school days until Christmas break, she couldn't afford to miss any of her tests or get behind in her homework.

So she made an agreement with herself. *If I don't feel better after I take a nice, hot shower, then I'll go back to bed.*

The shower seemed to perk her up, and she went to school with a package of Mom's cough drops in her purse. She actually felt okay until lunch, when she told Katie about Doug's phone call.

"So we missed our one opportunity," Katie said flatly.

"They'll start up again in January," Christy replied defensively. "I didn't know that was their final meeting."

"I'm not blaming you," Katie said. "I'm bummed, that's all. I had such a great feeling about being invited to a college campus and being considered on 'their' level."

"Is that why you were so eager to go?"

"Sure! Didn't it make you feel a little grown-up and, you know...kind of like the big kids were saying, 'Red Rover, Red Rover, send Katie and Christy right over'?"

"Not really, but I can see what you mean. Don't strangle me, but for a while I was thinking you wanted to go because of Rick."

Katie dropped her candy bar on her lunch bag and said, "Christy, how could you even think that?"

"I don't know. Maybe it's because I know Rick. He likes a challenge. You know that. I guess it seemed after our encounter with him in the mall parking lot that you became sort of a challenge to him."

"Challenge or no challenge, Rick isn't exactly my favorite person."

"I know."

"Rick and I couldn't be more opposite." Katie snatched up her candy bar and chomped into it for added emphasis.

To herself, Christy muttered, "Sometimes opposites attract."

"I heard that," Katie said. "Now can we talk about something else? Like the way Glen hugged me last night when I gave him the CD?"

"Oh, Katie! I'm sorry! I meant to ask you what happened. Tell me, tell me!"

"There's not much to tell. I gave him the CD after church last night, and he hugged me and said thanks. His mom was standing right there. It wasn't a big deal."

Christy's eyes scanned Katie's for more details.

"That's it. It was nice. I'm glad I gave it to him, but I wouldn't write a love sonnet about the experience. Speaking of sonnets, have you read that thirteen-page sonnet for English yet?"

Christy shook her head and slowly sucked her boxed orange juice through the thin straw. It surprised her that

Katie wasn't more excited about Glen. She didn't seem to be as interested in him as she had been a month ago.

Christy watched and listened to Katie the rest of the week. She didn't mention Glen once. Christy thought it best to wait for the right time before bringing up his name.

It was a grueling week of homework and three huge exams. By Friday Christy was so eager for school to end that she spent her last class writing out Christmas cards and working on her Christmas shopping list.

Half the class had ditched, and the teacher sat on the edge of his desk showing a clump of students his famous card tricks. Christy hoped to finish all her Christmas cards so she could mail them from work that night. With only a week left before Christmas, she hoped they would arrive on time. Alissa's card was going to Boston, and Paula's would be sent to Wisconsin, but the rest of her friends were in California, so their cards should arrive before the big day.

But what should she do about Todd? She had a card addressed to him at his address on Oahu, but would he get it if he was surfing all week like Doug said?

And what about a present? Last year she had painted a surfer on a T-shirt for him. He probably liked it because she had seen him wear it several times.

This year a painted T-shirt seemed like a dumb present. She was surprised she had thought it was such a great idea last year. Maybe she should just send him a card. It was probably too late to mail anything to Hawaii anyway. She should have thought of all this much sooner.

The final bell rang, and everyone cheered and joked, saying, "See you next year!"

Christy stuffed her cards in her bag and met Katie at Christy's locker as planned.

"Ready?" Christy asked. "I'd like to get to work a little early so I can mail my Christmas cards."

"I have everything," Katie said. "Let's go. Thanks for giving me a ride again. If my brother doesn't get his car fixed soon, I'm going to make my parents give him an ultimatum. He doesn't even ask. He just takes off in my car as if I don't have places to go, people to see."

"Why don't you ask your parents to get his car fixed for him as his Christmas present?"

"That's a good idea," Katie agreed as Christy unlocked the car doors. "By the way, what are you getting Rick this year?"

"Rick? Nothing!"

"Not even a card?"

"Well, maybe a card. I was going to send one to Doug, and I was thinking about adding Rick's name to it. I want to talk to him face-to-face and settle everything between us. I don't think a card would do much good."

"Sounds wise," Katie said, humming to herself the rest of the way to the mall.

Now Christy's curiosity was up. As they walked into the mall, she asked, "Katie, why did you ask if I was sending Rick a Christmas card?"

"Oh, no reason," she said.

Christy wasn't convinced. She felt suspicious the rest of the evening. It still bothered her that Rick had hung around and talked to Katie last Friday, and yet he hadn't given her a time when they could sit down and talk.

Maybe it was up to her to set the time. She had Rick's

phone numbers in San Diego and at his parents' home. She could call him and make him talk to her. But by the time Christy arrived home from work, all her fiery determination had died down to the same barely warm embers she had felt ever since they broke up. She would wait for him to call.

To her surprise, the next morning he did.

"Hi," Christy said, not at all sure what to say next. She decided to let him do the talking.

"Nice being out of school for Christmas, isn't it?" Rick said.

"Yes. Yes, it is."

"Well, are you working all next week?"

"I work Wednesday all day, but I have the rest of the week off."

"So Monday would be good to get together and talk," Rick said. It sounded more like a statement than a question.

"I think so. What time?"

Rick was silent for a minute. Christy wondered if she had asked the wrong question. For this to work, it had to be Rick's idea that they get together. She refused to give him any cause to think of her as one of his many old girlfriends who was trying to get back together with him.

"I don't know," Rick said suddenly. "I'll call you."

"Okay," Christy replied.

Then he hung up.

At first his abruptness made her mad. Then she thought about how he had sounded like he was trying to figure out how to talk to her normally. The whole time she had known him, he had been a smooth talker with lots of promises and flattery. Maybe Rick didn't know how to talk to her without an ulterior motive. Or maybe he was changing, and his new shy side was coming out. Did he really want to get together and talk, or was he doing this just for her? Could it be that hard for him to switch from boyfriend to friend and let their relationship go on, even if he didn't always have control?

I guess I'll find out Monday, Christy thought and hurried to get ready for work.

She arrived at the pet shop around 10:45. It was clear that the Christmas rush had begun. Christy rang up purchases for nearly two hours without a letup. Most of the sales were the seasonal promotional stuff, like kitty stockings filled with catnip and reindeer horns on a headband for a dog.

Christy didn't mind that it was so busy. She actually entered into the spirit of things and told the customers "Merry Christmas" when she handed them their bags.

Around one, Beverly, the other pet shop employee, came to relieve her at the cash register.

"Jon said he wanted to see you in the back," Beverly told her.

Uh-oh. Sounds like I'm in trouble.

Jon was slicing open a box when she stepped into the back room.

"You wanted to see me?"

"Yeah. Have a seat. I wanted to talk to you about the way you've been saying Merry Christmas to all the customers."

"Yes?"

"Well, Christy, not all of our customers celebrate Christmas. It could be offensive to them," Jon said.

"I'm only trying to be nice," Christy said defensively. "It didn't seem to bother anyone. Most of them said Merry

Christmas back. I think they like hearing it."

"Now, don't be defensive," Jon said. "Change it to 'Season's Greetings,' and no one will be offended, okay?"

Christy started to nod, but then she realized that deep inside, it wasn't okay.

"Okay?" Jon said again, looking for her agreement.

"No, it's not really."

Jon looked surprised and waited for her to explain.

Christy bravely put her thoughts into words. "Remember once you told me that if people believe something they should take a stand and not be sneaky about it?"

"Well, yes," Jon said. "That sounds like something I'd say. I'm sure I wasn't referring to this though."

"It applies to this," Christy said firmly, before she lost all her nerve. "At least to me, it does. It's not just a season that I'm celebrating. I'm celebrating Christ's birthday, and that's what Christmas is. Everybody knows that. How can that be offensive?"

"Christy, that might be what you believe, but that's not what everyone else believes."

"Then if they don't believe it, why can't they accept what I believe and say their own Season's Greetings back to me?"

"Okay, okay!" Jon said. "You win. You believe something, you're taking a stand for it, and I have to admit that I admire that. Go ahead. Stick with the Merry Christmas. How much can it hurt?"

"Thanks, Jon."

"That's okay. Now why don't you take your lunch break? It's been nonstop all morning. If you don't get away now, you might not get a chance."

Christy was about to leave when she realized that because

it had been so busy, Jon hadn't taken a lunch break either.

"I'll get something and bring it back," Christy said. "And what do you want me to bring for you? It's my treat."

Jon looked up, surprised at her offer. "Are you serious?"

"Of course I'm serious. I got paid today, remember? So what do you want?"

"Well, you know the Chinese place in the food court?"

Christy nodded.

"Go there and ask for Yun. Tell him Jon wants his usual. To go." Jon reached for his wallet.

"Got it," Christy said. "Hey, put your money away. This is on me, remember? Think of it as my early Christmas present to you." She emphasized the *Christmas* and looked at Jon for his reaction.

For a few seconds he met her gaze, a slight smile lighting his face. Putting his wallet back, he said, "Thanks, Christy. And Merry Christmas to you too."

Jon's response made her feel good all over as she quickly wound her way through the crowded mall to the food court. The line at the Chinese food counter was long.

During the five-minute wait to get to the front of the line, Christy forgot whom she was supposed to ask for. She scanned her brain, trying to find the name, and felt completely flustered when she reached the front.

"Hi," she said to the aproned clerk. "Do you know Jon?" The dark-haired guy looked at her funny and said, "Egg foo yong?"

"No, at the pet store. Do you know the guy who works at the pet store? His name is Jon." She could tell she wasn't getting anywhere.

A slender man with a kind face stepped up behind the clerk and asked, "Is there a problem?"

Christy noticed the name on the man's tag.

"Yun!" she said excitedly. "You're Yun."

The man looked at the clerk and then at Christy. "Yes, I'm Yun. Have been as long as I can remember."

Christy laughed, relieved that she hadn't blown her errand of kindness. "I work at the pet store, and I'd like to order the usual for Jon."

"Oh, Jon!" Yun said, his face lighting up. "Sure. I'll get it for you. Will there be anything else?"

Christy hadn't thought of what to order for herself. "I guess I'll have an egg roll. Oh, wait. Do you have those little, um...what are they called?"

The clerk stared blankly at her, and she became aware of the stares from the people standing in line behind her.

"Forget the egg roll. I'll just have the sweet and sour shrimp. Oh, and some rice. A small. Rice, I mean. A small rice and a small sweet and sour shrimp. Please."

The clerk handed her the ticket, and motioning to the right, he said, "Pay down there."

Turning to another employee near him, the clerk rattled off something that made the other guy laugh.

No need for a translation on that, she thought. *I'd know "ditz" in any language.*

Christy paid for the food, trying to be calm and gracious as Yun handed her the large bag.

"Here you go," he said, "And please tell Jon Merry Christmas for me."

Christy smiled and nodded. She would love to tell Jon that Yun wished him a Merry Christmas.

As she headed back toward the pet store, she tried to decide if she should hurry back or take a detour to see Katie, which had been her original plan for her lunch break. The smell of the hot food made the decision for her. She would wait and see Katie after work.

When Christy entered the pet store, she motioned to Jon by lifting the bag and tilting her head toward the back room.

"Go ahead," Jon said, pouring a box of rubber dog bones into a basket by the front register. "I'll be there in a minute."

She eagerly set up the Chinese picnic on the card table in the back room. Drawing in the feast's wonderful scent, she felt hungry enough to eat it all herself.

"I brought you a lunch guest," Jon said as he stepped into the back room. Christy peered around him, expecting to see Katie.

"Doug!"

"Hi, Christy!" he said, wrapping his arms around her in one of his famous hugs. "Guess I came at the right time."

Christy was so surprised that she was at a loss for words.

"You two go ahead and dig in," Jon said. Patting Doug on the shoulder, he added, "Help yourself to whatever you like. It's Christy's treat."

Doug pulled up a folding chair and said, "I already ate. Sure smells good, though. Maybe I will have a little rice. I stopped in only for a second. I'm on my way home for the holidays, and I wanted to see if we could set up something for next week." With a peek inside one of the white boxes, Doug asked, "What is this?"

"I'm not sure. It's Jon's 'usual.' This one is sweet and

sour shrimp, and this one is rice," Christy explained. "You want some?"

"Sure." Doug held up a paper plate for Christy to scoop the rice and shrimp onto.

She divided up the food and was about to take a bite when Doug asked, "Do you want to pray?"

"Oh, sure," she said, bowing her head and waiting for Doug to pray for her the way Todd always did. It was silent.

"Go ahead," Doug whispered. "You pray."

"Oh, you meant me." Christy bowed her head once more and quickly thanked God for the food.

When she looked up, Jon stood a few feet away.

"Don't mind me," he said, reaching for a box of doggie treats.

I wonder what Jon thinks of all this? Of Doug and me praying and everything?

"Remember how we all went ice-skating last year?" Doug asked. "Do you think we should do that again this year?" Christy vividly remembered that wild day with its mix-ups. She also remembered skating with Doug, supposedly to make Todd jealous. In the end, Doug turned out to be a great skater, and they had had a lot of fun together.

"Ice-skating would be fun. Or we could go to the movies, or maybe Heather would want to have another New Year's party," Christy suggested.

"Hey, you know what would be fun?" Doug said, swallowing a mouthful of rice. "We should all go to the Rose Parade!"

"That would be great!" Christy's face broke into a huge smile. "We always used to watch the Rose Parade in Wisconsin, and I grew up dreaming about going someday.

Seeing all that sunshine when you're bundled up and it's snowing outside makes California seem like paradise."

"The parade is a lot of fun," Doug said. "A bunch of us went two years ago and slept overnight on the street so we could have front row seats. It's time for us to go again. That takes care of New Year's. What else do you want to do next week? Do you want to get together on Monday? I thought it'd be fun to go sledding up in the mountains."

What's Doug asking me? Is he thinking about a group thing, or is he asking me out? Rick wanted to get together Monday. What do I say?

"Monday?" she asked.

Doug nodded and bit into a chunk of sweet and sour celery.

"By any chance did you and Rick talk about this? Because he said something about getting together on Monday. Did you guys already have something in mind to do as a group?"

"Oh, well not really." Doug looked disappointed. "I didn't know you and Rick were, you know...getting together. I didn't know you already had plans."

"We don't really. Rick suggested we get together Monday, but maybe he meant we could all get together, like you're saying. We could all go sledding."

Christy wasn't sure she was doing the right thing here, forfeiting her opportunity to talk with Rick. But the thought had entered her mind that if Katie came along, she might hit it off with Doug, and the two of them could kind of be together, and she could be with Rick.

"I'll stop by his house when I leave here. We'll see what we can come up with. Rick said you had a friend named Katie?"

"Yes, I wanted to invite her along to whatever we end up doing. Is that okay?"

"Great," Doug said, his warm smile returning. "The more the merrier! I'll look forward to meeting her."

Doug really was a great guy. Good-looking too. Tall like Todd but with broader shoulders and a more boyish face. Doug wore his sandy blond hair short on the sides, and he always looked as if he'd just combed it. He had a warm smile with perfectly straight teeth. The more Christy thought about it, the more she thought Doug and Katie might make a good couple. Doug had been interested in Tracy, one of Christy's beach friends. But that was a year ago, and it didn't appear that anything had come of Doug and Tracy's brief time of dating.

"I'll call you tomorrow afternoon and let you know what we've got going, okay? When are you coming up to Newport Beach?" Doug asked.

"I don't know yet. I'll find out before you call tomorrow," Christy promised.

Just then Jon walked in, and Doug rose to leave.

He shook hands with Jon and said, "Nice meeting you." Then he squeezed Christy's shoulder, "I'll call you tomorrow. See you."

Jon sat down and surveyed the feast. "So, where are the fortune cookies?"

Christy fished her hand around inside the bag until she found the two cookies. "Here you go."

Jon picked up the wooden chopsticks and started in on a box of the "usual," scooping up the noodles like a pro.

"You read yours first," he said.

Christy cracked open one of the cookies and read,

"'You do not yet realize what is before you.' That's silly," she said. "What's before me? A bunch of Chinese food. I think I'm capable of realizing that."

Jon shook his head, his mouth full of noodles. Pointing his chopsticks at Christy he said, "It's not what's before you at this moment. It's what was sitting here before you, before he walked out the door."

"Doug?" Christy asked, giving Jon a skeptical look. "I don't realize what Doug is? Of course I do. He's just Doug. He's always been there. What am I supposed to realize?"

Jon raised his eyebrows and glanced at Christy out of the corner of his eye. He didn't say a word but kept looking at her as he jabbed his chopsticks into the box of noodles and stuffed them into his mouth, slowly sucking in one long stray noodle.

4

I'm Not Dreaming of a White Christmas

On Sunday after church, Christy's family sat down to eat the roast chicken Mom had put in the oven on low that morning. Several weeks had passed since they had all sat down like this to a traditional Sunday family dinner. Everyone had been running in different directions, especially Christy.

"Your father and I have an announcement to make," Mom said as she passed Christy the spinach. "We talked with your Uncle Bob and Aunt Marti last night, and they've invited us to join them for a white Christmas!"

"What?" Christy asked, dropping her fork. "You mean we're going back to Wisconsin for Christmas? We can't! I have to work, and I have a lot of other things going on. Why can't we go to Bob and Marti's in Newport Beach like last year?"

"Christy, will you give your mother a chance to explain?" her father said.

He was a large man with rust-colored hair and matching eyebrows, big hands, a gruff voice, and a tender heart. "No, we're not going to Wisconsin, although your grandmother wanted very much for us to come. Maybe we'll see her next year. This year we're going to a cabin in the mountains that Bob and Marti have rented, and we're spending six days in the snow!"

"Six days," Christy moaned. "That's almost half the vacation!"

Christy's mom, a short, round woman with a plain face, gave Christy a disapproving look. "Yes, six days. We're going as a family to spend the holiday together. Your friends and your job will still be here when we come back. This is your father's first vacation all year."

Christy knew the look on Mom's face. Hushed up, Christy focused her attention on the food before her.

This is the worst possible Christmas I could ever have. I won't get to talk to Rick. I won't get to go to the Rose Parade with Doug and everyone. This is awful!

"Cool!" Christy's little brother, David, said. "Do we still have our old toboggan? Christy, remember how we used to sled down that hill out by Mr. Jansen's meadow? Don't you want to go sledding again?"

Christy shot a camouflaged sneer at her ten-year-old brother.

"Mom!" David yelped. "Christy looked at me!"

"Christy," Dad said in his firm voice.

"I'm just not real interested in sledding, that's all."

"Christy," Mom said, "it may take you a while to get used to the idea, but we are going, and it will be a wonderful Christmas."

"Okay," Christy said without looking up.

A year ago she might have fussed and tried to wiggle her way out of going. She knew now that it was better to agree and go along with the family plan, even if it wasn't her first choice.

"Try to have a better attitude," Mom advised.

"I have a good attitude," David said. He looked more like their dad every day. "When do we leave?"

"Wednesday," Mom said. "And I'm glad you're excited about it, honey."

"I can't go Wednesday," Christy interrupted as Mom smiled at David. "I have to work on Wednesday. We all had to agree to work one full day during vacation, and my day is Wednesday."

"Trade with someone," Dad said. "Find out who's working on Monday, and see if you can trade with that person. That way you can help your mother pack on Tuesday."

"But Dad, I can't work on Monday!" Christy spouted. "I already have plans."

"What kind of plans?" Dad asked.

"With Katie and some other people. We're going sledding. I hadn't asked you yet, but I was going to."

Mom and Dad exchanged the type of look that only parents know how to give each other.

"You just said you didn't want to go sledding with me," David said. Dramatically slapping his forehead, he said, "Women! They're all loony!"

Dad smiled, and Christy looked to Mom for support. "Mom, did you hear what David said? Why do you let him get away with stuff like that? Where does he learn these things? I never got away with talking like that when I was his age."

"David." Dad shook his head to show his disapproval. Christy thought her dad still looked like he was laughing inside.

"Okay, listen," Mom the peacemaker said. "Why don't you

call work and find out if you can trade days. That's the first step. After that we can decide about this group sledding trip."

"Okay," Christy sighed, excusing herself from the table.

"You're not finished, are you?" Dad asked. "You've hardly eaten anything."

"I'm not really hungry. May I be excused?"

"Sure," said Mom. "Go see what you can do about changing your hours."

Christy called Jon and explained the situation. She could tell by the noise in the background a lot of people were in the pet store. She realized this might not be the best time to ask him.

"Tomorrow," Jon said, after checking his schedule. "You can work tomorrow instead. I need you here from ten to six. See you then." He hung up before she had a chance to ask about any other options.

Well, there went my Monday.

Trudging down the hall to her bedroom, Christy closed her door and flopped onto her unmade bed, where she could pout in private.

Why does stuff like this always happen to me? Katie never has to go through this. She can do whatever she wants, whenever she wants. My parents are too strict! Now I'm never going to get to talk to Rick. And everybody is going to have a great day tomorrow, and I have to work. It's not fair!

The phone rang, and a minute later Mom called out, "Christy, telephone."

Oh, great. It's probably Doug calling with the final plans for tomorrow, and I have to tell him to count me out.

"Hello?"

"Hi, it's me," Katie's voice responded. "Guess who just called me?"

"Glen?" Christy ventured.

"No, he's long gone on his way to Oregon. Rick."

"Rick? My Rick? I mean Doyle?"

"Your Rick?"

"I didn't mean that," Christy said. "You know what I meant." Then turning the tables, Christy asked, "What's he doing calling you anyway?"

"He said he tried you, but the phone was busy," Katie answered defensively.

"I was only on it for three minutes," Christy snapped back.

"What's with you?" Katie asked. "What are you so upset about? Rick? You're ticked off that Rick called me?"

"No, it's not that. I'd never expect him to call you, but Rick can call whoever he wants. That's not what I'm upset about."

"Then what is it? Did I do something?"

"No, it's my family. They've made plans to go to the mountains for Christmas, and we'll be gone for six days starting Wednesday. I don't want to go, but I don't have a choice." She spoke softly so no one would hear her.

"It won't be that bad, Christy. You'll probably have fun. You'll be back for New Year's, won't you? Rick said we're all going to the Rose Parade and sleeping overnight on the street. I'm so excited! I've always wanted to do that."

"I'll be back by then, but I don't know if I can talk my parents into letting me go, especially since the plans include sleeping on the street."

"You haven't asked them though, have you?"

"Not yet," Christy admitted.

"You have to start asking about these things, Christy.

One of these days they'll surprise you and say yes to something. But you'll never know because you never ask them! Now listen to me. I have a plan. Start by asking them about sledding tomorrow. That's what Rick called about. They decided to go to Big Bear, and we're meeting at his house at eight. It'll be an all-day thing."

"I can't go," Christy said flatly.

"How do you know? You haven't even asked."

"Yes, I did. They didn't give me an answer because I have to work tomorrow from ten to six. I had to trade my Wednesday hours because we're leaving for the mountains Wednesday. The only option Jon gave me was to work tomorrow."

"Oh."

"See? It's hopeless. You get to do whatever you want, whenever you want, and I never get to do anything."

"Christina Juliet Miller, I can't believe you said that!" Katie snapped. "Who was it that went to Palm Springs and Newport Beach and Hawaii? Was it Katie Weldon? I don't think so! Would you like to take another guess?"

Christy remained silent.

"The only exciting thing I've done in my whole life is go to Lake Tahoe with the ski club last Thanksgiving. Now all of a sudden I have a chance to go to places like San Diego and Big Bear, and you're mad about it."

"I'm not mad," Christy said.

"Then you're jealous. Why? Because some of your friends are being nice to me and including me in their group! Is that so hard for you to accept?"

"No, that's not it at all! I'm glad you're getting to know some of my beach friends. They're all terrific, and I know they'll like you. It's just that you're being included and I'm being left out."

"Not on purpose, Christy. We're both being included. You can't go, that's all."

"That's what I'm upset about. I want more freedom. I want my parents to trust me more. I don't want to be tied down to a job. And most of all, I don't want to have all these responsibilities."

Katie paused before summarizing. "You want to be treated like an adult while you still have the freedom to be a kid."

"Yes, something like that. Seems to work for you."

"Sometimes. Maybe that's what happens when you're the youngest of three kids. It's probably harder for you since you're the oldest, and you have to be the first to break into new territory. It'll be easier for David."

"Don't talk to me about David. He just got away with this stupid wisecrack at the table, and I know if I would've tried something like that at his age I would've been sent to my room."

"Like I said, it's easier on the younger kids in a family."

"It's still not fair."

"So, what's fair in life?" Katie challenged.

"I don't know," Christy mumbled. "Not much, I guess."

"God is fair," Katie added thoughtfully. "Things that happen to us aren't fair from our perspective. I think in the end God evens things out when we leave the results to Him."

"I guess so," Christy said with a sigh.

"Come on, Christy," Katie said. "Snap out of it! You

need an attitude adjustment, girlfriend. And quick!"

"Oh, thanks a lot! Now you sound like my mother."

"Then erase that from your memory. You don't need an attitude adjustment. You need a friend. And I just happen to be one."

Christy let a smile lift her lips out of their pout.

Since Katie couldn't see Christy's response over the phone, she ventured another offering to her friend. "Remember? We're peculiar treasures, you and me. We have to stick together. And I've decided that because you have to work tomorrow, I won't go to Big Bear either."

"No, Katie, you should go. I want you to go. Really! You stayed home from San Diego because of me and that turned out to be a mistake. Don't turn down this opportunity. Go! Have a good time."

"Are you sure?"

"Yes. But will you do me one favor?"

"Anything! What is it?"

"Make a huge snowball and smash it into Rick's face for me!"

"Oh, my!" Katie joked. "Getting a bit feisty here, aren't we? I thought Rick no longer had the power to fire up your feelings."

"You're right," Christy agreed. "Forget I said that. You go and have a wonderful time and forget I ever said anything about Rick. Pretend I never met him."

"Pretend you never met whom?" Katie teased. "Rick? Rick who? I don't recall Christy ever mentioning a guy by that name."

Christy laughed. "Thanks, Katie."

"No, thank you for inviting me into your group."

Christy was about to say that it was originally Rick's idea to invite Katie to God-Lovers, but then she would be mentioning *that* name again, and she had more self-control than that.

"And we'll go to the Rose Parade together," Katie said. "You'll see. I'll call you when we get back tomorrow night, or if you're still at work I'll try to stop by."

"What about your job?" Christy asked. "I thought you had to work this week too."

"I do. But since I worked every afternoon and evening last week, they gave me Sunday and Monday off."

"Of course," Christy muttered to herself after she hung up. "Katie has Monday off, no problem! Not me. She's getting all the breaks lately. Why is God paying special attention to her and ignoring me? Not that she doesn't deserve it, but I deserve it too, don't I?"

Work on Monday wasn't too bad. Christy spent most of the morning in the back room marking sale prices on Christmas specialty items. The work was easy, and she didn't have to deal with the mob of customers out front. Still, she felt sorry for herself knowing that her friends were out having fun while she worked.

She had brought a sack lunch with her and didn't even leave the back room when Jon told her to take her break. Settling in at the card table with her peanut butter and honey sandwich, Christy picked up a magazine from Jon's mail pile.

Without realizing it, she had selected a surfing magazine. The cover copy announced, "This Month, the Big One's at Waimea."

A picture of a gigantic wave dotted with at least a dozen

miniaturized surfboards took up the rest of the cover. It looked like a huge blue fist was about to curl up its fingers and crush the antlike surfers.

Christy quickly found the feature article and pored over the photos and details of the surfing competition to be held that month on Oahu's North Shore.

Todd. He's there right now. Doug said it was this week. Todd's surfing waves like this!

She turned back to the cover and tried to imagine Todd on his orange surfboard, in the clutches of the ominous wave monster. It frightened her. Todd could die trying to surf a wave like that. He could die, and it would be weeks before any of them would ever know.

Oh, God, keep him safe! Protect Todd and don't let him get hurt. I want You to bring him home soon. Katie said You are fair. Please be fair to Todd and protect him. Don't do it for me though. Do what's best for Todd. But keep him safe, please!

5
Camera-Shy Christy

Christy looked at the wall clock behind the counter in the pet store. Six o'clock. *Time for me to get out of here. Where's Jon? I can't leave the register until he relieves me. I wonder if I should buzz him or just wait. He knows I'm off at six.*

Two customers stood in line. She decided to hurriedly ring up their purchases, hoping no one else would join them in line. The first customer had a large aquarium tank that Christy found awkward to get into a bag.

"Have you got it?" she asked the customer as she placed it in his arms.

"Yes, I do now. Thanks."

"You're welcome. Merry Christmas!"

"Merry Christmas to you," the customer responded.

The next customer slapped a bag of birdseed on the counter and muttered, "Took you long enough."

Christy recognized him as a frequent customer who seemed to love to complain. She and Jon referred to him as "Mr. Grouch."

Quickly punching the buttons on the cash register, Christy turned to the man with her brightest smile and said, "That will be $5.78, please."

The man handed her a five-dollar bill and a dollar and fumbled in his pocket. "Hold on, hold on. I have three pennies here somewhere."

His search produced two pennies and a button. "Hold on," he said, sounding even more irritated.

Christy remembered feeling some change in her jeans pocket earlier. She stuck her fingers in and found a penny, which she presented to Mr. Grouch with a smile.

"Here, I have an extra penny."

He scowled at her but ceased his pocket search. Christy quickly made the change and popped his birdseed in a bag. She handed it to him with another big smile and said, "Merry Christmas, Mr. Grou—"

Oh no! she thought in a panic, when she realized what she had done. *I almost called him Mr. Grouch to his face!*

The man snorted and strode into the mall as if he hadn't heard her or he didn't care.

Christy felt her cheeks burn red as she turned to the next customer, ready to ring up the person's purchase. To her surprise, that person was Doug.

"Hi. I didn't even see you come in. How was the sledding at Big Bear?"

Doug's cheeks were rosy from the wind. He wore a red-plaid flannel shirt and bib overalls that made him look like a kid who had been outside playing all day.

"Awesome! We had a blast. Everyone is over at the pizza place across the street. Katie said you finished work at six, so I thought I'd chance it and see if you could have pizza with us."

"She'd love to." Jon stepped behind the counter and reached for the phone.

"Yes," he said into the phone, "we have four Japanese fighting fish, and they're on sale until Christmas."

Christy smiled at Doug and said, "I guess my boss says I have to go. Let me grab my stuff. I'll be right back."

She slipped behind Jon and scooted to the back room to retrieve her purse. What she really needed to do was call her parents, and the phone in the back would allow her more privacy. As soon as she was sure Jon was off the phone, Christy dialed her home number. Her mom answered.

"Hi, I'm getting off work right now, and I wondered if I could have pizza with Katie and some other people." *There. That wasn't so hard. Why do I make asking to go places so hard? Wonder what she'll say. At least Mom answered rather than Dad.*

Her mom asked where Christy wanted to go and who would be there. Then she said, "Sounds like fun, honey. Think you'll be home by nine?"

"Yes. So it's okay?"

"Sure! Have a good time. Lock the car, and don't give anyone a ride home."

Christy hung up and thought how nice Doug was to include her in their get-together. Maybe she'd have a chance to talk to Rick. If not at the pizza place, then he might suggest they get together tomorrow before she left for the mountains. She didn't want to go through Christmas without resolving their relationship. Grabbing her backpack and jacket, Christy joined Doug up front, where he and Jon were laughing together.

"I'm parked out that way," Christy said, pointing behind her. "Do you want me to meet you at the pizza place?"

"Why don't we both go in my truck?" Doug suggested.

"I have a parking place right by the entrance. Then I'll bring you back here afterward to pick up your car."

"Okay," Christy said, fully aware of Jon's look of approval.

"Merry Christmas, Jon," Christy said as a customer stepped up to the counter. "I'll see you next year."

"That's right. You don't work again until the Saturday after New Year's. Hang on a second."

Jon totaled the customer's purchase of three doggie stockings and handed her the change. As soon as the woman stepped away from the counter, Jon pulled an envelope from the cash register drawer and handed it to Christy.

"May it never be said that I'm a total Scrooge. Here's your year-end bonus, Christy."

"Thanks, Jon!" She felt horrible for not buying him anything for Christmas. Even a plate of cookies would have been nice.

"Oh, and just to make you really happy—" Jon cleared his throat and glanced around to make certain no one could hear him except Doug and Christy—"May you have a joyful celebration of the birth of your God."

Christy, full of surprise, glanced at Doug and then back at Jon. "Thank you, Jon. And may *you* have a joyful celebration of the birth of my God." Then leaning closer and touching Jon's arm, she quietly added, "And may He become your God too."

Jon smiled his touché to Christy.

She waved and headed out into the crowded mall with Doug beside her and Jon's gaze following them.

"Amazing how irresistible you are," Doug said.

"What?"

"To Jon. There's something mysterious and appealing about a person who knows God and doesn't hide it. I can tell that you and Jon have talked about God, and Jon knows you're a God-lover. That's irresistible to people who don't know God."

"Oh," Christy said as they walked out the door to his truck. "I never thought of it that way. Jon knows how I feel about my relationship with God. He also knows I've been praying for him, and I think it makes him nervous."

"That's awesome." Doug unlocked the passenger door of his yellow four-wheel-drive truck.

Christy smiled to herself and climbed up into the seat while Doug jogged around the front of the truck and slid in on the other side.

"What?" he asked when he saw her grin.

"I can't believe you still say 'awesome.' That's one of the first things I remember about you when we met on the beach. Everything was awesome to you."

Doug laughed. He had a great laugh that came from a gurgling brook inside him, and when it splashed out, it refreshed those who heard it.

"Most things are awesome, when you think about them. It's because of God. He's an awesome God. I don't know a word that says it better."

Christy smiled back. It felt good to be with an old friend. It was a familiar, safe, contented feeling.

"Who ended up going with you guys today?" Christy asked.

"Your friend Katie, Rick, Heather, Tracy, and a guy named Mike, who's a friend of Rick's. We had an awesome time. Katie sure is fun. How come you never brought her up to Newport Beach?"

"I guess it never worked out. I'm glad she got to go with you guys. Sounds like she fit right in."

"She did. What a sense of humor!"

Doug's words proved true as they stepped into the restaurant and spotted the group at a large booth in the back. Katie had something on her ears, and the rest of the group was cracking up at her antics.

As Doug and Christy approached the booth, Christy saw that Katie had poked the bottoms out of two Styrofoam cups and placed a cup over each ear. Using her best Santa's-little-elf voice, she was coaxing them all to smile for the camera.

"Hi!" Doug greeted the merry group.

Rick and Mike barely noticed them. Tracy and Heather, two of Christy's beach friends, acted happy to see Christy, but they were so busy laughing at Katie that they merely scooted closer together in the booth and patted the corner for Christy to sit down and enjoy the show. Doug pulled up a chair at the end of the booth.

Katie continued, unembarrassed and apparently unaware of how ridiculous she looked and sounded. Christy could never act like that.

"Ah," Katie squeaked as she pointed to Christy, "my wardrobe assistant. May I borrow your earrings?"

With all eyes on her, Christy unclipped her dangling earrings. They were little green gift boxes tied with red ribbons. Tiny bells on them jingled when she shook her head.

Christy reluctantly handed them to Katie. They weren't valuable earrings, but she had bought them with her own money. She worried that Katie might unwrap the little boxes now just to get a laugh, and that would be the end of her earrings.

"Perfect!" Katie chirped, snapping the earrings onto the large, outer rims of the Styrofoam cups. The earrings now hung from her handmade elf ears, and the bells jingled when she wobbled her head back and forth. She looked so silly that even Christy started to laugh.

Out of nowhere, a guy from their high school stepped in front of their booth and snapped a picture of Katie. Katie, Christy, and Rick recognized him as Fred, the school yearbook's candid cameraman.

"Fred!" the three of them exclaimed in unison.

"Great!" Fred said. "I bet the school paper will be interested in using this as their January cover. I can see it now: 'What I Did During Christmas Vacation, by Katie Weldon, the Elf.'"

"Give me that camera," Katie squawked from her closed-in spot in the booth. "I want that photo destroyed. Get it, Rick!"

Rick stood up and spoke to Fred in a low voice. Fred smiled and nodded his head. Before Christy knew what was happening, Rick slid in next to Christy and, practically sitting on her lap, wrapped his arm around her and pressed his cheek against hers just as Fred snapped another picture and took off.

"Rick!" Christy shouted, pushing him off the edge of the booth seat. "He's going to put that in the yearbook!"

Rick dusted himself off and strutted back to his spot at the opposite end of the booth. "That's what I'm counting on, Killer."

Christy was furious. She wanted to tell Rick off right then and there. He had no right to push himself on her like he owned her. Everyone was looking at her, waiting for her response. Even Mike, who she hadn't met yet, looked amused at her expense.

"Come on," Doug suddenly said, grasping Christy by the wrist and urging her to her feet. "We haven't ordered our pizza yet. Do you like Canadian bacon and pineapple?"

Christy rose and let Doug hold her wrist as he led her to the order counter. Tiny tears bubbled up in her eyes as the anger over what Rick did surfaced.

As soon as they rounded the corner and were away from the group, Doug put both hands on her shoulders and said softly, "Are you okay?"

Christy blinked the tears back, looked up at Doug, and nodded. "I guess so."

"Rick thinks the world of you. You know that, don't you? I mean, talk about a godly woman being irresistible! You are absolutely irresistible to him. He doesn't know how to act around you because you're so different from all the other girls he knows. He doesn't mean to hurt you, really."

"I wish I could believe you."

Doug brushed his finger across her cheek to stop a runaway tear. "The problem is that you two need to talk things out. I know having your relationship unresolved must be killing you. Having lived with Rick all semester, I know it's been eating him alive. You both need to talk."

"I'd like to," Christy said. "But it hasn't worked out yet. I've told him I want to talk, but he can't seem to schedule it. We were supposed to talk today."

"Maybe you still can." Doug opened up his arms and welcomed Christy into his comforting hug. "You relax and leave everything up to ol' Uncle Doug."

6

Thanks a Lot, Uncle Doug!

By the time Christy and Doug returned to the booth, the first two pizzas had arrived, and everyone was eating as if nothing unusual had happened.

Katie had removed her elf ears, and the earrings, unscathed, waited on a napkin at Christy's place.

"I wish you could have come with us today," Heather said to Christy. "We had so much fun. These guys are maniacs!"

"Oh, right," Rick said, reaching for another piece of pizza. "And you three girls weren't a bunch of little maniacs yourselves on your run through the trees?"

Wispy, blond Heather giggled and described to Christy the run the three girls had taken. They had bounced off the slick path and headed into a clump of trees. Somehow they managed to maneuver through the obstacle course and ended up at the bottom of the hill without a tumble or a scratch.

The group chattered between bites of pizza, comparing wild stories and reliving the day's events. It was clear they'd all had a wonderful time.

Christy felt left out. The pizza she and Doug ordered

finally arrived. She listened to everyone else laugh while she mechanically bit into the hot, gooey cheese, which burned the roof of her mouth.

Reaching for a glass of water, she guzzled it down. It only helped a little. The roof of her mouth still felt red hot. No one had noticed her emergency, which made her feel even worse. If she weren't there, the party would have gone on without her.

Then the teasing began. Rick called Katie "Speed," and everyone laughed. Christy had no idea why that was funny. When he called Katie "Speed" a second time, she seemed to blush.

Christy could tell Katie loved the attention. The name had something to do with a run Rick and Katie had taken together on an inner tube.

Now Christy was really hurting. Rick had called her "Killer Eyes" for more than a year. That was his nickname for her, and nobody else called her that. It had seemed so sacred and special to have a name placed on her by Rick Doyle. Not anymore. Now Katie had a Rick nickname.

The conversation switched to plans for the Rose Parade. Rick announced that he was bringing a hibachi to barbecue their dinner, an ice chest, and his down sleeping bag.

"The girls should be responsible for the extra blankets and all the junk food," Rick said.

"Cookies!" Doug agreed. "You girls can bring lots and lots of cookies."

"How about it, Speed?" Rick asked Katie with one of his big smiles. "Think you can make us some more of those killer cookies?"

Oh, great! Christy thought. *My nickname has now been reassigned to a batch of cookies, and Speed over there is getting the credit for the last batch we made, which would have been chocolate-chip-less if I hadn't been there!*

The more the group talked, the more exciting the plans sounded. Christy really wanted to go. She would have to find a way to talk her parents into it.

Doug leaned over and asked Christy if she thought she would need a ride.

"I don't know. First I have to convince my parents to let me go." She smiled at Doug, appreciating his interest.

"Do you want me to talk to them?" Doug offered. "I can tell them about how things were the last time we went."

"Thanks, Doug. I'd better try first. I'll let you know what they say. We're going to be up in the mountains at a cabin for the next week. I'll call you when we get back."

"A cabin? That sounds pretty awesome."

"I guess."

Seeing Doug's sincerity made her realize how grumpy she must seem to him.

You're being a baby, Christy. Snap out of it. Join the fun instead of feeling sorry for yourself.

Christy was beginning to pull herself out of her dismal mood when Heather said, "I hate to be the one to break this up. It's been such a fun day. But Tracy and I have a long ride home, and we need to get going."

Everyone slowly slid out, and Doug said, "Mike, why don't you come in my truck with me? And Rick, would you mind dropping Christy off at the mall? Her car is still there."

Christy didn't look at Rick. She heard him say "Okay" in a casual way.

Rick positioned himself by the door, holding it open in

such a way that all the girls had to pass under his arm. The first three girls played along, sliding past Rick with smiles and giggles.

But Christy froze. She couldn't play along. A clear memory made her motionless.

She had been to this same pizza place before with Rick and Katie, about a year ago on a Sunday after church. Katie had been the center of attention that time too. And Christy remembered being quiet and thoroughly absorbed with Rick. That time she had passed under Rick's arm at the door and looked up into his brown eyes. She had thought she might melt. He had overwhelmed her with his charm.

She felt afraid to pass under his imaginary bridge tonight, lest he drop an invisible net over her heart and she became captured by him again. Her silent refusal must have come across loud and clear to him because he looked at her hard and then let the door go. It closed in Christy's face.

Jerking the door open for herself, Christy bustled through and joined the others in the parking lot. She would not let Rick get to her like this.

Why can't Rick agree to a middle ground for us? Why does it have to be all or nothing?

"So you'll take Christy back to the mall to get her car?" Doug repeated his question to Rick.

"Sure," Rick agreed, glancing over his shoulder at Christy and tossing her the car keys. "Get in."

He spoke the command in a lighthearted way, but the message was clear. Rick needed to be in control.

Does he have any idea how insulting he sounds? Is he doing this to me on purpose? Or is Doug right, and Rick really cares about me but can't show it because we broke up?

Christy obediently opened the door and slid into the comfortable, familiar passenger seat of Rick's red Mustang. She put his keys in the ignition and watched out the front windshield as Rick hugged Heather and Tracy good-bye. Then he hugged Katie.

The three girls hopped over to Christy's window and motioned for her to roll it down. She had been so absorbed with her confrontation with Rick that she hadn't even said good-bye to them.

Tracy reached her arms inside the open window and squeezed in to give Christy a hug around the neck. "Call me, okay?"

Heather waved and said, "I can't wait to see you on New Year's Day! We'll get all caught up then."

Christy waved as Heather and Tracy left. Katie opened the door, "Scoot forward. I'll get in the back."

Like a wildcat protecting her territory, Christy didn't move an inch. She stared at her clueless friend and in a low growl said, "Why can't you go with Doug and Mike?"

Katie looked amazed. Then, appearing to have caught on, she said, "You know, I love sitting in the front seat of that four-wheel-drive truck, sandwiched between two good-looking men, my legs all squished in such a dainty fashion. I much prefer it to riding in the backseat of this old clunker."

Katie called out to the guys who were saying good-bye to each other, "Hey, Doug, wait for me. I'm the peanut butter!" Rick turned and walked toward his Mustang with long strides, his expression stern. Christy felt her heart pounding. Maybe this wasn't such a good idea after all.

He lowered his large frame into the front seat and slammed his door. Without a word he reached for the keys.

He seemed to know that Christy had put them in the ignition, as she had done on several occasions when they were dating.

The car roared to life, and Christy held on while Rick peeled out of his parking spot. He turned to look at Doug out of his side window and honked and waved while the car accelerated past Doug's truck.

Christy noticed a small car pulling into the parking lot. She yelled, "Look out!"

The other car swerved to the left. Rick jerked the steering wheel to the right. The tires squealed. With another jerk, he turned the car and kept accelerating out of the parking lot. He changed lanes twice before coming to an abrupt stop at the red light by the mall.

Christy didn't dare say a word. She could hear Rick breathing heavily, and she knew he was mad. He drove to the section of the parking lot where Christy usually parked and found her car without saying anything. Conveniently, there was an empty space next to Christy's car. Rick turned in with a squeal of the tires, slammed on the brakes, and cut the engine, all in one motion.

Suddenly, it was quiet. Very quiet. Miserably quiet.

Christy wanted to scramble out the door and escape to the safety of her own car. Then she'd show him that she could squeal her own tires as she peeled out of the parking lot and away from him.

She couldn't do that though, because she knew this was what she had wanted for months: a chance to talk to Rick. She didn't think it would happen like this or that both their emotions would be at full throttle when they finally connected. Maybe it was a bad idea. The timing was off. She should wait for a better time.

"You wanted to talk," Rick said. "What did you want to talk about?"

Christy felt awful. "About us," she said softly. "But not like this. I don't want to talk when we're both so upset."

"I'm not upset," Rick said gruffly. "You wanted to talk, so talk."

"I…I'm not sure I can…" Her throat swelled shut, and she couldn't say a word. It took a gigantic effort to keep back the sudden deluge of hot, prickly tears.

They sat in silence for several minutes. Christy didn't dare move, lest the tears find a crack to slip through and spill down her cheeks.

Rick let out a deep sigh and in a calmer voice said, "I saw the car coming, Christy. I wasn't going to hit it."

"I know. I'm sorry."

"You don't trust me," Rick said. "You've never trusted me."

"That's not true."

"Yes it is. You don't trust me, and you've been afraid of me since the day we met. You never gave our relationship a chance." Christy tried to think of how to answer that. In some ways it was true. Rick overpowered her just because he was Rick. How could she explain that to him?

"Go ahead," Rick urged. "Admit that you never really made room in your heart for me."

Christy shook her head, trying to find the right words. Rick came on so strong. He made her feel things she had never felt with Todd. Todd would never push her like this. Why couldn't she talk to Rick the way she talked to Todd? Todd would understand her feelings.

"You never even gave me a chance, did you? Come on!"

Rick raised his voice. "You don't trust me. Say it!"

"That's not true. I do trust you, Todd."

Everything froze.

Todd! Oh no! I called him Todd! What have I done? Rick will never understand.

Rick stuck out his jaw and slowly turned his head away from Christy as if he had been slapped in the face. Calmly, he opened his car door and with even steps walked to Christy's side and opened her door.

She followed his unspoken instructions, still in shock that she had done such a thing.

He stood firm, a few inches from her, and calmly stated. "I'm not Todd. I'm Rick."

"I…I know, Rick. I'm sorry. I almost called a customer Mr. Grouch at work today," Christy began, but nothing she could say right now would make things better. "I don't know why I'm so mixed up with names today."

Rick acted like he hadn't heard her. With composure he said, "There will never be room for me or any other guy in your life until you've put him away."

He shut Christy's door, walked to his side of the car with deliberate steps, got in, and started up the engine. Before she could think of a way to stop him, he lurched the car from its parking spot and, with screeching wheels, sped away.

Christy's mind raced with thoughts of what to do. Part of her wanted to speed off after him and make him pull over his car and listen to her. She would find a way to make him understand and forgive her blunder. Another part of her wanted to give up on Rick forever and be done with running from him or chasing after him.

With trembling hands, she unlocked her car door and drove home cautiously, afraid of her own emotions. The most frightening thing was that she couldn't cry. She hurt too much to shed a single tear.

Maybe Rick was right. Maybe she had held on to the dream of Todd for too long. How could she move forward when her life was filled with memories of him? Before she reached home, Christy knew what she had to do.

She walked in the front door, said hello to her parents, and then rummaged in the garage until she found just the right size box. With another smile and a "good night" to her parents, she locked herself in her bedroom and began by tearing the poster from the back of her door.

It was a poster from Hawaii—a certain memorable bridge over a waterfall. She tossed the gift from Todd in the box and went straight for her dresser, scooping up the Folgers coffee can, which held a dozen very dead carnations—the first flowers she had ever been given by a guy. The coconut he had mailed her from Hawaii was the next victim tossed into the open box. Then the cable car music box from San Francisco, which always made her think of Todd. Next, another gift from Todd—a tiny, blown-glass Tinkerbell figurine from Disneyland—and then a T-shirt from her drawer that said "I Survived the Road to Hana."

Christy snatched her Winnie the Pooh bear off her bed and was about to plunge him into the box when she stopped. Holding the pudgy stuffed animal at arm's length, she told him, "I'm sorry, but you have to go too."

She looked at the Todd mementos in the box and then explained to Pooh, "I can't have all of you whispering to me in my sleep, telling me fairy tales about Todd. I'm a big girl now. I can't believe in fairy tales anymore." Christy tightly hugged Pooh. "Don't you see? What happened tonight with Rick was my fault. I should have sent you all away long ago."

With one last kiss, Christy stuffed Pooh into the box and closed the lid. As a hot tear escaped, she slid the box under her bed and out of her heart.

7

Snow Wars

Christy awoke the next morning feeling sad and alone. She ate some breakfast and then returned to her room to pack for the family's trip to the mountains. When the mail came, Mom brought three cards in for Christy. Christy examined the return addresses and opened the one postmarked Escondido.

It was a Christmas card from Teri Moreno, a girl from school Christy had met last year during the cheerleading tryouts. Teri wrote at the bottom of the card, "May your celebration of our Savior's birth be filled with joy."

Christy set it aside, feeling guilty for being in such an emotional slump. She opened the next card, which was from Alissa, an older girl she had met on the beach two summers ago. A long note on a separate sheet of paper fell out. Christy sat down to read it.

Dear Christy,

I'm having so much fun preparing for Christmas here in Boston! Since this is the first Christmas since I became a Christian, everything means so much more than it ever did. My mom is doing pretty well. She's gone without a drink for about three months. And she and my grandmother have been coming to church with me! I sent a present to baby Shawna yesterday. I think about her all the time and miss her so much. I know she belongs with her adoptive parents, and I know they love her as much as I do. Whenever I start to feel really bad about her, God gives me this unexplainable peace, and I feel like I can keep going. I pray for you all the time, Christy. I hope your Christmas is full of love, and joy, and peace.

Always,

Alissa

Christy stared at the letter, amazed. Alissa's father was dead, her mother was a recovering alcoholic, Alissa had given up her baby girl for adoption, and the baby's father had died in a surfing accident. If anyone had a reason to be depressed, it was Alissa.

Compared with her, Christy had it easy. Yet Christy was the depressed one, and Alissa sounded full of joy and hope—at least on paper.

Christy had to admit that last summer when she sat beside Alissa on the beach and listened to her pray and ask God to forgive her and come into her heart, Christy had wondered if it was real. Now Alissa was trusting God for more things than Christy was.

Maybe that's my problem. I haven't prayed much about all the stuff going on in my life.

Not feeling quite ready to pray, Christy opened the third card, which was from Paula, her childhood friend in Wisconsin. Out tumbled a stack of photographs. They were pictures Paula had taken last summer when she and Christy were in Hawaii with Christy's mom, David, her aunt and uncle, and Todd. The first picture was a waterfall with a bridge across the top, the same waterfall in the poster Christy had taken off her door. The next picture was of Todd on the beach with his arm around a surfboard. David stood on the other side of the surfboard trying to imitate Todd and look cool. The sky and water in the background looked pure, blue, and inviting.

Christy stared at the pictures for a long time, reliving the memories they each held.

Paula's card was signed simply, *Thought you might like a copy of these. Aloha and Merry Christmas! Paula.*

Christy wondered how Paula was really doing and guessed from her brief note that she was keeping her life to herself these days.

Christy set the three cards on her dresser where the mementos that reminded her of Todd had been. She decided the pictures only made her think more about him, so she pulled the box out from under her bed and added the photos to the collection.

With a heavy sigh, she whispered, "I know I'm not being very cheerful about Your birthday, Jesus. I'll try to think more about You and trust You more to work out all my relationships."

During the two-hour drive up to the mountains on Wednesday, Christy tried extra hard to be nice to her brother. She played a license-plate game with him until the road started to seriously wind, and her stomach felt a little queasy.

"Are we almost there?" David asked. "Where's the snow?"

"These directions indicate we have about a half hour before we reach the Blue Jay turnoff. We should see snow pretty soon," Mom said.

"There's some!" David exclaimed, pointing to a small patch on the side of the hill.

When they arrived at the cabin, the ground was covered with snow, and David was beside himself with glee. He was the first one out of the car. Packing a snowball with his bare hands, he threw it at the windshield and then quickly prepared another one for Dad as he got out of the car.

"Let's take our things in first, David," Dad said. "Looks like Bob and Marti are already here."

Christy stepped inside and gaped at the fully equipped, two-story deluxe home Bob and Marti had rented. It wasn't exactly the log cabin she had envisioned. She should have known. Her wealthy aunt and uncle were accustomed to the finer things in life, which included all the comforts of home wherever they went.

Marti stood on a small stepladder beside the fireplace, gingerly placing Christmas ornaments on a tree that reached to the vaulted ceiling.

"What do you think?" Marti leaned back slightly to admire her handiwork. "It's Santas this year."

Indeed, the entire tree was trimmed in a variety of Santa ornaments. Last year, Christy remembered, it had been lambs. Marti was the only person Christy knew who had a different theme for her Christmas tree every year.

"It's nice," Christy commented. "Are you all done? Do you need any help?"

"I believe I'm finished, dear. Wait until you see it with the lights plugged in. I used red lights this year. Gives the room a wonderful, festive glow."

Dad came in, carrying in a suitcase in each hand,

"Christy, could you help your mom bring in the smaller bags? Where do you want us to put all this, Marti?"

Marti descended from her decorator's loft and pointed up the stairs. "I thought you and Margaret would enjoy the morning glory room. It's the second on the right. David is in the daisy room at the far end of the hall, and Christy is next to him in the violet room."

"The rooms have names?" Christy asked, curious to know if the house really came labeled that way or if her aunt's dramatic flair had affected everything in the house.

"Oh, yes! This is a bed-and-breakfast. Bob knows the owners, and they went to London for the holidays. He rented it from them for a song. You'll be favorably impressed with the accommodations, I think. A fireplace in nearly every bedroom!"

"I can't wait to see my room," Christy said.

"Don't forget to help me with the bags," Mom reminded Christy.

Marti added, "Then your mother and I need to make a quick run to the grocery store to stock up on food for the week."

Christy hurried to carry in the bags and waved good-bye as Mom and Marti took off for the store. With anticipation, Christy grabbed her luggage and headed up the stairs to find her violet room.

She decided the first room on the right must be Bob and Marti's. In the center was a four-poster bed with a sheer canopy draped over the top and down the sides. Everything was in red roses and dark cherrywood.

She ventured on down the hall, the thick carpet crushing softly under her feet. The next room turned out to be her parents' morning glory room, with bright blue morning glories painted in a border trailing up the walls. The blue bedspread, rug, towels, and curtains lent the room a cheery look, and Christy knew her mom would like it.

Closing their door, she tiptoed across the hall, feeling as though she were exploring a great castle. The door on the left opened to reveal her violet room. Christy held her breath when she saw it.

It looked like something out of a storybook. In the corner, a fire glowed in the fireplace, and against the wall was a white wrought-iron daybed with a heart in the center of the back, frosted with a deliciously thick down comforter. Little bunches of violets were everywhere—violets tied with pink ribbon on the wallpaper, pressed violets in small, narrow frames on the nightstand, a soft blanket with embroidered violets over the antique trunk at the end of the bed, and even an oval throw rug by the door with a large clump of violets in the center.

But what captured Christy's heart was the window seat beneath the large double windows. It looked too enchanting to be real. She dropped her bags and approached the seat as if it would run away if she went too fast or startled it. Gently touching the narrow, cushioned seat and fingering the lace on the violet-covered throw pillows, she decided it was indeed real and hers for the next six days.

"Is the room to your liking, miss?" Bob asked, standing in her doorway.

"Oh, you startled me!" Christy said as she turned around. "Yes, it's gorgeous. I love it!"

Just then they heard hoots and hollers outside. Christy leaned her face close to the window and could see David pelting Dad with his meager supply of snowballs. Bob joined Christy in spying on the war about to break out.

"Come on," he said, tagging Christy on the arm. "We can go out the back through the kitchen and ambush them."

"Let me find my gloves." Christy quickly rummaged in her bag and then slipped the gloves on as she galloped down the stairs behind Bob.

Like two secret agent scouts, Bob and Christy crept along the side of the house until they saw Dad and David rapidly tossing snowballs at each other.

"All right, here's the plan," Bob whispered. "We need a fair supply of ammo before we rush them. Let's make a dozen balls each, store them here, and then we'll carry as many others as we can and still throw."

Christy gave her uncle a playful salute and set to work on her dozen snowballs. Next, she and Bob loaded more snowballs in the crooks of their left arms.

"On my signal." Bob held up his right hand and watched for a break in the skirmish between Dad and David. "Okay, now!" he ordered, snapping down his hand and running into the fray, hollering and throwing snowballs as if he were a ten-year-old.

Christy followed right behind him and lobbed her first shot at Dad. He was caught off guard, and the missile hit his right ear. David and Dad's surprise allowed Bob and Christy two more excellent shots before her brother and father retaliated. The battle raged, chilly and full of laughter, as Bob and Christy each took turns returning to the side of the house for ammo.

In a bold move, David cut across their lines, found their secret stash, and used the last few snowballs on them.

Bob managed to scoop an armful of snow down David's back before Dad called a truce.

Just then the car containing Marti and Mom turned into the long driveway.

"Quick," Bob said. "Everyone hide, and let's give the ladies a surprise welcome!"

David and Dad scrambled to hide together behind the family car while Bob slipped behind a tree. Not sure where to go, Christy headed for the side of the house but felt sure Mom and Marti had spotted her. She decided to play it cool and act as if she were out for a stroll.

"Hide, Christy!" David yelled in a hoarse whisper as Marti parked the car and turned off the engine.

Mom opened her door and greeted Christy with, "Are you out enjoying the fresh air?"

"Yes," Christy answered, scooping up a handful of clean snow in her gloved hand and licking it like a snow cone.

Marti exited her door, pulled a bag of groceries from the backseat, and said, "Where's Bob?"

Christy hesitated and then decided honesty was always the best policy. "He's hiding in ambush behind that tree over there."

"Christina," Marti scolded, "where do you come up with these things? Do teenagers take smart-answer classes in school these days?"

When Marti was a few feet from her, Christy held out her handful of snow, "There's something wrong with this snow. It doesn't smell right."

"What do you mean it doesn't smell right?" Marti asked.

Christy sniffed at the snow mound, "I don't know how

to explain it, but it doesn't smell like Wisconsin snow."

Mom lugged two sacks of groceries from the backseat and said, "Then, for heaven's sake, don't eat it, Christy. Snow isn't supposed to have any kind of smell."

Christy looked at her aunt with questioning eyes. "What do you think? Does it smell funny to you?"

Marti leaned over, ready to delicately sniff the white stuff. Christy playfully pushed the handful of snow into her unsuspecting aunt's face.

Dad, David, and Bob took that as their signal and sprang from their hiding places, yelling so loudly that Marti dropped her bag of groceries and ran into the house, screaming.

Mom planted her grocery bags in the snow and began to fling a few feeble balls at Dad. David snuck up behind her and shoveled a handful of snow down her jacket.

Letting out a yelp, Mom scooped up snow in both hands and showered the blessing back on David.

Mom, Dad, Bob, and David were all laughing and brushing the snow from their faces when Christy heard Marti calling to her from the window above her. "Oh Christy darling," Marti called. "Up here!"

Christy looked up just in time to see Marti tip a glass of water out the open window. Before Christy could move, the wet bullet found its mark and dripped down her face.

Christy shook off the startling wet surprise and called out, "Okay, okay! We're even, Aunt Marti." Christy waved her surrender at her aunt.

"That's the way I like it," Marti said with a satisfied expression.

Christy went inside to change and met Marti upstairs in the hallway.

"I couldn't resist the opportunity," Marti said with a giggle. "You're a good sport, Christy."

"So are you. You must have been pretty feisty when you were my age."

"Oh, I was!" Marti agreed. "Just ask your mother! Now, put on some dry clothes, and join us downstairs for cocoa."

Marti trotted down the stairs, and Christy thought, *Your poor mother!*

Once Christy was changed and seated at the kitchen counter, she asked, "Do you think we'll be able to do a little shopping somewhere up here today or tomorrow? I need to buy one more present."

She didn't want to mention that the only person she didn't have a gift for was her aunt, the person who had everything.

"The only shopping is at the Lake Arrowhead Village. I don't care to go there tomorrow," Marti said crisply. "It's Christmas Eve day, and the crowds will be unbearable."

"I could take you over," Bob said smoothly. "Or if you like small gift shops, I noticed one about a half mile down the road. I could take you down there, if you'd like."

"I could walk, if it's only a half mile." Christy accepted the mug of cocoa Bob held out to her.

"What's only a half mile?" Mom asked, joining them in the kitchen.

"A little gift shop. I still have one more present to get. Is it okay if I walk down there?"

"By yourself?" Mom asked.

"Mom, it's only down the road."

"I suppose it's okay. Thanks, Bob." Mom received her mug of cocoa. "You'll have to hurry, though. It's already after two. It gets dark faster up here in the mountains, so you would have to be back here before four, I'd say."

"That's fine. I'll leave right now."

"I imagine David will want to go with you," Mom said.

"Mother," Christy said with pleading eyes. "Please, may I just go by myself? He's not exactly a gift shop kind of kid."

"I suppose you're right. Just be careful, okay?"

"I will, Mom. I'll stay on the road, I'll be back by four, and I promise I won't talk to strangers."

Christy hurried to her room to grab her coat and some money.

Bob was waiting for her by the front door. "At the end of our driveway, turn left," he explained. "Then keep heading straight down the road for about a half mile, and you'll see the shop on the right. I think it's called the Alpine Gift Shop. Do you want me to pick you up in an hour?"

Christy was about to turn down his offer, but then she realized the walk there was downhill and would be quick and easy. But the walk back would be all uphill.

"Sure. My mom will probably feel better about that, won't she?"

Bob smiled. "I'll be there in an hour."

Christy trudged down the driveway before David noticed she was going somewhere. She turned left and kept heading down the cleared street. She was glad for the chance to think and pray, breathing out her prayers in misty puffs of cold air and listening for the answers in the crunch of gravel and ice beneath her feet.

The more she thought and prayed, the more she knew she wanted to be good friends with Rick and get all this tension between them resolved. And she didn't want to be jealous of Katie for having more freedom to do things and for being the center of attention all the time. She wanted Todd back in her life, or more accurately, she wanted to be back in Todd's life. She wanted his arm to be around her, not around his surfboard. And she wanted to feel close to God.

Is it possible to have all these at the same time? Maybe I need to set my priorities in order and reverse the list so God is at the top, with Rick, Katie, and Todd after that.

Into the cold winter air, she prayed, "I surrender to You, Father. I do this a lot, don't I? I'm glad You don't ever get tired of forgiving me for not trusting You completely. I don't want to run ahead of You. I want to walk with You. I want to hear Your voice and feel Your hand of blessing on my head."

8

Diamonds in the Sky

Christy found the Alpine Gift Shop right where Bob said it would be and eagerly entered the warm, fragrant shop. Her nose and ears needed a little thawing out from the cold air.

The small store connected to some kind of big lodge. Christy noticed that soft, Christian praise music was playing in the background.

She began to browse the darling displays of gifts. From the pictures with Scriptures on them and the assortment of T-shirts with Christian messages, she realized the shop must be run by a believer. It made her feel warm inside and at home.

She loved all the frilly little gift items like the white lace doilies and the stationery trimmed with wildflowers. There was a whole section of books, and an antique trunk bubbled over with stuffed animals.

An elegant white teapot caught her eye. It had a matching creamer and sugar bowl, but she didn't have enough money for the whole set. She also knew it was probably something she would like more than her aunt would.

A collection of angels by the shop's back door gave

Christy an idea. She chose an angel Christmas tree ornament that looked like it had been made from an old-fashioned lace handkerchief. Maybe one year Marti would decorate her tree in angels, and this could be her first one. The price was right, and Christy felt good about finding something unique and special.

She took the ornament up to the register, and a sweet-smiling lady with short, curly blond hair rang up the purchase. Christy smiled back, certain that the lady must be a Christian, even though Christy didn't know what to say to identify herself as one too. She thought maybe her smile back could be a secret message of kinship in Christ.

"Would you like this gift wrapped?" the lady asked.

"Sure, that would be great. Is there an extra charge?"

"No, it's complimentary." the lady turned to a tall, pretty teenager sitting in a chair behind the counter. "Could you find a box upstairs for this, Amanda?"

The girl had long, blond hair pulled back in a braid and wore glasses with light blue frames that Christy thought were flattering on her. She rose from her cozy spot and walked up the narrow stairs at the back of the shop.

Christy waited patiently, smiling again at the lady and noticing how much she resembled the teenager. Maybe they were mother and daughter.

"These are cute angels, aren't they?" the lady commented. "My mom makes these. She'll be glad to know we sold another one."

Amanda returned with a box, and the lady carefully laid the angel inside on a bed of tissue paper.

"Do you want me to get a bow for it, Mom?" the girl asked.

Christy thought how nice it must be for a mother, daughter, and grandmother to all be involved in running this fun little gift shop. And if they were Christians, as she suspected, they could at least say Merry Christmas to their customers without being corrected.

Christy thanked the mother and daughter and was about to leave when something inside compelled her to call out, "I hope you have a wonderful celebration of the birth of our God."

Amanda looked at her surprised mother and then back at Christy and said, "Thanks. You too!"

Bob was waiting in the car for her when she stepped outside, leaving the warm, spicy fragrances locked in the charming little shop. She told Bob how cute the store was and that it was run by a mother and her daughter.

She wondered how Mom, Marti, and she would do if they tried to run a shop together. The more she thought about it, the less pretty the picture became. Mom and Marti were so different—her mom was simple but sturdy, while Marti was all flair and fashion.

Christy especially noticed the differences between Mom and Marti the next night. It was Christmas Eve, and as the whole family ate dinner by candlelight, Dad read the Christmas story from the book of Luke. Bob and Marti respected Christy's family's tradition, although the looks on their faces showed Christy that they didn't see the miracle in the story.

Christy smiled, thinking of how Bethlehem must have been filled with Bobs and Martis that night, who hurried about their business, unaware of God's sudden presence among them.

When Dad read about the angel appearing to the shepherds, bringing "good tidings of great joy," Christy thought, *A whole city full of important, influential people, and God chose to wake up some lowly shepherds to announce His arrival.*

She glanced at petite, stylish Marti, who seemed poised like a rocket, ready to blast off to the presents under the tree the minute Dad finished reading.

I'd rather be a shepherd, Christy thought, feeling as if she and God had a little secret.

"This one's for Christy," David announced a few minutes later as he scurried around the tree, passing out gifts to the family.

Christy eagerly unwrapped the medium-sized box from her aunt and uncle and discovered a complicated, expensive-looking camera.

"Thanks," she said, not quite sure how to respond to such an unexpected gift.

"Your mom said you signed up for a photography class next semester, and I wanted to make sure you were prepared with the best equipment possible," her uncle explained. "I'll show you how to work it later. It's as easy as can be."

"Thanks."

She didn't know what else to say. The photography class had been almost an afterthought. It had sounded more interesting than some of the other electives offered, and she had been at a loss as to what else to fill her schedule with. Now she had an expensive camera to cement her elective-class decision. Maybe it would help her get a good grade.

"Another one for Aunt Marti." David handed Marti a small, long, narrow box tied with a gold ribbon.

"Bob, you shouldn't have," Marti protested. "I told you

all I wanted this year was a white Christmas. You already gave me that."

Bob grinned and said in his good-natured way, "I thought you needed a few snowflakes to keep with you all year long."

"Oh, Robert, you are the most wonderful husband in the world." Marti's long manicured nails slit the gold ribbon on the box and snapped it open.

With a gasp she exclaimed, "Oh, Robert, it's absolutely beautiful!"

Christy felt as though she were watching a commercial as Marti removed the sparkling diamond bracelet from the box and held it in the light of the red Christmas tree bulbs so everyone could see the glistening bracelet.

Bob looked at Marti proudly, pleased with his wife's reaction. "Am I forgiven for the snowball ambush?" he asked with a grin.

"Yes, yes, a thousand times yes!"

Out of the corner of her eye, Christy caught the expression on her dad's face. Dad was a dairyman, not a self-made real estate millionaire like Uncle Bob. When her parents married, they were so poor that Dad had given her mom a simple gold wedding band. Mom never even had an engagement ring.

How could her mom handle this so graciously? Mom had never received a diamond in her life. Yet here she sat, watching her sister ooh and aah over a bracelet filled with diamonds.

Christy's mother leaned over to Dad, placed her hand, the one with the simple gold band on her finger, on his leg and whispered something in his ear. Dad turned and looked at Mom. It was as if they each sent a love letter to the other with their eyes. It was beautiful.

No one else had noticed what had passed between Christy's parents because Bob, Marti, and David were busy trying to close the bracelet's clasp around Marti's slim wrist. Christy felt a little embarrassed, as if she shouldn't have been watching the intimate moment between her parents. At the same time, it made her feel warm and secure.

"Go ahead!" Marti said eagerly. "Someone else open a gift now."

"I will!" David dove for the largest box, which did indeed hold the video game set he had been hinting to Uncle Bob for. Another round of squeals and more hugs were lavished on Uncle Bob.

After all the gifts were opened, the wrapping paper crammed into garbage bags, and one last round of cocoa had been poured, everyone headed off to bed.

Christy carried upstairs her new ballet-style slippers and thick peach-colored robe from Mom and Dad. Bob had already been in her room, and a crackling fire filled the room with its amber glow.

After putting on her pajamas, Christy slipped into the new robe. She felt cozy and surrounded with warmth, ready to stretch out on her window seat.

Tonight no snow fell outside her treetop window. The sky had cleared, and she could see the stars. Tucking her legs under her and pulling the new robe tight around her middle, Christy undid the lock on the double windows and pushed them open.

The brisk night air ran in to greet her. She stuck her head out the open window, gazing up at the stars.

Those stars are Your diamonds, aren't they, God? They're beautiful—like diamonds scattered on black velvet. Why are they scattered? They should be gathered together to fill Your crown, not spilled out on heaven's floor.

For a long time she sat before the open window, watching the stars, breathing in the cold night air, and burrowing her hands in the large pockets of her plush robe. She felt small compared with the vastness before her. All her feelings from the past few days seemed to level out and, in a way, became insignificant when held up against thoughts of eternity.

When You were a baby, did You see that bright star over Bethlehem? Could You see it from Your manger bed? Did you know that star was shining for You?

In the stillness, something stirred in Christy's heart, something stronger than she had ever felt before. She felt deeply loved, as if Someone were calling her name without using a voice. It was an invisible communication of love, like her parents using only their eyes to speak to each other.

"I'm here," she whispered back.

That was it. There were no angels, no big celestial experience. Only the stars in the sky and the firm assurance deep within her that God loved her. It was Christmas Eve, and just like the shepherds, Christy felt she'd been included in a great, eternal secret. God is with us!

The next morning, when Christy awoke, she realized it was Christmas, and she was in her charming mountain bedroom. Then she remembered all the warm, close-to-God feelings she had experienced the night before.

She tried to put the feelings into words, as if she were writing a report to document the event. But she couldn't describe it. Besides, no one else needed to know. It was between her and God—something rare and sacred. Last night God had called her by name, and she had echoed back the love.

She could hear someone moving around downstairs and decided to pull on her robe and slippers and join whoever it was. She found Uncle Bob in the kitchen, making breakfast.

"Merry Christmas!" Christy greeted him. "Do you need some help?"

"Sure do, Bright Eyes. The pan on the stove is hot. Can you slide the bacon in there?" Bob placed a tray of homemade cinnamon rolls in the oven.

Within minutes, the cabin filled with the smells of bacon and cinnamon rolls.

"Better start some coffee," Bob advised. "These breakfast smells are sure to rouse the rest of the house in no time. Coffee's over there in the white bag. Can you hand it to me?"

Christy reached for the bag of gourmet coffee and drew in its rich fragrance before handing it to Bob. She loved the smell of coffee but had never liked its taste.

"It's Jesus' birthday," she said suddenly to her uncle.

He had typically slipped out of any conversation she ever tried to have with him about God. This morning she couldn't help but say something, still feeling God's presence.

Bob didn't respond.

"Did you ever think about how amazing it is that God laid down all His power and came to us on our level? He was God, and He let Himself become a baby."

Bob busily measured the freshly ground beans and pressed the coffeemaker's "On" button.

"I mean, that kind of love amazes me. To have it all and lay it aside so you can go undercover into enemy territory and rescue the ones you love. That's incredible, isn't it?"

Christy didn't care that her uncle wasn't responding. She was on a roll. God's love seemed so clear to her. "Especially because most of the ones God loved and came to rescue didn't even like Him. But He did it anyway because He loved them. He loves us. He never gives up. He never stops loving us."

Bob turned to face Christy with a tight grin on his face. "You make it sound pretty romantic, young lady."

"I think it is romantic. Jesus is like the ultimate Prince on a white horse coming to the rescue!"

"And I suppose you're the princess."

"Yes." Christy held her head high, "I am. And He saved me."

"What about her?" Bob said, taking several steps into the living room and reaching for a newspaper in the bin of fire-starter material. He held it up so Christy could see a picture of a small girl with huge eyes and a swollen stomach. The newspaper headlines gave statistics of how many had died of starvation that week in the little girl's war-torn country.

"Why didn't your Jesus ride in and save this little princess?" Bob asked.

Christy could feel tears come to her eyes—tears for the little girl and for herself. Bob's question had spoiled the aura of love she had been basking in.

Apparently recognizing how harsh his question had seemed to Christy, Bob tossed the paper down on the hearth and moved close to her.

"Don't get me wrong, Christy. There's your sweet fantasy, and then there's reality. I don't want you to get the two mixed up."

"God isn't a fantasy. His love is more real than anything," Christy stated.

Bob shook his head and gingerly flipped the popping bacon. "If your God is so full of love, then why would He allow that innocent child to suffer?"

Christy drew in a deep breath and answered honestly, "I...I don't know."

9

Spin Dry

"Let's go!" Dad called out as he carried suitcases to the car for the trip home.

Christy emerged from the cabin carrying a bottle of shampoo and said to Marti, already seated in her car, "I found this in your shower."

"Oh, toss it for me, will you? The bottle is wet, and I've already closed my suitcase."

Since the bottle was nearly full of expensive shampoo available only at salons, Christy made sure the lid was on tight and "tossed it" into the trunk of her uncle's car.

Bob carried the last suitcase over and swung it into the car trunk. "That should be it," he said, shaking Dad's hand.

Turning to give Christy a kiss on the cheek, he asked, "When are you going to come up and see us?"

"When do you want me to come?" Christy responded.

"Well, when do you have some time off work?"

"This week. I don't work again until the day after New Year's."

"Is that so?" Bob looked back at Christy's dad. "Why don't we take her home with us today? You folks can come up for New Year's Day, and we'll watch football on my new home theater system. What do you think, Norm?"

Dad thoughtfully scrunched his eyebrows together. "I don't know, Bob. You sure Marti doesn't mind?"

"Not a bit," Bob said. "We love having you any time. And you know how Marti feels about Christy. She's the daughter Marti never had."

"I suppose it would work out. You'd think we could have discussed this before the last minute when we're ready to leave."

Bob and Dad settled the details as if Christy weren't standing there. Not that she minded them making plans for her, especially since the plans were to go to Newport Beach. The problem was the Rose Parade. She hadn't brought it up with her parents yet, and she needed their permission before she could make any plans with her Newport Beach friends.

"Dad," she said. "I need to ask you something."

Dad looked surprised, as if he had just noticed she was standing there. At that moment Mom joined them.

"Would it be all right with you and Mom if I went to the Rose Parade with Katie and some other friends?"

Dad looked amazed. "When did you dream this up?"

"My friends started to make plans last week, but I was waiting for the right time to ask you."

Bob gave his approval. "Sounds like a great idea! The Rose Parade is a lot of fun for teenagers. They camp out on the street all night. It's quite a tradition with Southern California kids."

"They sleep on the streets?" Mom asked in disbelief.

"Sure. It's fairly safe. Sort of an all-night New Year's Eve party," Bob explained.

Marti, apparently noticing that she was missing out on something, left her warm spot in the car to join the rest of them.

"Sorry, Christy," Dad said firmly. "Tradition or no, you're not sleeping on the street to watch some parade."

Christy's face showed her full disappointment, and she blurted out, "I knew it. I don't know why I bothered to ask. Katie's going. She went sledding too. I had to work that day, remember? Katie wanted to go to the Bible study in San Diego at Rick and Doug's, and her parents said it was okay. But I didn't even ask you guys because I knew you'd say no. You always say no." Christy stopped to catch her breath.

"I think she should go," Marti spoke up. "After all, she is sixteen and very dependable. And I know most of her friends, and they are all to be trusted. If you're too strict with a child of this age, that child will rebel, you know."

Christy thought her aunt was kind of funny, spouting off her untried child-rearing ideas to Mom and Dad.

Dad looked at Mom, and Mom looked back at him. They seemed to have reached the same conclusion without saying a word to each other.

"We'll compromise on this one, Christy," her dad said, his eyebrows together again, this time with sternness. "You can go to the Rose Parade, but you can't sleep overnight. Either your mother and I will drive you up there early on the morning of the parade, or if Bob wants to, he can drive you."

"No problem," Bob said. "I'd be glad to take her."

"But she'll miss all the fun with the rest of the young people," Marti protested. "The party the night before is what it's all about."

Christy felt like saying, "Hush, Aunt Marti! Let's settle for what we got out of the bargain."

"It's too risky," Mom said. "Maybe when you're a little older, Christy."

"That's fine!" Christy jumped in before Marti had a chance to say anything. "I really appreciate your letting me go. You know it's something I've wanted to do since I was a little kid back in Wisconsin."

"Yes, I know," Dad said. "I'm glad you have the chance to go. Maybe we should plan on all going together as a family next year."

"Oh, Norm," Marti scolded, "what teenager wants to be seen with her parents at a place like that? It's strictly a teen party." Turning to Christy, she added enthusiastically, "Speaking of teen parties, I have the perfect solution. Why don't you invite all your friends to come over to our house after the parade to watch football with your uncle? I'll order some food, and we'll make up for you not being able to sleep over at the parade."

Dad had already lifted Christy's suitcase from the trunk and was walking with it over to Uncle Bob's car.

"We'll call you once we've made our final plans," Marti said to Mom and whisked Christy over to the car. "Bye, all!" Marti called over her shoulder, stepping out of the chill mountain air and into the warm car.

"Now, I thought I'd order one of those deli trays," she continued once they had settled into the car. "Those are always good for a group of hungry young men."

Christy waved good-bye to her parents and watched David appear from the forest, where he had been playing. David pointed at her and looked upset. She imagined he must be whining because she was going with Bob and Marti and he wasn't. Maybe there were some advantages to being the eldest.

Bob steered the car down the narrow, winding mountain road while Marti rattled on with her big party plans. Christy wondered if the party was really for her or for her aunt.

Two hours later they arrived at Bob and Marti's plush beachfront home, and Christy lugged her suitcase up to her familiar guest room. It was Monday afternoon, and New Year's Eve was three days away.

She had some arrangements of her own to make. First, she would call Katie and let her know she was in Newport and that her parents said she could go to the parade. Then she would call Tracy and see if they could get together over the next few days. Maybe she would call Doug too. And if she felt really brave, she would call Rick and try to talk things out on the phone so that when she saw him at the parade, things wouldn't be so tense.

Marti had other plans for how Christy would spend the next few days. Before Christy could even unpack her suitcase, Marti was tapping her nails on Christy's door and asking if she could enter.

Armed with a pad of paper and a pen, Marti planted herself on Christy's bed and said, "Let's start the guest list. How many total do you think we'll have, dear?"

"I'm not sure. Maybe six or seven."

"Oh, come on! Certainly you want to invite more than that."

Christy felt she had no way of knowing how many would be there. So she made up a number. "Seventeen."

"All right, then," Marti said, making notes. "Seventeen

guests. I'll order the large deli tray and several side salads. Most people like potato salad, don't they?"

"Yes, I'm sure they do."

"Now, for drinks we'll fill the ice chest with sodas and beer."

"Beer?" Christy questioned.

"For the college boys," Marti explained. "They'll want to drink beer with their potato chips while they watch TV, won't they?"

"Aunt Marti, you know my friends. They don't drink."

"None of them? Not even beer?"

"No! Besides, I would never feel comfortable having a party where alcohol was served. I don't want any beer at this party."

"All right," Marti said, sounding defensive. "I was only trying to help you throw a successful party at which everyone had a good time."

"I know, and I appreciate it. Really. With my friends though, just getting together is all they need to have a good time."

"You know, Christina." Marti put down the pencil. "You are a unique young lady. I was so different from you when I was your age. In case I haven't told you before, I have great admiration for your strong character. I believe you might make something of yourself."

"Thank you," Christy said. "And thanks too for offering to have the party. I appreciate all you do for me."

Looking back at her notepad, Marti pressed on. "Let's see, we'll need lots of snack foods too. Do you have any preferences? Chips? Candy? We can make a list, and I'll send Bob to the store tomorrow."

The list-making continued for nearly half an hour. Christy was eager to finish so she could make her phone calls.

But as soon as Marti finished with her lists, Bob joined them with a list of his own. "These are the movies playing in town tonight, and the times they start," Bob explained, showing Christy the long list. "If none of them appeals to you, we could rent a movie. I also thought we'd go out to dinner, since we're low on groceries. That is, unless you two ladies have already made other plans for the evening."

"No, dinner out would be fine," Marti said. "Why don't you make early reservations at the Five Crowns? I don't think we've taken Christy there yet."

"Okeydokey," Bob said. "Can you two be ready in an hour?"

"Certainly. And Christy, can you separate your laundry? You've probably run out of clean things to wear. Come to think of it, all you have with you are clothes for the mountains. We'll have to go shopping first thing tomorrow morning and buy you something to wear to the Rose Parade and then something to change into for the party."

"I'll call the restaurant," Bob said. "You check out that movie list, Christy, and let me know what you decide."

"I have to change." Marti sprang up from the bed. "Don't forget those dirty clothes, and try your best to find something nice for tonight. This is a classy restaurant we're taking you to. You might want to shower if you think you have time."

With that, Marti shut the door, leaving Christy in sudden silence. She sat for a moment, her head still spinning from all the instructions Bob and Marti had dumped on her.

Sometimes I wish my aunt and uncle would get a life and leave mine alone!

Christy gave up on plans to make her calls until tomorrow, realizing that being treated to dinner and a movie was nothing to complain about. She showered and dug through her stuff until she came up with a clean pair of jeans, a knit shirt, and a new vest Aunt Marti had given her for Christmas. She felt proud of herself for coming up with something out of her mound of dirty clothes.

Unfortunately, Marti, dressed in a green silk outfit, didn't share Christy's enthusiasm. "The shirt is all wrong with that vest. I knew I shouldn't have bought just the vest without getting the right kind of cotton shirt to go with it. Is that all you have? It's too casual. I told you this was a nice restaurant."

"I like it," Christy said. "I think it matches this vest you gave me perfectly."

"You both look terrific," Bob said. "If we want to make our five o'clock reservation, we need to leave now."

"You're right," Marti said, backing down. "But we'll take the vest along with us when we shop tomorrow and see if we can't find a better match for it."

Christy decided a smile was the best response. After all, how could she complain about her aunt's generosity?

Besides, she had learned long ago to protest only the big things, like her uncle's declaration that God couldn't be loving if He let that little girl in the newspaper starve to death. Christy was no closer to an answer than she had been on Christmas morning when he had asked her. Yet she knew he was wrong, and someday she would show him why.

In the meantime, it was hard to think of that starving

girl and fully enjoy her expensive dinner. Christy felt certain that the amount of money Bob was spending on her dinner tonight would feed someone in another country for a week.

Maybe that was part of the answer she would use on Uncle Bob one day. Maybe God, in His love, had provided an abundance, but people didn't share with those in need, so things became worse until the world ended up as it is today.

Christy liked that answer, although she didn't feel ready to spring it on her uncle.

"Did you decide on a movie?" Bob asked.

"None of the ones on the list looked very interesting. Would it be okay if we rented one instead?"

"Wonderful idea," Marti said. "I'm much more comfortable at home than in a sticky-floored theater. Besides, Bob's new television with the surround sound system makes our family room even better than a theater."

Marti was right. The effect of the huge screen and the sound coming from all directions was dramatic. Christy had selected one of her favorite movies, and the voices sounded as though they were right behind her. Even though she knew the story by heart, when the movie ended, Christy shuffled off to bed filled with warm, romantic feelings. In her opinion, all movies should leave the viewer with sweet, happy emotions.

The next morning she washed her face, pulled back her hair in a clip, and put on the same clothes she had worn the night before. Scooping up her pile of dirty clothes, she headed downstairs.

Just as her foot hit the bottom step, the doorbell rang.

She kept heading for the laundry room with her bundle but then realized no one was answering the door. Maybe Bob and Marti weren't up yet.

Retracing her steps, Christy bent her knees, reached for the doorknob, and pulled the door open far enough to see who was there. She heard a familiar rippling laugh before she could see over the heap of clothes in her arms. Doug was standing at the door, laughing at her.

"I thought you were the maid," he teased.

"I am, sir," Christy said in a high voice, hiding her face behind the mound of clothes. "Whom do you wish to see, sir?"

Doug cleared his throat. "Would you please inform Mistress Christina that Master Douglas is calling?"

"Yes, sir." Christy attempted a curtsy as she stepped backward.

But she didn't realize the hallway rug had bunched up. On her third step back, she lost her footing and slipped. Doug reached out to steady her, but it was too late. Both her arms flew over her head, ejecting all the laundry into the air. Just before she came down hard on her backside, her left foot got caught behind Doug's right leg, causing him to lose his balance and come crashing down on her leg.

Christy let out a shriek and then burst out laughing as all her dirty laundry showered down on them. One of her wool ski socks landed on Doug's head. Christy silently thanked the Lord that a sock, and not her underwear, had crowned him.

"Are you all right?" Doug asked in a gurgle of laughter, rolling his eyes upward to view the sock that was partially hanging down on his forehead.

Christy was laughing so hard she couldn't answer.

"What's going on down there?" Marti called from the top of the stairs.

Bob appeared from the kitchen, a spatula in his hand, asking the same question.

Christy and Doug were both so overcome with laughter that neither of them could speak.

Marti rushed to Christy's side and began to snatch up all the personal articles that had flown in the collision. Doug shook the sock from his head and pulled himself up. He offered Christy a hand to help her up. She was still laughing and felt certain her legs would give way if she tried to stand.

"Just a minute," she said, trying hard to compose herself. She stretched out her arm and took Doug's hand. He drew her up to a standing position and started to laugh all over again.

"What happened here?" Marti wanted to know.

"The doorbell rang, and I had my arms full of laundry," Christy managed to explain before feeling another surge of laughter rising to the surface.

"So, what was all this?" Bob said dryly. "The spin-dry cycle?"

Christy and Doug looked at each other and burst out laughing again.

"Honestly," Marti muttered, gathering up the rest of the clothes and marching off to the laundry room with her arms full.

"When you two can see straight again, I have some scrambled eggs ready." Bob lifted his spatula into the air and charged back into the kitchen.

Christy caught her breath. Wiping the laughter tears from her eyes, she asked Doug in her pretend maid voice, "Would you care for some breakfast, sir?"

"Sure," Doug said. "On one condition."

"What's that?"

He bent his knees, and before Christy realized what was happening, he placed one strong arm across her back and the other under her knees, scooped her up, and carried her toward the kitchen. "You let me do all the walking this time."

10

Just Friends

"How did you know I was here?" Christy asked Doug once she was safely seated in her chair at the kitchen table.

"I called your house last night. Your mom told me. She also told me you're going to the Rose Parade with us."

"To the parade, yes. Overnight, no."

"How are you getting up to Pasadena?" Doug asked.

"My favorite chef is taking me," Christy said as her uncle scooped a small portion of scrambled eggs onto her plate and popped two sausages next to it. "Oh, Bob? Have you met Doug? Doug, this is my Uncle Bob."

Doug extended his hand to shake Bob's, but Bob had a frying pan in one hand and a spatula in the other.

"Nice to meet you, Doug. Say when." Bob began to shovel eggs onto Doug's plate.

Christy watched as the plate became nearly covered with the mound before he said, "That looks great. Thanks."

"Do six of these sausages sound like a good start for you?" Bob asked. "I can make more. I have toast coming too."

"Sounds great. I sure appreciate this." Doug sprinkled pepper over his eggs.

"You know," Doug said to Christy, "I was thinking of driving up to Pasadena early that morning. You could come with me if you wanted to. I mean, if your uncle doesn't mind."

"You can call me Bob," he said, placing a plate of toast before them. "And no, I don't mind. It's up to Christy."

She looked at her uncle and then back at Doug. "You really weren't planning on going up that morning, were you, Doug? You wanted to sleep over ever since we started talking about this."

"I've done the sleepover part before. It's all right. It gets cold, though; you don't sleep at all; and the junk food only gives you a buzz for about the first four hours. By the time the parade starts, everyone is kind of burned out. I'd much rather drive up that morning. We can start early, stop along the way for breakfast, and then join our cranky, hungry friends. What do you think?"

"I know you're doing this to be nice, Doug."

"Okay, so I'm nice. Do you want to go with me?"

"Sure," Christy finally agreed. "I'll have to ask my parents to make sure it's all right with them."

Doug smiled and shoveled another forkful of eggs into his mouth. Christy glanced at her uncle. He winked at her, and she knew the matchmaker wheels were spinning in his head. It reminded her of Jon and the fortune cookie that said she didn't know what she had before her.

Could it be that Doug actually was interested in her as more than a friend? She wasn't sure she was ready to process that thought.

Marti made her grand appearance with her hair done and her makeup on. Christy introduced the two, and Marti said, "I'm sure I've seen you around before. Weren't you the one who stopped by in the yellow truck last year right after Christy and I returned from the hair salon?"

Boy, Aunt Marti, you should consider volunteering for the FBI! I'd forgotten all about that. You don't miss a thing, do you?

"Could have been me," Doug said. It obviously wasn't a monumental memory to him.

Christy remembered it because she had just come from the hair salon, and she and Doug were standing in the front yard talking. Doug had said her hair smelled like apples and leaned over to smell it just as Todd drove by. Christy had felt certain that Todd had seen her with Doug in their awkwardly close position.

Things sure change in a year. I was so embarrassed then. But this morning Doug falls all over me, and I think it's funny. Have I changed? Has Doug? What's different?

Christy remembered one other incident that happened that day a year ago. That's when Doug told her he was going to take Tracy out. Even though nothing seemed to come of their dating, Christy had noticed when they went out to pizza after the sledding that Doug and Tracy still acted like close friends. That's the way Christy wanted to be with Rick.

Christy decided that as soon as she could break free from Aunt Marti's schedule, she would see Tracy and ask her how she had managed to remain such good friends with Doug.

"I thought we'd go shopping first thing, Christy," Marti stated. "And Bob, I have a grocery list all ready for the party, and—oh, Doug, how rude of me!"

"What?" Doug asked. "Do you have a chore on your list for me too?"

"Of course not! I nearly forgot to invite you to my party. I mean, to Christy's party. We're having a party for Christy on New Year's Day right after the Rose Parade. I do hope you'll be able to come."

"Sure. Sounds great," Doug said.

"All your friends are invited, and we'll have lots of food."

"And football on my new TV," Bob added.

"Count me in." Doug finished his last crumb of toast.

Christy couldn't believe he had eaten everything set before him.

"Wonderful." Marti reached for her notepad on the counter. "That's one I can check off my guest list. Or rather, Christy's guest list."

Get a life, Aunt Martha!

"Sounds like all of you have a busy day planned. I don't mean to hold you up," Doug said, scooting back his chair. "I did want to ask you though, Christy, if you don't already have plans for tonight, do you want to have dinner with me over at Tracy's house?"

For a minute Christy thought he was asking her out to dinner, and she started to feel panicked, not knowing how to answer.

"Are you sure it's okay with Tracy and her mom?" Christy asked when she realized the offer was to go to Tracy's house.

"Of course. I told Tracy last night that you were here, and she asked me to invite you."

"I'd like to see her," Christy said. "If you're sure it's okay, then yes, I'd like to come."

"Great! Why don't I pick you up around 5:45?"

"Do you mean pick her up in your car or pick her up the way you delivered her to the breakfast table?" Bob asked with a mischievous twinkle in his eye.

Doug pushed himself back from the table and smiled down at Christy. "Whatever it takes," he said. "Preferably just in my truck."

Christy started to rise from the table. Doug put out his hand to stop her.

"Please, don't bother seeing me to the door. I'd like to make my exit a little less eventful than my entrance."

Christy smiled back, "As you wish, sir."

"Thanks again for the breakfast." Doug waved to Bob and Marti. Pointing at Christy, he said, "I'll see you tonight." Bob and Marti looked at Christy with knowing grins as they listened to Doug walk toward the front door.

The minute Christy heard the door close, she blurted out, "I know what you're both thinking, and you can stop right now!"

Bob and Marti exchanged innocent looks and playfully shrugged their shoulders.

"He's just Doug. We're just friends. He's being nice to me, that's all. Stop looking at me like that!"

Bob silently cleared the table. Marti scribbled something on one of her notes. Looking up with a straight face, she said, "Shall we go shopping, then?"

Christy obediently followed her aunt's schedule, waiting all day for Marti to say something about Doug. To Marti's credit, she didn't say a word.

They shopped for four hours, and Christy picked out two outfits, both on sale. They came home, and she finished her laundry and straightened up the guest room. Still

Marti said nothing. Bob coaxed Christy into a short walk on the beach later in the afternoon. She felt certain he would have some words of wisdom regarding Doug. But, no. Bob was silent too.

She actually felt relieved when Doug showed up. Now she could stop constructing explanations in her mind.

Doug opened the truck door for her, and she climbed in. The feeling of being free to come and go under Bob and Marti's unrestrictive care was something Christy always enjoyed. It always felt like a little vacation from the more confining rules of her parents at home.

Some letters lay on the driver's seat, and Christy picked them up so Doug could get in without sitting on them.

"Anything exciting in your mail today?" she asked.

She really wanted to ask if Todd had ever written to him, but she knew it wasn't likely.

"Sorry about that." Doug took the mail from her and stuck it in the side pocket on the inside of his door.

Then, pulling one letter out, he said, "As a matter of fact, yes. I received a letter today from Joab."

Doug handed her a piece of unusual brownish paper with tiny scribbled words written in pencil. It was hard to read.

"Who's Joab?" Christy asked as Doug started up the truck.

"He's a kid from Kenya. Here, I have his picture in my wallet." Doug opened the glove compartment, took out his wallet, and showed Christy a picture of a thin African boy about ten years old. He had a serious expression on his face and was wearing what looked like a school uniform.

"How did you meet him?" Christy wanted to know. She

recognized the look in Joab's eyes. It was the same haunting look of the starving girl in the newspaper. Only Joab looked much healthier.

"Our God-Lovers group started to sponsor him when school started. We put this big mayonnaise jar by the front door at our apartment, and everyone drops in pocket change. After about a month, I rolled all the coins, and we had almost thirty bucks, which was more than it costs to feed Joab for a month. Isn't he a cool kid?"

"Doug, that is so neat! I want to do that. How did you sign up for a kid?"

"A bunch of good organizations out there offer sponsorships. Here." He reached for the empty envelope Joab's letter came in. "You can have this. It has the address on the front."

Christy folded the envelope and tucked it in her back pocket. This was a way she could give back some of what God had blessed her with. Maybe she could even talk Bob and Marti into sponsoring a child. Why only one child? Bob could finance a whole orphanage.

Tracy's mom had made lasagna for dinner. When Doug took a fourth helping, Tracy poked Christy under the table, and they exchanged expressions of amazement.

After dinner, Tracy's dad and Doug went out to shoot hoops. Her mom said she would take care of the dishes, so Tracy and Christy retreated to Tracy's room.

"Where does he put it?" Christy asked. "And how could he possibly go outside and run around after eating like that?"

"I know," Tracy giggled. "One time last year Doug and I went out to dinner, and I was so embarrassed because he kept asking the waiter to fill the breadbasket. I think Doug must have eaten two loaves of bread plus a huge dinner."

"How long did you guys date?" Christy asked. "I mean, how long were you officially going together?"

"I don't know that we ever went together. It was...well, you remember. You were here then. We kind of went out for about two months—maybe less. It was really silly."

"That's about how long I went out with Rick. But he and I are barely speaking to each other now. How did you and Doug manage to keep your friendship?"

Tracy looked confused. "We were friends for a long time before I developed those crazy ideas about needing him to be my boyfriend. I don't know. The dating part was the strained part. The friend part has always been easy with Doug."

"It's not that way with Rick. With him, it's all or nothing. And right now it's nothing." Christy lay across Tracy's bed on her stomach, dangling her head and arms over the edge.

"I take it you two didn't talk the other night after pizza," Tracy said.

"No, I really blew it. I called him Todd."

"You called Rick Todd?"

"Well, he was coming on strong, pressuring me and saying I didn't trust him. I was thinking that Todd would never treat me like that, and then I slipped and called him Todd."

Tracy rolled over on her back and was silent for a moment before saying, "May I ask you a personal question? You don't have to answer if you don't want to."

"What?"

"Did you ever kiss Rick?" Tracy asked.

"Yeah, a bunch of times. Or, I guess if you want to be more accurate, he kissed me a bunch of times. We didn't do anything more than that, in case that's what you're wondering. Why? Didn't you and Doug kiss when you were dating?"

"No."

"No? You dated almost two months, and he never kissed you?"

"Doug has never kissed any girl."

"You're kidding! How old is he?"

"He turned twenty last month. Didn't you know that about Doug? The first girl he wants to kiss is his wife, and their first kiss will be at the altar on their wedding day."

"Really? I never knew that."

"I thought he and Todd had made some monk pact and that you knew about it." Tracy suddenly sprang to an upright position. "Wait a minute. Do you mean to tell me that Todd has actually kissed you?"

Christy sat up too, feeling a little self-conscious. "Only four or five times, always in front of other people."

Tracy looked at Christy with a glimmer in her eye. "I'm surprised. That really means something, Christy. I'm sure you're the only girl Todd has ever kissed."

The feeling of being special diminished when Christy realized that Todd wasn't the only guy she had kissed. At that moment she wished she had never dated Rick Doyle. She wished she could have the last few months to do all over again, knowing that she would do things a lot differently. Neither Rick nor any other guy would pressure her into being anything other than who she truly was from the heart out.

"Don't look so serious," Tracy said. "Hey, you know what they say, don't you? Sometimes you have to kiss a couple of toads before the handsome prince comes along."

11

The White Rose Parade

When Doug arrived at five on New Year's morning, Christy answered the door ready to go, with a blanket in one hand and a bag of cookies in the other.

She couldn't help but look at him differently than she had in years past. Doug had to be the only twenty-year-old guy in the world who fed starving children and was totally saving himself for his future wife. That kind of godliness was, as Doug had said, irresistible.

"My carriage awaits you, Princess." Doug playfully bowed at the front door.

"I'm leaving now," Christy called upstairs into the early morning stillness.

"Hold on," Bob called back from the kitchen. He emerged with a picnic basket bulging with the breakfast he had prepared for them. "I didn't know if you would find many restaurants open on a holiday. So I thought this might hold you over until you can find some real food."

"Thanks," Christy said.

"Thanks," Doug echoed, reaching for the basket.

"We'll see you and your gang after the parade," Bob said. "Have a good time!"

Christy waved good-bye and followed Doug to his truck. He had left the engine running and the heater on, so it was nice and warm inside. The hour or so drive to Pasadena turned into a picnic adventure. Christy kept Doug supplied with a steady stream of blueberry muffins and held his carton of orange juice so he could drink it without taking his hands off the wheel or his eyes off the road. Bob had provided a bountiful feast, and Doug, true to form, put it all away.

"I told my uncle about Joab," Christy said. "And I gave him the address and told him I was going to sponsor a child. I also told him I thought he should sponsor a few kids."

"How did he take that?" Doug asked.

"Pretty well, I think. He didn't say much. See, over Christmas we had this discussion about how could God be loving when starving people are in the world. I told him yesterday that I thought God had given him enough money to help do something about starvation, but he had to be willing to share his wealth."

"Whoa, Christy! Harsh attack, don't you think?"

"I felt strongly about it, and I wanted Uncle Bob to see that I was serious. I've always felt free to tell him whatever I think."

Doug flashed a smile at her, "I think you're right about sharing our money. But it's hard to think like Job in the Bible and say, 'The Lord gives, and the Lord takes away. Blessed be the name of the Lord.'"

Christy thought a minute. "Job was that guy in the Bible with all the trials, right?"

"Right," Doug said. "He lost everything, but he still hung tough and didn't blame God for his problems. In the end God blessed him over and above what he had before all the bad stuff happened."

"I don't know if I could have that much faith," Christy admitted.

"I know I couldn't," Doug said. "And God knows it too, because He hasn't done to me what He did to Job. God seems to have a measuring cup for each person and only measures out the dosage that's right. Pretty awesome, huh?"

"Do you think God really measures out a huge dosage to starving children, and do you really think they can handle it?" Christy asked, not convinced by Doug's answers.

"I don't know." Doug turned off the freeway. "I do know that He knows each one of them by name, and He promises to provide for everything He created. I also know that we're spoiled rotten, and we don't even know it. We expect God to be our own personal slave and bring us whatever we want whenever we ring the prayer bell.

"It's supposed to be the other way around," Doug continued. "He's God. He's awesome. He can do whatever He wants. He's the Master. We're the ones who are supposed to be the servants—His servants."

Christy knew she had fallen into the spoiled rotten category more than once. She knew she had treated God that way before, like her personal slave.

"So how does a person become a servant of God?" she asked.

"By surrendering. Offering yourself to Him."

"I seem to have to do that over and over," Christy admitted.

"Oh, me too. It's a constant thing. We have to keep

choosing if we'll serve God or ourselves. It's usually easier to serve ourselves."

"I'm just glad He doesn't keep track of how many times I ask Him for forgiveness," Christy said.

Doug smiled. "I know what you mean. God is pretty awesome, isn't He?"

Christy agreed, and looking out her window at all the parked cars lining the streets, she added, "I really appreciate your driving me up here today, Doug."

Her emotions had begun to flirt with the idea of what it would be like to go out with Doug like this on a regular basis. He was a special guy. After all, Bob, Marti, and even Jon seemed to think she should recognize what a treasure he was.

"I'm glad it worked out. You're like a little sister to me, Christy, and I enjoy keeping an eye on you for Todd." Doug glanced at her as if he weren't supposed to have said that.

Christy felt disappointed and not quite sure if she should feel insulted. It was embarrassing to have romantic thoughts about someone who saw himself as her bodyguard.

"Can I ask you something?" Christy asked, speaking fast before she lost her courage. "Are you interested in being with me because I'm your friend, or did Todd make you promise that you would guard me or something while he was gone?"

"What I said sounded kind of rude, didn't it?"

"I'm not sure what you were trying to say," Christy said.

"I like spending time with you, Christy, and I think you're a really awesome sister in the Lord. But I would never think of seriously dating you as long as that bracelet is on your wrist. Todd's my closest friend, and I'd never snake him."

Christy glanced down at the gold chain on her wrist and realized it was the one part of Todd she hadn't buried in the box with the rest of her souvenirs during her memorial service. She was so used to wearing it that she hadn't even thought to take it off.

"But did Todd put me up to this? No. I want to spend time with you because you're you and I value our friendship. I'm not much into dating anyway. Tracy probably told you I'm much better at being friends."

Christy appreciated Doug's honesty, and she knew they were both better off keeping their relationship just the way it was. Still, she couldn't help but wonder if anything would be different between her and Doug if Todd hadn't found his way into her heart.

She had met Doug and Todd the same day. What was it that made her and Todd close while it left her and Doug "just friends"?

"Oh, good!" Doug said. "There's a spot for us to park over there."

He pulled the truck onto a dirt area alongside dozens of other cars and turned off the engine. He and Christy loaded their arms with blankets, a small ice chest, and of course, the bag of cookies they had been saving.

They walked for several blocks until they came to Colorado Boulevard, where hundreds of people lined the streets, huddling in beach chairs with their sleeping bags pulled up to their chins. On one corner they passed a portable outhouse with a short line of people waiting to use it.

Christy noticed an older house with a wide front porch and a huge tree in the front yard. A hammock hung between the porch and tree, and two boys around her brother's age were wedged together in the hammock, covered with blankets and looking like a big cocoon suspended in the moist morning air.

Uncle Bob was right. Everyone sleeps outside waiting for the parade. If my parents could see this, they would know it would have been harmless for me to have done it too.

A few yards up, Christy noticed some college-age guys tossing a Nerf football in the blocked-off street.

"That looks like Rick," Christy said. "I don't know who that guy with him is though."

The guy receiving Rick's pass had on a navy blue sweatshirt with the hood pulled over his head, which made it difficult to determine his identity.

"You don't suppose..." Doug began and then stopped.

"What?" Christy asked.

"Oh, it's crazy," Doug said. "For a minute I thought the guy over there with Rick might be Todd. Todd always wears a sweatshirt like that."

Christy felt an immediate rush inside as if she had just taken a dip on a roller coaster with her eyes closed. *It can't be Todd. Can it? What if it is?*

"Hey, Rick!" Doug called out, waving.

Rick held the football and looked around.

"Over here," Doug yelled.

Rick spotted him and waved back. The other guy jogged over with him, and Christy eagerly tried to see who it was. He didn't run like Todd.

The guy pulled down the hood of his sweatshirt and

revealed flaming red hair that could only belong to Katie.

"Hi!" Katie greeted them enthusiastically.

Christy drew in a deep breath and felt her stomach do another dive.

"Where did you get that sweatshirt?" she snapped at Katie.

"It's my brother's. Why?"

"Oh, I just wondered." Christy tried to calm down. "So, where's everybody else?"

"We never found them last night," Katie said.

"You mean you and Rick stayed here all night, just the two of you?" As soon as she said it, Christy realized how accusing she sounded.

"Boy, what's with you this morning?" Katie asked. "Get up on the wrong side of the new year?"

"No, I'm sorry. Forget everything I said. Let's start over." Christy changed her voice to a brighter tone. "Oh Katie, hi! I'm glad we found you. How's it going?"

Katie gave Christy a questioning look, "Rick wanted to wait until you guys arrived before we went looking for the rest of the group since this is the street corner Doug told him to wait on."

Rick and Doug, their arms loaded with Rick and Katie's stuff, joined the two girls. Rick handed Katie her backpack and blanket.

"Ready to go on safari?" Doug asked. "The rest of the group has to be around here somewhere."

Feeling like a refugee, Christy fell in step behind Doug, and Katie did the same behind Rick. The guys led them out into the street, where it was much easier to walk without obstacles.

"I feel like people are looking at us as if we're part of the parade," Christy said to Katie. "I hope we find the rest of the group soon. This stuff is getting heavy."

"Look over there." Katie pointed across the street to a guy setting up a television camera on an adjustable metal platform.

"Hi, Mom," Katie called out, waving to the camera. "Happy New Year!"

Then, liking the idea of being in the middle of the parade route much more than Christy did, Katie started to goof off, waving to the little kids who lined the curbs.

"Good morning, little friends!" she said in her elf voice. "Rise and shine. The big parade is coming soon!"

"Stop it," Christy said in a mock scold. "They're starting to wave at you. They think you're part of the parade."

Katie laughed and waved back. "You've got to take your fans where you can find them!"

Then they heard someone calling, "Hey, Christy! Doug! Over here."

The foursome crossed the street as they spotted Heather and Tracy standing and waving at them. A group of about a dozen people Christy knew from previous beach gatherings was camped out beside the street. For the next ten minutes, there was a flurry of hugs, introductions, and explanations.

Once they settled in and wedged their blankets into the space available, Christy plopped herself down next to Tracy, "I feel like a pioneer woman who just made a six-month trek to California. Somehow this whole Rose Parade was a lot more glamorous from the comfort of my living room couch."

"So?" Tracy asked. "Did you talk to Rick yet?"

Before Christy could answer, Rick, who they didn't realize was standing behind them, stuck his head between them and asked, "Did I hear someone mention my name?"

"Oh!" Tracy said, startled.

She looked at Christy and then at Rick, "I was asking Christy if you two had a chance to talk yet."

Christy turned her head away from Rick.

"I don't know," Rick said. "Have we had our talk yet, Christy?"

"Not exactly," she said, still not looking at him.

"Then maybe you'd better step into my office." Rick offered his hand to pull her up.

Christy let him help her to her feet and gave Tracy a grimace that said, "Why did you say anything?"

Tracy smiled and blew Christy a kiss to send her on her way.

Rick led Christy away from the crowd and headed down a street that crossed the parade route. He stopped at a low cement-block fence that edged the front of someone's yard. Sitting down, he motioned for Christy to sit beside him.

She remembered the time last year when Rick sat with her on a cement-block wall at school and talked her into trying out for cheerleading. Today the damp chill from the cold cement shot right through Christy's jeans, and she shivered.

"Cold?" Rick pulled off his high school letterman's jacket and wrapped it around her shoulders before she could answer.

The jacket smelled like Rick. It felt like Rick's arms were once again around her. He was being so sweet and looked at her so tenderly. This was finally their moment to talk, and she had absolutely no idea what it was she wanted to say to him.

"You know, you're the only girl I've ever done this with," Rick said, a half grin pulling up the side of his mouth.

"Done what?" Christy asked.

"I've never talked to any of the girls I've dated after we broke up. You're the first one. Their friends would talk to me sometimes. Usually it was only to tell me what a jerk I was to their friend."

This was a vulnerable side of Rick she knew he didn't show often. Christy used her eyes to tell Rick to continue.

"Ever since junior high," he explained, "I'd go out with a girl, break up with her, and never talk to her again. Now that I'm in college, I have a bunch of girls who are good friends. And, you see, you're in the middle. You're not like any of the girls I dated in high school, and you're not one of the girls from our college Bible study. I don't really know what to do with you."

With Rick's jacket warming her and everything so tender between them, Christy wanted to say, "Take me in your arms and hold me. I'll be whatever you want me to be, Rick!" Fortunately, she remembered all the strained feelings, hurts, and insecurities from when they had dated. She remembered Rick's arrogant nerve when he took Todd's bracelet from her.

"Let me be one of your friends, like the girls at your Bible study," Christy said softly. "I want to be friends with you the way I am with Doug and these others. And I want you to be friends with Tracy, Heather, and Katie. I want us to all do things together and not have to feel weird because of what went on in the past."

"I want that too." Rick reached over and squeezed her hand. "Friends?"

"Friends," Christy agreed, squeezing his hand back. "Are you sure we're okay?" she asked as an afterthought.

"What do you mean?" Rick asked.

"The last time we tried to talk, you said that you didn't think I trusted you and that I'd never given our relationship a chance. Do you still feel that way?"

Rick let out a deep breath. "I guess it's no secret that I've always felt a little jealous of the place Todd has in your life. Maybe there's room for both of us. Maybe there isn't. You're going to have to be the one to decide. I don't see any harm in you and me being friends and you and Todd being friends, as long as that's what we all are. Friends."

Christy thought she liked the arrangement, even though something in Rick's voice made her wonder if he didn't want more from their relationship. For now though, Rick seemed willing to wait and be friends, and that's what she wanted from him.

She had a hard time believing this was the same Rick who had dumped her in the mall parking lot a week ago. Whatever it was that softened him, Christy was grateful for it and felt more relieved than she had imagined she would feel. Finally she could fully surrender this relationship to the Lord.

A vendor was heading for the parade route, carrying a flat of roses.

"We'll take one of those," Rick called out to the guy. "How much?"

"Five dollars each," the man said, displaying his assortment of colored rosebuds.

Rick pulled a crumpled five-dollar bill from his pocket and said, "Give me a red one."

"Red is for love," the man said with a satisfied grin, taking the bill and handing the rosebud to Rick. Christy remembered all the red roses Rick had given her while they were dating. Once they had died, she had thrown them all away.

Rick looked at Christy and then back at the assortment of buds. "Which one stands for friendship?"

The man reached for a yellow rose. "Yellow," he said, trading the yellow bud for the red one in Rick's hand.

"What's white for?" Rick asked.

The man didn't seem to mind all the questions. "Purity of heart."

"We'll take the white one," Rick said.

As soon as the vendor was on his way, Rick turned to Christy, "You're the first girl I've ever given a white rose to. Did you hear what he said? It stands for purity of heart, and that's you, Killer Eyes."

Christy accepted the white rose, swallowing a lump in her throat. It was the highest compliment Rick had ever paid her. This rose she knew she would keep.

12

Katie, You Didn't!

When Christy and Rick joined the rest of the group, Doug noticed them first. Holding out the bag of cookies Christy had made for him, he said, "Rick, you have to try these. They're the best ones yet!"

Tracy came alongside Christy, "So? How did it go?"

"Good," Christy whispered back. "I think everything is finally settled, and I feel good about it."

"That's what I wanted to hear," Tracy said. "Sorry if I kind of forced you into it."

"I'm glad you did," Christy admitted. "I don't think I would have talked to him otherwise. You did the right thing, Tracy. Thanks." Tracy was staring at the white rose in Christy's hand, and so Christy added, "Rick gave it to me. A gift of friendship."

Tracy smiled. "I'm glad that's settled. It's a good way to start the new year."

For the next hour, the group ate and talked, and the guys and Katie played more football out in the street. More and more vendors appeared, selling souvenirs.

Christy was content to sit on her blanket and watch the action going on around her. The morning warmed up quickly, and she shed her thick jacket.

Then official Rose Parade guards walked briskly along the street, shooing everyone back up on the curb. People began to press in closer, crowding Christy and Tracy together on their blanket. The spectators stretched their necks to see what was coming up the street.

They heard sirens. A group of motorcycle cops led the parade's way. Then the official white Rose Parade convertibles with dignitaries waving from the backseats rolled by.

"Who is *he?"* Christy asked when the first convertible passed them.

"Who knows," Tracy said. "Somebody important. Just wave at him."

Tracy and Christy laughed and waved, like two little kids sitting on the curb. The important person waved back.

The Marine Corps Color Guard and Band followed the cars and started to play just as they marched past Christy and the group. It was so loud that she wanted to cover her ears with her hands but refrained, since no one else was. The drums seemed to shake the ground and make her heart thump. She had been to parades before, but nothing like this.

The first float that came by amazed Christy. It was a huge green dragon with steam coming from its nostrils. The monster swerved down the street and came within a few feet of Christy. She could see up close all the layers of flowers carefully placed on the float's frame. The variety of colors and types of flowers was astonishing. The dragon's scales seemed real.

"Look!" Tracy laughed as she pointed at the dragon's legs. "Those are brussels sprouts!"

"You're kidding!" Christy responded.

"They really are. And look, they used brussels sprouts on the tail too! It's a vegetarian dragon!"

The group around Tracy and Christy laughed.

Doug, who was sitting on the other side of Tracy, said, "I give it an eight." He held up eight fingers and whistled.

Rick picked up on Doug's cue and held up eight fingers from his spot at the far end of their clump of friends. Christy noticed that Katie had planted herself in front of Rick's lawn chair, using his legs for a backrest. They looked awfully comfortable sitting together.

The next float appeared, and Doug and Rick, wearing matching sunglasses, slipped their glasses down their noses and looked at each other as if they were two official parade critics. Rick held up five fingers as the float motored by, and Doug gave it a six.

"That float deserves more than a five or a six!" Christy exclaimed to Tracy.

The float resembled a field of grass with giant wildflowers and a huge storybook spread open in the middle of the field. Animated butterflies escaped from the storybook, and a wobbly rainbow arched over the field, raining down colored glitter on the parade spectators.

"I give it a nine and a half." Christy held up to Doug nine fingers and half a pinkie.

"Naw," Doug said. "It's only a six. Wait until one of the award-winning floats comes by. You'll see."

As soon as the next float arrived, Christy held up seven fingers, to which Katie responded over the heads of their friends with a three. Rick gave it a four and Doug a five.

"Come on, you guys," Christy said. "That was a good one!"

"I'd give it a seven too," Tracy said.

"Well, I don't see your fingers up there," Christy teased.

Tracy stuck seven fingers up in Christy's face. "There!" she said.

A band from a Minnesota high school came by, and Rick started to whistle loudly, trying to get the attention of one of the girls playing a flute in the front row.

"That guy doesn't ever take a break, does he?" Tracy said, speaking loudly over the music.

Christy shook her head in response. "I suppose I shouldn't turn my back on him. That's what my boss, Jon, says." Christy and Tracy were speaking so loudly that Doug heard them.

"You should have seen Rick last semester with this girl who lived in our apartment complex. He never let up on her, and she told him to get lost in at least four different languages."

Tracy looked at Christy for her reaction. Christy carefully kept a straight face, looking at Doug as if she were interested in his amusing little story and eager for him to continue.

Doug started to laugh at some funny memory he had. Leaning closer to Tracy and Christy, he let them in on the joke. "Rick used to know when she did her laundry. I think she did it every Tuesday afternoon or something. Anyway, he would go down to the laundry room with a basket full of dirty clothes and wait for her, pretending he happened to be there folding clothes. He would come back to the apartment with neatly folded dirty clothes."

"And she never went out with him?" Tracy asked.

"She didn't even tell him her name!" Doug laughed.

"The guy can't handle being shut out."

"Hey," Rick called over to them. "Let's see those scores!" Rick was holding up a seven, and Katie had five fingers up in the air. The rest of the group had all joined in and were holding up their scores. Doug quickly checked out the float in front of them and gave it a six.

Christy didn't feel like playing anymore. Of course she knew when Rick went to college last fall he would meet girls and probably be his flirty self. But the first two months of school she was dating him. She felt sick in the pit of her stomach, thinking that while he was taking her to the beach on the weekends, he was chasing girls in the laundry room during the weekdays.

"Hey," Tracy said, giving her a poke in the side. "Are you okay?"

Christy nodded, but apparently Tracy could see right through her. "Don't let what Doug said about Rick bug you. You and Rick are friends now, remember? Don't let any bad feelings start up again."

"I was thinking that the girl in the laundry room was smarter than I was. She didn't fall for Rick's tricks. I feel foolish, that's all."

"Why?" Tracy wanted to know. "Because you liked a guy and went out with him a few times? I don't see any harm in that. You guys are friends now. There's nothing foolish about any of that."

"I feel like a fool because I believed everything Rick said. Why should I even believe what he told me this morning? Why did I so eagerly accept this rose from him?"

"You have to start somewhere." Tracy slipped her arm around Christy and gave her a quick hug. "Don't make such a big deal out of it. Oh, look at this float—a definite ten!" Tracy held up all ten fingers and whistled wildly with the others.

Tracy's right. I shouldn't make such a big deal out of everything. What Rick does or who he goes out with is no concern of mine.

By the time the next float approached, Christy had joined back in with the rest of the group in playing the rating game. Another band followed and then a float that turned out to be Christy's favorite.

Cinderella rode in an enchanted pumpkin carriage drawn by real horses. The carriage was completely done in roses and smelled wonderful as it passed by. It was a small float, it hadn't won any awards, and the Cinderella looked like she had been smiling and waving for too many miles.

Rick gave it a one; Katie a two; Doug and Tracy gave it a three and then slapped each other a high five for coming up with the same number.

Christy didn't hold up her hands at first. Then realizing that she was among friends and she should be free to express her opinion, she held up a perfect ten, thereby declaring to them all that she believed in fairy tales.

Rick noticed and, thinking it was a joke, joined in with Christy's ten, raising both his hands high over his head, standing up and whistling to get Cinderella's attention. The model in the float didn't pay any attention to Rick, and Christy tried to tell herself she shouldn't either.

She really did think it was a ten. So what if Rick made fun of her? What did he know about fairy tales, anyway?

After the Cinderella float, there was a lag in the parade. Someone behind them said there must have been a breakdown on one of the floats.

"Perfect opportunity to visit the little girls' room," Tracy said, rising to her feet. "Want to come with me?"

Christy stood and instructed Doug, "Save our places. Don't let anyone sit here, okay?"

Doug stretched his long legs over their blanket and set his small ice chest on the far corner of the blanket to mark the territory. "If I'm asleep when you come back, just wake me," he teased.

The two girls headed for the outhouse and were joined by Katie and another girl from their group named Katrina.

"That was a real cute joke, Christy," Katrina said. "Giving the last float a ten, I mean."

"I don't think she meant it as a joke," Katie said. "Christy happens to be the world's most hopeless romantic. You really did think it deserved a ten, didn't you, Christy?"

"Yes, I did," Christy said.

"Well, I kind of liked it a lot too," Katrina admitted. "But I wasn't about to let all those guys know."

"Why not?" Christy asked. "They're just guys. Some of them are as romantic as we are, if not more so."

"Who?" Katie challenged. "Rick?"

"No, I meant Doug," Christy said as the girls took their place in the long line at the portable restroom.

She lowered her voice as the other three girls tilted their heads in close. "Did you know that Doug is twenty years old, but he's never kissed a girl?" Christy whispered.

"No way!" Katie said.

"It's true," Tracy confirmed. "He says his first kiss is going to be at the altar on his wedding day."

"Is that romantic or what?" Christy asked.

"Can you imagine how special his wife is going to feel?"

Katrina asked in wide-eyed wonder. "She'll probably wish she had never kissed another guy."

"I know," Christy said. "I thought the same thing. Kind of made me wish I'd never kissed a guy before."

"Me too," said Tracy.

"Me too," said Katrina.

Christy knew Katie had never been kissed, but instead of Katie popping off with one of her usual jokes about not having that problem, she turned slightly away from the rest of the girls.

"Katie?" Christy asked.

Katie didn't look at her. Christy tried to be funny and said, "Don't you have anything to say here, Katie? You're the only one with virgin lips."

"Whatever," Katie mumbled.

The outhouse door opened, and Katie disappeared inside.

"I don't think Katie's as inexperienced as she may have led you to believe," Katrina said softly.

"Of course she is," Christy said. "I know everything about her. She's never had a boyfriend, and the few dates she's been on have been disasters. Glen, the guy at church that she likes, gave her a hug, but that was all."

Katie exited the restroom, and Christy stopped talking and waited for Tracy, who went in next.

Katie didn't look at Christy but instead spoke to Katrina. "I'm going to go back."

Christy felt awful. She obviously had embarrassed Katie in front of these girls Katie barely knew. It didn't quite seem like the honor Christy had meant when she called Katie "virgin lips." She tried to think how she would feel if she had never had a guy interested in her and her best friend had made a crack like that about her in public.

When the three girls returned to the group, Christy wanted to slip over to Katie and tell her she was sorry. It looked impossible though to maneuver through the jam of people without making a scene. Katie was tucked back in her spot, leaning against Rick's legs.

Tracy nimbly made her way back to their blanket, blazing a skinny trail for Christy to follow. The people behind them were not happy about letting them through to their front-row seats.

Doug straightened up when they arrived back to their little nest and said, "You didn't miss anything. A bunch of horses came by, that's all."

The next float finally arrived, pulled by a tow truck. "Let's hear it for the tow truck!" Rick started clapping loudly.

Christy noticed that Katie didn't jump right in and join Rick in his antics. She still seemed upset. As several more floats passed by, Christy kept looking over to see if Katie had snapped out of it, but Katie looked deep in thought.

Near the parade's end, Christy saw Rick lean over and say something in Katie's ear. Her bright smile instantly returned, and she playfully slugged him in the arm. She seemed her old self, and Christy felt relieved.

When the group started to pick up its stuff to leave, Christy reminded her friends, "You guys all know about the party at my aunt and uncle's, right?"

Everyone said yes. A few asked for directions, and one girl asked Christy if they should stop to buy any food.

"No. I'm sure my aunt has enough for an army."

"Your aunt doesn't know how these guys eat though," the girl said.

"Actually, she has watched Doug in action, so I think she has a fair idea." Christy smiled at Doug, who heard her comment.

"Okay." the girl linked arms with the guy beside her. "We'll be there. Thanks for inviting us."

"You're coming with me, aren't you?" Doug asked.

"I guess," Christy answered as she looked around for Katie. "Would it be okay if Katie came with us?" Christy was hoping to use the ride back to apologize to Katie for her insensitive comment.

"Sure, if one of you doesn't mind riding in the middle."

"I'll ride in the middle. Let me go ask her."

Christy wove through the mob and touched Katie on the arm. She was standing next to Rick.

"Katie, do you want to come with Doug and me?"

Katie looked at Rick and then back at Christy. "I don't know. I thought I'd go with Rick since the rest of my stuff is in his car and everything."

"Oh."

Rick stepped in and with his half smile said, "You can come with us, if you want. You can have the whole backseat to yourself."

Something about the way Rick said it felt like a slam to Christy. Why did he assume that Katie would be in the front seat and she would be in the back? Why was he stepping in and acting protective of Katie?

"Thanks." Christy forced a smile at both of them. "I think I'll go with Doug so he won't be by himself."

"Okay," Rick said, sticking his lawn chair under his arm and reaching for the ice chest Katie had in her hand. "We'll see you at Bob and Marti's. I remember how to get there."

Since he had on his sunglasses, Christy couldn't read his expression, but he sounded a little too arrogant and not at all like the tender person who had talked to her on the cement-block wall that morning.

"Ready?" Rick asked Katie, and the two of them headed down the street, with Rick carrying almost all their gear.

Katie didn't say a word to Christy or even look at her. She fell in step with Rick and marched down the street with him, her red hair shining in the late morning sun.

Something felt strange. Christy couldn't quite figure out what it was. She picked her way over the trash that people had left behind them and joined Doug and Tracy.

Tracy had found an empty paper bag and was going around picking up trash.

"Come on," Doug said. "They hire people to do that."

"We left such a mess though. Let me at least pick up the stuff from our group."

Christy joined her, and in minutes the bag was bulging with candy wrappers and empty soda cans.

"I can't believe how sloppy some people are," Tracy said. Looking up, she realized the rest of their group had disappeared, and only the three of them were left.

"Oh, I guess I'm going to need a ride back," Tracy said to Doug. "Looks like they all thought I had a ride. Good thing you two are still here."

Christy found another empty bag, and, after picking up enough trash to feel that she had done her good deed for the day, she said, "We'd better go or else everyone is going to arrive before us."

"You're right," Doug said. "We have a hike back to the truck, and the freeway will be jammed. Think you can leave that for the paid professionals, Tracy?"

"Okay, okay. I'm coming. Where's my sleeping bag?"

"Right here." Doug showed the tied-up bundle under his arm. He also had an ice chest, beach chair, two blankets, and Christy's jacket.

"Come on, Tarzan," Tracy said with a laugh "Let Christy and me at least carry the blankets."

Doug shared the load and led the girls back to the truck. It must have been at least a mile, and Christy's feet were starting to hurt. Before she could get in, Tracy slid into the tight middle spot and positioned her short legs to the side of the gears on the floor. Christy was about to argue, but Tracy was definitely smaller, and she did fit in that spot better than Christy.

As Doug had predicted, the freeway on-ramp looked like a parking lot, with cars stacked up for as far as they could see. He turned on the radio and settled back, apparently willing to take it all in stride. Tracy put her head back and closed her eyes, admitting that the all-night party was catching up with her.

Christy looked out the window and thought about Rick and Katie being together somewhere in this mess in his red Mustang. They had been together, just the two of them, all night, and Katie hadn't said a word about what it was like.

A couple of college students, a guy and a girl, were in the back of a pickup truck next to them. The girl looked like she was trying to sleep. Her head rested against the cab window, and her face was tilted up toward the sun.

A red light forced the pickup to stop, and the guy started to tickle the girl mercilessly. The girl flirted right back, smacking the guy in the stomach. Then he wrapped his arms around her and kissed her. The light turned green, and as the truck moved ahead of them, Christy saw the girl lay her head on the guy's shoulder as if settling back down for a nap.

It reminded Christy of the way Katie had planted herself in front of Rick's chair and had playfully punched him a couple of times during the parade. Suddenly, Christy knew why Katie hadn't admitted to never being kissed.

"Oh no! Katie, you didn't!" Christy spouted.

"What?" Tracy jerked forward out of her sleepy state. "What's wrong?"

"Nothing," Christy said. "I'm sorry I woke you. I didn't mean to say anything. I just thought of something, that's all."

Tracy went back to sleep, and Doug tapped his fingers on the steering wheel in time to the song on the radio.

Christy silently shouted to herself, *Katie, tell me you didn't kiss him!*

13

Marti's Party

"Welcome, welcome!" Bob greeted Christy, Doug, and Tracy at the front door nearly two hours later. "Looks like most of your friends beat you here. Did you have any problems?"

"I stopped for gas," Doug explained, "and then an accident on the freeway held us up. I guess everyone else made it through that stretch before the accident."

"There you are!" Marti appeared in the entryway. "Fourteen, fifteen, sixteen." She pointed her finger at each of them as she counted. "We now have sixteen guests. You said you were expecting seventeen, Christy."

"I think everyone is probably here, Aunt Marti," answered Christy. "What about my parents and David? Are they here yet?"

"No," Marti explained. "They decided not to come. I told your mom about our big party, and she decided it might be best if they sat this one out. I told her you could ride back to Escondido with Rick."

Oh, great! That's just what I need, a view from Rick's backseat of this budding romance between him and Katie.

"By the way," Marti said, taking Christy by the arm and

leading her into the family room, which was crowded with all her guests. "Who is that redheaded girl who arrived with Rick? Are they dating now? They make a stunning couple."

"That's my best friend, Katie." Christy pulled her arm from Marti's grip and got out of the noisy family room as quickly as she could.

She retreated to the kitchen. Heather was the only other person there. She was stacking two hefty sandwiches onto a plate. The selection and amount of sandwich preparations Marti had laid out on the counter was mammoth. It looked like enough food for 117 people.

"I don't know why I let those guys talk me into making these sandwiches for them. It's their seconds, not mine. Who do they think I am? Their personal slave?" Heather said.

"Then send them in here to make their sandwiches themselves," Christy advised.

Heather giggled, her wispy blond hair falling over her eyes. "I don't really mind. It's kind of fun actually. Besides, if I want to be great in God's kingdom, I'm supposed to be the servant of all, right?"

Christy grabbed a soda from the ice chest, "Yeah, well, as long as the guys know that verse applies to them too. They're supposed to serve us right back!"

"Good point," Heather said, carefully balancing the loaded paper plate and heading out the door. "I think I'll bring that point up at halftime."

Christy went over to the sink, filled a glass halfway, and popped Rick's white rose into the water. Placing it in the center of the kitchen table, she slid into a chair and nibbled on a potato chip from one of the six assorted bags before her.

She thought about Heather's servanthood quip and remembered Doug saying that people are supposed to be servants of God and not treat Him as though He were their personal slave. Doug also said the key was in surrendering.

"Okay, God," she prayed softly in the empty kitchen, "I surrender, again. Here I thought something might happen between Doug and me, but he sees me as his little sister. And then I thought I could patch things up with Rick and feel good about everything with him, but now I'm all upset that he likes Katie. I give up! I can't make things work out the way I want them to. I surrender all these guys in my life to You."

Just then Heather slipped back in and with a giggle said, "Oops! I forgot to get myself something to drink."

She scooped a soft drink from the ice chest and held it up in a good-bye gesture on her way back to the family room. She was almost through the door when she stopped, turned around, and looked at Christy.

"Are you okay?" she cautiously asked.

"Sure. Why?"

Heather sat down across the table from Christy. "Oh, no reason. Except that this is your party, and everyone is in the other room, but you're sitting here all by yourself."

"I had some thinking to do."

"About Rick and Katie and what's up with them?" Heather ventured, opening her can and taking a sip.

Christy smiled at her friend. "How did you know?"

"An educated guess," Heather said with a grin. "The last time I saw you with Rick you were trying to talk yourself into being glad you were going together. Then I saw him last week sledding with Katie and figured out real fast that some strange competitive thing was going on between them."

"Sounds about right," Christy said with a sigh.

"Then at pizza that night, it didn't exactly take a rocket scientist to figure out that you had broken up with him, he was ticked, and he was using all his immature stunts to get your attention." Heather took another sip, "You know, to be honest, I thought for sure that night when you two left together you were going to kiss and make up and get back together."

Christy smirked. "The exact opposite happened. I pushed Rick even further away. I didn't mean to. It just turned out that way."

"I think that means that deep down you wanted to send him away. You wanted to be done with your relationship with him." Heather looked at Christy for agreement.

"Oh, come on, Heather! You said the same thing when I agreed to go steady with Rick. Remember, in the bathroom at Tracy's house, when I was crying because I wasn't sure I'd done the right thing? You said I agreed to go steady with him because deep down I really wanted to."

"Well? Didn't you?"

"I don't know anymore. I wish I'd never gone out with him."

They paused while another girl slipped in and out of the kitchen, grabbing two sodas.

"Look," Heather said calmly, "I may not always be the best advice-giver, but I know that you need to forget the past and press on toward the future. That's not my stupid advice. It's in the Bible, so I know it's true."

Christy remembered reading that verse before. It was in Philippians. She'd read the short book of Philippians more than any other book in the Bible, except maybe for some of the psalms.

"You're right," Christy told Heather. "I need to look forward. After all, this is the beginning of a new year, right?"

"Right!" Heather said. "And if there is something going on between Rick and Katie, maybe the best thing to do is let it run its natural course. You don't know. They might really be good for each other. They say opposites attract."

"So I've heard," Christy said. "You're right, Heather. When I started going out with Rick, Katie was supportive of me. She didn't really agree with my dating him, and every now and then she'd let me know her opinion. Still, she never stopped treating me like her best friend. I think it might be my turn to be a servant and treat her like my best friend, even though I'm not crazy about her going out with Rick."

"And you can tell her that honestly," Heather added. "Katie didn't hide her opinion of Rick while you were dating him. Tell Katie honestly what you think."

"Okay. I will. Thanks, Heather. You always seem to pop up at the right time. I really appreciate you."

Heather smiled. "Good! Because that's my New Year's resolution—to learn to be the servant of all. I'm glad to have been of service."

Christy felt relieved and almost ready to face the mob in the other room when the kitchen door swung halfway open and the back of Katie's red head appeared.

"And Speed," Rick's voice boomed over the clamor in the other room, "don't forget the mustard this time!"

"Yes, Master," Katie responded, playfully bowing from

the waist. She spun around with a huge grin, which vanished when she spotted Christy.

The two friends locked gazes.

Heather slipped from her seat and said, "You know, Katie, I was just going to make myself a sandwich. Can I make that one for Rick, and you can do something else? Like, say, maybe take my place at the table and help Christy guard all those potato chips?"

"Turkey with everything, including mustard," Katie said, handing the empty plate to Heather. Her eyes still fixed on Christy, Katie headed for the table and said, "I already know what you're going to say."

"No, you don't."

"Yes, I do."

"No, you don't!" Christy said firmly. "You don't know what I'm going to say."

"Okay," Katie said. "Fine. What would you like to say to me?"

"First, I want to apologize. My crack about 'virgin lips' at the parade was stupid, and I'm sorry I said it."

Katie looked away.

"Will you please forgive me?" Christy asked.

"Sure," Katie said, still not looking at Christy. "Don't worry about it."

"There's more," Christy said. "You're my best friend, Katie. We have to stick together."

Heather left with a plate of sandwiches. In the crook of her elbow were two sodas. She gave Christy a thumbs-up sign as she disappeared.

Christy thought she saw a tear fall from Katie's eye onto her lap.

Christy continued. "If you like Rick, that's fine with me. Really. I talked with him this morning, and I feel like things are settled between us. We're just friends. He can be interested in whoever he wants to be interested in. And if that's you, then that's great!"

Katie looked up. There were tears in her eyes. "You really mean that?"

"Yes, I really mean that. It's hard because I don't want you to get your feelings hurt by Rick the way I did. But you and I are different in a lot of ways, and you might be good for him. And he might be good for you. I don't know. I don't want to come between you two. Your friendship means more to me than that."

Katie pressed her lips together and looked like she might be swallowing hard to keep from crying. In a cracked voice, she said, "He kissed me, Christy."

"I know," Christy answered softly.

Katie's green eyes suddenly flared up. "How did you know? Did he tell you? That jerk!"

"No, Rick didn't tell me. I just knew. I know you, Katie, and I could tell. Not at first, but I figured it out."

"It wasn't like you think," Katie began. "I didn't know he was going to do it. It was New Year's, you know. Everyone on the street was having this big party, and at midnight we all counted down, and then all of a sudden Rick kissed me. Everyone was kissing. It was New Year's!"

"Katie, I know. You don't have to explain anything to me. It's fine!"

"But it's not fine! He came at me so fast and strong, I didn't know how to respond. And the worst part is, you were right about the virgin lips, up until last night. I'd never been kissed. And Christy, I've been so jealous of you! I never thought any guy would want to kiss me, least of all someone like Rick."

Christy reached for a napkin on the counter and handed it to Katie to blot her eyes. "You deserve the best guy in the world, Katie."

"Do you know how awful it feels to be kissed for the very first time and think you can't ever, ever tell your best friend?"

"I'm sure my virgin lips comment didn't help."

"It wasn't even that. It was the horrible, mixed-up feelings of wanting to feel so special, because in my wildest dreams I never pictured a guy like Rick ever kissing me, and then he does. And then I felt awful."

"Don't feel awful," Christy said. "Try to see it for what it was. It was your first kiss, and that's a very wonderful thing. It was New Year's, and there's nothing wrong with a quick little kiss at midnight." Christy scanned Katie's face for the truth as she delicately asked, "That's all it was, wasn't it? One little kiss? I mean, you guys didn't sit and make out all night or anything."

"Of course not!" Katie looked offended. "We sat up all night and played cards with the people next to us and told stupid elephant jokes. It was the most fun New Year's I've ever had."

"Then there's no reason to feel bad."

"I didn't until you guys started saying all that stuff about Doug never kissing a girl," Katie said. "But then I think he's a little extreme. I mean, isn't there someplace in the middle where you can kiss every now and then, and it doesn't mean you're a loose woman?"

"I'm not sure. I guess so," Christy said. "I admire Doug though. I think he's going to make his wife feel so special."

"Yeah, on their wedding day she'll feel really special," Katie said. "But I would imagine she'll feel like dog meat all the months they date and during their engagement if he never kisses her. I mean, I don't think there's anything wrong with light kissing to show your affection. It's all the other stuff that I think should be saved for marriage."

"I agree. And you could be right about Doug being a little extreme. For someone like Doug who's such a natural hugger, it does seem he would be a little freer with his kisses. Still, I admire him because he's made a decision and stuck to it. Plus, it seems he and Tracy didn't have much trouble switching from dating to friends because they didn't have any of that physical stuff to try to erase from their relationship."

Katie reached for a potato chip, obviously feeling better. "I admire that," Katie admitted. "I also admire you and Todd, and I don't see how his kissing you a few times made it any easier or harder when he left for Hawaii. That guy is in your heart. I think you'd feel the same way about him even if he'd never kissed you."

"You could be right," Christy said with a sigh.

"Of course I'm right!" Katie said, picking up steam. "If you want to know my opinion, you should take your own advice, Christy, and hold out for a hero, no matter what the state of his lips—virgin or not."

Christy laughed, "Okay, I will, as long as you take the same advice, and you hold out for a hero too. I'm not saying that Rick isn't that hero. He could be. I don't know. But promise me you'll settle for nothing but the best."

Katie's bright smile returned, flashing her agreement and making Christy feel much better.

Remembering her earlier prayer of surrender, Christy thought, *This servant stuff might not be so hard after all. God sure has a way of working everything out when I let Him.*

"Shall we join the party?" Christy asked Katie just as an unusually loud roar rose in the family room.

"Must be a major touchdown." Katie grabbed a bag of chips and fished for a can of soda in the ice chest.

"Listen," Christy said. "That's Marti screaming. She's not much of a football fan. And that sounds like Tracy shouting. They must be having a pillow fight in there."

"Come on!" Katie urged, grabbing a slice of cheese and sticking it in her mouth. "Grab the M&M's, and let's show those guys a real pillow fight!"

Christy grabbed the jumbo bag of M&M's. Just as they were about to exit the kitchen, the door swung open. Uncle Bob stood before them, his face red with excitement. Around his neck he wore a Hawaiian lei made from plumeria that were no longer white but looked brown and travel-worn.

"I think you'd better come out here, Christy," Bob said. "It appears guest number seventeen has just arrived."

14

Counting Stars

"Todd!" Christy screamed, throwing the bag of M&M's into the air and racing past her uncle into the family room. There, encircled by his shocked friends, stood a tanned, sun-bleached blond Todd. Around his neck hung half a dozen crushed leis.

"Todd!" Christy called out again, sprinting across the room. The group of friends stood back, making way for Christy.

When Todd heard her calling his name, he pulled away from Heather's hug around his neck and looked for Christy. Those silver-blue eyes that Christy had dreamed about met her gaze across the room. Todd's face lit up, and he opened his arms to receive her embrace.

Just before Christy reached him, she spotted a white sling on his left arm. With great self-control, she curbed her hug to a modified side squeeze on his right side.

"What happened?" she breathed into his ear, her tears giving way and trickling down his T-shirt.

"It's nothing. Here," he said as she pulled back. "This is for you, *Kilikina.*"

Feeling the warmth of hearing him call her his special Hawaiian version of her name, Christy watched as Todd looped a plumeria and orchid lei off his neck and placed it around her neck, kissing her once on each cheek.

"Aloha, Kilikina," he said softly.

The tropical fragrance of the plumeria set off a cascade of hopes, joys, and dreams in her heart. "You're back" was all she could say.

Todd's gaze left her face and locked on the gold bracelet circling her right wrist. A huge grin spread across his face. He kissed Christy again on her damp cheeks and said, "Yes, I'm back."

"Well? Tell us what happened!" Marti said, eagerly wedging her way into the circle. "Are you through with surfing for a while?"

"Looks like it." Todd raised his sling for emphasis. "Here, Marti. You need one of these."

He began to remove one of his leis for her when Marti protested. "Oh, no, give them to the younger girls first. Look, Katie doesn't have one yet."

Katie shyly stepped forward, and Todd presented her with a lei, kissing her on the cheek in the Hawaiian custom. Christy thought it looked like Katie was blushing. Oddly, Christy didn't feel jealous. She knew Todd's kisses on her cheek, even in front of everyone, were different from what the others received.

The football game was forgotten as everyone started to ask Todd questions.

"Whoa!" Bob said. "Let's let the poor guy catch his breath. Are you hungry, Todd? Come into the kitchen and get yourself something to eat."

The group followed Todd into the kitchen, and he answered questions along the way.

"I arrived this afternoon—an hour ago. Doug's mom said you were all over here. I was on standby out of Honolulu, and they had an opening on a flight early this morning."

Marti handed him a soda as Bob spread some mayonnaise on a French roll. "What do you think, Todd? A little of everything?"

"Sure, that would be great." He sat at the table, popped open his soda, and took a long drink.

"What happened with the surfing?" Doug asked, joining the others crowded around the table.

Christy had managed to slide in and take the empty chair next to Todd. She scooted closer to him so Tracy could wedge in next to her. That made room for Rick to slip a bar stool in on the end.

"Surfing was outrageous," Todd said, a smile lighting up his tanned face.

His skin was so dark. Even in the summer Christy had never seen him this bronzed. And his hair looked almost white. She noticed it was a lot longer than she had ever seen it, especially in the back, where it curled at the nape of his neck. Todd looked different—really good, but different.

"The championships..." Doug said, bringing Todd back from his apparent daydream of the foaming waves. "What happened? Did you drop out?"

"Sort of." He chomped into the huge sandwich Bob placed before him.

Everyone waited while Todd chewed and swallowed.

"Great sandwich," he said to Bob. "*Mahalo.*"

Come on, you surfed-out beach boy! Christy thought. *Stop being so easygoing and tell us what happened.*

"The big ones came in at Waimea last Monday afternoon," Todd began, gulping his soda. "Man, you can't imagine the feeling of standing on a beach you've stood on day after day and looking at an ocean you only played in before. All of a sudden everything is changed. The waves are so outrageous. When they crash on the sand, you can feel it through the bottoms of your feet."

The group bent in closer. Todd took another bite, smiling at each of them with his eyes.

"Nobody went out right away. You have to get psyched up for waves like that. You know it's going to be a wrangle between you and the wave. Only one of you is going to win. You have to make sure it's going to be you before you go out there."

"Is that how you hurt your arm?" Heather asked.

Todd took another bite and another swig of soda. Instead of answering her, he continued the story. "Kimo was ready first. I think Kimo was born ready."

"Now, who is Kimo?" Marti asked.

"The guy I went to school with when I grew up on Maui," Todd answered and took another bite.

Christy filled in for him while he ate. "Todd stayed with Kimo over there. The two of them always wanted to get on the pro surfing circuit, ever since they were kids. Kimo has a house on the North Shore of Oahu."

"More like a shack," Todd said with a laugh. "A lot of times we just slept on the beach because his apartment was so full of cockroaches, centipedes, and geckos. It was hard to sleep at night with all the local critters crawling across my face."

Christy could easily believe Todd had spent the last few months sleeping on the beach and living off the land. He certainly looked like an island boy. Knowing him as she did, she imagined such a life must have been a dream come true for him.

"So Kimo takes this wave on, and he makes it!" Todd's eyes grew wide. "I mean, this is like riding down the side of a four-story building, and he makes it look like nothing. Now we're all psyched. If Kimo can take it, we all want a ride."

"Was this part of the competition?" Tracy asked.

"No, competition wasn't supposed to start until the next day. The waves showed up early. We all paddled out, feeling the spray on our faces. There it is, man! This monstrous wall of pure blue, and we all know it's the day of reckoning."

Christy remembered the cover on the surfing magazine with the huge wave, shooting the surfboards to shore like toy arrows. She also remembered that it was a Monday. Todd said they were surfing the big waves on a Monday. *I wonder if the Monday I prayed for Todd at work was the same Monday he's talking about?*

"Eddie catches it on the outside," Todd continued, "and in seconds he's shot out of the water like a rocket, with his board right behind him. Before I even have a chance to feel the fear, it's my turn, and all of a sudden, I'm on it. I'm riding this monster to shore! I'm riding it!"

"Weren't you afraid that you were going to be killed?" Marti asked. "Didn't you think of that, Todd?"

Todd smiled, "Actually, I thought of Elijah."

"Elijah?" Marti asked. "Who's that? One of your surfing friends?"

"No, you know, Elijah, the great man of God in the book of First Kings. Remember? He stood in a cave on the side of a mountain waiting for the presence of the Lord to pass by. First a wind came that tore the mountain apart, then an earthquake, then a fire. But God's presence wasn't in those natural things. Finally, Elijah heard a gentle whisper, and he knew that was God's voice speaking to him."

Marti blinked and glanced around at the group of teens nodding their understanding. Obviously, Marti had never heard that Bible story before.

"That's what I felt like," Todd said. "There I was, standing in the hollow of this mountain of a wave, everything crashing around me, and then right here," he said, patting his chest, "I felt this total calm, and I knew God was about to do something."

Everyone remained still, waiting for Todd to continue. His expression looked a little glazed as he said, "That's when I saw Kimo's board shooting past me, and I couldn't see Kimo anywhere. So I plant my feet, and I ride this killer wave. It felt like Jell-O under my board. I could bend and turn that wave any way I wanted to, and it carried me like a baby in a basket. I rode it all the way to shore, man! Do you know what I'm saying? A wave like that only comes once in a surfer's life. This was my wave!"

"What happened to the other guys?" Tracy asked.

"When I hit the sand, an ambulance was there, and two lifeguards were pulling Eddie out of the water. They started CPR, and I started to pray and scan the water for Kimo."

"Oh, how awful!" Marti spoke up. "Why did you boys ever do such a foolish thing? You could have all been killed!"

"I'm not afraid of anything in creation," Todd answered. "I know the Creator."

"What happened to Kimo and Eddie?" Christy asked. "Were they all right?"

"Kimo came up spewing chunks, and Eddie came real close to going to hell," Todd said bluntly.

One of his grins spread across his face, and he said, "Then they both got saved, right there on the beach!"

Christy and most of the others knew what Todd meant and expressed their joy and amazement. Marti, however, looked to Bob for an explanation. Bob only shrugged his shoulders.

"The paramedics were able to revive them, you mean?" Marti said.

"Oh yeah, their lives were spared, and I'm sure the paramedics helped out with that. But they both surrendered their lives to God, right there on the beach, with the waves spraying them and a whole crowd of people watching. It was the most incredible thing I've ever seen!"

"These guys you were staying with this whole time weren't Christians?" Doug asked.

"Not when I got there. That's mostly what I did for the last four months—tell them about Jesus. When I left yesterday, five of them had laid down their weapons and surrendered to God. It was like a revival, man!"

Marti looked perturbed, and in an effort to change the subject, said, "You still haven't told us about the competition. How did your tryouts go? That's what you worked so hard for, wasn't it?"

"I didn't go," Todd said, munching on his last bite of sandwich.

"What?"

"Hey, I surfed *my* wave on Monday. I'll never surf another wave like that—ever. Kimo got saved. That's what I went for."

"I don't understand," Marti said, looking to Bob for interpretation.

"What about your arm?" Bob asked, motioning to the sling. Todd held it up and said, "Centipede. I got bit last week and ended up in the hospital. Seems I'm more allergic to centipedes than I am to bees."

Christy jumped in and told everyone how Todd was stung by a bee last summer on his foot and how it swelled up twice its size. "He has to carry around this kit to give himself an injection or else he stops breathing."

"Now I have two kits," Todd joked. "A bee antigen kit and a centipede kit."

"We're all glad you're back and in one piece," Tracy said. "Think you'll stay around for a while?"

"I have to get into school somewhere."

"Where do you want to go?" Doug asked.

"Any place where I can transfer my credits from the University of Hawaii."

"That shouldn't be too hard to find," Doug said. "Have you considered the ever-popular San Diego State?"

"As a matter of fact, I have."

"It just so happens Rick and I lost our roommate at the end of last semester. We're looking for somebody to start paying rent on that empty room. What do you think, Rick? Did we just find our third amigo?"

Christy couldn't believe this was happening. It was freaky enough when Rick moved in with Doug last fall. But the thought of the three of them sharing the same apartment was too much.

Rick sounded casual when he answered, "Sure. He looks harmless enough. But can he cook? Or do we feed him bananas and coconuts off the tree?"

Christy wondered if this living arrangement would really work. Could Rick see Todd as anything but a competitor? Time would tell.

The group around the table started to break up. The guys headed back to the family room to see what had happened in the game. And Doug and most of the girls stuck around to ask Todd questions about Hawaii and what it was like to go to college there.

Christy had felt her stomach grumbling for the last half hour and thought it was the excitement over Todd. But with a glance at the clock, she realized it was dinnertime. All she had eaten since the muffins in Doug's truck that morning were a few potato chips.

As she folded the thin slices of roast beef onto her piece of bread, Christy caught Todd looking at her while still answering questions. She pointed at the food and mouthed the words, "Do you want another?" Todd nodded, and she eagerly set to work making him a masterpiece. It felt so good to have him back.

But Christy really felt like a princess when everyone started to leave. She had already asked Katie and Rick if she could catch a ride home with them, and Rick had agreed nicely, without making any comment about her sitting in the backseat.

Todd came up beside her and asked, "Would it be okay if I drove you home?"

She was about to protest that it was a long drive and he must be tired, but no words formed on her lips. She only smiled at him and nodded her appreciation.

Once they had said good-bye to everyone, gathered Christy's things, and thanked Bob and Marti several times, Todd and Christy stepped into the cool January night. He led her half a block down the street to where he had parked his Volkswagen van, Gus the Bus.

He opened the side door and tossed Christy's suitcase inside. Even the door's sound filled her with memories.

She recalled the first time she had ridden in Gus. Thinking Todd had asked her for a date, she had dressed up. But he had arrived with Gus loaded with people all casually dressed, and off they went to a concert at his church.

Now Todd opened her door, and this time she climbed into an empty but musty-smelling van and adjusted her position so she wouldn't sit on the rip that had begun in the seat.

"Smells like Gus needs a bath," Christy said when Todd got in.

"He's been locked in my dad's garage since I left." Todd started up the engine and drove a few blocks, sniffing the air. "Oh, I think I know what it is," he said, pulling into a gas station and jumping out.

He pulled out a pizza box from under the driver's seat and gingerly lifted the lid with his bandaged arm.

"If that's what I think it is." Christy eyed the box Todd had snapped shut, "I don't want to know how long it's been under there, and I don't want to know what color the fungus is."

Todd jogged over to a trash can and dumped the moldy pizza.

Returning, he said, "It's kind of a shame to waste a perfectly good science experiment like that. Your little brother could have gotten an A with that one."

"Todd, do you know how gross that is?"

He laughed, "You should have looked at it, Christy. You really missed a miracle of nature!"

"I can think of other miracles of nature that I prefer over a five-month-old piece of pizza."

They talked and laughed for the first half hour of their drive down the coast. Somewhere near San Clemente, Todd pulled off the main highway and drove on a bumpy dirt road up the side of a deserted hill. City lights were behind them, but the farther up Todd drove, the darker it became. He coaxed Gus over several huge ruts in the road. Suddenly, the road leveled out, and they were on a flat surface.

"Where are we?" Christy asked.

"You can't see it in the dark, but that's Tressels down there."

"Tressels?"

"Surfing spot," Todd explained. "It's a good one."

This is it? You risked my life to bring me up this road to show me a surfing spot I can't even see in the dark?

"Come on." Todd reached for Christy's jacket in the backseat. "I want to show you something."

Christy got out carefully, unable to see if she was about to step on firm footing or fall off a cliff.

"What way did you go, Todd? I can't see anything."

"I'm up here," he called, and she looked around to see

how his voice could suddenly be coming from above her. "I'm on top of Gus. Come around to the back, and I'll give you a hand up." Christy felt her way along Gus's side. Once she reached the back, she placed her foot on the bumper.

"There's a little thing to put your foot on," Todd instructed. "Good, you've got it. Now give me your hand." He helped her up, and Christy, still unsure of herself, crawled over to where he had spread out her jacket. She sat down and waited for Todd to join her.

He sat down close beside her and said nothing. Christy remembered when they had sat nearly this close on the beach several months ago. It was the morning Todd had announced he was going to Hawaii. He had told her he was selfish to try to hold on to her and wait for her to grow up. And then he put his hand on her forehead and blessed her.

That was a horrible morning. It was basically where they had left off.

Tonight, just like that morning, Todd said nothing. He stared at the stars.

In the past, such silences had made Christy nervous, wondering what he was thinking, wondering if she should say something.

Now she didn't mind the stillness. Todd was here, beside her. They could be together and be silent. The main thing was that they were together.

Christy tilted her head back and looked at the stars.

"Last time I watched the heavens like this was on Christmas Eve," Todd said.

"Really? Me too! We were in the mountains on Christmas Eve, and I sat for a long time and looked at the stars out my bedroom window," Christy told him.

"Imagine," Todd said, "we were looking at the same stars the same night except I was sitting on a beach five thousand miles away. What were you thinking about that night?"

Christy wished she could tell Todd that she had been thinking about him and dreaming about when he would come back. She couldn't lie, so she told him, "I was thinking about Jesus, when He was a baby. I was wondering if He noticed the bright Bethlehem star from His manger."

"Do you know what I was thinking about?" Todd asked. Without waiting for her to answer, he continued, "I was thinking of Abraham."

Christy wished he had said he was thinking about her. Still, why should she be surprised that Todd would think of something spiritual and bizarre on Christmas Eve? *After all, I was thinking about Jesus watching stars from His manger. Oh no, maybe I'm starting to think of everything in spiritual terms like Todd!*

"Remember how God made him a promise?" Todd interrupted her thoughts.

"Wasn't he supposed to become the father of a great nation?" Christy asked.

"Right. Father of a great nation—a guy who had no kids. It seemed like a big joke. Then God told him to step outside his tent one night and said, 'Look up in the heavens, Abe. Count the stars if you can. That's how many descendants you're going to have.'"

"I remember that story," Christy said.

"Well, did you know that after God made that promise, He turned silent? God didn't speak to Abraham again for years and years."

She had always enjoyed Todd's insights into God, and

tonight they seemed even more wonderful with the sky above them ablaze with the very same stars God had pointed out to Abraham that holy night thousands of years ago.

"Don't you see?" Todd said. "God made one promise, and He disappeared. Can you imagine how Abraham felt year after year? He had no kids. He had no proof God had ever talked to him. All he had was a bunch of silent stars up in the sky to keep counting and keep believing that God really did make him a promise."

"That takes a lot of faith," Christy said.

"I want to have faith like that," Todd said, turning to Christy.

His voice became low and serious. "I don't know exactly what it is God has promised me about you, about us, and about what the future holds."

Christy could feel her heart pound faster. She had waited two years for Todd to verbalize some kind of commitment to her. Could this be it?

"I believe that God has planned for us to be friends—close friends. I promised you I'd be your friend forever, Kilikina. I want to have faith like Abraham that whatever that means to God, He'll work it out for us in His time. I want to keep listening for God's voice."

Then, slipping his arm around Christy and drawing her close, Todd said, "For now I guess we keep counting stars."

Christy snuggled her head on Todd's shoulder and whispered softly into the starry night, "Then this is where I want to be. Right beside you, forever counting stars."

BOOK NINE

Seventeen Wishes

To Ethel Herr,
who taught me with her life
that I can never love too much.
And to The Parts of Speech Critique Group,
with wonderful memories of all the years
we sat together with our feet beneath Ethel's table.
I thought we were learning to write.
Now I know we were learning what love looks like
when it's dressed in grace.

1

Act Natural

"Are you sure you told the guys we were coming this afternoon?" redheaded Katie Weldon asked her best friend, Christy Miller, as they ascended the outdoor steps of the apartment building.

"Of course. I told Todd yesterday we would leave right after church. He said it would take about an hour to drive down here," Christy answered, her long legs taking the stairs two at a time. "The directions were really clear. I'm sure this is the place."

"Number twelve is at the end there," Katie pointed out. Then striking her usual athletic stance, she knocked on the door. No one answered. Katie looked into Christy's distinctive blue-green eyes with an unspoken, "Well? What do we do now?"

Christy bit her lower lip and scanned the piece of paper in her hand. "I know this is right. Knock again. Louder."

Katie pounded her fist on the door and called out, "Hey, Rick, Doug, Todd. We're here!"

Still no answer.

Christy brushed her nutmeg-brown hair off her forehead and cautiously peered in a window. From what she could see, no one was inside. "What should we do?"

"They're probably playing a joke on us. They know what a big deal it was for you to talk your parents into letting you come to San Diego. They're probably trying to freak us out. You know, the 'big college guys teasing the little high school girls' trick."

Katie sounded so confident of her answer that Christy almost believed her. But then Katie usually sounded confident.

"Should we find a phone and try to call them?" Christy suggested.

"Lower your voice," Katie warned. "If they're in there, they can hear what you're saying."

"I don't think they're here. Maybe they ran to the store or something." Christy looked around.

Below them she noticed a cement courtyard with a swimming pool surrounded by lounge chairs. "Why don't we go down by the pool and wait for them?"

Katie surveyed the situation, her bright green eyes scanning the apartment complex for any sign of life. "Doesn't it seem weird to you," she whispered, "that for a place that's supposed to be crawling with college students, nobody's around?"

Christy was starting to get the heebie-jeebies. "Come on. Let's go down by the pool. At least we won't look so obviously lost standing by their door with our luggage."

"Oh yeah, we'll look real natural lounging around the pool wearing jeans and clutching our luggage. If anyone from these other apartments sees us, they'll probably think we're homeless and call the police," Katie sputtered as she followed Christy down the stairs to the pool.

"Then let's put our stuff back in the car."

"Good idea. I'm starting to feel like an orphan. Why would they ditch us like this? You'd think one of them could manage to leave a note or something."

The two girls stood at the trunk of Katie's car while she fished for her keys. "Did I give you my keys?"

"Very funny," Christy said. "Of course I don't have your keys. Stop goofing around and open the trunk."

"I can't find them."

Christy let out a sigh. "Did you leave them in the car?"

They both peered in the front window and at the same time noticed the keys dangling from the ignition. Of course, all the doors were locked.

"Good, Katie. Real swift! Now what are we supposed to do?" Christy snapped.

"Hey, relax, will you? I've done this before. All I need is a coat hanger."

"And where are we supposed to find a coat hanger?"

"Let's try the Dumpster over there."

She opened the gates to the garbage area and began to rummage through trash bags.

Christy stood nervously beside the car, guarding their gear. Now they really looked like a couple of bums with Katie sifting through the trash.

This was supposed to be a nice, simple Memorial Day weekend in San Diego to visit the guys' God-Lovers Bible study and to have a fun trip to the zoo. It's turning into a disaster!

"Found one!" Katie lifted her prized coat hanger into the air. A rotten banana peel clung to her arm.

"Nice work," Christy said. "Now why don't you try to leave the rest of the garbage in the Dumpster?"

Katie beamed a victory smile as she shook off the banana peel and straightened out the hanger. She cheerfully gave Christy a rundown of the last time she had locked her keys in the car.

"I was at work, and I had to go in the mall to find a clothing store that would give me a hanger. I figured out that time how to make the loop on the end just right so it'll catch on the knob there. Good thing my car is so old. Your car doesn't have locks like this. We'd be stuck if it was your car."

Christy kept glancing around, aware that now they looked like homeless, garbage-digging hoboes and car thieves.

"Can you hurry it up, Katie?"

"I almost have it." She gingerly wedged the hanger between the window and door frame,then maneuvered the loop over the lock button. Her tongue stuck out slightly, and she squinted her eyes.

Christy thought Katie looked like she was playing one of those games at the video arcade where the player has to manipulate a metal claw inside a glass cage to pick up a small stuffed animal. Christy could never win that game. She had ceased wasting her quarters on it long ago.

Not Katie. She was always up for a challenge. Anytime, anywhere.

"Almost," Katie breathed between clenched teeth as the two girls pressed their faces against the car window, pleading with the loop to connect with the black peg.

"Hey!" a loud voice called out behind them.

They jumped and spun around. They were surprised to see that the big voice belonged to a petite Asian girl.

"Are you Todd's friends?"

She had a bag of groceries in her arms and apparently had arrived on foot, which explained why they hadn't heard her approach. Her long, silky black hair hung over her shoulders, and she peered at them with a delicate smile.

"Yes!" Christy said eagerly. Then feeling obligated to explain what they were doing, she quickly added, "We locked the keys in the car, and we're trying to get them out."

Katie continued recounting their adventure. "We went to the guys' apartment, but no one was there. We thought maybe they were playing a trick on us, which would be typical of those guys, but they never jumped out and said 'Boo,' so we thought we would put our stuff back in the car."

The girl listened as they rattled on with their nervous explanations.

"That's when we found out the keys were locked in the car," Christy said.

Then becoming aware of how silly they must sound, like two inexperienced high school girls babbling on to this independent college woman, Christy lowered the pitch of her voice and tried to sound calm. "So do you know where the guys are?"

"At the hospital."

Christy felt like a huge fist had just reached into her chest and squeezed the air out of her lungs. She found just enough breath to ask, "Is it Todd? Is he okay?"

"It was Rick," the girl replied.

The fist released her lungs, and she let out a wobbly sigh.

"Rick?" Katie said, looking like the invisible fist had just grabbed her by the heart. "Is he okay? What happened?"

"I'm sure he'll be fine. He hurt his arm when the guys were in the pool this afternoon. They were doing handsprings off the diving board, and Rick had some kind of competition going. He twisted his arm the wrong way."

"Sounds like Rick," Christy said under her breath.

"We'd better go to the hospital," Katie said, urgently returning to her mission of retrieving the car keys. "Do you know how to get there?"

"I don't think it would help much for you to go. Todd and Doug took him more than an hour ago. I imagine they'll be back before you could get to the hospital."

"Got it!" Katie popped the door open and reached for the keys. "Are you sure we shouldn't go?"

"I guess you could if you wanted. I think they'll be back any minute though. Or you could stay here and help me with dinner. I told the guys I'd have a spaghetti feast for them when they came back."

Christy turned to Katie, who still looked worried, and said, "The way this afternoon has been, I don't think you and I should be driving around San Diego trying to find the hospital. It seems to me we should stay here and help..." She paused, realizing she didn't know the girl's name.

"I'm Stephanie," the girl filled in the blank for her. "And you must be Christy. I've heard a lot about you."

Christy felt her cheeks warming. "And this is Katie."

"Did you happen to hear anything about me, say, from Rick maybe?" Katie asked.

Stephanie smiled a delicate, mysterious smile. Her face reminded Christy of a soft pink apple blossom.

"Rick has lots to say about a lot of things. Perhaps he has mentioned you."

Christy glanced at Katie, concerned about the way her friend might take such an answer. A bit of a relationship had sprouted between Rick and Katie at the Rose Parade on New Year's Day, but that was five months ago. Katie had tried to further the relationship since then, but nothing had brought Rick back into her life. This weekend was designed to be the test. Christy could tell it hurt Katie that Rick hadn't spoken of her the way Todd had talked about Christy. But then Christy and Todd had almost two years of relationship history to draw from.

"I guess we'll stay then," Katie decided, locking the door again, this time with the keys in her hand.

"Bring up your suitcases," Stephanie said. "You're both staying with me tonight. I'm in number ten. Two doors down from the nuthouse."

"Thanks for letting us sleep at your place," Christy said. "Todd told me he would make arrangements with one of the girls in the complex. I'm just glad you're the first one we ran into!"

"It's pretty quiet around here," Stephanie explained as they headed for her place. "School was out more than a week ago, and almost everyone has gone home for the summer. I work at the same restaurant as the guys. The Blue Parachute. Did they tell you about it?"

Christy nodded. Katie looked a little left out.

Stephanie unlocked her apartment door. "We all agreed when we took the jobs to stay until June so the restaurant could switch over to its summer help. Here we are," she announced, opening the door and revealing a tidy, nicely decorated apartment.

"Welcome to my humble home. Please make yourselves

comfortable. My roommate left yesterday, so the empty room is all yours."

Christy and Katie lugged their bags into the bedroom on the right. The only thing in the room was a standing lamp in the corner.

"Todd didn't tell me we were supposed to bring sleeping bags," Christy whispered.

"I'll ask Rick if I can borrow his," Katie said. "Maybe Stephanie has one too."

Soft classical music floated into their room, and the girls followed its sound back to the living room where Stephanie had turned on the stereo.

"This is a really cute apartment." Christy surveyed the blue and white striped futon couch, the hanging lamps covered with blue and peach flowered fabric, and the variety of intriguing pictures on the walls.

One of the larger pictures caught Christy's eye. A young woman was wearing a long, pink, lacy dress, with her hair puffed on top of her head like a cloud. From the surrounding garden scenery, it looked like summer, and the woman was seated on a bench, wistfully looking out to the ocean.

"I love this picture!" Christy said.

The scene stirred something inside her. It was the hint of another time and place. A time when women were praised for looking feminine and being dreamers. A place for tea parties and parasols and wearing long, white gloves for a stroll in the garden.

I think I was born a hundred years too late.

"Thanks," Stephanie called out from the kitchen, where she was unloading her groceries. "Would you two like something to drink? Have you ever had iced ginseng tea?"

The two girls made a face at each other and cautiously approached the kitchen.

"Whatever you have is fine," Christy said graciously.

"Do you happen to have any Coke? Pepsi?" Katie ventured.

"I don't," Stephanie said. "But I'm sure the guys do. I have a key to their place. Do you want to go over and get some?"

"Are you sure it's okay?" Katie asked.

"I'm sure they won't mind. They gave me the key because they kept locking themselves out. Sometimes those guys seem like Peter Pan and the Lost Boys, and they think I'm their Wendy."

Christy liked Stephanie. She seemed awfully sweet. There was an international flair about her, and she was intriguing.

"Come on," Katie said. "Let's go raid the guys' refrigerator. This ought to be fun."

Stephanie handed them the key. As Christy turned it in the guys' door, she looked over her shoulder to make sure they hadn't returned.

"Doesn't this feel sneaky to you?" she asked Katie.

"Yeah, it's fun! Let's freeze their underwear or something."

"Katie!"

"What? It was only a suggestion."

"Where do you come up with these things?" Christy asked as the door opened, and the two of them glanced around the room. "What a mess!" Christy said under her breath.

The two spies entered slowly and took in the full spectrum. To their right, in the kitchen area, were folding chairs at a card table with a box of sugary cereal in the middle. Surrounding the box were three bowls with puddles of pink soured milk from the dissolved cereal. A half-full bottle of generic cola stood next to the cereal box.

"I feel like Goldilocks," Christy whispered.

"Me too," Katie giggled. "Let's see where the three bears sleep."

"Katie!"

"I'm not going to steal their underwear, I promise. I was only kidding. Come on. I'm curious."

They stuck close together as they made their way through the living room, which hosted a long brown couch, an overstuffed plaid chair, a small TV balanced precariously on a cement block bookcase, and an old trunk covered with surfing magazines, which served as a coffee table in the center of the room.

"Very stylish," Katie quipped. "It's the ever popular 'early slob' decor."

Christy noticed Todd's orange surfboard in the corner, serving as a coat rack at the moment.

"This must be Rick and Doug's room." Katie peeked around the half-opened door on the right.

Two unmade beds hugged the walls. The floor between the beds was covered with clothes, books, empty potato chips bags, and a neon yellow Frisbee. A bike was tucked behind the door, and a guitar was propped up in the corner with a Padres baseball cap balanced on top.

"How can you tell?" Christy asked.

"Easy. The guitar is Doug's, and the bike is Rick's."

"Todd plays the guitar too."

"This doesn't look like Todd. Come on. Let's see what the room of a surf rat looks like."

Christy felt hesitant to follow Katie. Doug and Rick were two of the neatest dressers she knew. If they could live in such a messy room and appear so tidy in public, then what would "Mr. Casual's" room look like?

"Christy," Katie called from the bedroom on the right, "you have to see this!"

Christy looked into Todd's room but couldn't believe what she saw.

The room was immaculate.

"Do you really think this is Todd's room?" she whispered.

"What's that?" Katie pointed to a peculiar box in the center of the room. Standing only a few inches up from the floor, the large, wooden-framed box was covered with a rippled sheet and had a neatly folded blanket at one end.

"It's too small to be a water bed."

Katie poked it, and the substance under the sheet gave way. "It feels like..." She pulled back the corner of the sheet and announced, "It is. It's sand. I don't believe it!"

Christy joined in the examination and felt Todd's unique sand mattress.

Katie started to laugh. "Only Todd would sleep in a giant kitty litter box!"

"I'll bet it's really comfortable," Christy said, quickly coming to his defense. "After sleeping out on the Hawaiian beach while he was in the surfing competition, he's probably more comfortable in the sand than on a mattress."

Katie turned to Christy and smiled, her bright green eyes doing a merry dance. "Like I said, only Todd."

Christy noticed a grouping of pictures and posters on the wall behind the bed. In the center was a poster of a waterfall on Maui where Todd, Christy, her friend Paula, and her little brother, David, had spent a day last summer. The three other posters were surfing shots. A half-dozen photographs surrounded the posters, all stuck to the wall with thumbtacks.

"They're all of you," Katie said. "Look at that. All these pictures are of you."

Christy was amazed. Over the years she had sent Todd a picture here or there, but she never would have guessed he would save them or would create a place of honor for them.

"Isn't that your picture from the eighth grade?" Katie pointed to a wallet-size picture at the top.

"Oh no, look at that! It's from ninth grade. That is such a pathetic picture. I must have sent that to him right after we met. That's about the time he left Newport Beach and went to live with his mom in Florida."

Katie took a close look at the small photo and then looked at Christy. "May I just say you've improved over the years?"

Christy laughed at the little-girl expression on her face in the picture. Her hair was long then, almost to her waist, and hung straight down in an uncomplimentary fashion.

"This one must be tenth grade," Katie said. "That's when I met you, when you moved to Escondido. Look how different you looked with short hair! It was too short then, if you ask me. I like the way you wear your hair now."

Christy had been growing her hair out ever since she had let her aunt talk her into whacking it all off the summer before her sophomore year. Now, at the end of her junior year, it was past her shoulders.

"I can't believe Todd has all these pictures. I don't even remember sending some of them to him," Christy said. "I do remember this one though." She pointed to a snapshot of the two of them at the Hawaiian waterfall in the poster.

"Listen," Katie said. "Is that them coming?"

Christy heard the thump of heavy footsteps coming down the corridor outside the apartment. They both heard loud, male voices approaching.

"Do you think they'll go to Stephanie's first?" Christy asked.

"Why? They don't know we're here. It sounds like they're coming inside. Quick, hide!" Katie dove for Todd's closet. The minute she opened it, a mound of clothes and junk tumbled out, showering her with damp swimming trunks and a sprinkling of sand.

"Ewww!"

"Shhh," Christy said. "They're coming in!"

Katie quickly stuffed the clothes back into the closet and whispered, "What should we do?"

"Act natural!" Christy stood perfectly still in the middle of Todd's room, her hands behind her back and a nervous grin pasted on her face.

They could hear the front door of the apartment open. One of the guys said, "Hey, it was unlocked. Is somebody here?"

"What should we say?" Katie asked under her breath. She took her place by Christy's side, looking like her mirror image, with hands behind her back and a goofy grin frozen on her face.

Christy could tell by the pounding footsteps that the three bears were about to discover them. There was no way to look anything other than stupid.

"Katie, think of something. Quick!"

2

Mr. Gizmo

As Christy and Katie heard the guys coming down the hallway toward Todd's bedroom, Katie, quick thinker that she was, shouted, "Surprise!"

Christy quickly joined in. "Surprise!"

She spotted Todd's screaming silver-blue eyes opened wide in surprise. He started to laugh, and in two giant steps, he had his arms around Christy. She hugged him back, her ear pressed against his chest where his deep laugh rumbled. She wondered if he could feel her heart about to pound out of her chest.

"You sure surprised us!" Todd said, giving Katie a quick hug. He ran his fingers through his bleached blond hair.

Doug and Rick followed with hugs for both the girls. There were lots of explanations and laughter and lots of sympathy, especially on Katie's part, when they saw the bandage around Rick's sprained wrist.

"So Stephanie knows you're here?" Doug asked. He stood a little taller than Todd, but not as tall as Rick.

Seeing the three of them all lined up, Christy realized Rick was the most striking of the three. His dark, wavy hair, deep brown eyes, and athletic build had been the obsession of many girls at her high school last year, including her. No wonder Katie couldn't get Rick out of her mind. In any room, any situation, his looks commanded full attention.

If Christy hadn't dated Rick for a short time and experienced some of the not-so-pleasant sides of his personality, she too might have been staring at him now the way Katie was.

As far as Christy was concerned, she would choose Todd or Doug over Rick any day. Katie, she knew, would have to come to her own conclusion on that, just as Christy had.

"We were supposed to be raiding your refrigerator for soda," Katie explained, her blunt-cut copper hair swishing dramatically as she looked to Christy for support and then back at the guys. "Only we thought we would do a little room inspection first. We were pleased to find your kitty litter box so nice and clean. Only one question though. Where's the cat?"

Doug started to laugh at Katie, who was pointing to Todd's bed as though she were a game show model showing off the showcase of prizes.

Doug had a clean-cut appearance, with his sandy blond hair that always looked like he'd just had it cut. He was good-looking in a boyish way and appeared younger than his twenty years. The most outgoing of the three guys, Doug was known for his hugs, which he gave out generously.

"Try it," Todd challenged Katie. "Lie on it and see how it feels."

Katie, ever the good sport, lay down on the sand bed as they all watched. She wiggled her back until she had formed the perfect support.

Folding her hands over her stomach, she said, "Okay,

I'm convinced. This is the perfect bed. Did you invent this, Todd?"

"Not much to invent," he said. "A couple of boards, a couple of sandbags, and a blanket. I don't think the patent office would recognize it as a true invention."

"You didn't go in our room, did you?" Doug asked.

Katie and Christy exchanged glances.

Christy said, "We'll never tell!"

"I told you we should have picked up," Doug said to Rick out of the side of his mouth. "Todd had the right idea."

"What do you mean?" Rick said. "Todd just threw everything in his closet."

"We could have done that too," Doug said with a smile. "Might have impressed them."

"If I'm going to impress anyone," Rick said confidently, "it's going to be with my other attributes. Not with my housekeeping skills."

"Obviously," Katie said under her breath.

"I heard that," Rick said.

Christy watched carefully to see if anything might be starting up between the two of them.

"And which of your fine attributes are you going to start with?" Katie teased, getting up from the sand bed. "Perhaps your wonderfully coordinated skills on the diving board?"

"No," Rick countered quickly. "My skill at keeping girls off balance." As he said it, he gently pushed Katie with his good hand so that she toppled back into the sand pit.

Katie gave Rick a firm look of indignation, but Christy could tell Katie was feeling honored to have been the object of Rick's teasing.

"Todd," Katie asked from where her bottom was planted in the sand, "may I show your roommate a handful of your bed? In his face?"

"It's up to you," Todd said. "I'm going to see if Stephanie needs any help with that spaghetti."

"I'll join you," Christy said.

"I'm right behind you," Doug echoed. "What did you need from our fridge? Drinks and what else?"

Christy and Doug followed Todd to the kitchen, leaving Katie and Rick alone. She could hear Katie's muffled voice teasing Rick and then laughter. So far, so good.

Doug opened the old gold-colored refrigerator and pulled out a couple two-liter bottles of soda. The rest of the refrigerator's contents looked like they might fit nicely into the penicillin family of molds.

"Do you guys ever clean out this thing?" Christy ventured.

"Todd did once, didn't you, Todd? Couple of weeks ago, I think," Doug said. "We're all moving out next week. We'll dump everything then."

Todd was standing by the card table, shaking the box of cereal and looking inside. "Did you guys find the toy yet?"

"Don't think so," Doug said. "What is it this time?"

"Some kind of plastic gizmo that walks down windows," Todd said, his face brightening as he stuck his hand inside.

Christy could tell by the way his one dimple appeared on his right cheek that he had found the treasure and was pretty pleased with himself.

"Check it out." Todd tore the clear wrapper from the gizmo with his teeth and tossed the critter against the window. "It's Mr. Gizmo!"

Sure enough, Mr. Gizmo walked. The first row of tiny suction cups on its feet stuck to the smooth window for a moment and then released as the next row hung tight. It gave the appearance of "walking" down the glass.

"Cool," Todd said, sticking the treasure in the pocket of his shorts. "You two ready to go?"

"We're ready," Rick answered, appearing in the living room with Katie in a headlock under his good arm. With his bandaged hand he pinched her cheek.

Christy would have been furious if Rick had ever treated her like that. Katie gave every indication she was in heaven. *Maybe they are good for each other.*

The group filed out the door, and Christy noticed a large mayonnaise jar half filled with coins on a shelf. Doug had told her about that jar. The guys used it to collect money for a young boy they supported in Kenya. Christy had seen a letter that ten-year-old Joab had written to Doug and the guys. She also knew Doug carried a picture of Joab in his wallet and showed it around as if he were the proud big brother.

"Guess what, Doug?" Christy said as Todd locked the door and they followed Rick and his crutch, Katie, down the corridor. "I wrote to the organization that set you up as a sponsor for Joab. My family and I adopted a four-year-old girl from Brazil. Her name is Anna Maria. I never thanked you for giving me the information. So thanks."

"Awesome!" Doug slipped his arm around Christy and gave her a quick Doug-hug. "Isn't it amazing how little it takes to feed and clothe those kids?"

"Steph," Rick called out at the door of apartment number

ten, "open up! It's the Rickster. I've come to collect your sympathy."

"Yeah, right," Stephanie said, opening the door and giving Rick a playfully disgusted look. "Like I'd ever give you anything, least of all sympathy."

Rick let go of Katie and stepped into the apartment, continuing his lively flirtation with Stephanie as if Katie didn't exist.

"Aren't you going to kiss it and make it better?" Rick held out his sore paw to her with a pout on his handsome face.

"When pigs fly!" Stephanie tossed back at him.

Rick then wrapped his good arm around Stephanie's shoulders and walked into the living room, still pleading for her sympathy.

Oh no, look out, Katie! When you put your heart out there on the edge of the wall, it doesn't take much for it to do the ol' Humpty Dumpty crash.

Katie seemed fine. She went in the kitchen and stirred the pot of spaghetti sauce as if she had been asked to do so. Christy had never admired her resiliency more than she did at that moment.

"We brought some sodas," Doug said, offering the two bottles for Stephanie to see before he placed them on the counter.

"Want me to finish making this garlic bread?" Todd picked up a knife and sliced the loaf of French bread where Stephanie had left off.

"Sure," Stephanie said, turning her back to Rick and joining them in the kitchen. "Christy, could you help me get a salad going?"

Todd, Stephanie, Christy, and Katie all worked

together in the narrow kitchen while Doug and Rick planted themselves on the sofa and turned on the TV.

"Their home away from home—in front of my TV," Stephanie said to Christy, motioning to Rick and Doug over her shoulder. "If you ever want to make sure you have lots of attention from guys in your apartment complex, all you have to do is be the only one who gets cable."

"I'll remember that." Katie helped Todd wrap the pungent garlic bread in foil. Katie waved her hand above the bread to clear the strong aroma and asked sarcastically, "Are you sure you used enough garlic, Todd?"

"It's good that way. You'll see. It's my secret recipe. Butter, mayonnaise, and lots of garlic."

"And only three thousand calories a slice," Stephanie said with a wink as she turned on the oven and handed Katie a cookie sheet for the bread. "It's good. Trust me. Todd's made it before. That's why the kitchen wallpaper is starting to peel."

Even though she knew Stephanie was kidding, Christy glanced at the wallpaper. There was nothing wrong with it. Every little peach heart stood in place.

Christy liked the way Stephanie used lots of hearts in decorating the kitchen. She especially liked the heart-shaped basket hanging on a nail above the sink. Peach ribbons were strung through the sides with a bunch of silk flowers attached at the bottom.

Christy liked colorful decor like that and thought how fun it would be to decorate her own apartment some day.

When they all sat down to eat a little while later, she decided one day she would have straight-back wooden chairs with padded cushions at her kitchen table, just like

Stephanie's. And she would serve her guests on blue and white dishes, just like Stephanie.

Todd was right. The bread was delicious, as was the spaghetti and everything else. The conversation around the tightly packed table remained lively. Everything about this gathering made Christy feel grown-up and included in her circle of college friends. It felt completely different from being a sixteen-year-old living at home with her parents and eleven-year-old brother.

Oh no, Christy suddenly remembered. *I promised I would call home as soon as we arrived!*

"May I use your phone?" she quietly asked Stephanie.

"Sure. There's one in my bedroom."

Christy slipped into Stephanie's room and closed the door. She felt awful for being so forgetful.

Mom answered, and Christy quickly explained about the guys not being there, the keys being locked in the car, meeting Stephanie, and Rick's sprained wrist. When she finished, there was an uncomfortable pause on the other end.

"Honest, Mom, that's what happened, and that's why I didn't think to call."

"Oh, I believe you," Christy's mother answered. "It's just that with all that has gone on during the last few hours, I'm not sure I'm ready for all the adventures you may face between now and when you come home tomorrow night."

"Mom," Christy tried her best to sound mature and responsible, "there's nothing to worry about. I'm really sorry I didn't call sooner. Everything is fine, and I'm sure the rest of our visit will be uneventful. I'll call you tomorrow before we leave to drive home. I really appreciate you and Dad letting me spend time with my friends like this."

"Well, have a good time and remember all the things we talked about."

"I will, Mom. Don't worry. I'll be fine."

Christy sat for a moment on the edge of Stephanie's bed after she hung up. She couldn't help feeling a little like a baby in this group where all of them were living on their own except Katie and her. Katie's parents not only let her go on this trip, but they also gave her the car with a full tank of gas and told her to have fun. Katie didn't have to check in with them.

Christy felt fully aware of that ever-present invisible rope that connected her to her parents. The older she became, the more rope they let out and the more they encouraged her to go exploring on independent experiences like this overnight trip to San Diego. Still, that invisible rope kept her anchored to them. In situations like this, when she had to check in, the rope seemed to pull awfully tight, right around her stomach.

Then she had a thought that was even more sobering. *Really soon I'm going to be eighteen. I'll be in college and living on my own like Stephanie. What will it feel like for that rope to be cut?*

Christy decided to be grateful for the linkage while she had it. She felt secure, knowing that the invisible rope to her parents was intact and taut. It would be gone soon enough.

Katie doesn't seem to have any ropes attached to her, Christy thought. *That must feel scary. Like you wouldn't know for sure if someone is going to be there to pull you in if you go too far.*

Joining the others, Christy pitched in and helped to clear the table and dry the dishes. Doug washed and Todd put them away.

"Look how lovely my hands are after using this new dish soap!" Doug said in a high-pitched voice, holding up his bubble-covered hands.

"How's this for squeaky clean?" Doug rubbed his finger over the back of one of his plates, continuing to act out his commercial.

"Wait, I have an idea." Todd snatched the plate Christy was drying. He pulled Mr. Gizmo from his pocket and threw it on the back of the plate. Mr. Gizmo started to walk down the plate.

Doug whistled his applause. "Good show, good show! Now try it on the refrigerator."

Todd did, and it worked again.

More cheers and whistles came from Doug, and Christy joined him with eager applause.

"The oven door," Doug challenged.

Mr. Gizmo met the challenge.

"Now the true test—can he walk on the ceiling?"

Todd tossed Mr. Gizmo onto the ceiling.

Fwaaap! He stuck perfectly, but he didn't walk. He didn't move at all.

"Boo! Hiss!" Doug appraised the immobile Mr. Gizmo.

"What are you guys doing in there?" Stephanie called from the living room.

"It's the Mr. Gizmo Olympics," Doug said. "And our favorite contender just experienced a major setback."

"I'll get it down," Todd offered, pulling over one of Stephanie's chairs with the flowered cushions.

"Don't stand on that," Christy scolded. "It's too nice to stand on."

"What do you suggest?" Doug asked. "Waiting for gravity to keep its law?"

Christy had an idea. She twirled the dish towel in her hand and snapped it toward the ceiling, just missing Mr. Gizmo. But the towel gave off a loud, cracking sound.

"Good thinking." Doug snatched another towel from the handle of the refrigerator and snapped it in the air. "Take *that,* you Mr. Gizmo, you!"

"You missed," Todd told him, reaching for a towel and giving it a try.

Before Christy knew what was happening, she was stuck in the middle of a towel-snapping war between Doug and Todd.

"Whoa! Wait a minute! How did I get between you guys?" she cried out, trying to break loose from the circle. It was no use. They had her surrounded.

Christy began to snap them back, but they were faster and more experienced at this. On impulse, she scooped both her hands into the bountiful soap bubbles in the sink. With a mound of the white fluff, she glanced at Doug and then at Todd.

"Okay, who's going to get it first?"

Before she could decide which one to "suds," Doug slid his hand under hers and pushed the whole mound into her face. Some of it went up her nose.

Christy let out a squeal and wiped the suds from her eyes in time to see Doug and Todd giving each other a snap of their towels over her head. Just as their towels came down, so did Mr. Gizmo—right on the top of Christy's head.

They all started laughing, and Todd grabbed the toy out of her hair.

Just then someone knocked on the door. As Christy blew bubbles out of her nose, seven college students entered the apartment and greeted everyone. Christy reached for the towel in Doug's hand and finished mopping up, feeling embarrassed.

"You okay?" Doug asked, pulling her over to the corner of the kitchen.

"I think so," Christy said, looking up at him. "Did I get it all?"

"Here." Doug took the towel and gently wiped under the corner of her right eye. He then smoothed down the top of her hair where Mr. Gizmo had landed.

"Good as new," he announced. Taking her by the hand, he said, "Don't be shy. Come meet the rest of the God-Lovers."

Christy smiled and greeted the three girls and four guys who had just arrived. She tried to think of a way to remember all their names.

There was another knock on the door, and two more girls entered. One of them was really outgoing as well as gorgeous. She went right to Rick and asked about his bandaged wrist. She soon made up for the lack of sympathy Rick had received from the rest of them.

Everyone found a seat on the floor or by pulling over one of the kitchen chairs. No one said it was time to start. They all sort of fell into place as if this was a familiar habit for all of them. Christy noticed that Todd had disappeared, and she wasn't sure where to sit. Katie was right next to Rick on the couch with the blonde on his other side and her friend next to her. Doug seemed to be in charge. Stephanie was on the floor talking with one of the guys.

Christy slipped into an open spot by the wall near the front. A lifetime of familiar "left out" feelings joined her in the corner and kept her company. As long as she was wrapped up in those feelings, she couldn't make the effort to start chatting with anyone. She was the visitor. They should greet her. No one did.

Todd came back in with his guitar and Doug's. The two of them sat on chairs in front of the TV and took a few minutes to tune their instruments.

Three more girls showed up, and one of them wedged in next to Christy.

"Hi, I'm Beth," she said.

"I'm Christy."

"Nice to meet you. Are you visiting?"

"Yes," was all Christy could explain before Doug spoke up.

"I'm glad you guys are all here tonight," he said. "As you know, most of the God-Lovers have taken off for the summer. This is our last time together until next fall. I thought it would be good if we spent some time thanking God for the awesome stuff He's done in our lives this past year."

Todd started to play his guitar, and Doug joined him in strumming Rich Mullins's song "Our God Is an Awesome God." Somehow Christy knew that would be Doug's favorite song since *awesome* was his favorite word.

She knew the song and sang along with the others, feeling a little amazed that so many college students were sitting there, openly singing their hearts out to God. One guy toward the front had his eyes closed and both arms slightly lifted in a gesture of praise to God.

Christy couldn't explain it, but somehow after that first song and then listening to Todd open in prayer, she felt all her defenses dissolve. The people in this room were Christians. All of them seemed to be there to worship God. These college students were some of her brothers and sisters in Christ. Even if she never saw them again, she would spend eternity with them in heaven. She felt included in God's family.

Doug started to strum the next song, which Christy didn't know. Instead of feeling left out, she quietly closed her eyes and bowed her head to listen while everyone else sang.

Eyes have not seen. Ears have not heard.
Neither has it entered into the heart of man
The things God has planned
For those who love Him.

For two hours they sang and prayed and talked about what was going on in their lives. Then Doug read some Bible verses and talked about waiting on God and trusting Him for the future. Everyone seemed to get into what he had to say, especially since most of them were taking off in different directions the next week. Not many of them knew what the future held.

After Todd closed in prayer, everyone started to visit with each other. Christy, feeling warmed by the sweet spirit of the group, walked around and met everyone she hadn't been introduced to before. She had never been this outgoing, and to her surprise, it wasn't that hard.

"Do you want to come out to coffee with us?" Beth

asked. "A bunch of us are going. Your friend Katie said she would come, and I'm sure Stephanie is coming."

All Christy's warm feelings disappeared. One of her agreements with her parents for this trip was that she wouldn't go out after dark. It seemed like such a silly rule now. If her parents had been there, they would have seen how responsible all these people were.

Still, if she went without asking, she would be breaking her agreement. Maybe she could call and explain the situation, and they would understand and give her permission to go.

Christy glanced at the clock on the kitchen wall: 9:45. She knew her parents were probably in bed. Her dad worked at a dairy and had to be up early every morning. He usually went to bed before she did. It would *not* be good to call and wake him to ask a favor like this. Still, if she didn't ask...

"Come on, Christy. We're going to the Blue Parachute," Katie said enthusiastically. "Grab your purse and let's go."

Todd was talking to some people in the kitchen. It would help if she knew whether or not he was going.

"Ready?" Doug asked, coming alongside her. "We're all going. You want to ride with Todd or me?"

"I...I'm not sure," Christy said. She hated having to make decisions like this. Especially when she knew that either way she would come up the loser. Which was the worse to lose? Her friends' approval or her parents' trust?

3

Elephants, Monkeys, and Snakes

"*Okay, I'll go.*" Christy regretted her impulsive words the minute she said them.

My parents will never know. I won't tell them. We're only going to a restaurant. What could happen? They would understand if they met these guys.

"I have room," Todd called out to Doug and Christy, "if you both want to ride with me. Stephanie is going with me."

Christy numbly followed the rest of the group down to the parking lot and watched Katie laugh and joke with Rick on their way to his classic red Mustang. She was one of three girls riding with Rick.

Todd opened the side door of his old Volkswagen bus called Gus. Glancing at Christy, he asked, "Are you okay?"

"Sure," she answered quickly, certain her guilt showed all over her face. She never had been good at sneaking around. She was especially bad at lying.

Doug moved in for a closer look into Christy's eyes. "No, you're not," he said. "Something's wrong. What is it, Christy?"

"It's just that I had an agreement with my parents that I

wouldn't go out after dark once Katie and I got here. I know if they were here, it would be different. They would let me go."

"But they're not here," Todd said, sliding shut the van's door.

"We'll stay too," Doug said.

"I have stuff to make banana splits," Stephanie said. "Not enough for the whole group, but it should be enough for the four of us."

"You guys don't have to stay," Christy said. "I'll stay, and you guys go."

"Why would we?" Todd asked.

"Don't worry about it, Christy," Stephanie said. "These guys don't care where they go as long as food is involved. It'll give us a chance to talk, and that will be nice."

Todd flagged down Rick, who was about to peel out of the parking lot. He jogged over to Rick's window and, bending down, explained the situation to Rick. Christy could feel Rick's gaze as he looked past Todd at her.

She was sure he was remembering all the rules her parents had laid down for her when they were dating.

That's right, everyone gawk at me, she thought. *Here I am: Christy Miller, the biggest baby in the world!*

Katie's lighthearted laughter rippled into the air. Todd patted the side of the car three times, the way a cowboy pats his horse's side. With a squeal of tires, Rick peeled out, hurrying to catch up with the other cars that had already left.

As the four of them headed back for Stephanie's apartment, Christy felt an overwhelming urge to keep apologizing. "I'm really sorry, you guys. Thanks for doing this for me."

Doug slipped his arm around Christy, "What kind of God-Lovers would we be if we didn't support you when you have an opportunity to honor your parents?"

"I still feel bad for holding you guys back. Really, if you want to go, that's fine. I could stay here by myself."

"Christy," Todd said, "shake it off." He shook both his hands in front of her for emphasis. "You're the only one making a big deal of this."

She might have felt reprimanded or embarrassed by such a comment from someone else. Not from Todd. She could take it from him, and when she did, something inside her calmed down.

Stephanie welcomed them all back into her kitchen, where they set to work creating masterpiece banana splits, topped off with a whipped cream fight.

Stephanie started to talk about how she was going back to San Francisco next week to spend the summer working at her father's computer store.

"Her parents came over from China," Doug explained to Christy. "It's an awesome story. Her dad was handed a Chinese Bible by some guy who smuggled it into the country. It was the first time he had ever heard of the Bible. He read it and gave his heart to the Lord and then found some other Christians who were meeting in an underground church. That's where he met Stephanie's mom."

Stephanie jumped in. "Actually, they had met at the university, but neither of them knew the other was a believer."

"That's amazing," Christy said, licking the chocolate sauce off the back of her spoon. "How did they end up in San Francisco?"

Stephanie launched into the story of all the hardships her parents endured trying to get out of China. "They were extra motivated when my mom was pregnant with me. They had to leave before the pregnancy became obvious."

Todd leaned over and explained to Christy, "Mandatory abortion. It's China's way of population control. They already had one kid, and that's the allotment per family."

Christy's eyes grew wide. "You mean you would have been aborted if your parents had stayed there?"

Stephanie nodded.

Christy had heard vague stories before of how hard life was in other countries, but she had never met anyone who had "escaped" and come to America.

"So obviously your parents made it out of the country," Christy said.

"I was born four months after they arrived at my uncle's in San Francisco, so all I know are the dramatic stories. The hard part now is that here we are in a country where we're free to worship God, and one of my younger brothers wants nothing to do with Christianity. I think that's been harder on my parents than anything else they've been through."

Christy thought about Stephanie's words later that night as she lay on the floor in her sleeping bag. Katie and the others hadn't returned yet, and Christy couldn't sleep. She felt like she had grown up more that night than she had during her entire junior year of high school. The conversation with Stephanie had sobered her and caused her to realize how easy it was for her to be a Christian. She had never been challenged to do anything dangerous because of her faith.

Another part of the grown-up feeling came from being

on her own, around college students. It made her feel independent, even though she hadn't been free to go out with everyone. Still, she was away from home, making new friends, and making good decisions. This was one night when growing up seemed like an honorable, wonderful experience.

Just then the front door to Stephanie's apartment opened. Through the half-open bedroom door, Christy could see Katie's silhouette standing there, whispering to Rick.

As Christy watched, Rick braced his good arm against the door frame and bent his head to be eye-level with Katie. Christy knew the move well. He had assumed the same stance with her more than once, right before he had kissed her. His hovering position had the effect of making the girl feel sheltered and yet vulnerable at the same time. She wasn't sure she could watch what would happen next.

But she did.

Rick kissed Katie. Instead of just receiving it, Katie looped her arms around Rick's neck and kissed him back. He pulled away slightly, and Katie removed her arms. Christy could hear muffled whispers, and then she saw Rick back up and wave good-bye.

"See you in the morning," Katie said softly.

She closed the door, and Christy could hear her humming.

Oh, Katie, I don't want Rick to break your heart!

Christy pretended to be asleep when Katie stepped into the room. She was sure it was well after midnight, and this would not be the time to have a heart-to-heart talk with her best friend.

I'll wait to see how things go between them tomorrow at the zoo. I haven't said one discouraging word to her about him yet. But if he treats her badly tomorrow, that's it. I'll do everything I can to break them up!

The next day, it took Christy more than an hour of walking around the zoo before she began to relax and quit working so hard at being super-sleuth.

Relaxing was difficult for several reasons. Rick appeared to be ignoring Katie or, at best, treating her like she was an annoying little kid. Katie didn't seem to notice. She came off as exceptionally loud and flirty. Twice Christy noticed Katie linking her arm with Rick's, but he didn't allow the connection to remain for long.

Plus Christy felt strained because there were five of them. Stephanie had to work, so Christy, Katie, Rick, Doug, and Todd went on the zoo adventure. A group of five was a lot harder to maneuver than four or even six.

By the flamingo lagoon at the main entrance, the group decided to ride the tram. Katie slid in next to Rick, Christy sat across from them, and Doug scooted in next to her. With no room for Todd, he had to sit on another seat next to some tourists who spoke only Japanese.

They disembarked and headed for the giraffe exhibit, the five of them mixed in with all the other tourists. It didn't feel like they were their own group at all.

Katie reached the exhibit first, "Look at the baby giraffe! Isn't he cute?"

Doug stepped next to Christy, slipped his arm around her, and pointed to the grove of tall eucalyptus trees. "Look at that one giraffe twisting his neck around the tree. Doesn't he look like he's trying to play hide-and-seek but the tree isn't quite thick enough?"

Christy laughed with Doug, but at the same time she was aware that Todd was walking off to the side by himself. Katie had again grasped Rick's arm and was stretching her neck, trying to entertain Rick with her giraffe impression.

Rick didn't look impressed.

Christy felt uneasy, as though it were up to her to make sure everyone was getting along and having a good time.

Stop it, she finally scolded herself in front of the koala exhibit as she watched a baby koala clinging to its mother. *You're not everyone's mother here, Christy. Relax and enjoy the day.*

"I want to see the elephants," Todd said. "Anybody have an idea which way we go?"

Doug pulled a folded zoo map from his back pocket and began to give directions. Rick pulled away from Katie and joined Doug, bending over the map.

"Do they still have the sea lion show?" Rick asked. "That was my favorite when I was a kid."

The three guys huddled around the map, and Christy cautiously sidled up next to Katie. "I didn't get to ask you how everything went last night," she said in her best lighthearted voice. "Did you and Rick have a good time?"

Katie looked cross, but she answered calmly, "Yeah, it was great. We all had a good time."

Christy decided to venture a more direct statement. "You and Rick seem to be getting along okay."

Katie grabbed Christy by the arm and jerked her several yards away from the guys. She had tears in her eyes. "He doesn't like me, does he? Last night I thought something might be starting up between us, but all morning he's been pulling away from me and looking at me like I'm an idiot."

"You're not an idiot, Katie."

"I feel like one. Why did I ever want to start up a relationship with him? Why is it so important for me to get him to like me?" Now she was crying.

Christy stood close to Katie so the guys couldn't see her crying. "It's okay, Katie. Really. You don't have to get Rick's approval. You don't have to try to make him like you. Just be yourself. You're wonderful just the way you are. If Rick recognizes that, great. If not, it's his loss."

Katie sniffed and wiped her damp cheeks with the back of her hand. Her bright green eyes looked like two emeralds at the bottom of a deep pool.

"Will you make me a promise?" Christy asked.

Katie nodded.

"Promise me you won't let Rick use you. He does that to girls, and you know it. I don't think he does it on purpose. He can't pass up a challenge, and sometimes I think once the challenge is gone, so is his attention. Do you know what I mean?"

"I know, I know. And you have every right to tell me these things, Christy. These are the same things I told you when you were dating him last year."

"Yes, I know," Christy said. "I didn't listen to you very well then, and I wouldn't blame you if you didn't listen to me now. But I still want you to promise me that you won't let Rick use you. You don't deserve to be treated badly by any guy."

Katie wiped away the last tear and peeked over Christy's shoulder at the guys. A smile returned to her face. "Look at those three," she said. "You'd think we were one of the zoo's attractions the way they're standing there cautiously observing us. If we stay here long enough they might throw peanuts!"

Christy looked at them and laughed with Katie. "Come on," she said. "Let's both try starting this adventure all over, okay?"

"Did you ever notice," Katie said, still eyeing the guys, who looked as though they didn't know how to approach this rare female species, "how many things come in threes?"

"Like the three bears?" Christy asked.

"And three musketeers and three blind mice and," Katie added with a burst of laughter, "the three stooges!"

Christy motioned with a nod of her head as they started to walk back to the guys. "Which one do you want? Larry, Moe, or Curly?"

"You girls all right?" Doug asked, leaving the pack and approaching them.

"Sure," Katie said. "We were just discussing movie stars."

Christy tried to suppress her giggles and smiled at Todd, who shot back one of his warm, understanding smiles.

"How about visiting a famous star?" Doug asked. "It says a dancing elephant is here. Want to go visit him?"

"Sounds good." Katie ignored Rick and smiled brightly at Doug. "Lead on into the jungle, O great trail master."

Doug and Katie led the way, and Christy followed, sandwiched in between Rick and Todd. The awkward five-some dynamics returned.

"Why does he do that?" Katie asked a few minutes later when they stood watching the dancing elephant sway back and forth with his ankle chained to the ground. "Does that thing hurt him?"

"It doesn't seem to," Todd said. "I think he hears his

own music and goes with it. Pretty cool, huh?"

Christy knew that when it came to someone hearing his own music and "going with it," Todd was king. He and the dancing elephant seemed to have a lot in common.

"How about some real animals?" Rick said. "Where are all the lions and tigers? Don't they have any snakes here?"

"We already passed the lion, remember? He was snoozing. The monkeys are over this way," Doug said. "Let's check them out first."

Katie whispered to Christy, "Notice how each guy wants to see the animal he's most similar to?"

Christy nodded and smiled back.

"And did you notice how Rick wants to see some snakes?"

"I know! Remember how Jon, my boss at the pet store, used to compare Rick to a snake?"

"Well, I'm glad I came to my senses before he wrapped his coils around me!" Katie said a little louder.

Christy put her finger up to her lips and whispered, "Shhhhh!"

"'Ssssss' is more like it," Katie whispered back.

"What's with all the secrets, you two?" Doug asked.

Todd answered before Christy or Katie had a chance. "It's a girl thing. Makes them feel in control when they have secrets. You know they're whispering about us."

"You don't know that," Katie said, challenging Todd's philosophy. "We could be talking about something else."

"Like what?" Todd asked.

"Like, well...like anything," Katie answered with her hand on her hip. "Besides, you wouldn't know because, like you said, it's a girl thing."

Christy was glad they had stepped in front of the gorilla exhibit so the subject could change. A great, gray-black lowland gorilla sat on his haunches on a rock before them. His hands were folded under his chin, and he appeared to stare at all the zoo visitors.

"Look at that guy," Doug said. "You'd think he got up today just so he could sit there and watch the tourists walk by."

"He's not moving an inch," Todd said.

"I'll make him move." Rick picked up a peanut off the ground and tossed it at him.

"Don't throw things," Christy said. "Can't you read all the signs around here?"

"Look," Doug said. "He didn't flinch. The guy is a rock."

"The guy is smelly," Katie said, plugging her nose. "Can't you smell him?"

"I thought that was Doug," Rick teased.

"Ho, ho, very funny, Mr. Stuff-All-Your-Gym-Socks-Under-My-Bed."

Rick laughed. "I wondered what happened to all my socks."

"You guys," Todd said, reading the information sign in front of the gorilla. "It says here they have a 'distinct body odor that is unmistakable and quite offensive to humans.'"

"And then it has Doug's name at the bottom, right?" Rick said.

Doug slugged Rick on his unbandaged arm.

"Actually, it says, 'The odor does not stem from lack of cleanliness. In the wilds, the odor helps gorillas locate each other.'"

The guys all started to laugh as if it were the funniest thing they had ever heard.

"Must be a guy thing," Katie whispered to Christy.

"They are so weird! They'll laugh at anything," Christy whispered back.

"Come on," Rick said. "I want to see the snakes."

Christy and Katie broke into their own bout of laughter.

"Don't even try to understand them," Todd said, leading them on to the next exhibit. "It's a girl thing."

4

Katie's Idea of a Good Time

Two weeks later, as Christy and Katie were driving home after their school yearbook–signing party, Katie asked, "What was with Fred? He made such a big deal about signing your yearbook. What did he write?"

"I don't know." Christy shook her head and then motioned to her book in the backseat. "Something like 'keep smiling and see you next year on the yearbook staff.'"

"Are you going to join the staff next year for sure?" Katie reached for the yearbook.

"I signed up, but I still don't know if I want to. I could because I have that really good camera my uncle bought me for Christmas."

"I'm sure you could take better pictures than the ones Fred took this year."

"Do you really think so?"

"Oh, I don't know." Katie opened her yearbook to the winter break section and held it up so Christy could see the center photo. "Let's see. There might be a little stiffer competition here than I realized. Fred did have a real talent for getting those candid shots."

"Get that picture out of my face," Christy said, refusing

to look. Fred had taken a photo at a pizza place over Christmas break. It was enlarged as the center of the photo collage. The picture was of Christy sitting on the end of a booth, and Rick sitting halfway on her lap with his arm wrapped around her. Rick looked like a model, of course. Christy looked like someone who just had ice cubes slipped down her back.

Next to that picture was a small one of Katie goofing off that same night in the pizza place. She had Styrofoam cups on her ears and was pretending to be an elf. It was a much funnier photo than the one of Rick and Christy, and Christy wished the yearbook staff had used that one instead of hers to highlight the junior class collage.

"I guess if I join the yearbook staff I can at least have a say about the pictures they use," Christy said.

"Might not be a bad idea after this picture." Katie flipped to the ski club page and pointed to the photo of Christy ramming into the ski instructor. Her skis had veered between his legs, and her face was buried in his chest.

"Why did they put my name under the picture?" Christy said with a moan. "No one would have known it was me if they hadn't done that."

"Don't complain. You have more pictures in here than I do."

"And that's a good thing?"

"Sure it is," Katie said. "You're becoming popular. I think it started when you turned down the cheerleader position last year and the whole school knew you did it just so Teri Moreno could take your place. Did you even want to try out again this year?"

"Not at all," Christy said. "Isn't that strange? Last year

all I could think about was cheerleading, and now it's the last thing I'd want to do."

Christy pulled into the driveway of her house. "You want to come in for a while?"

"Sure. So what do you want to do?"

"What?" Christy asked as they walked up the steps to her front porch. The jasmine on the trellis was in bloom, and its sweet fragrance filled the air with memories.

"What do you want to do?" Katie repeated. "You don't want to go out for cheerleading, you might go on yearbook staff in the fall, but what do you want to do this summer?"

"Work, I guess. And go to the beach and spend time with you and Todd and everyone."

Christy opened the front door and greeted her mom, who was sitting on the couch watching TV and mending clothes.

"Hi, Christy. Hi, Katie." Mom spoke in a soft whisper.

The light from the floor lamp hit her dark, curly hair in such a way that it made the gray strands shine like silver threads woven into a black woolen cap. "Dad's already asleep, and David should be."

"We'll be quiet," Christy promised.

It was difficult since their house was so small, and the three bedrooms all connected to the same hallway.

Once inside Christy's room with the door closed, Katie asked again what Christy planned to do during the summer. Christy scrutinized her friend's face before answering.

"Would I be correct in guessing you already have an idea of what we should do this summer?"

"How did you guess?"

"I can read you like a book, Katie Weldon. If I'm correct, right now you're thinking of something courageous, adventurous, daring, and slightly wacky."

"Who, me?"

Christy positioned her pillow against her headboard and leaned back. "The last time you had that look on your face, you talked me into joining the ski club and going to Lake Tahoe."

"I'm not talking about skiing this time. I'm talking about summer camp."

Christy hadn't been to summer camp since she was in junior high. She liked the idea the minute Katie said it. "Where? When? With the youth group at church?"

"Yep. I signed us up last Sunday after you left. I wasn't sure you would like the idea because I thought you might be planning on spending as much time with Todd as you could."

Christy let out a sigh. "You know, Katie, things never change with him. I feel like our relationship has hardly moved forward an inch since he came back from Hawaii. That was more than five months ago. Things seem the same as they were last year."

"At least he's consistent."

"Consistent? Boring is more like it."

"I wouldn't complain if I were you," Katie said. "Todd is there for you. He's always there for you. Shall we compare my last year of relationships?"

Katie lay on her back on the floor, counting on her fingers. "Let's see. There was Glen, the missionary kid from Ecuador who liked to talk on the phone, hugged me twice, and promised to write when he left for Quito two months ago. Of course, I haven't received a single word from him, and he must think I have no social life since I've written him four times."

"That's okay," Christy said. "I'm sure he'll write. Mail from South America probably takes a long time."

"Then there's the Rick experience. Kick me in the head if I ever start to like him again! Aside from one New Year's Eve kiss and one and a half kisses at Stephanie's apartment in San Diego, all I ever got from Rick was a severe blow to my self-esteem. I'm sure he thought it was better mine than his.

"There you have it," Katie concluded. "My sizzling love life! At least you have Todd. Nice, consistent, friend forever, won't mess with your mind, guards your heart, Todd."

"I guess," Christy reluctantly agreed.

Katie sat up and gave a tug on Christy's bedspread. "Stop your whining, girl! Can we have a reality check here? You have it great and don't know it."

Christy didn't try to explain her feelings to Katie. They were hers alone. Feelings of wanting to be romanced. When she had dated Rick, he had brought roses and said incredibly tender things. Todd never said mushy stuff or touched her hair and gazed in her eyes the way Rick had. But with Rick, it felt like a game, and she was the prize.

If Todd would only throw a little tender romance into their close, honest, consistent relationship, it would be perfect. He seemed to be holding back, and so of course, she held back too.

"Hello?" Katie waved her hand in the air to get Christy's attention. "Anybody home?"

"I'm sorry. What were you saying?"

"Summer camp. I think we should go to summer camp."

A warm sensation washed over Christy. A feeling of sitting around a campfire at night, of picking wildflowers, and of splashing into a sun-toasted lake. A feeling of mysteriously meeting someone in the woods. Someone new. Someone handsome and tender who would write her long, romantic letters and hold her hand in the moonlight.

"Excuse me," Katie said. "Am I, like, having a one-sided conversation here?"

"No, I'm listening. Summer camp. We're going to summer camp. We're going to have a fantastic time at summer camp. I'm ready. Let's go!"

Katie's mouth turned up into a smile. "I don't know about you, Christy. I think you're asleep with your eyes open. Perhaps I'd better leave you alone to finish your dream without interruption."

Katie rose to her feet. "July fifth to the eleventh. Call Luke this week at church and tell him you agreed to go. He'll be glad. I'll see you later. Sweet dreams!"

Letting herself out, Katie left Christy with a swirl of exciting summer camp thoughts. She would have to ask her parents, request time off from work, and make sure she had enough clothes for the entire week. Maybe this summer would hold some adventure after all.

The next Sunday, Christy talked to Luke, their youth pastor, and asked some questions about the camp.

"It's called Camp Wildwood, and it's about two hours from here," the big, bearded, lovable youth pastor answered. "You'll have eleven girls in your cabin. Your tuition is paid, but I'm afraid I'll have to ask you to come up with twenty dollars for the transportation."

"That's no problem. And I already have the week off from work, so I'm all set."

Luke gave her an appreciative smile, "You know, Christy, I really am glad you're willing to do this."

"Willing? Are you kidding? I can't wait! I love going to camp."

"I'm glad. I think it'll be a good week. I want you to know how much I appreciate you and Katie for signing up. Not many of the other students are willing to give up a week of their summer."

"Well, they don't know what they're missing," Christy said. She thought it was great that the church was sponsoring the teens who wanted to go by paying for their tuition.

That afternoon, Todd came over, and they went to the beach. Even though summer was supposed to have arrived, it was chilly, and a thin mist of ocean fog hovered above the sand.

"Carlsbad is such a different beach from Newport," Todd commented as they sat together on a blanket and looked out at the waves. "It's hard to believe it's only sixty miles down the same Pacific coast from Newport. It feels like I'm on the Atlantic."

"Why?" Christy slipped on her sweatshirt and wrapped the end of the blanket around her bare feet. "Because it's so cold today?"

"No, it's the way the waves break. They seem to come in at a different angle here. I don't know. Could be the weather too. Although it's not unusual for it to be like this in June."

At Christy's home in Escondido, about a half hour drive from Carlsbad, it had been warm and sunny when they had left. She had put on shorts and a T-shirt over her bathing suit. Her wise mother had tossed her a sweatshirt on her way out the door.

The wind whipped the sleeves of Todd's T-shirt. He seemed comfortable enough. Christy had never really noticed before, but the hair on Todd's legs looked white-blond and was super curly. He didn't even have goose bumps.

"I'm cold," Christy said.

Todd took his gaze off the ocean and looked at her in surprise. "You are?"

Christy smiled at his amazed expression and rubbed the goose bumps on her bare legs. "Yes, I am. I don't come with a built-in fur coat like you do to keep me warm." She playfully reached over and pulled one of the hairs on his leg.

"Ouch!" he said. Then noticing her smooth legs, he asked, "Why do girls do that, anyway? Shave their legs, I mean."

"So they'll look nice. You know, smooth and feminine."

"But then you get cold."

"Never mind," Christy said. "Actually, we do it so that guys will feel sorry for us when we say we're cold, and they'll put their arms around us and warm us up."

"I have a better idea." Todd stood up and offered Christy his hand. "Let's walk."

Todd's hand felt strong and secure as they strolled down the beach together. Her legs were still cold, but inside she felt warm and content. That's how things had been between her and Todd for the last few months. More than brother and sister, not quite boyfriend and girlfriend.

She felt Todd's thumb rubbing the chain on the gold ID bracelet she wore on her right wrist. He had given it to her a year and a half ago with the word "Forever" engraved on it. It was Todd's promise that they would be friends forever. As it was, their relationship had gone through many ups and downs since they first met two summers ago. But Todd's promise had remained. He always treated her like a close friend. It was just that sometimes, like now, Christy wanted more.

"What are you thinking about?" she asked him.

"About Papua New Guinea," Todd answered. "I was wondering what angle the waves come in there."

What did I expect? Ever since I first met Todd, he's been dreaming of being a missionary to an island full of unreached natives. He's such a surfer boy. I bet if I cut him, he would bleed saltwater. Why did I think he would be thinking of me?

"What were you thinking?" he asked.

The question surprised her. Although she asked him for his thoughts often, he rarely asked her. Maybe Todd was becoming a little more like Christy as they spent more time together. She knew she was becoming a little more like him.

"I was thinking about us and wondering what the future held." One thing Christy had learned was to be honest with Todd.

There was a pause. Then Todd squeezed her hand and said, "Me too."

Christy felt her heart beat a little faster.

Todd stopped walking and turned to face her. The filtered sunlight shone on his face, illuminating his clear silver-blue eyes and highlighting his square jaw. His expression remained sober, and no dimple appeared on his right cheek.

"But you know what, Kilikina?"

Christy always melted when he called her by her Hawaiian name.

"If we spend all of today thinking about tomorrow, today will be gone, and we will have missed it."

Christy knew he was right. As much as she wished he would wrap his arms around her, hold her tight, kiss her hair, and tell her that all his future plans included her, she knew he wouldn't. Todd was reserved when it came to physical expression. It was part of his honesty. He once told her that he would never purposefully "defraud" her.

When she asked what he meant, Todd said, "I won't deliberately arouse a desire in you that I can't follow through on honestly, before God."

She knew that if their relationship had been full of hugs and kisses and whispered secrets about their future, her desires for him would have been aroused past the point of no return.

As it was now, they could walk away from their relationship today, and besides missing each other's close friendship, they would have no regrets about making promises they weren't able to keep or painful memories from having become too intimate.

"Then let's enjoy today," Christy said, her eyes smiling at Todd. "I'm glad we can be together. We'd better keep walking though. I'm starting to get cold again."

Todd squeezed her hand and started down the beach. They spent the next two hours collecting shells, digging for sand crabs, and playing foot tag with the waves. It really was a wonderful afternoon.

When they arrived at home, Mom had tacos waiting for

them and a message that Katie had called.

Christy didn't call Katie back until the next morning. The conversation was short, and Katie's news sent Christy back to bed on her first Monday of summer vacation.

"Christy," Mom called, tapping on her bedroom door, "are you okay?"

"Come on in, Mom. I'm bummed. Katie can't go to camp. Her parents won't let her because it's a church activity. Isn't that crazy? They let her take off and do all kinds of stuff you guys would never let me do, but they won't let her become too involved in church. It has to be hard for her, being the only Christian in her family."

"Do you still want to go?" Mom asked.

"Sort of. Not as much as before."

"Maybe we can call Luke and see if some other girls that you know are going," Mom suggested.

"Okay," Christy sighed. "But it won't be as much fun without Katie."

Christy didn't get around to calling Luke. When she saw him Sunday at church, she asked him who else was going to camp.

"You and Katie were the only two girls from the youth group."

Christy couldn't believe it. Their high school group had 250 people in it.

"I'm sorry Katie isn't going. We really need counselors. That's why I appreciated you both signing up."

"Counselors?" Christy squeaked. "Katie signed us up to be counselors?"

"For junior camp," Luke explained. "We need counselors for the fifth-grade girls. You thought Katie signed you up for high school camp? That isn't until the last week of August. Does this mean you want to drop out too?"

Something about the way Luke worded it made Christy feel like she would be the flake of the year if she withdrew only a week before camp. Especially since Katie had backed out.

"No, I'll go." Christy tried to sound like it didn't make much difference to her. "I have the time off from work, and you need counselors. I'll go."

A huge grin spread over Luke's face. "Thanks, Christy. I knew I could count on you! It'll be a real stretching experience, you'll see."

"That's what I'm afraid of," Christy muttered.

The next Sunday, when she arrived in the church parking lot with her luggage and sleeping bag, she knew she wasn't up for this stretching experience. A sea of fourth- and fifth-grade kids ran through the mounds of luggage, yelling, hitting, tattling, and clearly presenting Christy with a glimpse into her next week.

It took more than an hour to organize the troops, load their luggage, and get everyone on the bus at one time. Christy sat in the seat right behind the driver, hoping to ignore most of the spit wads, smacking gum, and rude little boys. She realized her main goal this week would be to avoid getting gum in her hair.

Katie, I'm going to get you for this one!

The crazy part was that this was Katie's type of activity. She loved being the center of attention with a bunch of kids and had a way of getting them to follow her easily. Those were Katie's special gifts, not Christy's.

A young girl ran screaming from the back of the bus and dove into the empty seat next to Christy as if her life depended on being protected from whatever was chasing her. Christy readjusted her legs to accommodate the flying banshee and asked in her sternest voice, "What is going on here?"

"Eeeeeeek!" the girl squealed, ducking and covering her head with her arms.

A cute kid with bright eyes and dark blond hair skidded down the aisle and slugged the girl in the back.

"Stop that right now!" Christy demanded.

"She took my candy," the boy hollered.

"Is that true?" Christy asked the girl, who was still bent over at the waist. Her matted hair hung over her face. The girl only giggled.

Christy asked again, "Did you take his candy?"

The girl kept giggling as Christy grabbed her by the shoulders and pulled her upright, revealing the stolen candy in her lap.

"Give it back," the boy spouted, grabbing the stash of candy bars and marching to his seat at the back of the bus.

As instantly as the seat beside Christy had filled, it now emptied. Giggling, the candy robber hopped up and returned to where her friends sat.

Christy felt a rush of relief when two college-age guys boarded the bus. With booming voices, they got the kids' attention and commanded them to settle down. To Christy's amazement, they did.

One of the guys announced the rules for the bus ride to camp. The other one asked them to bow their heads and close their eyes because he was going to pray for their trip to camp.

Christy added her own prayer at the end. *Lord, could You assign me a couple of extra guardian angels this week? I think I'm going to need them.*

5

Camp Wildwood

Two hours later, when the bus rolled under a rustic wooden sign that read "Camp Wildwood," Christy felt an urge to jump bus and run for home. The word *rustic* would be a polite way to describe the camp. Christy's cabin was at the end of an uphill trail that made luggage-hauling miserable. Her fledglings followed her up the narrow, dusty trail, squealing and sobbing and making enough noise to scare off any wildlife for miles.

Somehow Christy knew the only wildlife she would experience this week would be in the form of pillow fights at three in the morning, frogs in her sleeping bag, and raids from the boys' cabins across the creek.

"Okay, girls," she called out as they stepped into their home sweet home. "I'm taking the bunk on the bottom here by the door. Everyone find a bunk. If you fight over who's on top, we'll swap positions halfway through the week."

The girls took to their nesting with lots of noise. Christy tried to let them solve their own problems while she smoothed out her sleeping bag. She found a note from her mom tucked inside.

May you have sweet dreams every night. Love, Mom.

Christy smiled and tucked it in her backpack. She pulled out her notebook just as two of the girls were about to exit.

"Whoa! Where are you going?" Christy stopped them. Suddenly she understood why, at the camp counselors meeting last night, they had made such a big deal about the counselors taking the bottom bunk by the door. It was the best spot to serve as a door guard.

"Out," the blond one answered.

"Not yet," Christy told her. "We have to have a cabin meeting first."

The girls acted as if she had just ordered them to eat raw brussels sprouts and marched off to their bunks, pouting.

"Okay, everyone come sit on the floor. We're going to have a quick cabin meeting, and then you have free time until dinner."

"Can't we sit on our bunks?" asked a girl with ebony skin and big black eyes.

"Well, all right. As long as I can see all of you. Wait, I have an idea. Everyone sit on the top bunk. That way we can all see each other."

"I just made my bed," the girl across from Christy complained.

"I'd rather sit on the floor," another said.

"Can we eat in the cabin?" The request came from a plump blonde who, from the chocolate smears around her lips, looked as though she had been eating ever since they left the church.

"No, it's one of the rules. The food attracts ants and other critters we don't want to invite into our cabin. Come on," Christy said, hoisting herself onto the empty top bunk above hers.

She realized if one of the bunks was empty that meant one of the girls hadn't made it to the cabin. Rather than leaving to find the lost sheep, she thought she had better go through her meeting as planned. Her list of campers would reveal who was missing, and then she could go after that person and at least know who she was looking for.

"Quiet down, girls. You two in the back on the bottom bunk, could you join us please?"

It was the blonde and her friend who had tried to escape earlier.

Christy looked over her list of names, "This will be a short meeting. I need to find out who's who. When I call out your name, please raise your hand."

"We're not back in school," the plump one said.

"What's your name?" the girl across from Christy asked.

"I'm Christy. Christy Miller."

"Do you have a boyfriend?" the blonde in the back wanted to know.

"Well, actually," Christy hesitated, "let's talk about all that stuff later. First I need to find out your names." She started down the list. "Amy?"

"Present, Teach," mocked a girl across the room. She wore dangling earrings that looked a little too large for her small ears. Her coffee-colored hair was pulled up in a high ponytail, spilling over her head like a water fountain. With every movement, her hair and her earrings jiggled. She reminded Christy of a wild tropical bird. Even her "Present, Teach" sounded as though a "gawk" should be attached to the end.

"Jocelyn?"

The black girl raised her hand. "That's me." She looked as though she would be gorgeous once she grew into her strong features, like her eyes.

No eleven-year-old should be allowed to have eyelashes that long. She'll never have to spend a penny on mascara.

"Sara?"

"What?" the petite blonde answered. She looked like a Skipper doll. Her wavy blond hair ran free all over her head, and her ginger eyes seemed to take in everything with a glance. Sara's T-shirt had the word "So?" printed on the front.

"Ruth," Christy called out.

"I like Ruthie better," the girl on the bunk across from her answered. "I hate my name. It sounds so blah."

"I like your name," Christy said. "It's the same as my grandmother's."

Some of the girls started to giggle, but tears welled up in Ruthie's eyes. "See what I mean? Your grandmother! Nobody my age is named Ruth."

She had a plain face, a long flat nose, and braces. Her skin was perfect, smooth, and without a freckle. Her light brown hair hung straight to the tip of her shoulders and was tucked behind her ear on the left side.

"Well, I like your name," Christy said, hoping to repair any damage she had done in the first fifteen minutes of their week together.

Christy called out the rest of the names. The only one who didn't answer was Jeanine Brown. She ran through the rules about camp boundaries, staying away from the guys' cabins, and not raiding cabins. Her confidence wasn't too high that any of the rules would be followed.

"Any questions?"

"Yeah," said Sara. "Do you have a boyfriend?"

"Sort of," Christy said. "And that's the best answer you're going to get from me. Now go enjoy your free time until dinner, and I'll look for all of you at the dining hall."

"Dining hall?" Jocelyn laughed. "Here it's a mess hall."

"Okay, fine. The mess hall. When the bell rings, go right to the mess hall. And wash your hands before you come in, okay?"

The girls were already elbowing their way out the door. Amy, the bird, called over her shoulder, "Yes, Teach."

Hopping down and tucking away her notebook, Christy kicked her big green duffel bag under her bed and headed out to find the missing Jeanine Brown. Halfway down the trail she heard the familiar squeal of the perky little thief who had collided with her on the bus on the way up. Christy went off the main trail and soon spotted the girl dashing from her hiding place behind a tree and running straight for Christy.

"Hide me!" she shrieked, grabbing Christy by the waist and using her as a shield.

"Give it back," hollered the boy she had harassed on the bus. He was galloping through the woods toward them.

"Never!" the girl shouted, giggling and pinching Christy's middle as she ducked behind her.

"She took my pocketknife," the exasperated boy said.

Christy jerked free of the girl's clutches, spun around, and in her firmest voice said, "Hand me the knife right now."

The girl sobered, pulled the deluxe Swiss army knife

from the pocket of her jeans, and handed it to Christy with a repentant expression.

"What is your name, and who is your counselor?" Christy asked the boy.

"Nicholas. Jaeson is my counselor."

"Fine. At the counselors meeting tonight I'll give this to Jaeson, and he can give it back to you if he thinks you need it this week. As for you, who is your counselor?" she asked the sober-faced girl.

"I don't know."

"What cabin are you in?"

"I don't know."

"Where did you put your sleeping bag and luggage?"

"Down there, by the bus. I didn't know where to go."

"What's your name?" Christy closed her eyes as she waited for the answer. She already knew what it would be.

"Jeanine Brown."

Nicholas took off into the woods, and Christy let out a sigh. "Come with me, Jeanine. I'm Christy Miller. I'm your counselor. Our cabin is at the top of the hill. Let's pick up your stuff."

"Oh, good!" Jeanine said joyfully. "I was hoping you would be my counselor."

Christy didn't feel she could return the compliment to her soon-to-be bunk mate. "Good," was all she managed to say. "Let's get going; it's almost dinnertime."

At least at dinner all her girls showed up. Amy wanted to sit by Christy at the large round table, and Sara squabbled with Jocelyn over who would sit on the other side. It was nice, in a way, to be fought over. Then Christy reminded herself that this was the first night and the first of many meals they would share. She hoped not every meal would be accompanied by so much hassle.

The food was good, better than she had expected. Amy dropped one of her dangling earrings in the bowl of applesauce as it was passed around, and Christy had to fish it out with the serving spoon. Before she could stop Amy, she had licked off the earring and poked it back in her ear.

"Do we have free time after dinner?" Jocelyn asked.

"Yes, but remember you have to stay in the camp boundaries. I'll be in a counselors meeting, so if you have any problems, wait for me outside the door of the lodge. We should be done in about an hour."

"Yes, Teach," Amy replied solemnly, her hair falling down on her face and touching the ends of her eyelashes.

The first question the camp dean, Bob Ferrill, asked in the counselors meeting was if their campers knew the counselors' names.

"Yes," Christy volunteered in the room of five of her peers. "Except one of them keeps calling me 'Teach.'"

"Don't worry," the dean said. "We've heard worse around here. Now we want all of you to meet each other. I prefer you call me Dean Ferrill rather than Bob or Mr. Ferrill."

The girl next to Christy was Jessica, and the other girl counselor was Diane. The guy counselors were Mike, Bob, and Jaeson. They each told where they lived and a little bit about themselves. Mike and Bob were two college guys from Christy's church. Jaeson was from the same church as Jessica and Diane.

Dean Ferrill explained that several of the campers were what he called "potentially high maintenance" because they were from difficult home situations. He explained that some of them would be acting younger than their age because of their emotional challenges.

"We're not going to label these kids because we want all of them to be treated equally, but we want you to know that you may have expectations of your campers that are higher than what some of them are capable of handling. Be patient. Love them all the same."

He went over the schedule for the evening, stressed the camp rules again, and then prayed. Christy thought his prayer was touching, especially when he prayed for each of the counselors and for the campers as if the salvation of each kid was the most important thing in his life. Christy knew she could survive the week with him on her side.

As the meeting broke up, Christy approached Jaeson. "Hi, I have something to give you. I forgot it back at my cabin. It's a pretty sophisticated pocketknife I confiscated from one of your boys. His name is Nicholas."

"Yeah, Nick said one of the girls wouldn't leave him alone."

Jaeson looked like he was born to be a camp counselor. He had an athletic build and short black hair, with facial features that seemed chiseled out of stone. His sunglasses hung around his neck on a black foam strap, and on his wrist were half a dozen leather "friendship bracelets" the campers had learned to braid at craft time.

"Why don't you bring it to the meeting tonight? I'll keep it for him."

"Thanks," Christy said.

She hurried up the trail to her cabin to grab her sweatshirt and the knife before the meeting started. When she opened the cabin door, three of the girls scampered like frightened mice.

"What are you guys doing?" Christy scanned the room for a clue. She spotted her makeup bag open on Amy's bed.

"Hey, what are you doing in my things?" She looked at her bunk and saw her duffel bag was open with some of her clothes pulled halfway out.

The three culprits, Sara, Amy, and Jocelyn, stood frozen.

Sara spoke up. "You said you were going to be in that meeting for about an hour. You weren't gone that long."

"Wait a minute," Christy said firmly, feeling her temperature rising. "The meeting has nothing to do with this. You got into my things without permission." She noticed that Amy appeared to have awfully pink cheeks and black smears around her eyes.

"Were you in my makeup, Amy?"

"Yes, Teach. But I was going to put it back."

"That doesn't matter," Christy spouted, looking at the three of them sternly. "You *do not* get into other people's things! Do you understand me?"

The three solemnly nodded.

"Amy, go wash your face. Sara and Jocelyn, put my things back the way you found them. *Now!*"

The girls fled to obey the orders. Sara knelt to repack Christy's bag and started to sniffle.

"You're mean," Sara said under her breath. "I wish you weren't our counselor!"

Christy felt like saying the feeling was mutual when she noticed what Sara was wearing. "Is that my sweatshirt, by any chance?"

Sara pulled the sweatshirt off and threw it on the cabin floor. "I was only trying it on. I wasn't going to really wear it!"

Snatching it up, Christy shook it out and put it on. Then grabbing her backpack, she felt inside for the pocketknife, which was still there. The girls finished zipping up the bag of now-crumpled clothes and rose to their feet. Sara was still crying, and Jocelyn's lip was lowered in a pout.

"We're sorry," Jocelyn said. "We won't do it again."

Something inside Christy told her to take both girls in her arms and hug them. Maybe these three were some of the ones who had special needs. But she was too upset at the moment. Instead Christy took two steps backward and ordered them to get their jackets and come to the evening meeting with her. Maybe the evening's message would straighten them out.

The girls obeyed, still sniffling. Amy met them at the door, her face scrubbed and her expression almost frightened.

"Get your jacket and come with us," Christy said firmly.

She marched them down the hill to the meeting, making them sit with her instead of with their friends. The singing was lively and fun, but Christy's three prisoners didn't join in. They sat quietly through the speaker's message.

Christy began to feel bad for coming down so hard on them. She knew they were still thinking about what had happened in the cabin and not paying attention to the message. As soon as the meeting was over, she told them they were free to go to the mess hall for the evening snack.

Just before the girls left the building, Jaeson came up to

Christy and asked about the knife. She took her backpack off her shoulder to retrieve the knife and accidentally swung it too far, hitting Jaeson in the chest.

"Oh, I'm sorry! I didn't realize how heavy it was."

Jaeson appeared unaffected. He reached over and gently squeezed Christy's shoulder. "You're going to get a muscle spasm before the week is over if you keep carrying that around."

"I'll lighten the load tonight," she promised, noticing that the three girls had reappeared by her side. They were apparently curious as to what was going on between their counselor and this buff guy, who was touching her in public.

Christy handed Jaeson the pocketknife and said, "I told Nick you would decide whether to give it back to him."

"No problem," Jaeson said. "Thanks for catching it for me."

"Can I try on your sunglasses?" Sara looked up at Jaeson, her ginger eyes bright with admiration.

"Maybe tomorrow," he said kindly. "You'd better run over to the mess hall if you want to get any cookies before the guys scarf them all."

"Are you coming?" Sara asked.

"Sure, we'll go with you," Jaeson said. "Come on, Christy. They always have peanut butter cookies on Sunday nights. They're the best."

"You've done this before, I take it," Christy said as they were escorted across camp by three sets of big ears.

"This is my third year. I started last week, and I'm staying until the end of July. How about you?"

"This is my first time as a counselor. I'm not sure I'm

going to be very good at this," she admitted, still feeling bad for the way she had treated the girls.

"Oh, you're the best counselor we've ever had, isn't she?" Sara asked the other two girls. "And she's pretty too, isn't she, Jaeson?"

Christy felt her cheeks warming. How could these little girls change their opinion of her so instantly?

Before Jaeson could answer, Amy popped in with, "And if there's anything she needs to learn about camp, you can teach her. 'Cuz she's our Teach, so you can teach her. Get it?"

By then, thankfully, they had arrived at the mess hall, and Jaeson graciously said, "If I can help you out in any way, let me know. I'm sure you'll have a great week."

"Oh, she will, won't you, Teach?" Amy answered enthusiastically before running off with the other girls in a fit of giggles.

That night it took two hours for the girls to settle down. Even then, Christy worried that one of them might fake being asleep and sneak out the minute she dozed off. She lay half awake, half asleep, listening for rustling in the silence.

After some time, she checked her alarm clock with her flashlight: 1:25.

I'm never going to wake up at six! And this is only the first night.

The second night didn't go much better. The day was packed with activities for the campers. Christy thought for sure with all the swimming, horseback riding, and archery, combined with last night's late hours, the girls would willingly tumble into bed.

No, they wanted to talk. About boys.

"You girls are only going into the fifth grade. You're too young to be so interested in boys," Christy said from her bunk once she had gotten them all in bed and the lights out.

"People mature faster now," Sara informed her. "We're much more grown-up than we were last year. When did you first start to like guys?"

Christy had to think back. She remembered going to summer camp with her best friend, Paula, right before they went into seventh grade. When she thought about it, she and Paula did spend most of that week trying to get the boys' attention.

"It doesn't matter," Christy said. "The point is, there's lots more to do at camp than occupy yourselves with guys. Besides, none of them seems to be very interested in you girls yet. You see, girls mature more quickly than boys."

"We know all that, Teach," Amy said from her bunk across the dark cabin. "Tell us stuff we don't know."

"Stuff you don't know?"

"Yeah, like what it's like to be kissed by your boyfriend," Sara said.

"She said she only 'sort of' had a boyfriend," Amy interjected. "I think Jaeson wants to be your boyfriend."

All the girls joined in a noisy chorus of agreement and approval.

"Hush," Christy said. "We have to be quiet or Dean Ferrill will come up like he did last night and tell us to settle down. I don't want to get in trouble again."

"Don't you think he's cute?" Jocelyn said in a loud whisper.

"Who?" Christy played it cool. "Dean Ferrill? Sure, I

suppose he's cute, for a man who's old enough to be my father."

"No, not him. Jaeson."

"You know what, girls?" Christy said sternly. "It's too late to have a discussion like this. I want you all to quiet down and go to sleep."

A round of complaints followed.

"I mean it!" Christy said gruffly. "All of you settle down right now."

Just then there was a loud knock on their cabin door. Dean Ferrill's voice boomed out. "Is everything okay, Christy?"

"Yes," Christy answered. "The girls were just going to sleep, weren't you, girls?"

Someone faked loud snoring, and another girl said, "Hey, stop knocking on our door! We're trying to sleep in here."

"Good night, ladies," the dean said firmly. "I don't want to have to come back up here to check on you again."

"You won't have to," Christy promised. "We're going to sleep now."

The girls remained quiet as they listened to Dean Ferrill walk away from their cabin.

All of a sudden, into the stillness, Sara called out, "Hey, Dean Ferrill, Christy thinks you're cute for an old guy!"

6

What You Can Never Do

"How are you doing, Christy?" Dean Ferrill asked the next morning at the counselors meeting.

"Pretty good. I apologize for Sara's comment last night."

"Don't worry about it. How do the girls seem to be responding spiritually?"

"Not much, I'd say. I could use some pointers on what I should be doing."

"What are your plans for cabin devos?" Jessica asked. She carried herself like a model, with straight posture and gentle movements. She had excelled during the swimming competition the day before.

Her caramel-colored hair was back in a ponytail today, and her delicate face looked as though she followed a strict skin-care program. Without a touch of makeup she looked beautiful.

"Cabin devos?" Christy asked.

"Devotions. What are you doing with the girls at night before you go to bed?"

"Yelling at them," Christy answered, half joking, half serious.

"Devotions really help to calm them down, and I think you'll get the most open responses from them then," Jessica said. "Would you like to get together during free time this afternoon? I could give you some ideas."

"Great! I'd appreciate that."

Christy thought she noticed Jaeson smiling at her. She wondered if it was because he was thinking she was inexperienced or if he was being nice. The meeting again ended with a wonderful prayer time for the campers. Christy felt certain something of eternal value would have to break through with her girls soon, the way everyone was praying.

That morning at recreation, Christy's girls went up against Jaeson's boys at archery. Christy didn't look forward to the competition. She hadn't shot a bow and arrow since she was in junior high. Thankfully her girls had come to expect her to be the expert in everything, and right now she appreciated all the votes of confidence she could get from them.

The girls all lined up, facing the stacks of hay with the target tacked to the center. Christy picked up a bow and showed her girls how to hold it and aim for the target. She let the arrow fly. It whooshed a grand total of about three feet and landed uncomfortably close to Jaeson's foot.

The campers broke into laughter as the red-faced Christy made her way to the boys' side to retrieve her wayward arrow.

"Sorry," she muttered to Jaeson. "I don't know what went wrong."

"You had your elbow down. Hold it up flat like this," Jaeson said, demonstrating with the bow in his hand.

Christy tried to imitate his stance and elbow position. It

didn't feel right. "Like this? Or higher?" she asked.

"May I?" Jaeson put down his bow and stepped over next to Christy. He put his muscular arm around her shoulders and placed his hand on top of hers. "Pull back like this," he instructed. "Keep your elbow up. Do you feel that?"

Christy was starting to feel something, all right. She felt the eyes of her campers drinking in the scene before them. She knew she would never convince them that he was only helping her.

"Now try," Jaeson said, stepping back.

Christy let go of the taut string, and the arrow zinged through the air, hitting the white part of the circle.

"All right! Good job!" Jaeson praised. "You guys all see that?"

A couple of the older boys said, "Yeah, we saw it, Jaeson. You sure you don't want us to leave so you two can be alone?"

Jaeson ignored the comment. He put his arm around the shoulders of the first boy in line and demonstrated the correct position the same way he had with Christy.

She approached her flock of twittering birdies with a serious expression. "Who's first?"

The girls had giddy expressions in their eyes as they whispered among themselves.

"Sara," Christy called. "You try it first."

Christy wrapped her arm around Sara and imitated Jaeson's correct archery stance. She hoped the girls would think this was the way everyone was taught how to shoot an arrow, with your arm around them.

Ignoring all the "Cupid" comments, Christy patiently

showed each girl how to shoot. She was amazed at how readily the girls responded as she put her arm around them. They seemed eager to please her, and she began to see them in a different light. Not as brats, but as babies away from home and needing a big hug.

When their time was almost up, Christy glanced over at the boys and saw Jaeson watching her. He smiled and gave her a thumbs-up sign.

She felt like during the last few days she had been building up a reservoir of wonder about Jaeson. She wondered if he liked her. She wondered if he was looking at her across the mess hall. She wondered if he would be at the pool during free time.

With Jaeson's thumbs-up, the reservoir of wonder overflowed, flooding her with thoughts of Jaeson, Jaeson, Jaeson.

At lunch she looked for where he was sitting before she chose her table. The rule was only one counselor at each table. She thought if she spotted him right away, she could sit at the table next to his so their chairs would be back to back. Her plan worked. There was an empty table next to his and an empty chair behind him. She slid in quietly, as if she didn't notice he was there.

"Hi," Jaeson said. "Did you see the final score on the archery practice?"

"No, I didn't. How did we do?"

"Your girls beat my guys by ten points."

"You're kidding! I never would have guessed it," Christy said, smiling. "Thanks for all your help."

"Anytime," Jaeson smiled back.

Just then the mess hall doors opened, and the campers

were let in. They ran like escaping guinea pigs, not sure where they were going but feverish about being the first one to get there. Christy's girls filled in at her table in record time and took turns poking each other with their elbows.

Jessica came over to Christy's table with two adoring campers holding on to each arm. "Where do you want to meet after lunch?" Jessica asked above the roar.

Christy shrugged, looking to Jessica for a suggestion.

"How about the lodge?"

Christy nodded, and Jessica surrendered to the persuasion of her two-arm fan club.

When Christy went to meet Jessica in the lodge as arranged, she kept checking over her shoulder to see if Jaeson might be following her. He seemed to be headed in the direction of the craft barn. Maybe she should go over after her meeting with Jessica—to check on any of her girls that might be there, of course.

"First," Jessica said when they had seated themselves on the old couch, "I'm not trying to tell you how to relate to your girls. I know you're doing a great job. I didn't want you to think I was trying to step in this morning and tell you what to do."

"I didn't think that at all. I need all the help I can get!"

For half an hour Jessica made some good suggestions about how to put a devotion together and what worked best for her last year when she was a counselor for the first time.

"It's actually easier this year with the group I have. They're the youngest batch, the ones just going into fourth grade. Some of them are having a hard time because this is the first time they've been away from home on their own. And they're not real good about their hygiene without being reminded. But they're not real boy-crazy yet. At least not all of them."

"They sure like you," Christy said.

"Well, I think I'm learning from some of the mistakes I made last summer. I didn't realize until after camp what I did wrong, and I'm trying to do it differently this year."

"Can I ask what it was?" Christy asked cautiously. Jessica seemed so approachable that she thought it would be okay to ask such a personal question.

"Christy, I'll tell you, there is one thing you can never do."

Just then Christy's little boy-chaser, Jeanine, burst through the lodge's door, clutching a baseball cap in her fist. With ear-shattering squeals, she ran behind the couch and pleaded, "Don't let him get me!"

Outside the door, Nick obeyed the "No Campers" sign and stayed outside, peering in for a glimpse of Jeanine.

"That's it!" Christy shouted, jumping up and demanding the cap from Jeanine. "This has gone on too long. Give me the cap. Now leave the poor kid alone, and don't take anything else of his. Do you understand me?"

Jeanine handed over the cap with the look of a scolded puppy. "I'm sorry," she said in a small voice.

Christy stomped over to the door and delivered the cap to Nick, who looked slightly annoyed. Two of his friends joined him and stood on either side for moral support.

"Will you tell her to stop it?" Nick asked Christy.

"You know what, Nicholas. It's only a game if both of you play. If you stop playing, it won't be fun to her anymore, and I guarantee she'll stop."

"Not likely," one of Nick's bodyguards mumbled.

Nick slipped the cap back on his head, and the three of them trudged off to the baseball field. Christy watched them go and almost laughed aloud. They were miniature versions of Todd, Doug, and Rick.

Elephants, monkeys, and snakes. Oh my.

When Christy turned around, she discovered Jeanine had taken her place next to Jessica on the couch. Jessica, the experienced counselor, was stroking the young girl's hair out of her face and speaking to her softly. Jeanine drank in every word.

"Okay, I'll try it." Jeanine hopped up and gave Jessica a look she never would have given to Christy. A look of true admiration and appreciation. Then she rushed out of the lodge.

"What did you tell her?" Christy asked, retrieving her seat on the couch.

"I told her that instead of taking things away from Nick, maybe she should try giving something to him to get his attention. She's off to make a friendship bracelet at the craft center."

"That was brilliant. How did you think of that?"

"It's what I was about to tell you before she burst in here. The one thing you can never do is love too much."

"Never love too much?" Christy repeated.

"When I left camp last year, I realized I had done a lot of the 'right' things as a counselor, but I hadn't loved the girls in my cabin as much as I could have. Do you know what I mean?"

Christy flashed back to when she had caught the girls going through her clothes. Yes, she did know what Jessica meant.

"You see," Jessica said, "you can't argue with love. When this week is over, what will the girls remember? The squabbles? The team races on the last day? What the speaker said?"

"I'm sure they'll remember some of that," Christy said. "I remember some of that from my days as a camper."

"But what do you remember the most?" Jessica asked. "Not just about camp, but about your whole life? I think we remember the people who loved us."

Christy took Jessica's advice to heart. She knew her new friend was right. Eagerly making her way to the craft barn after their meeting, Christy wondered how that advice might apply to Jaeson. What would he remember about her when camp was over?

More and more thoughts collided in her head as if all her emotions had gathered and were holding court in her brain. She was the one on trial. The prosecuting attorney's voice said she was silly and immature to chase after a guy at summer camp when she had Todd waiting for her at home. Another emotion stepped up as her defense witness and claimed that she had the right to build relationships with any guy she wanted to, and this was all part of camp.

Just as she was about to enter the craft barn, Christy imagined all the girls in her cabin as the jury. Their squeaky voices were raised in a loud "Not guilty" inside her head. She felt free to take that step into the craft barn and see what happened next.

She noticed Jaeson right away. He looked up and saw her at the same time.

"Christy," he greeted her. "Just the person I wanted to see. Can you help these girls with their bracelets? I'm supposed to meet my guys at the pool in five minutes."

Sara, Amy, and Jocelyn beamed their approval at her and started to talk all at once. Christy stepped over to the side of the table where the three of them were nearly finished braiding their friendship bracelets.

"Can you tie mine?" Sara asked. "I'm all done. Do you like it? Does it look right?"

"Yes, it's very nice." Christy tied the two leather straps around Sara's thin wrist. "You did a nice job."

Jaeson squeezed Christy's shoulder, "Thanks a million for helping me out here. I'll see you later. At the pool, maybe?"

"Sure, we'll come to the pool," Amy answered for her. "Won't we, Teach? We're really done, aren't we, you guys?"

"I'll see you," Jaeson called over his shoulder as he took off for the pool.

The minute Jaeson was out the door, Sara smiled at Christy and said, "Jaeson asked if you had a boyfriend, and we told him no because you never told us if you really had one or not. We told him you liked him, and he said he liked you."

The three girls gathered around Christy with their eyes twinkling.

"So? Do you like him?" Amy asked.

Christy wasn't sure how much of all of this she should believe. She decided a strong, direct answer might work best. "I think Jaeson is a really nice guy. He's a strong Christian, and that's a very important quality to look for in a guy."

"We knew it!" Sara squealed. "We knew you liked him! Come on. Let's go to the pool."

Jocelyn and Amy held out their arms for Christy to tie their bracelets and then joined Sara, racing up the hill to their cabin to put on their bathing suits.

Christy realized Jeanine must have gotten sidetracked because she wasn't busily making her bracelet for Nick. Either that or she had been so enthusiastic that she had already finished it and rushed off to present it to her "boyfriend."

Taking a few minutes to close up the craft barn, Christy headed up the hill. The girls met her halfway, already suited and with towels under their arms.

"We'll see you there!" they shouted and scampered on down the hill to the pool.

When Christy met them a short time later, they were having a water war with Jaeson and his guys. She wasn't sure she wanted to step into the middle of their combat. To her relief, the lifeguard blew his whistle and said they were getting too rowdy and had to get out of the pool. She put down her towel on the warm cement.

Her three little drowned rats were the first ones out, complaining and arguing about how the boys weren't playing fair. They wrapped themselves in their towels and sat down right next to Christy, hurling rude comments at the boys.

Jaeson planted himself in the middle of his guys and tried to calm them down. He glanced over at Christy, smiled, and shrugged as if to say, "What am I supposed to do with these clowns?"

Christy smiled back.

"He likes you," Sara said, lifting Christy's left hand and pressing down on Christy's fingernails. "Are these real? I mean, are they yours?"

"Yes, they're mine and they're real."

"They're so long!" Sara exclaimed as Amy and Jocelyn crowded in to feel Christy's nails.

"Not really," Christy said.

"They're longer than mine," Amy said. "How do you make them grow?"

"First of all, try to stop biting them," Christy suggested.

"I bite mine all the time," Jocelyn confessed.

The girls continued to compare their nails with Christy's and each other's. Christy peered over their heads and noticed Jaeson talking with the lifeguard. The lifeguard blew his whistle, signaling for everyone in the pool to stop where they were.

"We're going to put up the volleyball net in the shallow end," the lifeguard announced. "Everyone who wants to play volleyball go in the shallow end. Everyone else stay in the deep end."

Apparently volleyball was Jaeson's idea, because he had already pulled the net from the storage cupboard, and his boys were helping him to set it up.

"I don't want to play with them," Amy said. "They always cheat. We'll stay here with you."

Christy's fan club positioned their towels closer to her, overlapping her towel and dripping all over her.

"You want to play?" Jaeson called out to Christy from the shallow end as soon as he had the net in place.

"No!" Sara answered, grabbing Christy by the arm.

The other girls followed her lead. "She's staying here with us."

Christy felt a strong urge to break free from these wet, clinging urchins, but Jessica's advice prompted her to stay.

This was a chance for her to show these girls she loved them. Besides, she wasn't much of a volleyball player on land. She had a feeling the water wouldn't improve her skills.

Now it was Christy's turn to smile and shrug back at Jaeson. He gave her one of his thumbs-up signs and tossed the ball into the water. For the rest of free time, Christy hung around the pool, watching Jaeson, talking to her girls, and wondering if Jaeson would come over and talk to her. He never did, but he looked at her a lot.

At dinner, Christy arrived in the mess hall before Jaeson and took a seat at an empty table, watching the door. He soon came in and headed right for Christy.

"There you are," he said, taking the seat that backed up to hers at the next table. "Your girls told me you didn't have one of these yet."

Jaeson used his teeth to remove one of the leather friendship bracelets from his wrist and offered it to Christy. "You're not an official Camp Wildwood counselor unless you have one."

"Thanks." Christy held out her left wrist for Jaeson to tie on the bracelet. Her "Forever" ID bracelet circled her right wrist, and she didn't think the two bracelets mixed.

While Jaeson tied the thin leather straps, the doors opened and the campers ran in. Christy's girls flocked to her table in time to see him finish tying on the bracelet and give Christy a big smile, which she returned. That's all it took for them to all start whispering about how Jaeson and Christy were now going together.

The eager group of matchmakers made sure that Christy sat near Jaeson in the evening meeting and that they walked to the mess hall together for evening snack.

Christy had to admit that it was fun playing the role of heroine. Six of her girls had now permanently attached themselves to her and led her by the arms wherever they wanted her to go, telling her how pretty she looked or how much Jaeson liked her.

Jaeson seemed to enjoy being a hero too. Christy could tell he had been through this kind of treatment many times before because of all his years as a counselor. She knew it must be like this for him every week of camp. She also figured she was one in a long line of girl counselors who were destined to be Jaeson's girlfriend for the week.

It didn't matter. Christy was having too much fun to think of why this game should end.

The next morning she found it hard to wake up. It was Wednesday, halfway through the week. They had been warned in a counselors meeting that this was when it would all begin to catch up with them.

The girls seemed to have no problem bouncing out of bed though. Christy pulled her sleeping bag over her head and tried to catch a few more Zs.

"Aren't you going to take a shower?" Sara asked, rocking Christy by the shoulder. "You always get up and take a shower."

"Just let me sleep five more minutes," Christy pleaded. "Five more minutes."

"But it's almost six-thirty," one of the girls said. "You have to get to the mess hall before seven so you can get a table next to Jaeson's."

"Oh, I do, do I?" Christy asked, throwing back the sleeping bag and facing seven curious faces peering at her.

"Yes," they all agreed. "He really likes you, and he

would be mad at you if you didn't get there in time."

"Oh, he would, would he?" Christy pulled her legs from her snug cocoon and forced them into the cool morning air and onto the cluttered wood floor.

"You guys, this place is a mess," Christy scolded. "We only received five points yesterday for cabin cleanup. Today I want us to get all ten points. That means everyone has to pick up her junk and put it away."

"Here, wear this," Amy said, pulling a T-shirt from Christy's bag, laying it on her sleeping bag, and smoothing out the wrinkles with her hand.

"And your jeans shorts," Jocelyn advised.

"Okay, okay! You girls get yourselves dressed. And don't forget to pick up all your junk." Christy was beginning to dislike this part of the day when she couldn't go to the bathroom or wash her face without bracing herself against the morning chill on the hike to the restrooms. Throwing on her clothes and grabbing her towel and makeup bag, she headed out the door.

"We'll go with you," four of the girls echoed. "Wait for us."

Christy stood outside the cabin door, shivering and waiting for her entourage to get its act together. The girls joined her, all chattering brightly as they trudged through the dirt.

When Christy arrived in the bathroom, Jessica was already there with her fan club. She looked fresh and pretty and ready to start the day.

"How do you do that?"

"What?"

"How do you manage to look so awake? I'm exhausted."

"We got to bed on time last night, finally," Jessica said. "I cut my devos short. How did yours work out last night?"

Christy plunged her washcloth into the cold water and washed her face as quickly as she could. "Brrr!" she patted dry with her musty-smelling towel. "Devos went well, I think."

The campers were all scurrying around the bathroom. A few huddled around the sink next to Jessica and Christy and imitated the older girls' wake-up routine by splashing cold water on their faces and responding with the same "Brrr!"

"They were great!" Jocelyn answered for Christy. "We talked all night."

"I tried your idea of getting acquainted by each girl telling about her family. We went too long, but they all had lots to say. I think I know them a lot better now."

"And she likes us more too," Amy added. "Don't you, Teach?"

Jessica and Christy exchanged smiles.

"You can never love too much," Jessica whispered in Christy's ear. Then gathering her things, she said, "You're doing a great job, Christy. I'll see you at breakfast."

Christy felt warmed inside and encouraged. Maybe she was going to make it through this week after all.

7

Tippy Canoe

Wednesday zoomed by with the usual routine of the counselors meeting, morning Bible study, and the whole afternoon free. Christy planned to spend the afternoon at the pool with her girls since Jaeson said he was going to be there. But when she went up to the cabin to put on her bathing suit, she found Ruthie on her bunk bed crying.

Christy sat on the edge of Ruthie's bed, ducking her head to fit under the top bunk. She placed her hand on Ruthie's back and slowly rubbed it. "Are you okay?"

Ruthie's sobbing slowed to a sniffle. "Nobody here likes me."

"Yes, they do. Everyone likes you. I like you very much," Christy said.

"Everybody has her own friends here. I don't have anybody. Nobody asked me to go with them. They all took off without me."

Christy kept rubbing Ruthie's back and stroked her light brown hair back from her peaches-and-cream face. "I'm sorry," was all Christy said.

She thought of plenty of advice to give Ruthie about

how she should be the friendly one who pursues the other girls and how it wouldn't do any good to lie here feeling sorry for herself when there was so much outside for her to do. But Christy remembered the times she had felt left out, lonely, and sad. It had always helped to throw herself on her bed and have a good cry.

What she didn't like was when her mom had come in and told her how she should act or what she should be feeling. Christy always wished her mother would just let her cry and feel sad with her for a few minutes.

Christy sat silently rubbing Ruthie's back as she finished getting out all her tears. Eventually the only sound was a few sniffs from Ruthie into her damp pillow.

"Here." Christy reached over to her backpack on the floor and pulled out a packet of tissues. "Try one of these instead of your pillowcase. You're going to have to sleep on that thing tonight, you know."

Ruthie accepted the tissue and blew her nose. "You probably think I'm acting like a baby."

"Not at all," Christy said, handing her another tissue. "I think you're a lovely young girl turning into a beautiful young woman."

The girl honked her nose loudly as she blew. "Sorry." She repressed a giggle at how loud her nose sounded.

"That's okay," Christy said. "You feel better?"

Ruthie nodded and offered a smile.

"Good. Now what do you want to do this afternoon? You and I can do it together."

"I wanted to go out in a canoe, but nobody else wanted to go with me."

"I'll go with you," Christy said.

"Are you sure?" Ruthie asked. "Wouldn't you rather be with Jaeson?"

"No, I'd rather be with you."

Ruthie sprang from the bed, her hope renewed, and led the way to the door. Christy followed, feeling pleased with Ruthie's comeback. On the trail to the lake, Ruthie slipped her hand into Christy's and gave it a squeeze. Christy squeezed back.

"How did you get so good at knowing what to do when a girl is crying?"

"I happen to be the pity party expert," Christy said. "When I was your age I used to cry about stuff all the time."

"And you don't cry anymore?"

"Sure, I still cry, but not as much. I still have some of the same feelings that used to send me to my pillow when I was younger, but they don't make me cry as much anymore."

Ruthie let go of Christy's hand and skittered a few feet into the woods, where she picked a small yellow wildflower and brought it back to Christy.

"Thank you, Ruthie." Christy slipped the flower behind her right ear. "And I really do like your name. There was a Ruth in the Bible, you know. There's a whole book written about her because she was such a loyal friend. That's how I'll always remember you: Ruthie, my loyal friend."

Ruthie flashed a rare full smile, revealing her mouthful of silver braces. She looked like a different girl from the sullen one who had told Christy she hated the name Ruth.

They walked through the clearing onto the gravel beach by the lake. Ruthie was the first to notice that two of the other girls from their cabin, Sara and Jeanine, were there.

Christy knew if Jeanine was here, Nick probably wasn't far away. Sure enough, Christy spotted Nick and his two friends at the boat shack, apparently getting a canoe.

"Why don't you ask those two girls if they'd like to join us on our canoe ride?" Christy suggested to Ruthie. "I have a strong feeling at least one of them would like to."

Ruthie ran off to invite Jeanine and Sara while Christy headed for the boat shack. Not until she was in front of the shack did she notice that Jaeson was the one behind the window passing out life vests.

"Christy, just the person I wanted to see. How do you feel about taking these guys for a canoe ride? I told Mike I'd fill in for him here until four."

"She's taking us out," Jeanine answered, stepping up to the window with Ruthie and Sara.

"We could take one of the guys," Jeanine added, flashing a grin at Nick.

"Nope," Jaeson said. "Only four to a canoe."

Jaeson looked at his watch and then back at Nick and his two friends. "I probably shouldn't do this," he said, "but you guys have gone out before, and you pretty much know what you're doing. I'll let you three go by yourselves. Christy, can you keep an eye on them and try to stay close to them out on the lake in case of any accidents?"

"Sure, that's fine," Christy said.

"And I'll be right here watching you guys," Jaeson added, handing out the life preservers. He caught Christy's wrist when she reached for her preserver and gave it a squeeze. "Thanks. You're a honey."

Christy's campers heard him say it, and they huddled close to her as they walked over to the canoes.

"He likes you!" Jeanine declared nice and loud.

"Shhhh," Christy said. Then bending close to Jeanine, she asked, "How's it going with you and Nick?"

"Okay, I think. He hasn't hit me yet today."

"And you haven't taken any more of his things, have you?"

"No. I gave him a bracelet like Jessica said, but he's not wearing it."

"That's okay." Christy gave her a little squeeze around her plump orange life vest. "I'm proud of the way you're acting."

Jeanine beamed.

It took Christy's troop longer to launch their boat than the boys. They suddenly had four captains and no mates. Jaeson came over and helped by giving their canoe a good swift push. Christy sat at the front with a paddle in her hand, Ruthie took the middle bench, and Jeanine and Sara insisted on sharing the backseat, each with a paddle in the water.

"Make sure you paddle in the same direction," Jaeson called out as they began to bob on the calm lake.

"Farewell!" Sara cried out dramatically, standing up and turning to wave good-bye to Jaeson.

"Sit down!" they all yelled at her as the canoe began to tip.

"Okay, listen," Christy called over her shoulder. "All of you follow my lead. If my paddle is in the water on this side, then you put your paddle in on this side. And the same over here." She demonstrated for them, hoping none of them would guess that she hadn't been in a canoe since she was their age. Even then, it was with her Uncle Tom in Minnesota, and he had done all the paddling.

The crew followed orders, and everything seemed smooth. No problem.

"Let's catch up with the boys," Jeanine said, eagerly paddling on her side. The canoe swerved to the left toward the shore.

"We have to paddle all together," Christy said. "Remember what I said? Follow my lead."

She dug her paddle into the water for three strong strokes on the left side of the canoe to straighten them out and at least point them in the boys' direction. Christy switched her paddle to the right side, but apparently the girls weren't watching. Sara and Ruthie kept paddling on the left. It seemed they were getting nowhere.

Christy barked out more instructions. The canoe gently drifted toward the middle of the lake, no thanks to their efforts.

"Look at the ducks!" Sara said. "They're coming right up to the canoe. Let's sit here and watch them."

"No, we need to catch up with the boys," Jeanine objected. "Remember what Jaeson said. We have to stay with them, and they're headed for the other side of the lake."

"What's over there?" Christy asked.

"That's where they have the counselor hunt on the last full day," Sara explained. "All the counselors row over in canoes and hide, and then we run around the edge of the lake to find them. Whoever finds their counselor first has to get their counselor's sash and run all the way back to the boat shack."

"But the counselors get to try to beat them," Jeanine added. "They come back in their canoes and have to plant their flags by the boathouse."

"Sounds like a lot of fun," Christy said.

"Whoever loses has to serve the food at the banquet on the last night. We have team captains, and if the campers lose, they serve the counselors, who all sit together at one table."

"And if the counselors lose?" Christy asked.

"Then they have to serve all the tables."

"Well, I hope we win. I wouldn't mind having dinner served to me," Christy said. "Paddle on the right, girls. We're starting to drift too far."

They worked their way across the lake, improving as they went, until they almost caught up with the boys. Christy could feel strange muscle twinges in her upper arms. She never would have guessed paddling was such hard work or that this small lake was so far across.

"How are you guys doing?" Christy called out when they were within a few yards of the guys' canoe.

"We're fishing," Nick said. He pulled his stick out of the water and revealed a brown string attached to it with a wiggly worm at the end. Christy thought their Tom Sawyer fishing pole looked quite clever.

"Ewww!" Sara said. "That's a worm."

"Duh," said one of the boys.

"I hate worms," Sara said.

Nick dangled the fishing pole over toward the girls' canoe so Sara could look at the worm close-up. It came within a few feet of her face, and she screamed.

"Hey!" Jeanine yelled when she looked closely at the brown string attached to the stick. "That's the friendship bracelet I made for you!"

"Turned out to be good for something," Nick said, laughing.

"I want it back!" Jeanine yelled. "I worked hard on that. You're not supposed to use it for a fishing line!"

Jeanine stood up and lunged for the line, which Nick jerked away. Before Christy knew what was happening, Jeanine toppled from the canoe and into the lake.

"Jeanine!" Christy screamed, turning around and trying to steady the topsy-turvy canoe. Sara stood and tried to reach for the soaked Jeanine.

Ruthie leaned back to compensate for Sara's weight being thrown to one side, but it was too much of a compensation. The canoe tottered to the left, dumping Ruthie into the lake, and then to the right, dumping Sara in after Jeanine.

"Girls!" Christy called out futilely. The canoe rocked back and forth, and Christy tried to steady it as the three drowned rats, buoyed up by their life vests, each tried to pull themselves into the canoe on opposite sides. The girls were laughing and didn't seem to mind the dunking a bit.

"Wait!" Christy cried. "Stop! This isn't working. We're so close to shore, why don't you swim in, and I'll pick you up there?"

The girls, still laughing, willingly dog-paddled the short distance to shore and waited there for Christy, dripping wet and shivering.

The boys were laughing so hard that they didn't hear Christy tell them to stay put while she went for the girls. They must have decided their best course of action was to get as far away from the girls as they could, since they knew retaliation would be on the girls' minds. The boys took off, paddling full speed back to the boat shack, leaving Christy to manage the rescue landing by herself.

The girls helped pull their canoe into shore and stiffly tried to get in. That's when the laughing stopped and the complaining began.

"They made us fall in," Jeanine sobbed. "I'm going to get back at them."

"I'm cold," Sara complained. "Didn't you bring a towel?"

"It's back on the other side," Christy said. "Once we get over there you can use it."

"But it's so far," Ruthie moaned. "We're going to freeze to death."

"It's not that cold," Christy said. "Try sitting in the bottom of the canoe. You'll keep out of the wind better that way."

"But there's water in the bottom," Sara said.

"That's okay," Christy coaxed them. "You're already wet. It won't hurt you."

The girls wedged themselves into the hull of the canoe and crossed their arms in front of them around their bloated vests, trying to keep warm. Christy, at the helm, tried her best to maneuver the canoe across the lake. It seemed impossible to move the canoe in the direction she wanted it to go. Without anyone paddling at the rear, the canoe floundered through the water, more motivated by the wind and waves than by Christy's determined efforts with the paddle. She was definitely doing this the hard way.

Her complaining crew kept giving her advice about which side she should be paddling on and why she was doing it all wrong. Christy endured the remarks for ten minutes and then lost it. "Would one of you like to try this?" she barked. "It's not exactly easy."

"I'll help you," Ruthie offered. She rose to sit on the middle seat and stuck a paddle into the water on the same side as Christy's. Together they plunged the canoe through the water and made some headway.

Ten minutes later they reached the shore. By then the girls were mostly dried out. The boys had landed a good fifteen minutes earlier and had long since disappeared.

Jaeson met them at the shore, wading waist deep in the water to help bring in their canoe. He lifted each of the girls from their floating prison and offered his hand to Christy so she could step out onto the gravel. She felt like an incompetent counselor, having dumped her girls and lost track of the boys. If she had fallen in herself, she might have felt better at this moment. At least she could have been another victim and not the responsible person.

Jaeson held on to her hand and drew her close. In a low voice he said, "Would you be interested in a free canoe lesson?"

A smile returned to Christy's face. "Why?" she teased. "You think I need one?"

"It's up to you," Jaeson said. "I thought you might want a little edge on the campers for the counselor hunt on Friday."

"Okay, you talked me into it. You say when, and I'll be there."

"I'll let you know tonight at dinner." Jaeson gave her hand a squeeze before letting it go.

At dinner, Jaeson and Christy sat back-to-back in what had become their usual spots at the tables. During the meal Jaeson leaned back four times to make comments in Christy's ear. It was hard to hear him above the roar of the campers. But it didn't really matter what he said. Just the attention was fun.

She did notice when dinner was over that he hadn't mentioned a time for the promised canoe lesson. Maybe he had forgotten. Christy tried not to feel discouraged. After all, this was only Wednesday, and they had the whole next day to practice, since the race was on Friday.

"Come play softball with us," her girls urged, pulling her by the arms from the mess hall. "We have to hurry! We only have a half hour free before the evening meeting starts."

Christy let the girls lead her out to the baseball field where some of the campers had already started up a game. When they saw her coming, they all insisted she be the pitcher. She was good at hitting the ball, but she wasn't too confident that her pitching would win any awards.

Taking her place on the mound and winding up, she let the softball fly over home plate. *Thump!* One of the girls from Jessica's cabin hit the ball, and it sailed to center field. Her teammates cheered, and the girl took a playful bow when she made it safely to first base.

Another windup, and the next girl made contact with the first ball Christy pitched. Same with the next hitter; the bases were loaded. A timid, skinny fifth-grader stepped up to the plate next, and Christy threw three of the gentlest, slowest balls she could throw. The girl swung at all three and missed.

"One more pitch," a deep voice called out from the side of the field. It was Jaeson. He stepped up behind the discouraged little hitter, wrapped his arms around her, and showed her how to hold the bat the right way.

"Okay, Christy," Jaeson called out, his arms still around the batter. "Give us your best shot."

Christy pretended to be spitting on her hands and sending signals to the catcher.

"Come on, pitcher," Jaeson yelled, "let us have it!"

With a dramatic windup, Christy let the ball go. It was a ridiculous pitch that landed almost four feet away from the plate on the left side. Everyone laughed, including Christy.

"If that's your best," Jaeson heckled, "we don't want to see your worst."

"I was just testing you," Christy called back. "Wanted to see if you would swing at anything. Here comes a good one."

Christy pitched a nice, slow ball straight over home plate. With Jaeson's help, the girl smacked the ball almost all the way to the woods. Everyone cheered as she ran the bases with Jaeson by her side. The other three runners came home with hoots and hollers.

A fielder threw the ball to second base just as Jaeson and the girl touched third. Now it was a battle to see if they could make it home. Jaeson picked up the girl, carrying her under his arm like a football, as he charged home. They made it a few seconds before the ball did, and Jaeson put the girl down firmly on home plate, like an explorer planting a flag and claiming the land.

A small crowd of campers had gathered, and everyone was still cheering when the next girl stepped up to bat. "I want Jaeson to help me too," she said.

"Naw, you can do it yourself. Go ahead and try," Jaeson coached from the sidelines.

With the first pitch, the girl looked as though she deliberately swung and missed. Perhaps she hoped her lack of coordination would bring Jaeson to her side.

"Come on!" he called out. "I know you can do better than that."

She positioned the bat over her shoulder and turned to Christy with a fierce look on her face. Christy wanted to laugh. This girl was taking the game more seriously than it was intended. Christy gave her an easy low ball, and the girl hit a grounder that dribbled right back to Christy. Watching the girl run to first base out of the corner of her eye, Christy made sure she was almost there before snatching up the grounder and tossing it to first base. The girl was safe. By the look on her face, she was quite proud of herself.

In the distance, they heard the camp bell ringing, which was their signal to go to the evening meeting. Everyone groaned. Christy's girls complained that they didn't have a chance to bat.

"Can we finish our game tomorrow?" they asked.

"Sure," Christy agreed. "How about tomorrow right after lunch?"

"You were too nice to them," Sara said. "You were trying to make them win."

"She would pitch the same way if you were up to bat," Jaeson said, coming to Christy's defense and joining them as they headed back to main camp. "That's what counselors are supposed to do—be fair to everybody."

The girl Jaeson had helped around the bases now had a hold of his arm and looked like she intended to remain attached permanently to him. Sara grabbed Jaeson's other arm.

Looking up at him with her ginger eyes, she pleaded,

"Will you play with us tomorrow afternoon? Pleeeease?"

"Sure," Jaeson said, catching Christy's eye and giving her a big smile. "Christy and I make a good team, don't you think?"

That comment prompted a round of agreement from the girls, including Jocelyn's bright statement, "Why don't you two get married? Then you could do this every day for the rest of your lives."

"Hey, yeah!" Jeanine agreed. "You could build a little cabin over there in the woods, and we'd all come and stay with you. You could take us canoeing and play baseball every day."

Christy was too embarrassed to look at Jaeson, but she could feel his amused glance. Fortunately they were back at camp and could file into the meeting hall with the rest of the campers. The singing started a few minutes after they walked in. Christy's girls, full of energy, sang loudly, nudging each other and making up their own hand motions to go along with the motions they had already learned. Christy looked across the room and noticed Jaeson sitting with his boys. He turned and gazed back at her, giving one of his thumbs-up signs. She smiled back, hoping her girls hadn't noticed.

Then Christy spotted a film projector set up in the back. She remembered Dean Ferrill telling them at the counselors meeting that they had a movie for the kids tonight that should get them thinking. At devos that night the counselors were supposed to take advantage of the film's message to see if any of their campers wanted to make a commitment to Christ.

The lights were out, and the movie started. Christy felt a

firm hand on her shoulder. Jaeson whispered in her ear, "Come with me."

Christy slipped out without her girls noticing and followed Jaeson. As soon as the door to the meeting hall closed behind them, he took Christy's hand and said, "Time for your canoe lesson."

"Now?"

Jaeson, still holding her hand, pulled her along with him as he jogged toward the lake. "Now's the best time. Right after sunset. The water is smooth, and it's nice and quiet."

"But are you sure this is okay?" Christy puffed. She couldn't help but feel they were sneaking off, leaving their campers behind. They would get in trouble for this, she just knew it.

"We'll be back before the movie is over. It won't be a problem. Trust me."

Jaeson kept a firm hold on her hand as they wound through the woods. They arrived at the boat shack winded. He had the wild look of an adventurer in his eyes when he handed Christy her life jacket and paddle. She still felt they were doing something wrong and would get caught.

"Are you sure this is okay, Jaeson?"

"You want to learn to canoe, don't you? Now's your golden opportunity. Just look at the lake. Isn't it beautiful?"

She had to admit that Jaeson was right. The lake looked like the polished floor of a ballet studio, with the fading golden lights of the summer evening dancing across it.

"Get in," Jaeson ordered when he had positioned the canoe halfway into the water.

Christy carefully balanced her way to the front bench

and held on, trying to keep the canoe steady. Jaeson dropped his full weight on the back bench and used his paddle to push off from shore.

Suddenly it was quiet. The only sounds were the calm water rippling up against the canoe's side and the evening chorus of bullfrogs and crickets along the shore.

"Jaeson," Christy whispered, "are you sure we should be out here?"

"Relax, will you? I've done this a bunch of times." Then Jaeson's voice became softer, "Isn't it beautiful out here? I love this. Come on. Relax, Christy. I promise tonight will be the highlight of your whole week."

Christy's fingers clutched the paddle in her lap. Her eyes darted back and forth across the darkening waters as they headed for the middle of the lake.

Relax, huh?

8

Moonlight Picnic

When they reached the middle of the lake, Jaeson said, "Now, the first thing you need to know is how to hold the paddle. I noticed you were holding it like this today."

He showed Christy in the dim light that he had both hands on the neck of the paddle. "You need to put one hand on the top like this and the other right about here."

Christy held up her paddle and followed his instructions.

"Good. I knew you would be a fast learner. When you're in the canoe alone, you have to paddle from the back if you want to control which way it goes. You were trying to steer it from the front this afternoon. Watch."

Jaeson dipped his paddle in the water on the right side, and as he gave a mighty stroke, the canoe lunged forward. Another stroke on the left side, and the canoe charged again. Jaeson kept the canoe going straight from his control point at the back.

"You try it," Jaeson said. "Turn around and face me, and your end will become the back of the canoe."

Christy lifted one long leg and tried to swing it over to

the other side without tipping the canoe. It felt terribly awkward. She managed to get both legs over and sat facing Jaeson. It was too dark to see his expression clearly, but she thought he was smiling at her.

Does he think I'm a klutz or what? I can't tell if he's smiling at me or laughing at me.

"Are you right-handed?" Jaeson asked.

"Yes, why?"

"I have a theory that you'll have more strength paddling on your left side, because your right hand will be on top of the paddle, and that's your strongest. So start your paddle on the left side. Remember to put your hand on top."

Christy followed his instructions.

"Good. Always start with a strong stroke, and then switch to the other side and give it another strong stroke."

Christy did, and Jaeson praised her. "See how different it feels when you're at the back of the canoe? You have much more control."

"You're right," Christy said. "Thanks for the lesson."

Jaeson started to scan the treetops on the other side of the lake. "It won't be here for another ten minutes," he said. "Good thing I brought provisions for us."

"What won't be here?"

"You'll see. Thirsty?" Jaeson reached for a bundle on the floor in the center of the canoe.

Christy had noticed it when she had climbed in but thought it was just a blanket. He undid the bundle and revealed a variety of "provisions."

"What's that?" Christy asked.

"Our moonlight picnic," he said, placing a lantern onto the center seat. He lit the wick inside. Jaeson pulled out a glass and scooped up some lake water and placed it next to the lantern. He picked up a dozen squashed wild-flowers from the bundle and dunked them in the vase.

Christy laughed at his creativity. "This is charming, Jaeson."

"Charming?" he repeated. "It's been called many things, but I think I like charming the best so far."

Christy took it from his comment that during his years as a camp counselor, he had taken more than one girl out for a moonlight picnic. She wondered if tonight was any different for him. Was she special to him? Or was she just another girl counselor he could flirt with for the week? She wanted to be his favorite, the only girl he had ever done this with. She wanted it to be romantic and as wonderful for him as it was for her.

Jaeson handed Christy an opened bottle of mineral water and a napkin.

"Thank you, kind sir," she said, playing along with the fun.

"And now for the best part," Jaeson announced. "Peanut butter cookies saved from Sunday night!"

He handed Christy a cookie that was about seventy-five percent there.

"That's the biggest one," he said. "They get a little crumbly after the second day."

Christy laughed. "This is great, Jaeson! How fun. Thanks for bringing me out here."

She bit into the cookie and listened to the sound of the lake gently lapping at the side of the canoe.

"Oh, I almost forgot." Jaeson rummaged through the bundle and came up with a portable CD player. He popped in a CD, cranked the volume all the way up, and balanced it on the middle seat with the earphones pointed in Christy's direction. The music came out soft, just loud enough.

"A little music," he said.

Christy felt like giggling; this was all so fun. A breeze blew over them, bringing with it the cool, pungent smell of moss, with just a hint of coconut tanning lotion.

"So," Jaeson leaned back slightly and took a bite out of his cookie, "tell me your dreams."

"What?"

"What do you wish? What are your dreams for the future?"

Christy was caught off guard. Whenever she dreamed of the future, the dreams included Todd. She couldn't tell that to Jaeson. Not here with the music and lantern light and everything.

"I don't know if I really have any dreams or wishes for the future," she answered.

"Sure you do. You have to. Everyone has to have a dream. Do you want to hear mine?"

"Sure," Christy said.

"I want to be a pilot. I want to fly my own plane. Not those big commercial airplanes or military jets. I want a little plane. I'd even be happy as a crop duster. That's my wish."

"Have you taken any flying lessons?" Christy asked.

"No, but I have some information on them. I'm saving up my money because they're not cheap. Maybe by this fall I'll start lessons."

"That's a good dream." Christy took a sip from her bottle. "I bet you'll make a great pilot."

"Your turn," Jaeson said. "What's your dream?"

"Well, I only thought of one thing. I've never told anyone this before, I don't think."

"You can tell me. All secrets shared on moonlight picnics are safe with me." Jaeson reached for another cookie and listened intently, waiting for her answer.

"I'd like to go to England. To Europe, actually. I've always wanted to visit a real castle and go for a ride in a gondola in Venice. That's my dream," Christy said, feeling brave.

"That's a jolly good dream," Jaeson said with a British accent. "You do have a bit of a Mary Poppins look about you. I'm sure your wish will come true."

Just then he spotted something over the top of Christy's head. It was easier to see his expression now, and Christy noticed his face lighting up with delight.

"Here he comes," Jaeson said. "Look!"

Christy turned around and saw what Jaeson was so excited about. The moon, a big, fat, buttery ball, had just popped over the treetops and was dripping its golden light onto the lake.

"Right on time." Jaeson gently paddled the canoe around so Christy wouldn't have to look over her shoulder.

"It's so beautiful!" Christy whispered as they watched the moon rise over the lake and shine on them like a searchlight. Everything around them took on a hazy, amber glow, and for some reason it felt warmer.

They sat in silence, enjoying the night show and listening to the muted melodies floating from the CD player. Christy knew Jaeson had been right when he said this would be the highlight of her week. Still, as wonderful and romantic and peaceful as everything was, thoughts of Todd crept into the fantasy evening.

There's nothing wrong with me being here with Jaeson and enjoying this romantic moment with him. It doesn't change anything between Todd and me.

Just then Jaeson leaned toward Christy, his hand reaching for her face.

Is he going to kiss me? What should I do?

Jaeson's hand brushed against her cheek. "There. You had some cookie crumbs on your cheek."

"Oh," Christy's hand flew to her cheek and brushed away a few tiny crumbs Jaeson's hand had missed. Her skin felt hot to her touch, and she hoped Jaeson couldn't see her blushing in the moonlight.

"When do we need to leave to get back before we're missed?" She tried not to sound as nervous as she felt.

"Oh, about now. Are you sure you want to go? This is the most peace and quiet you'll have for the rest of the week."

Christy wanted to stay. She wanted to float on the quiet lake for hours and stare at the moon and share her secret dreams with Jaeson. She wanted the fantasy to go on and on. But inwardly the struggle was growing. Should she be here, alone with Jaeson? Would they get in trouble for leaving the meeting? Would she do or say anything with Jaeson that she would later regret?

"I guess we should go back," Christy said with a sigh. "This has been wonderful, Jaeson. The music, the flowers, the moonlight. I love it. I loved being here with you."

"Thanks. I'm glad you liked it." He extinguished the lantern light. "I'll take you back. Remember, though, it was your choice, not mine."

He lifted the bunch of flowers from the vase and handed them to Christy. "To remember me by."

She took them and said, "I'll keep them, Jaeson, and I know I'll never forget you or tonight."

She could see his smile in the moonlight and felt content and a little relieved that things had gone just as far as they had and no farther.

Dipping her paddle into the water, she asked, "You want me to practice paddling us back to shore?"

"Good idea. Remember to start on your left side."

Christy tried to remember all of Jaeson's pointers as she plunged the paddle deep into the water and headed them for shore. It was a lot easier than her afternoon experience had been, and in no time, Jaeson's end of the canoe scraped up onto the gravel.

"Excellent." Jaeson hoped out and pulled them up on shore. "I'll put the gear away if you want to head on back. Or you can wait for me if you want."

The thought of wandering through the dark woods by herself didn't thrill Christy, so she helped Jaeson put the stuff back where it belonged. He stuffed the picnic bundle into a corner in the boat shack. Christy couldn't help but wonder if it would sit there until next week, when Jaeson would take another girl counselor out on the lake.

He took her by the hand again, and they hurried back to the meeting hall where the campers were just beginning to stream out the open doors and run for their snacks.

"See?" Jaeson let go of her hand and joined the throng headed for the mess hall. "No problem."

Christy almost believed everything was okay until devotions in her cabin that night when she was supposed to discuss the movie with her girls. As they all started to jabber about it, Christy had no idea what they were talking about. Quickly taking another direction, she asked the girls to be quiet and listen so she could tell them her testimony.

"Why do they call it a testimony, Teach?" Amy asked.

"Well, I guess because you're telling something that happened to you and you're letting people know that what you're saying is true," Christy explained. Then she went on to tell the girls how she had grown up in a Christian home.

"How can a house be a Christian?" Sara popped off.

The other girls laughed, and Christy calmed them down, saying, "Of course a house can't be a Christian. What I meant is both of my parents are Christians, so I grew up going to church."

"Me too," Ruthie said, and several other girls chimed in that their parents were Christians too.

"It wasn't enough for me to just know about God," Christy said. "I had to invite Him into my life. I did that when I was fifteen. I prayed and asked God to forgive all my sins and to come into my life. He did, and since that time I've slowly been changing and becoming more the person God wants me to be."

"How can there be a Christian school?" Sara asked. "The people who go there could be Christians, but the school can't become a Christian."

The other girls joined in with their opinions on the difference between a school of Christians and a Christian school. Christy felt certain none of them had heard her testimony, and even if some of them had, it didn't seem to matter much to them.

"Okay, girls. That's enough. I'm going to turn out the

lights, and everyone needs to be in her sleeping bag." She snapped off the light and climbed into bed.

"Now I'm going to pray, and if any of you wants to pray, you can. We'll all be silent for a little bit so anyone who wants to can pray, and then after a while I'll close, okay? Let's pray."

It was silent for about two seconds, and then one of the girls gave a loud snort, which prompted lots of muffled giggles. Then someone else did her best to manufacture a belch. Jocelyn whispered, "Stop kicking my bed, Sara."

"Girls," Christy said firmly, "we are praying."

It became silent. Completely silent. None of the girls prayed, so Christy jumped in after two minutes of silence. She prayed specifically for each of the girls, the way they did in the counselors meetings. Then she prayed for the other campers, the counselors, the camp staff, and the campers who would be coming next week. Her prayer lasted more than five minutes, and when she finished, not one girl was still awake.

Well, she thought, *that's one way to get them to sleep at night!*

Christy fell asleep immediately and had wonderful dreams about being in a rowboat on a placid lake with swans swimming around her. Behind her was a huge storybook castle. She held a lacy parasol and twirled it with her white-gloved fingers. Across from her sat a man dressed in a tuxedo who was pouring tea into a china cup. When he asked if she would like one lump of sugar or two, he looked up, and she saw that it was Todd.

When she woke up with the alarm at six the next morning, she felt rested. Bouncing out of bed, she headed to the restroom for a brisk morning shower. Jessica was already there, and Christy told her about her new devotional tactic for praying the girls to sleep.

"The only bad part was they didn't pay attention when I gave my testimony, and none of them prayed. I don't think any of my girls are interested in spiritual things."

Jessica wrapped a towel around her wet hair, and pouring some astringent on a cotton ball, she began her facial-cleansing routine. "I think the next step is for you to spend time with each of them one-on-one and find out where they are."

"How can I do that? It's Thursday already. That's not much time. Besides, what do I say? 'Let's have some quality time. We've got three minutes. So tell me if you're saved or not, and if you want to be or not.'"

Jessica laughed. "Not like that, Christy. Just sit down with each of them individually, tell them you care about them, and ask if there's anything they want to talk about. We don't know which ones are ready to give their hearts to the Lord and which ones aren't. God knows. All we need to do is give them an opportunity to talk about it and offer to answer their questions."

Christy combed through her wet hair. "You're right. I'll figure out a way to get together with each of them. I hope you know that if you weren't here giving me all this good advice, I'd be completely lost."

"I'm sure you would do fine," Jessica said. "I'm glad we're here together though. I want to be sure to get your address so we can stay in contact after camp."

"Me too. My friend Katie is never going to believe I said this, but I'm glad I came. It's been a great week."

"It's not over yet! We still have to live through the counselor hunt tomorrow."

The hunt was the first thing they discussed at the meeting that morning.

"I suggest," Dean Ferrill said, "that you each take a hike over to the other side of the lake sometime today and scope out a hiding place. This will help save a lot of time tomorrow when you get over there."

Since Christy had promised the girls she would pitch at their softball game after lunch, she wasn't sure when she would have a chance to hunt for a spot. Fortunately it was hotter than usual that afternoon, and after three innings, both teams were ready to quit and find a cooler sport. The minute one of them suggested volleyball in the pool, they all disappeared, leaving Jaeson and Christy alone to put away the equipment.

"You coming over to the pool?" Jaeson asked.

"Actually, I thought I'd better find myself a good hiding place across the lake."

"Good idea. I'll go with you. I can show you some places I've used before."

They walked around the lake rather than taking a canoe. At one spot where the trail became narrow, Jaeson reached his hand behind him, offering it to Christy. She felt comfortable holding Jaeson's hand.

"Here's one spot I used last year," Jaeson said, stopping and pointing straight up.

"Where?" Christy asked.

"Up there. This is an easy tree to climb. It was a lot of fun because the kids never thought to look up even though I showered them with pine needles."

"I'm not much of a tree climber," Christy said hesitantly. "Do you have any other suggestions?"

"Sure. Follow me."

Jaeson led her through the woods, pointing out five possible hiding spots. She liked the last one best and decided that was the one for her. It was a hollowed-out tree trunk behind a huge tree that grew close to the trail. The campers would have to go off the trail and around the tree to find her. She thought it would be good to bring a towel along so she wouldn't have to sit on the moldy bark inside the tree.

Jaeson took her hand again and began to lead her back. He stopped at the good climbing tree and said, "I think I'll try going up again this year. Worked great last year."

He then coached Christy on canoe strategy. She loved this feeling. The birds were singing above them, the shimmering lake was peeking at them from behind the trees, and she was on an afternoon walk, hand-in-hand with the cutest counselor at camp. This is what Christy dreamed camp would be like. Nothing of her previous life seemed to matter now. She had two more days at Camp Wildwood, and she intended to enjoy every minute of them.

9

View from a Hollow Tree

At dinner that night, Jocelyn wasn't eating. Christy asked her if she felt okay.

"My stomach hurts," she said.

Christy felt her forehead, "You feel pretty warm. Let's get you over to the nurse's office."

Turning to Jaeson, who sat behind her as usual, Christy asked, "Can you keep an eye on my girls? This one needs to see the nurse."

With her arm around Jocelyn, Christy escorted her from the noisy mess hall and across the grounds to the nurse's small white building.

When they were only a few yards away, Jocelyn said, "I think I have to throw up."

"Can you make it to those bushes?" Christy asked, helping Jocelyn walk a little faster.

They made it just in time for Jocelyn to be sick. Christy turned away and held her breath. This was a part of camp counseling she hadn't planned on. Rummaging through her pockets, she found a tissue. Still holding her breath, she held it out to Jocelyn and said, "Here."

Jocelyn groaned and started to cry as she wiped off her mouth. "I feel awful!"

"We're almost there, honey." Christy wrapped her arm back around Jocelyn and coaxed the sobbing girl along.

Fortunately the nurse must have heard them coming because she opened the door and helped Jocelyn to a clean cot.

"Her stomach hurts," Christy explained. "She threw up out there in the bushes."

"You poor little thing," the nurse said, placing her hand on Jocelyn's forehead. "What did you eat today?"

"She didn't eat any dinner," Christy said.

"What about during free time? Did you have any snacks?"

Jocelyn slowly nodded her head and listed half a dozen snack foods and types of candy bars she'd eaten.

The nurse placed a cool washcloth on Jocelyn's forehead and whispered to Christy, "Sounds like a case of junk food overload. I'll give her something to settle her stomach, and she'll be fine."

Christy patted Jocelyn on the arm, "You do what the nurse says, and I'll check on you later, okay?"

She was about to slip out when the nurse said, "Could you do me a favor? Would you fill up the bucket on the side of the building and then wash down the site where she vomited?"

Christy shuddered as she doused the spot with a bucket of water. This was definitely the part of being a counselor she could do without. For good measure, she filled a second bucket and poured it over the area so no signs of the accident remained.

I'm glad I got her out of the mess hall when I did!

The doors to the mess hall opened, and the Camp Wildwood wild campers scattered to make use of their short free time before the evening meeting.

Oh, great, dinner's over, and I didn't finish eating. Actually, I don't feel like eating anymore.

Christy had planned to spend time with her girls individually today, but with the baseball game and the walk with Jaeson, the afternoon had flown. Jeanine was the first of her girls she spotted exiting the dining hall. She caught up with her and asked, "Do you want to do something?"

Jeanine looked at her funny. "Like what?"

"I don't know. Go for a walk, sit by the lake, and talk."

"Why?"

"Well, just so we can have some time together." Christy scrambled for a better approach.

"We've been together all week," Jeanine said. "We're bunk mates even."

"I know, I just thought maybe, well...never mind."

"No," Jeanine said, clutching Christy's arm. "We can do something if you want."

Now Christy wasn't sure who was the leader and who was the follower. "Why don't we just go out in the woods and talk. I know where there's a bench not far from here."

"Okay," Jeanine said cheerfully. "If that'll make you feel better."

Christy led Jeanine to the bench. She had planned her opening line during their walk and sprang it on Jeanine. "I want you to know that I think you're wonderful, I care about you, and I want to know if you have any questions about God."

Jeanine looked at her a moment before answering. "Nope."

"Okay, that's fine." Christy had no idea where to go next with her big witnessing opportunity. "So you feel like everything between you and God is fine?"

"Yep. My parents prayed with me when I was little, Jesus lives in my heart, and I know I'm going to heaven. Do you think you could braid my hair like that other counselor Jessica braids her girls' hair?"

"I could try," Christy floundered.

Why don't any of these girls want to talk about spiritual things?

"Good." Jeanine turned her back to Christy and scrounged in her pocket. "I have a rubber band here." She proceeded to extract at least two dozen rubber bands from her pocket.

"What are all these for?" Christy asked, trying to smooth Jeanine's matted mane with her fingernails before she pulled all the pieces together in a French braid.

"Jessica told me to try giving something to Nick instead of taking stuff from him, you know? I tried it with the leather bracelet, but you know how that turned out. So now I'm giving him something else. A rubber band in the back of the head whenever he's not looking. He still doesn't know it's me."

Christy was glad Jeanine couldn't see her face. She couldn't repress her smile.

"How come guys don't start to like girls at the same age as girls start to like boys?" Jeanine asked, patiently holding her head still.

"I don't know. Maybe God is giving the girls an extra year or two to polish up their manners. That way, when the guys are old enough to be interested in them, they'll be the kind of girls worth being interested in."

"I never thought of it that way," Jeanine said, genuinely persuaded. "Will you teach me how to have better manners?"

"Sure, if you'd like. Hand me a rubber band." Christy tied off the end of Jeanine's braid.

Then Jeanine turned eagerly to face Christy. With her hair off her face, Jeanine was a pretty little girl.

"First, I'd say lose the rubber bands. I don't think that's going to help with Nick at all. Next, try to chew with your mouth closed and not to talk when you have food in your mouth."

"What else?" Jeanine asked.

"Well, sitting up straight always helps."

Jeanine immediately straightened her back and held her head up high. "Like this?"

"Yes, that's very good. I might mention screaming next. There's a place for screaming. Like in the pool or on a roller coaster. But for the most part you don't need to scream a lot during the day just for the sake of screaming."

Jeanine nodded solemnly. "What else?"

"That's a good start. Always try to say kind things and be considerate of others."

Jeanine beamed, looking anxious to take off and try some of her new charm techniques on Nick. Just as she was about to hop up, Christy touched her arm and asked, "May I bless you, Jeanine?"

"Bless me? But I didn't sneeze."

Months ago, one chilly morning on the beach, Todd had placed his hand on Christy's forehead and blessed her.

At the time she didn't want the blessing and didn't receive it well. But his act had stayed with her all this time. For some reason Christy felt the urge to bless this girl, who was blossoming into a young lady right before her eyes.

"Just close your eyes," Christy instructed. She then placed her hand across Jeanine's forehead, "Jeanine, the Lord bless you and keep you. The Lord make His face to shine upon you and give you His peace. And may you always love Jesus first, above all else."

Jeanine opened her sparkling eyes. A big smile spread across her face. "That was neat!" she said. "What does the 'love Jesus above all else' mean?"

"It means in every situation you face as you're growing up, may you fall in love with Jesus and love Him more than you love anything else."

"Thanks, Christy." Jeanine hopped up and impulsively gave Christy a hug. "You're the best counselor in the whole world!" Then off she ran down the trail.

Christy sat for a moment, thinking about the advice she had just given. She wished she could say she already had that kind of love for Jesus. She did love Him, but she wanted to love Him even more. Todd once said that was good because it meant she was "hungering and thirsting after righteousness."

Even though her talk with Jeanine hadn't gone the way she had planned, she felt good. She had given Jeanine what she needed, and maybe the blessing would help Jeanine feel loved.

Christy sat with Amy, Sara, and Ruthie at the evening meeting. She was glad Amy and Sara had included Ruthie into their little group. Christy quietly told Amy and Sara in the cabin that night that she liked the way they were being good friends with each other and with other girls in their cabin. Both girls looked pleased and proud.

For devotions, Christy read them her favorite psalm—Psalm 139. Then she talked for a few minutes about how much God loved each of them and how much He wanted them to promise their hearts to Him.

Christy felt like her "message" had gone well and anticipated lots of discussion afterward—and hopefully a conversion or two. She gave her closing line and waited for their responses.

All of them had fallen asleep except Sara.

Christy tried to hide her disappointment as she asked Sara, "Do you have any questions?"

"Yes," Sara said. "Has Jaeson kissed you yet?"

"No, of course not."

"Why not? You like him and he likes you."

"Sara, that's not enough of a reason to kiss a guy. When you give away kisses, you're giving a little part of your heart that you can never take back. You have to be careful that you don't give away too many pieces too soon or to the wrong person."

"You *have* been kissed before, haven't you? What was it like? Did you close your eyes?"

"Sara, let's talk about this later. I think we both need some sleep, okay?"

Christy pulled up her sleeping bag over her ears and only heard a muffled response from Sara about how nobody ever wanted to talk about it. Promising herself she would talk to Sara tomorrow about kissing, Christy fell asleep.

She floated in and out of a confusing dream in which

Jaeson tried to kiss her and she didn't know how to respond.

Friday dawned overcast and chilly. It was the first morning Christy put on jeans instead of shorts. She passed on the chance to have an invigorating shower and pulled her hair back in a ponytail rather than washing it. Her neck was stiff. She felt like she had been at camp for six months instead of six days.

Everyone at breakfast seemed on edge too. Perhaps it was because this was the last full day of camp or because it was cold and rainy outside. Whatever it was, the mood hung over the camp all morning. At lunch two of her girls argued over the last half of a grilled cheese sandwich until one of them fell backwards with her chair. If Christy hadn't rushed over in time to hold them back, there would have been a major fight.

"Here." Jessica offered Christy's table a plate of sandwiches. "My girls aren't very hungry."

Jocelyn grabbed the first sandwich. Ever since her recovery early that morning, she had been eating everything in sight.

Jessica then confided in Christy over the roar of the savage campers, "I don't like it when they get this way before the counselor hunt. You would think they were out for blood!"

"Our blood, I suppose," Christy answered.

Jessica nodded and headed back to her table of sassy whiners, who kept asking when they could leave so they could go to the snack shack and buy candy bars.

The instant they burst out of the dining room, the sun popped through the clouds and looked as though it would stay around all afternoon. Within minutes Christy felt boiling hot in her jeans and sweatshirt and decided to change into shorts before the counselor hunt. She also wanted to take along a towel to sit on inside her tree.

The cabin was a disastrous mess. The girls hadn't worked on it at all during cabin cleanup, and since Christy was in the counselors meeting during that time, she hadn't been there to motivate them. They had lost points for the mess, but her girls didn't seem to care.

Christy hurried down to the lake. Six canoes were lined up on the shore with a bright flag mounted on the stern of each. Christy was assigned the canoe with the orange flag and tied the matching orange strip of cloth to her waist. She was to relinquish this sash to the first camper who found her.

Dean Ferrill gave the rest of the instructions, and Christy mounted her "trusty steed" with a surge of excitement. With paddle in hand, she waited along with the other counselors for the signal.

"On your mark, get set..." Dean Ferrill's shrill whistle blew, and Christy plunged her paddle into the water on the left side, just as Jaeson had told her. She got a good, swift start and was ahead of the other girls by several yards in no time. With each stroke she felt the muscles in her upper arms stretching and letting her know that she was giving it all she had.

Christy was glad she had changed into her cutoff jeans and her Camp Wildwood T-shirt when she felt the sun beating down on the tops of her legs. The sun's intensity seemed double because of the reflection off the water.

From the shore behind her, Christy could hear the

shouts from the campers. They were to stay put until the first counselor's canoe touched the shore on the opposite side. Then they were released to run around the lake and find the counselors.

Jessica was right. From the way the campers' yells and screams echoed across the lake, they did sound like they were out for blood.

Near the middle of the lake, the three guys overtook Christy and passed her, all three stroking in unison, with their canoes lined up neck and neck.

Then Jessica passed her and called out, "Keep going, Christy. We're almost there."

Christy paddled harder, keeping her canoe straight and aiming for a nice, big open spot on the shore. Jaeson hit the shore first. Then Mike, Jessica, and Bob. Right behind them, Christy's canoe made the welcome sound of hitting mud and gravel. She hopped out, pulled her canoe to shore, and ran with soggy tennis shoes to her hiding spot in the hollowed-out tree.

She found the tree with no problem but realized she had left her towel in the canoe. From the echoing sounds of the wild campers running around the lake, she knew she didn't have enough time to go back to retrieve it.

With her muddy tennis shoe, she tried to scrape out some of the gunk on the floor of her hiding place. It seemed she was leaving more mud inside than she was managing to get moldy bark out. The campers' voices sounded closer.

Christy gave up and wedged herself into the triangular hideout. Drawing her long legs up close to her chest, she wrapped her arms around them and tried to make herself as small as possible. Then she tried to slow her breathing down to a calmer pace.

The inside of the tree was actually kind of interesting. A few inches from her face, the wood appeared to be rippled in several layers around the opening of the trunk. It smelled musty but in an earthy way that didn't bother her.

As a child, Christy had always liked stories about woodland critters who lived in the trees. She pictured one of her storybook elves or dwarfs being delighted to use her hideout as his home.

The first camper's footsteps came pounding down the trail right behind Christy's tree. She held her breath but feared her loudly pounding heart would give her away. Several more ran by, yelling and screaming, and Christy actually felt frightened. Not that they would find her; that was the game. But what if they were so wild this afternoon that they thought it a good idea to tie her up and leave her there?

She wiggled slightly, trying to improve her position. The bark was poking her and she felt tingles up and down her legs, probably from them falling asleep. As her eyes adjusted to the darkness of her cave, Christy realized that the bark in front of her face appeared to be moving. She looked closely and discovered a nonstop string of red ants marching across the entrance, only inches from her face.

With great control she kept herself from screaming or even moving an inch. Another hoard of campers thundered behind her down the trail. She kept silent. Then she felt that tingly sensation from her legs move up her arms and onto her hands. At that moment, she realized she was covered with ants.

"Yiiiiii!" she screeched, ejecting herself from the tree and jumping around in the woods, slapping her arms and legs in a futile effort to get the ants off her.

Two girls from Jessica's cabin found her in the midst of her furious dance and ventured carefully toward her. "Can we have your orange strip?" they asked cautiously.

"Come and get it," Christy said, still shaking and stamping her feet. Dozens of red ants fell to the ground. But it wasn't enough.

One of the girls timidly drew near and snatched the end of the orange cloth. As she pulled it from Christy's waist, another dozen ants emerged and raced down the cloth and up the girl's hand.

Now she too was screaming and shaking, doing the Christy ant-dance.

"What are you two doing?" the other girl asked. "I'm taking this back to the other side!" She grabbed the orange cloth, shook it out, and took off running.

"You're supposed to get in your canoe and beat her back," the girl explained.

"I can't," Christy wailed. "I still have ants in my pants!"

"Maybe if you run to the canoe, they'll fall out, and then if there are any left, you can sit on them and squish them all."

Christy was close to tears. "They sting. My legs feel like they're on fire!"

"Then jump in the water," the girl suggested. "Look, they bit me too." She held out her hand, revealing a baker's dozen red spots.

"This is awful!" Christy cried. "Are you okay?"

"I'm going to go to the nurse."

"Good idea." Christy slapped herself on the legs as she raced to the canoe. Then, because the cool lake water seemed like the only thing that could possibly stop the stinging, she jumped in and came up soaking.

"Christy!" Jaeson called out as he ran up and pushed off the canoe next to hers. "What are you doing? Get in your canoe! Come on! I'll push you off. We can paddle together."

In spite of her misery, she jumped into her canoe and let Jaeson push her off, knowing she had no time to explain. With quivering arms, she numbly followed Jaeson's shouted-out instructions.

"Paddle left. Paddle right. Come on, Christy, faster!"

Her hair was dripping in her face, and her legs were shivering and burning at the same time. She glanced at her arms and saw the red marks beginning to swell.

"Paddle left. Paddle right. Faster!"

"I can't keep up!" she cried out to Jaeson. "You go ahead."

Jaeson pulled out in front of her, and with a quick thumbs-up, his strong arms shot his canoe through the water like a well-aimed arrow. He made it to shore and planted his flag before his runner arrived. Since he was the first counselor back and most of the campers were still on the other side, it seemed a hollow victory with so few to cheer for him.

Christy paddled slowly but steadily, trying with all her might to ignore the increasingly painful stinging in her arms and legs. She still was a ways from shore when her arms gave out. "Come on, Christy," Jaeson called. "You can do it! Paddle left. Paddle right."

She tried, but it seemed pointless. Her chest was heaving from being so winded, and her head began to throb. The breeze nudged her a few feet closer to shore as she tried to catch her breath.

"Come on, Christy," Jaeson called again. "Your runner is almost here! Only a few more paddles."

Christy stroked three times on each side of the canoe and seemed to drift backward rather than forward. She looked to the shore and saw Jaeson waving his arms and coaching her to give it full steam.

Just then the girl with Christy's orange strip in her hand shot through the woods and crumpled on the gravel as she plunged her strip of fabric into the hole meant for Christy's flag. The score was now counselors one, campers one.

Hanging her head, Christy realized how dizzy she felt. Hearing a splash in the water, she looked up and saw Jaeson swimming out to her canoe. He took hold of the rope in the front and towed her the twenty feet to shore.

"I'm sorry," Christy apologized, reaching for Jaeson's hand to help her out.

"Christy, what happened? You're covered with red spots!"

"Ants," she breathed out, feeling completely exhausted. Her soggy tennis shoes slipped on the gravel, and Jaeson caught her just before she fell.

"You're going to the nurse," he said. "Put your arm around my shoulder. I'll help you walk to camp."

"Are you okay?" Dean Ferrill asked when he came over and saw Christy's polka-dotted skin.

"I'll take her to the nurse," Jaeson offered. "Cheer the rest of the counselors in for us, okay?"

Limping and leaning against Jaeson for support, Christy felt ridiculous to have been defeated by a bunch of stupid ants. She said nothing all the way to the infirmary. Jaeson talked the whole time about other mishaps he had seen at camp over the years, everything from broken collarbones to split lips. Somehow nothing he said made her feel better.

"Red ants," Jaeson told the nurse when she opened her door. The nurse took a quick look at Christy's arms and said, "Oh my, this doesn't look good."

"Wait till you see this." Christy exposed the back of her raw legs to the nurse.

"Oh, my gracious! What did you do, girl, sit on their convention center?"

"I think so." Christy tried hard to smile but without much success.

"I'll check on you later," Jaeson promised and left Christy in the hands of the sympathetic nurse.

"Let's get you in the tub and make sure all those critters are off you," the nurse said. "I hope you didn't have any special plans for the evening, because I'm afraid you're not going anywhere for a while."

A few minutes later Christy lowered herself into the lukewarm tub, anticipating a soothing sensation. Instead, the water felt like a thousand needles were plunged into her flesh. She itched like crazy.

"Whatever you do," the nurse called to her through the closed door, "don't scratch. I've put something in the water to draw out the poison. If you scratch, you'll only spread it."

The camper from the woods with the ant bites on her

hand had arrived, and the nurse was checking her hand as Christy soaked.

"I hope you know," Christy called back, "that this is about the worst torture a person could ever go through."

"I know. I'm sorry. But it *will* help. Trust me."

At that uncomfortable moment, Christy knew she had no other choice.

10

Sara's Promise

After drying off and putting on some clean clothes, Christy lay on her stomach on the infirmary cot so the nurse could smear her spotted legs with a cold, gooey lotion. She wanted to cry. This had to be one of her life's all-time worst experiences.

Covering Christy with a sheet, the nurse instructed, "Don't move. Stay on your stomach, and try to get some rest."

It's funny, but I never thought much about wanting to sleep on my side or my back until she told me I could only lie on my stomach.

Christy wiggled and clenched her teeth. How could she rest? The lotion stung almost as bad as the ant bites.

"How's the patient?" Dean Ferrill's voice called from the front door.

"Trying to rest. She was attacked pretty severely," the nurse said. "You can go on in and see her if you like."

The dean had to walk all the way around to the front of Christy's cot and squat down on one knee so he could look her in the face.

"You okay?" he asked with such a tender tone that Christy couldn't hold back the tears.

"I'm fine," her voice said, but her tears told him differently.

She blinked, trying to stop from crying. Then she realized she couldn't use her hands to wipe the tears from her face because the pink lotion would get in her eyes.

"Here." Dean Ferrill recognized her dilemma and reached for a tissue. He wiped her eyes for her. "You're going to be fine in a day or two."

"Who won?" Christy asked.

"The campers won this year. They're pretty happy about it too."

"It's because of me, isn't it?" Christy said.

"No, don't think that. You did a great job. You gave it all you had. I'm proud of you."

Christy rested her pink hands under her chin on the pillow. "At least I don't have to serve tables tonight."

The dean smiled at her joke. "So that was your motive for sitting on the world's largest ant farm?"

"There must be easier ways," Christy said, feeling a little better.

"Actually, you've been working hard serving your campers all week, and I think you've done a terrific job. I'd love to have you as a counselor anytime."

"I don't feel I accomplished anything spiritually with the girls. I tried talking to them about their relationship with God, and I even sat down with some of them one-on-one. Either they said they were already Christians, or they didn't want to give their hearts to the Lord, or they just didn't get it."

The dean's face took on another one of his understanding expressions. "Christy, you've done your part. You've told them how to receive eternal life. How much they understand is up to God. And how they respond is up to them, not you."

"But none of them responded. At all."

"You don't know what's going on in their hearts. We've planted lots of seeds in these kids this week. Some of them might sprout a week from now, some ten years from now. That's God's business."

"I just wish I could do more," Christy said with a sigh.

"You can. You can pray. Always pray. Actually, it looks to me as though you're in a pretty good position to pray for us during the rest of the evening."

Christy wished she could see her "infirmity" with as much of a spiritual reason as Dean Ferrill did. After he left she thought about how he might be right. She couldn't do anything else tonight. She couldn't serve tables at dinner or practice with the counselors for their closing night skit. She couldn't even have her final night of devotions with her girls. The camp secretary was going to stay in Christy's cabin that night so she could remain in the infirmary. About the only thing she could do was pray.

Wiggling her still-stinging legs under the rough sheet, Christy tried to find a comfortable spot for her head on the pillow and began by praying for Jaeson and the other counselors. She prayed for her girls, all the other girl campers, and then all the boy campers. She prayed for the kitchen staff, office staff, leaders, and bus drivers. It didn't seem she had left out anyone except maybe herself.

She wasn't sure what to pray for herself. A quick recovery? For the sting to go away? Death to all red ants on planet Earth?

"Can she have visitors?" Christy heard Jaeson asking the nurse.

"Sure, go on in. She can't move, so why don't you take this stool. You can sit by the head of the cot."

Christy tried to twist her neck around without moving the rest of her body. She saw Jessica holding a plastic cup with wildflowers and Jaeson following her with the nurse's stool. "Hi," she greeted them, trying to sound cheerful, while fully aware of how silly she must look with pink polka dots all over her face and arms.

"You poor thing." Jessica planted herself on the floor cross-legged and held up the cup of flowers. "I wonder where I can put these so you can see them."

"Right there on the floor would be fine. Thanks, Jessica. They're pretty."

Just then, a chorus of boys' voices started to sing under the slightly opened window. "The ants go marching one by one, hurrah, hurrah. The ants go marching up Christy's legs, hurrah, hurrah."

"Hey!" Jaeson yelled, opening the window all the way and sticking his face out where they could see him. "You guys are in big trouble! I've got all your names. You're going to get it!"

The boys immediately scattered. Jessica pressed her lips together to try to keep from laughing.

Christy broke the silence with a ripple of laughter. "That was pretty clever of them," she said.

Jaeson and Jessica laughed with her.

"Are you feeling any better?" Jessica asked.

"A little, I guess. Sorry I won't be able to help you guys serve tables. And I'm really sorry I made us lose the race."

"Don't worry about it," Jaeson said. "I feel awful since I'm the one who showed you that hiding place. I promise there weren't any ants two years ago when I hid there."

"It's not your fault, Jaeson. I should have looked before I crawled in or at least worn jeans. I was going to take a towel, but I left it in the canoe. I feel bad because I'm letting you down with the dinner and the counselors' skit and everything."

"We were able to rework the skit. It's going to be fine. The main thing is that you get better, Christy."

"I'll try," she said.

"We need to get ready for dinner," Jessica said. "We'll check on you later, okay?"

"Oh, Jessica, if you have time, could you braid Sara's hair? I promised I'd do it for the dinner tonight."

"Sure. Anyone else you want me to check on for you? I think the camp secretary is already up in your cabin."

"No. Just tell them all I said hi, and I'll see them in the morning."

Jessica adjusted the cup of flowers on the floor so they faced Christy. "I think the purple ones are the prettiest," Jessica said. Then kissing the tip of her finger, she touched the "kiss" to the end of Christy's nose.

Christy smiled up at her and said, "That's about the only place on me that didn't get bit!"

Jaeson and Jessica left. She felt awfully alone.

"I'm going to dinner," the nurse announced about fifteen minutes later. "I'll bring something back for you. Are you too warm or too cold?"

"No, I'm fine. I'm getting a little stiff though. Can I at least turn on my side?"

"It'd be better if you could wait. The majority of your bites are on the back of your legs, and I want them to remain exposed to the air."

"Okay," Christy sighed. "Are you sure you didn't find this remedy in some medieval book of tortures under 'How to Drive a Person Crazy'?"

"At least you still have your sense of humor," the nurse called over her shoulder as she left.

Yeah, my sense of humor and I are going to have a great time tonight.

Christy tried to pray again, going through and remembering everyone she could think of at camp. Near the end, right after she prayed for the bus driver, she dozed off and didn't wake up until she heard the door open.

The nurse must be here with my dinner. I'm not exactly hungry. I sure could use something to drink though.

Soft music began to play behind her, and she twisted her head to see Jaeson, dressed in a crisp white shirt with a black bow tie, walking toward her. He had a white towel draped over his arm, and in both hands he balanced a tray decked with his CD player, a can of 7Up with a straw sticking out of it, and a plate of chicken, mashed potatoes, and green beans.

"Dinner is served," he said in his best British butler voice. "I asked the nurse if I could bring this to you for her."

Christy should have felt delighted and honored by Jaeson's clever display of attention. Instead, she felt helpless, lying there with her painted clown face, not even able to cut her own meat.

"You didn't have to do this," she said.

"Oh, yes I did. It's the camp rules. If one counselor

causes another counselor to end up in the infirmary, said counselor must serve the invalid dinner."

"I'm not exactly an invalid."

"Oh, really? Then you'll just have to pretend for me. Do you want a drink?" Jaeson sat on the stool, balancing the tray in his lap and cutting up Christy's chicken into little pieces. He seemed perfectly content to continue acting out his part.

That's when it hit Christy that everything with Jaeson that week *had* been pretend. The moonlight picnic, talking about their dreams, all his smiles at her on the archery field and at the pool. They were pretending to be boyfriend and girlfriend for the week. Tomorrow she would leave, and Jaeson would start the game all over again with some other girl next week.

"Is that what all this is to you?" Christy asked. "One big game of pretend?"

"What do you mean?" Jaeson scooted closer to her cot and used his knees as a table for Christy to eat off of. He handed her the fork and smiled.

"I mean, I don't know anything about you, and yet you've treated me all week like I'm you're girlfriend."

Jaeson looked surprised. "Why? Because I taught you how to shoot an arrow and showed you the moon from a canoe?"

"I'm not accusing you of doing anything wrong," Christy said, realizing how unkind her statement must have sounded to a guy who was nice enough to bring her dinner. "I've been playing along the whole time. I've liked doing things with you and holding hands and the moonlight picnic and everything. It's just that tomorrow it's going to be all over, and it'll seem like it was just a dream."

"That's how it is," Jaeson agreed. "You'd better start on the potatoes. They're going to be cold soon."

Christy took a forkful of potatoes and regretted the way she had blurted out her thoughts.

"Dreams aren't bad, are they?" Jaeson said cautiously. "If you both know you're playing the same game, then it's okay, and nobody gets hurt, right?"

Christy thought that somehow it didn't seem right or feel right. She didn't know how to say it in a way that would make sense to Jaeson, so she took a bite of chicken. "This is good. Thanks for bringing it to me. I guess I was hungrier than I thought."

"You're very welcome. And if you're upset about anything I said or did this week, I'm sorry. I wasn't trying to hurt you. I just wanted to enjoy the week with you."

After Jaeson left, Christy lay alone in the quiet room thinking about his words. Why should they bother her? She had played the camp romance game. She had wanted to. Why did her heart feel achy now?

It must be that I'm leaving tomorrow and this whole dream will disappear. What will I have left of my relationship with Jaeson? He hasn't indicated that he would ever want to see me again or that he would write or call. Take me out of the week and put in another girl, and I'll bet he would do everything the same with her. Next week he probably will.

Christy decided that she and Jaeson had had a dream relationship. It had started in her head, and she had convinced her heart it was real. Tomorrow it would be gone, evaporated like a morning mist. And she already knew it would not be her head that would be sad, but her heart. This dream relationship would leave her craving more.

She had plenty of time to contemplate all of this while she lay on her full stomach, listening to the sounds of the evening meeting floating through her window. From the roar of the campers' laughter, the counselors' skit must have been hilarious. The singing sounded good. Much better than it did when she sat in the middle of her girls and heard their high voices singing as loud as they could. From her position across the camp, the distant music sounded sweet. She hummed along softly when she recognized the songs they were singing and realized for the first time that every song they had learned that week was Scripture put to music.

What a great idea! Without knowing it, the kids have learned a dozen Bible verses this week.

The last song they sang was Christy's favorite. She had heard it for the first time more than a month ago at the God-Lovers Bible study. From her cot she softly sang along.

Eyes have not seen. Ears have not heard.
Neither has it entered into the heart of man
The things God has planned
For those who love Him.

Christy thought about her dreams, her fantasies, and her wishes. If the words to the song were true, which they had to be because they were from the Bible, then her dreams for her life were nothing compared to God's dreams for her. Her part was to love God. And that was a true dream relationship that started in her heart and went to her head. Why was it that she kept having to relearn this same lesson?

Drifting off into a peaceful sleep, Christy dozed for

some time before being awakened by the disturbing awareness that someone else was in the room, watching her.

She snapped her head up and squinted, looking around in the dark room. "Who's there?"

"It's me. Sara." The tiny voice came from behind her.

"What's wrong, Sara? Are you okay?" Christy asked, trying to wake herself up and remember why she was here and who Sara was.

Suddenly the light snapped on, and Sara stepped over to the stool and plopped herself down, ready to talk.

"I'm glad you're awake," Sara said. "Everyone else is at the campfire, but I had to talk to you."

Christy slowly opened her eyes, hoping they would adjust soon to the light. "Does anyone know you're here?"

"I asked Jessica, and she said it was okay. She fixed my hair for me tonight for the dinner. Do you like it?"

Christy peered at the pesky little "Skipper" doll. Jessica had made two thin braids on each side of Sara's hair and tied them together in back with a thin, pink ribbon. It looked like a fallen halo, and the rest of Sara's wild blond hair billowed out beneath it.

"It's darling," Christy said. "What did you want to talk about?"

"Well, you know," Sara said shyly.

Christy remembered her promise from the night before to talk to Sara about what it was like to kiss a boy. She let out a deep breath. To think this little "angel" woke her up to ask about kissing was more than Christy had patience for at the moment.

"Sara, I don't know if this is such a good time."

Sara lowered her brown eyes and looked disappointed.

"I mean, isn't there someone else you could talk to after the campfire? Jessica, maybe?"

"I guess," Sara said slowly. She stood up, shuffling her feet and stalling by the door. "It's just that you said if we ever wanted to talk about giving our hearts to Jesus, that you would be happy to talk to us."

"Sara!" Christy cried out. "Don't leave! Come back here and sit down."

Sara plopped back down on the stool, looking surprised.

"I'm sorry," Christy said. "Of course I want to talk to you about Jesus. I thought you were here to talk about kissing."

"Oh, no," Sara said, the sparkle returning to her eyes. "I already asked Jeanine. She kissed Nick today in the woods during the counselor hunt, and she said it was kind of yucky. She only kissed him on the cheek when he wasn't looking, but she said it tasted like salty mud." Sara gave a little shiver. "I don't think I want to kiss a boy for a while."

"Good." Christy laughed. "It's better to wait until the boy is old enough to see the benefit of bathing more than once a month. It's also a whole lot better when it's the boy's idea too and not just yours. That will take a few years, though. Be patient."

"Don't worry, I will," Sara said.

"You wanted to ask me about how to become a Christian?" Christy prodded.

"Yeah. How do you do it?"

Christy was about to launch into a detailed explanation of how our sin separates us from God, how Christ is the sacrifice that paid our debt, that salvation comes from repenting of our sins and trusting our lives to Christ. But then a little voice in her head reminded her that the campers had been hearing that all week from the speaker. Sara wasn't asking *why* she needed to give her heart to the Lord; she was asking *how*.

"God already knows what you're thinking, Sara. Do you want to ask Jesus to forgive your sins and come into your heart?"

"Yes."

"Then tell Him."

"Isn't there a special prayer, or something I'm supposed to do?" Sara asked.

"No, this is between you and God. You be honest and tell Him you're sorry for all the things you've done that made Him sad. Then tell Him you want Him to rule your life."

"That's it?"

"Yes," Christy said, "because, you see, it isn't your words. It's what's in your heart that God looks at."

Sara started to cry. "That's what I want. I want God in my heart."

"Then let's pray, and you tell Him." Christy reached her stiff arm over to Sara and held her hand.

As she listened, Sara told God she was sorry. She asked Him to forgive her and come into her heart and ended with a hasty "Amen."

Looking up at Christy with tears sparkling in her eyes, Sara said, "I don't feel anything."

"I didn't either when I gave my heart to Jesus. But it's not a feeling. It's a promise. God will keep His part of the promise and forgive you. Now you have lots of years ahead to keep your part of the promise and fall in love with Him."

"I think I do feel different now," Sara said. "I feel good that I finally did it. I've been wanting to ever since that night in the cabin when you talked about this."

Christy looked into Sara's innocent face. She felt a ball of joy catch in her throat. "You know what, Sara? The Bible says that all the angels in heaven are rejoicing right now because you've just joined God's family."

"Really?"

"Really!"

"I didn't know I meant that much to God."

"Oh, Sara." Christy felt a tear of joy escape and skip down her cheek. "If you only knew! If you only knew!"

11

Seventeen

"So who was the letter from today?" Katie asked Christy as the two of them were driving in Katie's car a few weeks later.

"Sara," Christy answered. "I found a card with the meaning of her name on it and sent it a few days after camp. Sara means 'Princess.' She said in her letter she put the card on the wall above her bed."

Christy glanced at Katie and could tell by the way her jaw was twitching that she was clenching her teeth. Whenever Katie held something inside, her cheek would ripple in tiny spasms.

"Is it still hard on you that I got to go to camp and you didn't?" Christy asked cautiously.

The last time she had brought up the subject, Katie had cried.

"It's getting better. I'm glad all your campers are writing to you. Sounds like they really love you a lot," Katie said. "I hope someday my turn will come to be a camp counselor. I know it sounds crazy, but that's a major goal for me."

"It doesn't sound like a crazy goal, Katie. Maybe next year. I can't help but think that God will honor your heart's desire. Especially since you honored Him by abiding by your parents' wishes this year."

Katie shook her head and changed lanes as they neared Newport Beach. "Now, Christy, you know that God doesn't work in such predictable patterns. But doesn't it seem ridiculous the way my parents see things? I mean, here we are, driving alone in my car an hour and a half to Newport Beach to stay for the weekend, and they didn't even ask where I was staying, for a phone number, or anything. Yet when I wanted to go to camp, they said no simply because it was associated with the church. They said they didn't want me to get too involved with religious people. Why are they like that?"

"Maybe they've seen too many weird things that have been labeled a church-thing even though Christianity had nothing to do with it," Christy suggested. "Think of all the horrible stuff on the news, and then they show some murderer who says God told him to do it. I think a lot of people have the wrong idea of what a true Christian is."

"I guess you're right. Now I understand why Doug said they named their group the God-Lovers."

"I think you're right," Christy said. "I heard him say once that his main goal in life is to love God. That must be how he came up with the name. By the way, let's be sure to call him right when we get to my aunt and uncle's to tell him we'll be there all weekend. I told Todd we were coming, but I don't know if he told Doug."

"I told Doug," Katie said.

"You did? When?"

"Oh, last week sometime. I just happened to be talking to him. What time is it?"

"You didn't tell me," Christy said, her curiosity aroused. "Did you call him, or did he call you?"

"Does it matter?"

"Maybe."

"Okay, I called him. There's no law against calling a guy, is there? Do you know what time it is?"

Christy checked her watch and smiled at her defensive friend. "It's 1:15, and no, there's not a thing wrong with it. I kind of like the idea of you and Doug together."

"Really?"

"He's a great guy, and I think you two make a cute couple."

"Now that I'm over Rick," Katie added. "Which, I might say, didn't take very long."

A smile crept onto Christy's face. She kept her thoughts to herself, but soon realized her best friend could read her mind anyway.

"I know what you're thinking. And you're right. Rick was one of those phases we all have to go through while we're growing up. Now that I have that out of the way, I'm ready for a real relationship."

"With someone by the name of Doug, perhaps?"

"Perhaps."

"You have my blessing on that one," Christy said. "So our plan is to get there, call Doug and Todd, and set up something for the four of us to do tonight."

Now it was Katie's turn to smile and keep her thoughts to herself. Only this time Christy couldn't read her best friend's mind. Katie kept a shadow of a smile on her face all the way to Uncle Bob and Aunt Marti's. But she began to act jittery when they arrived.

"We'll get our stuff out of the trunk later," Katie stated, looking down the street as they shut the car doors and started up the walk to Bob and Marti's luxurious beachfront house.

"What are you looking for?" Christy asked.

"Who, me? Nothing." Katie laughed when she said it. A nervous laugh that made Christy think maybe Katie was hoping to see Doug's truck already there.

"I'll ring the doorbell." Katie skipped a few steps ahead of Christy and pressed the doorbell three times. She looked over her shoulder again and smiled at Christy.

No one came to the door.

"We could just walk in," Christy suggested. "This *is* my aunt and uncle's house, you know. Come on."

"No, wait." Katie grabbed her arm. "I'd feel better if we waited for them to answer the door."

Again Katie pressed the buzzer. *Ring, ring, ring.* It was as if she were trying to signal in some kind of secret code.

Christy heard the rush of feet running up behind her. Before she could turn around, someone covered her head with a pillowcase and grabbed her hands behind her back.

She screamed and kicked her left foot into the blackness. "What's going on, Katie?"

"You're coming with us," a deep, gruff voice behind her said.

She could tell by the grip that a guy held her hands. Her heart was pounding from the surprise of it all, but she wasn't really afraid. This kidnapping had all the marks of something Katie had cooked up.

The guy led her down the front steps and what seemed to be over toward Bob's garage. She heard the garage door open and a truck engine start up. Katie was whispering something about "in the back."

Next thing Christy knew, she was being hoisted into the back of what she imagined to be Doug's truck, with the mysterious guy next to her holding her hands to keep her from removing the pillowcase. The truck backed out of the driveway with a bump and sped down the street at what seemed to be an alarming speed.

"Where are we going?"

"You'll find out," the gruff voice said.

The truck turned a corner so quickly that Christy thought she might fall over. Then came another quick turn and another. She had no idea where they were. Another fast turn caused her to lean against her captor. Before she could balance herself back to a sitting position, they flew over another bump and came to an abrupt halt.

"Get out," the voice ordered.

For the first time, she felt frightened. She had been so sure the kidnapping was something Katie had arranged for her birthday, which was in two days. But she was all turned around and had no idea where she was. She felt panicky.

The guy practically lifted her out of the back of the truck. Christy could feel another hand on her upper arm, helping her down.

"Okay, you guys," she said with a nervous laugh. "This is all real funny." She tried in vain to peer through the weave on the pillowcase.

Her escort led her in a circle on what felt like asphalt beneath her feet. Then he directed her to take one step up, then one step down, then a few steps to the right. Christy could hear the ocean, so she knew they couldn't be far from her aunt and uncle's house. But where? Who was holding her hands and directing her to walk forward with baby steps? It didn't feel like Todd. Doug, maybe? But then who was driving the truck?

They went a few more steps, and Christy thought she smelled her uncle's aftershave. "Uncle Bob, I can smell you," she blurted out.

Christy heard Katie's squelched giggle, but no one else made a sound. At first she thought it was just her guide and Katie. Now it seemed more people were around her, watching her, trying to muffle their footsteps. How many more? And where was she?

"This way," the gruff voice directed, urging her to the right. "Up two steps."

She knew her feet were now on cement. She felt a strong ocean breeze, and she could hear the roar of the waves. Christy was certain that more people were around her. She could hear whispers and feet shuffling. Through the dense pillowcase she thought she smelled the scent of matches.

Another step forward, and she felt something light and buoyant brush across the left side of her head. It was a strange sensation. A strong urge came to bat at it, but her hands were still held firmly. Christy managed to catch a peek of gray cement at her feet when she looked down through the opening of the pillowcase.

Where am I?

With an unexpected yank, the pillowcase came off her head, her hands were released, and a loud blast of "Surprise!" nearly knocked her off her feet.

A crowd of all her beach friends stood before her on

Uncle Bob and Aunt Marti's wildly decorated patio, singing "Happy Birthday" and beaming over their big surprise.

Todd held out a huge birthday cake. It was loaded with pink frosting roses and seventeen lit candles. Todd's silver-blue eyes met hers as the song ended.

With a smile he said, "Go ahead, Kilikina. Make a wish."

Catching her breath, Christy stared at the cake. A tiny little runner in her brain took off sprinting for her "wish" file and pulled out the first thing it found there. Then the runner dashed back from the file to present her with her wish.

I wish I could go to Europe, she thought, and she blew out the candles with one big puff.

Everyone clapped. Todd set the cake down on the patio table, where Aunt Marti set to work cutting slices and inviting the guests to scoop their choice of ice cream.

Christy laughed with her friends as they chattered about how shocked she looked when they took off the pillowcase.

"I want to know who put that thing on my head," Christy said.

"Me," Doug admitted. "You and Katie came too early, and your aunt told us to think of some way to stall you."

"We had to drive you around the block," Bob added. "Hope you weren't too shaken by the experience."

"I figured it was you guys, of course." Christy looked at Doug. "But I couldn't imagine what was going on or where we were."

"Your uncle drove my truck," Doug said. "Can't say he's the smoothest person I've ever met when it comes to shifting gears."

Katie handed Christy a huge piece of cake with a mound of chocolate chip ice cream smashed into the pink rose on top. "Did we surprise you?"

"Slightly! When did you plan all this?"

"Your aunt called me last week, and we put our heads together. That's why I acted so casual when you invited me to come here for the weekend. I kept the secret pretty well, don't you think?"

"No kidding! I had no idea. Thanks, Katie. I was definitely surprised."

"That's for later," Katie said, pointing up.

Christy looked up at the pink pig piñata strung from the slatted wood covering over the patio. She noticed that the whole patio was laced in crepe paper streamers and dozens of bright-colored balloons. It kind of looked like a five-year-old was having a party, but she liked it. She knew her aunt had thrown herself into making the party a success.

All of Christy's beach friends were there: Heather, Tracy, Brian, Leslie, Doug, Todd, and a few others. But Christy glanced around and noticed Rick wasn't anywhere in sight.

"Everyone," Marti called out, waving her hands above her head to get their attention. Being petite was not an advantage to her at this moment. Her best advantage was that she had managed to keep a youthful flair about herself.

"As soon as you're finished with your cake and ice cream, there's a trash can over in the corner. The ice chests in both corners are filled with cold drinks anytime you want one this afternoon. Bob and Todd are going to set up the volleyball net, aren't you, boys?"

Bob gave Marti a playful salute. "One volleyball net coming up."

"We'll open gifts after the barbecue tonight," Marti continued. "And this sliding door will be open all afternoon if you need to come in to change or anything. Now all of you have fun on the beach, and remember to use your sunscreen."

"I'll get our stuff out of the car," Katie told Christy. "Are you still surprised?"

"I think I'll be in shock for the rest of the day!"

Katie smiled, "Good." As she turned to go, her copper-colored hair swished like an oriental fan whispering open.

Christy couldn't finish her humongous piece of cake and asked Todd if he wanted the rest of it. He held up his hand and shook his head.

"Try Doug," he suggested. "He has a higher tolerance for pink sugar roses than I do."

"Todd!" Bob called out from the sand a few yards away. "Are you going to help me with this?"

"Sure!" Todd called back. Then giving Christy a squeeze on the elbow, he said, "See you on the beach."

It took Christy and Katie only ten minutes to change into their bathing suits and cover-ups in the guest room and scamper down the stairs to join the group.

As they stepped out onto the sand, Christy said, "I noticed Rick isn't here."

"Is that a problem?" Katie said.

"I don't know, is it?"

Katie stopped, her feet burrowing down in search of cooler sand. "What is that supposed to mean?"

"Did you not invite Rick because of how things turned out between you two? I mean, he's close friends with Doug and Todd. He's going to hear about the party."

"I asked Doug to call him," Katie explained. "I didn't want to talk to him. He told Doug he might show up later in the day. We planned this to be a daylong party, in case you hadn't figured that out. Your aunt is the ultimate party woman. She bought steaks for everyone for the barbecue and stuff for s'mores around the campfire. She rented a stack of movies in case anyone wants to stay up for a marathon movie night. I'm not going to hold my breath, but Rick might show up later. If he does, I promise to be civil to him."

"Okay, that makes me feel better. As long as you invited him, that's the main thing. What he does with the invitation is his choice. I just don't want him to feel shut out."

"Don't worry. I may not cherish the thought that I once was somewhat interested in Rick—"

Christy interrupted with a roll of her eyes at Katie's understatement.

"But I have a good teacher showing me how to be friends with a guy after the crush is over."

"Who, me?"

"No, the Little Mermaid," Katie teased. "Of course you."

Christy thought back to what a great teacher Jessica had been to her at camp, "You know, I think once we figure out what real love is, it becomes clear that we can never love a person too much."

Katie looked thoughtful. Then tilting her head, she looked at Christy and said, "Is this what happens when you're about to turn seventeen? Your mind fills with deep ponderings, and you can suddenly explain the meaning of life to the rest of the world?"

Before Christy could answer, a bright orange volleyball flew through the air, bopping Katie on the top of her head.

"Hey!" Katie called out, spinning around, scooping up the ball and looking to see who threw it.

"Over here!" Todd called. "You're on our team, Katie. You want to play, Christy?"

She hesitated. Christy had never been good at sports like Katie was. But this was her birthday party. She imagined a person should be able to overcome at least some of her self-consciousness by the time she turned seventeen.

"Sure!" she hollered back at Todd. "Which team am I on?"

"I need you over here," Uncle Bob said.

For the next hour, an intense game of volleyball ensued. Christy had a lot of fun, even though she didn't get the ball over the net too many times. Doug, Bob, and two of the other girls on her team made up for Christy's less-than-stellar performance. In the end, Todd and Katie's team won.

Todd somehow came up with the idea that the winning team should throw its opponents into the ocean. Before Christy realized what was happening, Todd single-handedly wrestled her down to the shore with a little boy grin plastered all over his face.

Christy screamed and wiggled, but Todd held her arm tight. Just when her feet touched the cool, foamy part of the wave at the shoreline, she thought she had a chance to make a break for it. That's when Doug rushed up behind them.

"Yahoo!" Doug screeched, wrapping his gorilla-length arms around both Todd and Christy and taking them with him on his kamikaze plunge into the wave.

The three friends came up for air, laughing, dripping, and splashing each other. Doug dove under the water and grabbed Christy's ankle. She pulled away and surprised Doug with a splash of water in his face when he surfaced. Another wave crashed on them, tumbling them all to the shore.

Christy stood in the wet sand, still laughing and wringing the saltwater from her oversized T-shirt, which now clung to her.

"Ready for another dip?" Doug asked.

"Maybe after I get the sand out of my ears," Christy said. "But I noticed Katie looking awfully relaxed over there." She pointed to Katie, who was lying stomach-down on her beach towel.

"Say no more," Doug said.

He and Todd charged through the sand, startling Katie from her rest. Within minutes they had pulled their three-point plunge maneuver into the ocean.

Christy retreated to Katie's now-vacant towel next to Tracy and Heather and tried to dry off.

I guess some things never change, she thought, remembering summers past on this same beach when she and these girls had watched Todd and Doug perfect their "throw the screaming girl into the ocean" routine.

Christy stretched out her long legs on the towel and felt the hot July sun drying up all the salty beads on her legs. Planting the palms of her hands behind her in the sand, Christy gazed out at the shimmering blue ocean. Katie's red hair popped up from under a wave. Next came Doug with his contagious laugh dancing toward her on the ocean breeze.

Todd, like a playful dolphin, rode the next wave to the shore. Then emerging from the water, he tilted his head back and shook his sun-bleached blond hair so that all the droplets raced down his back. Christy had watched Todd shake his hair that way many times, but this was the first time she noticed what a distinct Todd-thing it was.

I'm glad some things don't change. I wish I could be this age, on the beach, with these friends, for the next fifty years. I don't want things to change. Ever.

Christy realized she was wishing almost the opposite of everything she had wished before. For years she had wished things would be different, especially that her relationship with Todd would change and move forward. Now she wanted it all to stop and stand still so she could observe and enjoy every little pinch of her life.

She knew the empty feeling when a camp romance ends. She knew the heady pleasure of dating a guy like Rick. And she knew the exquisite treasure of Todd's forever friendship.

Christy tilted her head back and felt the sun kissing her face and neck. She remembered Todd's blessing that she had passed on to Jeanine: "May the Lord make His face to shine upon you and give you His peace."

At this moment, Christy knew His forever peace. She felt His face shining upon her. With her eyes closed and a smile tiptoeing onto her lips, Christy silently made seventeen wishes. And all of them started with Todd.

Can't get enough of ROBIN JONES GUNN!

Christy Miller COLLECTION

VOLUME 1

Book 1: Summer Promise

Fourteen-year-old Christy Miller has the dream summer ahead of her in sun-kissed California , staying with her aunt and uncle at their beachfront home. Aunt Marti loves to shop, and those surfers are cute—especially Todd. Christy promised her parents she wouldn't do anything she'd regret later, and some of her beach friends are a little wild. But Todd and his "God-Lover" friends are giving Christy a new image of all things eternal. Can this summer live up to its promise?

Book 2: A Whisper and a Wish

Christy's family has moved to California just in time for her sophomore year of high school. But they're not in Newport Beach, where she spent the summer. Instead they're an hour and a half away and Christy has to start all over making friends. Despite an embarrassing escapade at a slumber party, things are going pretty well...until some midnight fun leads to a trip to the police station. Does God really hear every whisper? Does He know our every wish? Then why is it so hard to know who your friends really are?

Book 3: Yours Forever

Christy is back at Aunt Marti and Uncle Bob's house on the beach for the entire week between Christmas and New Year's...and Todd is in town, too! The cute surfer completely captured Christy's heart last summer, and she's eager to spend every possible minute with him. But soon Christy and her aunt are barely speaking, and it seems like all her friends are mad at her, too—including Todd! Is he hers or isn't he? And why would God let things get so tangled?

ISBN: 978-1-59052-584-5

Christy Miller COLLECTION

VOLUME 2

Book 4: Surprise Endings
With prom just around the corner, Christy gets swept away making plans for her dress and the entire event. But her dreams turn to bitter disappointment when her parents tell her she won't be allowed to attend, and Christy watches in tears as Todd takes another girl. Can Christy leave a space in her heart for God to fill, or will she keep looking to others for her happiness?

Book 5: Island Dreamer
Celebrating her sixteenth birthday in Maui and holding hands in the moonlight with handsome Todd don't exactly meet Christy's romantic expectations. The problem? Her best friend Paula. As soon as Paula sees Todd, she never takes her baby-blues off the goal of winning him. Can Christy put aside her jealousy and fears? And will Todd choose Christy and their longstanding relationship over Paula and her flirty maneuvers?

Book 6: A Heart Full of Hope
Christy's starting her junior year going steady with a handsome guy who carefully plans each date to show Christy she's wonderful. And Christy is dazzled by him. But when her parents restrict her activities and insist Christy find a job, her boyfriend is upset by her parents' strict rules. Can he and Christy work out their problems? Or will her parents ruin everything?

ISBN: 978-1-59052-585-2

Christy Miller COLLECTION

VOLUME 4

Book 10: A Time to Cherish
Juggling the stress of not having enough time with Todd, trying to understand Katie's relationship with Michael, and making Doug happy forces Christy to evaluate what's most important to her. Can Christy find a way to keep her friendship with Katie even though they're not in agreement on much anymore?

Book 11: Sweet Dreams
Christy is relieved her senior year is over. She and Katie have made up, and Christy's dreams of growing closer to Todd are coming true. Suddenly, Christy finds herself having to make what might be the most difficult decision of her life—one that could end every sweet dream she ever possessed. Will Christy find the strength to do what she knows is right?

Book 12: A Promise Is Forever
On a European mission trip with her friends, Christy can just see herself traveling across different countries and talking to new friends, like Sierra Jensen. But when tensions among the group set in, memories of Todd constantly swim in Christy's mind. Then she's sent to Spain alone while her friends travel elsewhere. Will Christy face her fears of the future? And can she truly trust that God has great things planned for her even when all seems lost?

ISBN: 978-1-59052-587-6

Join Jessica, Terri, Lauren, Alissa, Shelly, Meri, Leah, and Genevieve as they encounter love, life, and a growing faith in the small town of Glenbrooke.

Read excerpts from these books and more at WaterBrookMultnomah.com!

About the Author

Just like Christy, Robin Jones Gunn was born in Wisconsin and lived on a dairy farm. Her father was a school teacher and moved his family to southern California when Robin was five years old. She grew up in Orange County with one older sister and one younger brother. The three Jones kids graduated from Santa Ana High School and spent their summers on the beach with a bunch of wonderful "God-lover" friends. Robin didn't meet her "Todd" until after she'd gone to Biola University for two years and had an unforgettable season in Europe, which included transporting Bibles to underground churches in the former Soviet Union and attending Capernwray Bible School in Austria.

As her passion for ministering to teenagers grew, Robin assisted more with the youth group at her church. It was on a bike ride for middle schoolers that Robin met Ross. After they married, they spent the next two decades working together in youth ministry. God blessed them with a son and then a daughter. When her children were young, Robin would rise at 3 a.m. when the house was quiet, make a pot of tea, and write pages and pages about Christy and Todd. She then read those pages to the girls in the youth group, and they gave her advice on what needed to be changed. It took two years and ten rejections before *Summer Promise* was accepted for publication. Since its release in 1988, *Summer Promise* along with the rest of the Christy Miller and Sierra Jensen series have sold over 2.3 million copies and can be found in a dozen translations all over the world.

Now that her children are grown and Robin's husband has a new career as a counselor, Robin continues to travel and tell stories about best friends and God-lovers. Her popular Glenbrooke series tracks the love stories of some of Christy Miller's friends. Her books *Gentle Passages* and *The Fine China Plate* are dearly appreciated by mothers everywhere. Robin's bestselling Sisterchicks novels hatched a whole trend of lighthearted books about friendship and midlife adventures. Who knows what stories she'll write next?

You are warmly invited to visit Robin's websites at: www.robingunn.com and www.sisterchicks.com. And to all the Peculiar Treasures everywhere, Robin sends you an invisible Philippians 1:7 coconut and says, "I hold you in my heart."

Don't Miss the Next Chapter in Christy Miller's Unforgettable Life!

Follow Christy and Todd through the struggles, lessons, and changes that life in college will bring. Concentrating on her studies, Christy spends a year abroad in Europe and returns to campus at Rancho Corona University. Will Todd be waiting for her? CHRISTY AND TODD: THE COLLEGE YEARS follows Christy into her next chapter as she makes decisions about life and love.

CHRISTY AND TODD: THE COLLEGE YEARS by Robin Jones Gunn

Until Tomorrow • *As You Wish* • *I Promise*

SISTERCHICK®

Adventures by

Robin Jones Gunn

"A friend loves at all times…"
—PROVERBS 17:17A (NASB)

SISTERCHICKS
in Sombreros
Robin Jones Gunn
SISTERCHICKS
Down Under
Robin Jones Gunn
SISTERCHICKS
Say Ooh La La!
Robin Jones Gunn
SISTERCHICKS
in Gondolas
Robin Jones Gunn
SISTERCHICKS
Go Brit
Robin Jones Gunn
SISTERCHICKS
in Wooden Shoes
Robin Jones Gunn